The Lost Books of Benjamin
3 Benjamin 1:1-78

When Leaning Towers Fall

Novel 1 of 12 in the 3rd Book of Benjamin

B. Albertill

When Leaning Towers Fall, published May, 2023

Editorial and proofreading services: Highline Editorial, New York; Taylor Morris; Gina Sartirana

Interior layout and cover design: Howard Johnson

Cover concept by Ruth Angulo

Cover and interior illustrations: Lisa Marie Brennan

 **SDP Publishing**

Published by SDP Publishing, an imprint of SDP Publishing Solutions, LLC.

ISBN-13 (print): 979-8-9856475-3-2
ISBN-13 (e-book): 979-8-9856475-4-9

Library of Congress Control Number: 2022923610

Printed in the United States of America

*For the Lorelei. How did I
ever exist without you?*

When told to go back home, Ruth remained determined not to be sent away. She said, *Don't tell me to turn back or to leave you. Where you go, I will go. Where you stay, I will stay. Your people will be my people. Your God will be my God. Where you die, I will die and there with you I will be buried. May the Lord punish me ever so severely if anything but death separates you from me.*

—Ruth 1:16–17

Acknowledgments

When Leaning Towers Fall, the first novel in the Third Book of Benjamin (3 Benj. 1:1-78) within the *Lost Books of Benjamin* (LBoB) series, could not exist without the support of so many people. Hence, sincere gratitude must be given to many, including my wife, the Lorelei, who helped me shape and hone characters, served as my plot-sounding board, and (with go-bag-in-hand) traveled with me throughout England, Germany, Poland, and Italy to visit all the leaning towers. To Steve and Hilda, who helped me photograph and document the French regions of the story arc. To Letitia and Thierry, who brilliantly hosted the LBoB gang, numerous times for dinner and lodging in Péronne. To my creative editor and contributing author, Cathleen Salsburg-Pfund, who has been there to shine and polish the novel's creative delivery. To my developmental editor, Taylor Morris, who provided timely sage meaningful guidance for novel depth and structure, as well as Gina Sartirana for the eagle eye proof-checking help. To my illustrator, Lisa Brennan, who took my chicken scratch and converted them to powerful images, as well as to Ruth Angulo who helped start the creative concept for the cover image. To my interior layout and cover design guru, Howard Johnson, who provided me the mallet and chisel to release my literary work in aesthetically-sound hard copy. To my publisher, Lisa Akoury-Ross at SDP Publishing, who very early believed in the beauty of this book and the series and has patiently allowed me the pacing to make an idea tangible to the masses. Also, I must give thanks to my triune God who has blessed us and kept us in His hands, as well as being the inspiration for all things done in this novel and throughout the LBoB series.

Table of Contents

Prologue

In Europe today, army physician-scientist historian—Mickey Peronne—awaits the results of his medical evaluation and potential ejection from active service. Working with the Defense Intelligence Agency (DIA), Mickey's wife, Loni, impatiently waits for data from her secret sources, all the while wondering whether her address will be soon changing. Operationally moving from one desert location to another, Mickey's physician-historian colleague Russell Lange leads his team in covert intelligence-gathering. Last, Mickey's physician-historian colleague, Suzanne Coletrane, prepares lessons once taught by the teaching team trio of Mickey, Russell, and Suzanne at the army medical history schoolhouse in Maryland.

Unbeknownst to all of them, there are strange underground rumblings. What was once hidden for ages now lies uncovered. What was kept secret now lays open to discovery. Danger and intrigue are hiding in every corner as the lines defining friends and enemies become blurred. As the world clock ticks, the race between good and evil begins. Can a once-effective team be timely reassembled? If so, will former colleagues mesh smoothly to take on the mission?

1

Tiles Without Smiles

Leaning Tower of Niles
Chicago, Illinois
Current day

"I can't do it." Father Judas panted. "It's ripping my bones from their sockets." Father Judas couldn't hang on to the banister for much longer. Looking down through his flapping robes, he saw a sea of inlaid brick on the ground below. Although patterned beautifully, the brick tiles would do nothing to cushion his landing should he plunge the forty feet. *What made me think that this harebrained escape plan would even work?*

Several minutes ago, the evening seemed like every other. The wind blew through the banister posts on the porch of the leaning tower. Overhead, another in a long line of airplanes shattered the evening quiet as it screamed into the sky. They carried passengers from nearby Chicago's O'Hare International Airport to destinations as far away as Pisa, Italy. Amidst the intermittent noises, Father Judas nevertheless felt safely blanketed in his solitude.

"What a life, Sister." The father sipped his tea. "I know it's not your lovely Romania, but for me it's blissful heaven."

"Father Judas," the Cistercian nun straightened her pleats, "please don't say that; it makes what I have to say that much harder."

"The preceptory has denied my tenure here as tower keeper, right?" Father Judas's natural facial ruddiness grew deep scarlet.

"Believe me, Father, it's not a reflection of the work you've done."

"I knew this was coming." Father Judas firmly set down his teacup. "That is why you returned the fish to Europe earlier this year. Isn't it?"

"Look, the Americans have promised they will keep an eye on the leaning tower here." The sister smiled kindly. "We really could use your talents either in Germany, Poland, or Romania."

"I guess I need to come to terms with the idea of returning to Europe." Father Judas frowned.

"It's better that way." The Cistercian sister stood. "I will begin the transfer arrangements for you tonight."

13

"No need to rush off, Sister. My only remaining task for the evening is the five-thirty latching of the door for the night."

"Thank you kindly, Father, but I will return at first light with your travel papers." The Cistercian sister followed the father down four levels to the tower entrance.

"I'll leave the light on until you pass through Leo I and Leo II," Father Judas said.

"Pardon?"

"Sorry." Father Judas pointed down the walkway. "It was my attempt at humor."

"Ah! I get it … the paired stone lions." The sister waved. "Good evening, Father."

"At least for one of us, Sister," Father Judas mumbled as he closed and bolted the door securely, went back upstairs, and poured himself a second cup of tea. Halfway through it, a grinding, screeching, and snapping of metal reached his ears.

"Whaaa?" Father Judas bolted to his feet as his teacup toppled. "Think! At least I still have power," said the father as the lights flickered and went off. Father Judas grabbed the phone. "It's dead!" His breath spasmed.

I have no more than a few minutes before the intruder makes it here, to the wall safe. Father Judas's swirling dark hair caught the outside breeze as he rapidly vacated the room. Leaving his shoes behind, Father Judas scampered onto the balcony as fast as his stocking feet could carry him. He paused and took a quick backward glance. *Okay, tower keeper's protocol dictates that I leave the wall safe door hanging wide open. Done. Now it's time to take care of me.*

Standing out on the balcony, he listened nervously to footsteps clicking on the concrete floor inside the tower. The footsteps were brisk and close, echoing from the level below him. *No matter how many times I have practiced this active intruder evasion drill, my gut tightens. I can't breathe.*

"Father God," he whispered, "in the name of your Son and the Holy Spirit, I know not what I have done to bring such evil to myself, but I ask you to protect me. If it is by my hand that all this has transpired, I ask you to forgive me—"

The slamming of the wall safe door interrupted him in mid-prayer. Father Judas quickly reviewed his actions. *Everything needed to be done has been done, according to protocol. Let me think. Open the wall safe … done. Press the audible alarm … done. But without power … did help get notified? Slip out the door onto the balcony … done. All good. Now I wait.*

After rounding yet another level up the spiral staircase connecting the circular balconies, Father Judas again paused to listen. *They are still plundering the room on the fourth level. Wait! What's that?* Father Judas caught the additional echoes of footsteps coming up the spiral staircase toward him. His gut knotted even tighter. *Sounds like multiple intruders coming after me. What now?* Fearfully, he pressed his knuckles into his face as he peered beyond the balcony's ledge. *Only one option.* The sound of quickening footsteps pressed ever nearer. Father Judas took the rope belt off his robe, tied it into a knot around the base of the banister post, and eased himself down the side of the tower. *Even if I can't make it to the ground, I might be able to swing myself onto the balcony below as they proceed onward to the top.*

Suspended in midair, Father Judas's shoulders ached from the weight of his body as well as the sweat-laden black-over-white Cistercian friar robe. Further, it seemed that all the moisture from the night air, along with his perspiration, added additional poundage to his already overloaded shoulder joints.

"Take my hand, Padre. Nothing you have is worth dying for," a voice said from above.

"How ... would you ... know?" Father Judas grunted.

"Hurry. Take my hand," said the thug. "Those old shoulders aren't going to hold out much longer. That's a long drop. Hate for you to break something important."

"Okay ... okay, but I can't let go of the rope."

"Don't worry, Padre, just don't move. We'll pull you up." It wasn't long before Father Judas stood back on the fifth-level landing of the leaning tower, rubbing at the pain in his aching shoulders and looking into the empty souls of lidless-eyed men without conscience.

"I guess some gratitude is in order." Father Judas searched the two faces.

"Absolutely, Padre. Aren't you trained to forgive and forget—turn the other cheek or something like that?"

"Yes, I suppose that anyone, even one who saves the very life he endangers, deserves a modicum of gratitude. Thank you."

"Oh, we don't need *words* of appreciation, Padre. We only need to have that which you possess."

"What do you mean?"

"Hand over the fish. That'll be all the thanks we need."

"All this is about seafood?" Father Judas bit his lower lip.

"Do you really want to play games with me, Padre?"

"Games? What are you talking about?"

"Look, the sister said—"

"You talked with the sister?"

"She said that the fish wasn't here."

"Well, there you go," Father Judas scowled. "Why are you asking questions that have already been answered?"

"Well, you see. The sister also said that the tower was empty ... locked for the night ... yet here you are ... still open for business. It makes a body think that the sister may have been confused."

"I trust you have done nothing to harm—"

"Don't worry. She's with God," the thug grinned. "You will be too ... soon ... if you don't cough up the fish."

"Haven't we just been through all this?"

"Look, Father, neither of us has the time for this. We want the fish that you took from the wall safe."

"I assure you, gentlemen. I took nothing from the wall safe."

"Priests shouldn't lie, Padre. So says the Ten Commandments in the Good Book."

"How dare you play clergy with me?"

"I'm not, Padre. However, I do know that you are bound by it to tell me the absolute truth. That being said, where is the fish?" Leaning forward, the thug hissed. "Understand this, Padre. We are willing to sacrifice a life to find it."

"Mine, I suppose?"

"What can I say? There seems to be a connection between priests and martyrs. They just seem to go hand in hand—or neck in rope." Father Judas suddenly felt a loop of his rope belt cinch around his neck.

"Padre, we will have the fish that came from the wall safe."

"I have no fish," Father Judas panted as the rope's tension lessened. "I took nothing from the wall safe. Jesus is my witness."

"I know that there is truth within you, Padre." The thug tapped Judas's chest. "Give it to me or I will be obliged to dig for it."

"This is so sad." Judas set his chin. "You can't understand that much of what is sought is hidden in plain sight."

"Like the truth, Padre?"

"I know in my heart that I have only spoken the truth to you."

"Okay, we'll do it your way. Bare the padre's chest. Let's see if we can find what truth resides inside the heart of our soon-to-be dearly departed priest."

2

Judging Characters

Heidelberg Hospital
Heidelberg, Germany

"Instead of a human, why can't I be a plant, just for today?" Dr. Mickey Peronne pressed his forehead against the cool glass of the front window of the hospital entrance. He looked beyond this doorway of Heidelberg, Germany's US Army military hospital and past the hedges. Inside him burned yet another in a continuous string of life failures. His army career had just unexpectedly ended—a perfect capstone joining his failure as a Templar and also as a husband.

Magnified by the distortions in the hospital glass panel, Mickey's unhappiness looked larger than life. His pronounced, tanned Native American features accented an imposing six-foot frame which was odd since he was solidly a French-Canadian mix. His salt-and-pepper military haircut bracketed a usually confident face which, until only recently, belied his true age to be in the mid-fifties. Even now in this medical failure to meet retention standards, he maintained his sharp soldier's appearance.

"Bad news runs in streaks," sighed Mickey as he noted an approaching figure.

"Talking to yourself," Luis Toro-Calderon pointed, "or to your reflection in the glass?"

"I guess both." Mickey twisted his mouth. "They seem to agree that bad news breeds only more bad news."

"That's for sure," Luis replied as his eyes surveyed the piece of paper in his hand. "But I'm no judge. There might be some folks who would see bad news and think it to be good news."

"What are you saying, Luis?"

"I'm just thinking out loud." Luis tucked the paper into his military uniform's cargo pocket. "I take it that the Templar thing you said you wanted didn't play out."

"Correct," said Mickey. "Last month it was announced that the Templar position of grand secretary of the US National Templar Organization had been selected."

"And your name wasn't attached to it?"

"No. It wasn't." Mickey frowned. "This post was two steps from the lead position of grand prior."

"Sorry about that, Mickey."

"If that wasn't enough, some lab results just came in."

"I take it that wasn't good news either."

"Correct again, Luis."

"Well, Mickey, I wish I could chat longer, but this paper I just read will need to be briefed soon." Luis tipped an imaginary hat. "I know there's a lot of stuff going on with you, your career, Loni, and such—"

"What do you mean, about Loni?"

"As you know, I work for this installation's general and his chief of staff. I know a lot about a lot of folks." Luis patted Mickey's shoulder. "You are a man of unparalleled character. All will work out for you."

"Thanks, Luis." Mickey watched as Luis headed down the long hospital hallway toward the adjacent building where the general had his office. "I wish I had good news to share with Loni," he murmured, placing his head back against the cool glass. *What was that Luis said? There is bad news that could be seen as good. That would be nice for a change.* Having passed the lab on his way out, Mickey reviewed his and Loni's lab results in the folder he had clutched in his hands. *Just two weeks ago, her fertility studies were all normal.* He addressed his reflection. "Well, we can see now who the problem is then, can't we." He closed his eyes. *Why has God turned against me?*

He willed his eyes open again and searched through the window glass for Loni, his lovely wife, whom he left seated on the steps beyond the manicured shrubbery. He had hoped that when they again met, the news he would bring would be uplifting. *It's certainly not going to be.*

Loni Leigh Meriwether Peronne, the slender five-foot daughter of the former commander of the Leighton Barracks Installation, was now in her late forties and not one cell of her body revealed senescence beyond thirty-five. Mickey knew every curve—from her burnt sienna-and-café, thick, full, shoulder-length hair to each painted toenail. Her fair complexion complemented his olive, tanned appearance.

Mickey's doldrums grew as he watched Loni sitting on the uncomfortable stone entrance stairway, sliding her crucifix pendant back and forth on its chain. He could imagine the growing pain of Loni's hips. It didn't matter how much she adjusted her position; he did not see her smile. *Even if her hip pain subsides, her headache won't.*

From his vantage point at the glass, Mickey could well see the flushed appearance of his wife's face—her telltale sign of a headache. He watched her finger spiral the lock of hair at her temple. Mickey understood his wife better than he understood himself. Despite any pain she felt, he knew Loni would remain stalwartly in place. All she needed was to find some quiet time to exert mind-over-matter and the opportunity to pray away the discomfort.

In the quietness of the morning, this should have been easy. However,

Mickey could see Loni's concentration wavering. *Her work requirements are ever-pressing, and my string of failures just makes her world worse.* As Mickey continued to gaze, he noticed Loni glancing to the inside of her wrist at her watch. *I told her I would be gone twenty minutes, tops.* Mickey looked at his watch. *Because bad news takes more explaining, that statement was made forty-five minutes ago.*

Mickey wanted to go and tell her the recommendation of his medical board so that at least that news wouldn't be hanging over her head. *I want to go. I do. It's just that my legs won't budge.* With the ending of his army career for medical reasons, he knew Loni would remain in angst. Picking at his cuticles, Mickey hardly noticed the child walking by, hand-in-hand with her soldier mother. The playful cherub tugged at Mickey's trouser pocket, beaming a smile which, unfortunately, did little to change Mickey's sullen mood.

If indeed I was a plant today, I would be a thistle—thorny, prickly, and most definitely a pain to anyone who made contact with me.

3

Reading Between the Lions

Heidelberg Hospital
Heidelberg, Germany

I hate everything about hospitals. I always have. Dr. Loni Peronne, remote viewing analyst for the Defense Intelligence Agency, was not usually asked to sit on hospital steps to review briefing notes. *It was amazing to think that I ever married a man whose workplace, by design, would involve a hospital.* Although quite uncomfortable, she preferred the stone steps outside to the more comfortable seating inside any hospital waiting room.

Today had the potential to be a really bad day for her husband. *Today Mickey will find out if he is medically fit enough to continue in military service, despite his past deployment injury.* Loni knew how much he loved wearing his digital-pattered camouflaged business suit. If not found medically fit for duty, the pain he would feel would far surpass these cold stone steps. *I hope cold stone steps, sore hips, and a headache are the worst of it today.*

Twirling the wisp of hair at her right temple, Loni looked down at the papers in her lap from a file she received from a DIA briefing yesterday. Loni reread the notes she had scribbled in the margins.

> The murdered body was identified as the tower keeper at the Leaning Tower of Niles.

Loni remembered wondering initially where along the Egyptian Nile River this leaning tower sat. She recalled the answer given at the briefing: Chicago, Illinois. *Who knew that a leaning tower actually existed in the United States? Before yesterday I certainly didn't.* She had been quite happy in her ignorance that there was only one leaning tower in the world, and it quietly sat in Pisa, Italy. Now there appeared to be two towers, one of which was presently stained with the blood of a murdered priest. Add to that the mystery of a missing nun. She glanced down again.

The deceased, a Father Judas Lenz, was from Schriesheim, Germany.

Incredible. Schriesheim is literally just a few miles north of here. In fact, every day Loni drove through Schriesheim on the way to and from the Peronne home in Altenbach and her office in Heidelberg.

The brother of the deceased is a tower keeper in Germany.

How can that be? Is the whole family in the tower-keeping business? Could this be a case of sibling rivalry gone sour? Loni's final notation really made her finger spiral at her temple.

The German tower also leans.

What are the odds of that? Of the three leaning towers she now knew existed, two were connected in a US-based murder case which had literally landed in her lap. Whatever the odds were, Loni knew the clock was ticking. She whispered as she counted on her fingers, "Including today, we have four more days to figure this thing out before we have to turn it over to the local German authorities and the international press."

By her own marks on the page, the words *Heidelberg* and *brother* were circled. Loni locked her hands behind her head in a backward stretch, rolling back her shoulders. She closed her eyes to recall the photograph shown of the tower keeper hanging by his neck from a rope tied to the staircase handrail five stories up. *His belly entrails hung out from the front of his body, dripping into a pool of bowel contents and blood. His body had been sliced open right through the belly button—from his neck to his pelvis.*

In the photo's foreground squatted a criminal investigator. His jacket and equipment were marked with the initials ICD. The kneeled investigator appeared to be referencing a manual while hovering over equipment centered between two low-lying stone lions. From the angle the photograph was taken, it just wasn't clear the exact testing that was being performed there at the murder site.

Loni again stretched to clear her mind. She felt the bones of her neck crack with relief. Almost instantly the pressure in her head dissipated, and the warmth in her cheeks began to cool. With a temporary reprieve from the headache, Loni flipped her notes to page two.

The notes on the second page seemed to refer to times, locations, and places which just didn't make sense right now. Loni forced herself to read on until eventually she got to the point where she couldn't remember what she had just read. She stared at her notes, but the words wouldn't link into any real meaning. She stretched again, shutting her eyes tightly in a deep yawn. It didn't get better.

"Can't get work from a dead horse," Loni murmured.

There would be time to relook and rethink the murder later. Right now, she had a husband who was missing in action. Hoping to see a sign of life, Loni opened up her eyes, blinked hard and looked back at the swooshing automatic entrance doors which graced the front of the hospital. There was some evidence of movement, but it was only a soldier with her child leaving the hospital. Loni's eyes strayed back to the pages in her lap.

"Maybe I *can* get some work from a dead horse."

With two fingers at either side of the bridge of her nose, Loni laterally wiped the moisture from her eyes. Slowly, she moved her hands back in the direction of her lap. She continued to read.

The DNA from the deceased was over two thousand years old.

This is absurd and obviously a testing error. Two thousand years? How could that be? Loni recalled all the questions which had flown around the briefing room. No matter how the question was asked, the answer was always the same. The DNA had been tested on-site and retested by the Investigation Criminal Division labs. On every result the conclusion could only be that the deceased was more than two thousand years old.

My Lord, this isn't news a person sees every day. More importantly, this was not information which needed to be given to a foreign government or the international press. There were significant unresearched questions here which did not have any plausible answers. Loni shook her head and bit at her lower lip. *I wish I could get Mickey's take on this. His analytical mind is so keen. Unfortunately, he doesn't have a need-to-know.* It was her job to know. In fact, it was her job to gather raw data and make sense of the jumble so that others could take decisive action. Right now, that bridge from raw data to final actions lay absent for two reasons: the data was badly convoluted, and Loni just didn't have the mental focus right now to unscramble it.

Loni looked down at her watch. Before her eyes could focus on the watch hands, the sound of electric doors opening diverted her gaze rearward. Framed in the cool darkness of the open hospital doors stood her husband, Mickey. His face had a remarkable absence of joy.

While folding and creasing tightly the confidential DIA notes, Loni's eyes moved quickly to inspect his face and read the answers to the questions of the day. *Is Mickey fit for duty and destined to remain a soldier tomorrow?* She captured the answers amidst the drawn, sallow features of one very unhappy army family physician and husband.

Loni sat breathlessly as she watched her husband suck in a deep draught of the morning air. Racing through her mind, she formulated response after response which might be adequate to unclench those whitened knuckles. Before she could arrive at the right response, Mickey had closed the gap between them. She rose slowly from the stone step but before she could turn to face him, she heard Mickey speak.

4

Yes Pain and No Gain

Heidelberg Hospital
Heidelberg, Germany

"I've seen lightning strike victims look happier, Loni," Mickey grimaced while folding and stuffing the lab folder into his cargo pocket. "How's the headache?"

"Lightning … what?"

"Your cheeks, they're flushed. You have a headache. How's it going?"

"The headache? Oh yes, it's alive and doing quite well. I'm fine too. I'm a survivor. Mickey, honey, this is not about me. This is about you and the lightning bolts you've been dodging. The question is, how are *you* doing?"

Mickey watched Loni take his hand. *Her hands are so warm. No matter what I say, she will know by my icy hand that I am not fine.* His thoughts raced to find the correct response to let her know that their lives in the active military had just ended. Despite all the time at the window in preparation for the moment, he stood speechless. *Besides my fingers, maybe the coolness of the window glass froze my brain.*

"Honey, Mickey, talk to me." Loni held her breath until she saw Mickey's lips begin to move. She released it slowly as he broke the silence.

"I wonder if we can really call it news if—" Mickey's voice went oddly vacant.

Mickey took in a deep breath to further explain but all the words in his head vanished. With lungs full of air and postured to speak, he stood silent, empty. He stared hard at his legs that had been injured in combat.

"I don't know whether it still can be called news." Following Mickey's gaze, Loni set her jaw. "That part is not important. The fact is that we now know the answer for sure. The waiting is done, and the worst is over. We can make plans to move on from here. Isn't that what we really needed today?"

"I'm not sure I needed to know today that I am not fit for duty." Mickey groaned. "But there, I've said it. Maybe now the worse is over." Mickey flashed a fake smile, knowing deep inside that the worst was yet to come. What followed next would be the final professional nail in the coffin. He had to go receive the

23

official final out-briefing from the hospital commander, Army Colonel Huston Birdsong. Career military officers always dreaded such humiliation. It always ended with well wishes and the cordial slap on the back. It was the military equivalent of receiving a gold watch for twenty years of civilian service.

They both always knew that one day, Mickey would have to face this parting event as eventually all military service comes to an end. But neither Mickey nor Loni ever dreamed that it would come about as an adverse ruling from a medical evaluation board from an injury sustained from combat heroism.

Mickey watched numbly as Loni placed a tightly folded piece of paper into a zipped pocket in her purse. *Probably a bucket list of things she wants in life.* Certainly this news wasn't on that list, and neither was a discussion on setting a retirement date. Mickey heard his wife groan as she stood up from the stone hospital steps and stretched her wincing hips and lower back. Before she could speak, he cupped her face in his hands. He pressed his cheek against her forehead, then placed a kiss over each eye, and a last kiss lightly on her lips.

"You can join me at the commander's office if you like," said Mickey while kissing her in this, their special way.

"Just like Ruth said to Naomi, where you go so shall I. Your commander shall be my commander."

Mickey then took her by the shoulders and squared her off in front of him. He spoke with the first semblance of confidence he could muster all day.

"We may not have started this military career jointly, but we will certainly go together and inter it into its final resting place."

"It sounds like you're feeling adventurous, Indiana."

"What can I say? Life with us seems to be just that—a never-ending, whip-cracking adventure."

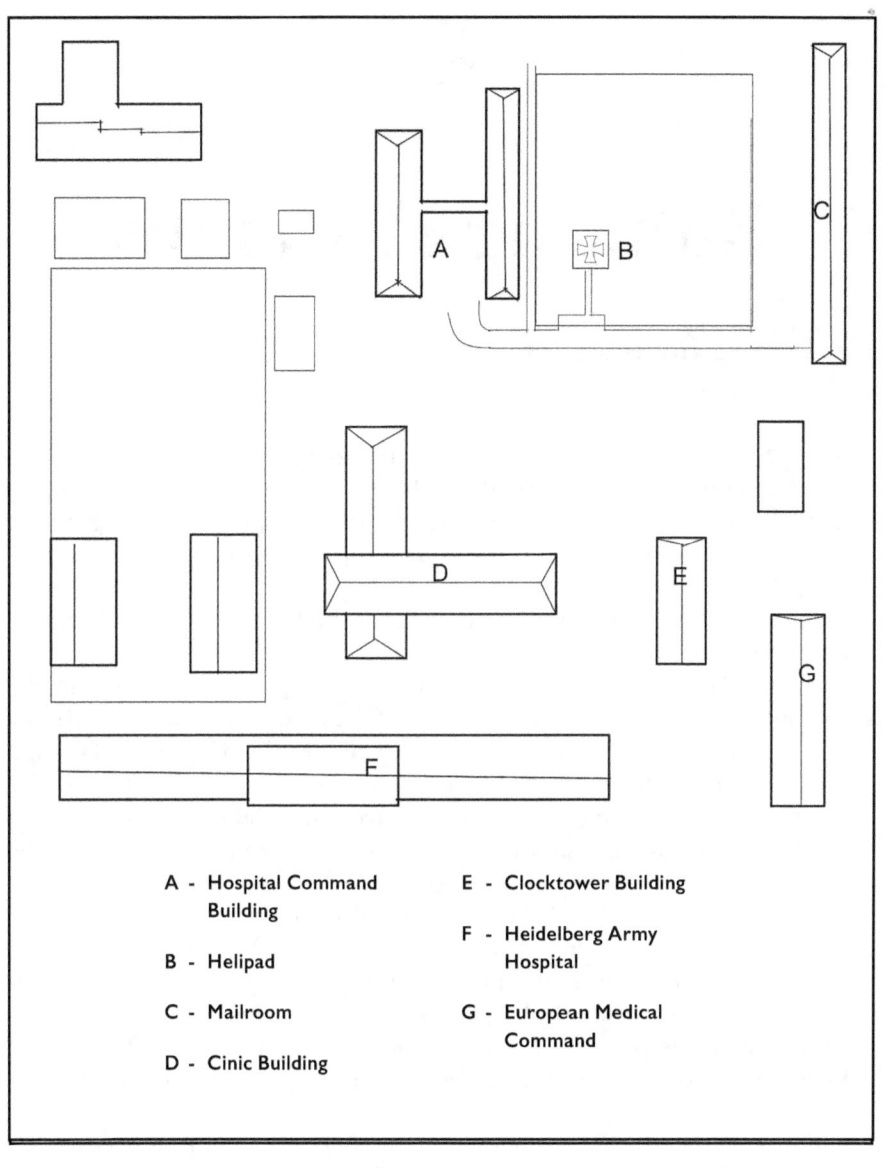

A - Hospital Command
    Building

B - Helipad

C - Mailroom

D - Cinic Building

E - Clocktower Building

F - Heidelberg Army
    Hospital

G - European Medical
    Command

Map of Caserne

5

Building H-Bombs

Heidelberg Hospital grounds
Heidelberg, Germany

"Many a career has been sunk by the torpedoes originating from the hospital commander's office, Mickey." Loni forced a laugh as the pair left the hospital's entrance, heading away across the hospital grounds.

"I guess that's why the commander's headquarters is shaped like an H."

"Huh?"

"You know … an H-bomb?" Mickey flicked his fingers upward, adding the corresponding sound.

"It's good that we're making light of it now. I imagine reality will eventually set in and humor will be the first casualty." The remaining walk took Mickey and Loni from the main hospital through the multileveled Heidelberg Hospital clinic building directly to the H-Building. There, one entire wing of the *H* was dedicated solely to the hospital's chief executive and his staff elements.

Loni paused a moment as the command suite arched in front of them. She looked for silent instructions from Mickey now that they had arrived at the place that she knew he dreaded most. In a few moments, he would be face-to-face with the hospital commander. Loni acknowledged Mickey's nod signaling that he would go alone from this point to face dismissal from the commander. Most of the walk over from the hospital, Loni had been mentally reviewing her DIA briefing notes and now, as she went to the seating area, her tongue was clamped to the floor of her mouth, but her mind was streaming in her DIA world uncontrollably.

Why would anyone want to ritually kill a tower keeper who was, in fact, an ordained priest? It wasn't enough just to snuff out his life. There was an additional need to mutilate him. Why the humiliation? What statement is being made here? Beyond this mystery, what's the explanation for the presence of DNA whose carbon age spanned two thousand years? Is it just coincidence that the tower keeper's home was previously in the Heidelberg area and that his brother is a tower keeper of yet another leaning tower located here in Germany?

Loni's mind drifted back to the three middle school years she had spent in this very town when her father was stationed here as a NATO staff officer. It seemed to her that Germany was more her home than the United States since most of her developmental years were spent in the towns of Bamberg, Heidelberg, or Würzburg.

In fact, it was in the town of Würzburg, at Leighton Barracks, where she spent her high school junior and senior years. It was also the place where she, young Loni Meriwether, fell in love with a young army officer named Michael Peronne whom everyone called Mickey. He was so austere, striking, and just drop-dead handsome. *It might have been nice if he had even noticed me back then. He would have been quite a catch.*

Today at fifty-five, Mickey was still a quite a catch. *Now, even better than his good looks, Mickey has brilliance which over time has developed him into an acknowledged military and theology history expert.* The truth of the matter was that Mickey knows history. Considering the nature of the DIA murder case on the current docket, having access to a history whiz kid was a good thing for Loni.

There had to be a way for her to pose her burning history questions to Mickey without *really* asking him. Even if she could think of the manner, now wasn't the moment. Mickey's body and mind were locked in the present and most painfully imprisoned in smoldering discontent.

6

Noted

Heidelberg Hospital Commander's Office
Heidelberg, Germany

"I'm not clear why you don't understand, Dr. Peronne." Without lifting her eyes from her computer, the hospital commander's secretary, a German civilian assigned to the US Army, toggled on her keyboard as the white-knuckled Lieutenant Colonel Doctor Mickey Peronne stood impatiently at her desk. "You can either wait in here or sit outside and wait. The choice is yours." Working for a full-bird colonel hospital commander gave Frau Heinz the leeway to be less than awed by any subordinate ranking officer, which included everyone assigned at Heidelberg Hospital.

"Look, Frau Heinz." Mickey sat on the edge of the chair. "There are times when the needs of others outweigh the needs of the one."

"You're talking about my Henry, yes?" Frau Heinz folded her hands in front of her keyboard.

"Not long ago, when you called my staff in a panic because Henry couldn't be awakened, I didn't balk." Mickey drew in a deep breath. "I canceled my morning appointments and made a house visit."

"Henry wouldn't wake up."

"I know, I remember." Mickey scooted the chair forward. "He was off the far end of the bed, between the bed frame itself and the wall."

"It was horrible to see him that way—his nose pressed against the wall."

"Yes, Frau Heinz. It was my staff and I that returned Henry back to the bed so he could lie in state with the dignity he deserved."

"He was a crew member for the Golden Knights," the secretary said of the army's show and competition parachute team. She stifled a sniffle.

"Yes, he was, and he had a right to be remembered with honor worthy of that station." Mickey inched forward again. "As you know, German law required that he could not be removed from the house for twenty-four hours."

"Yes, Dr. Peronne, to assure he was dead." Frau Heinz shivered. "It's an old law. It's one that was held over from olden times when people who were thought to be dead suddenly came to life."

"The art of medicine has come a long way from those days."

"Yes, but the legal system hasn't." Frau Heinz wiped her eyes with a tissue. "At least it's no longer a three-day wait."

"Do you remember how much you struggled with being in the same house all night long with your dearly departed Henry?"

"I struggled badly, Dr. Peronne. As much as I wanted to be with him, the thought of laying all night next to a corpse frightened me."

"That's right, Gertrude. We talked … just like we are talking now…"

"Yes, I stayed the night with Henry. I held him in my arms one last time. Thanks to you I had closure, Dr. Peronne."

"Right now, Gertrude, I need the same closure from you." Mickey stood. "I would appreciate if you could—"

The phone rang.

"Excuse me, Dr. Peronne, I must take this call." Cradling the phone on her far shoulder while executing a smile, she resumed working on the keyboard. Somehow, amidst this marked demonstration of multitasking, she managed to silently pass Mickey a folded note upon which was written his name.

"What is up with folded notes today?" Mickey murmured under his breath. A quick glance through the open commander's door revealed that the hospital commander, Colonel Birdsong, was nowhere in his office. Mickey unfolded the note and read the last thing he wanted to see. Crumpling the little yellow square, he rapped his knuckles respectfully on the secretary's desk in traditional German courtesy and exited the commander's suite.

As he stepped out the door, he looked for his devoted wife. Loni was nowhere in sight, but the click of a closing ladies' restroom door to his left caught his attention. Realizing it was his turn to wait, Mickey looked for a comfortable place to sit. Loni's unscheduled trip to the powder room had just bought him a few minutes of private thinking time.

7

Good, Bad, and Unbridled

Heidelberg Hospital H-Building
Heidelberg, Germany

*G*ertrude, send Dr. Peronne to meet me in the general's office ASAP.

"That's what it said, all right," Mickey whispered. Nervously he glanced at the ladies' room door before pulling open the creases of the balled-up note he had just received from the commander's secretary. *No need to keep staring at these words. It doesn't change them, and it doesn't make me feel any better.* Mickey tried hard to focus on any silver lining this dark cloud might have to offer. *Meeting with the colonel in the general's office? This can't be good.* However, Mickey could not to let his thoughts carry him away. He needed a tincture of the optimism that defined Loni. *She's been that way as long as I have known her.*

✠ ✠ ✠

At Würzburg High, Loni was the head cheerleader while I was a brand-new army officer. He chuckled. *Oh, I noticed her girlish flirtations and yes, I was indeed attracted to her … but I knew it would not be wise to go messing around in the very sandbox where I worked. That was a smart decision.* Mickey nodded. *Many, many years later, we met again. That time, there was nothing to stop the sparks from flying. Loni was no longer girlish but had blossomed into the beautiful woman that I have come to love deeply.*

Today, as his wife, Loni fulfilled Mickey in every way but one—motherhood. Mickey tried hard not to dwell on this failure of his.

Being careful not to drop the note, Mickey began pulling on the length of each digit of his hands. His mother always said that if the fingers felt the same afterward, then the problems or failures were still there. After a couple cycles of pulls, the fingers usually became tingly. She had espoused that this was because the shortfalls were disappearing into thin air. Much to his chagrin, Mickey had started on round three when he noticed some peripheral movement.

"Everything good, Mickey?" Loni's voice was a salve that, given enough time, could smooth out the creases of the now sweaty, rumpled note still in his hand.

"I thought you left me," Mickey replied.

"No worries, honey. If I left you, you'd still come following after me, right?" Mickey could feel a smile brewing behind his tight lips. He maintained silence.

"Judging by that scowl, I'm guessing that we still have unfinished business."

"Scowl? What, this face, a scowl? This is my seriously pondering look. It's what army officers do when they have to go from the hospital commander's office to meet with the medical commanding general."

"Why do we have to go to General Framingham's office?" Loni's voice quavered. Mickey noted Loni's hand tremble. He softened.

"No scowl, see?" His voice soothed. "I'll tell you along the way."

"Is it going to be good news? Honestly, Mickey, I really don't think I can take any more bad news. It's just that I—"

"It is never news when you know the answer going in," Mickey interrupted unflinchingly.

"So you know why we are going to see the general."

"Not ... exactly."

"I see." Loni tightened her lips. "Cannons to the left and cannons to the right, so 'rode the six hundred' on 'into the valley of Death.'"

"Hey, I'm the army historian—"

"*Were* the army historian." Loni hardened her features. "Looks like I'll be on point from here."

"Then lead on, Loni, 'half a league, half a league, half a league onward.'"

8

Sted and Limpy

Heidelberg Hospital grounds
Heidelberg, Germany

"Colonels call for lieutenant colonels to stand before their desks, Loni." Mickey puffed as he picked up the pace across the hospital grounds. "Generals call for colonels to stand in front of theirs."

With a sense of newfound urgency, Mickey and Loni briskly crossed the caserne to the building which housed the one officer who did, indeed, outrank the hospital commander. The European medical commander was the resident one-star medical general who gave directives which all hospital commanders in Europe had to follow.

"Wasn't it General Framingham who ordered the initiation of your medical board, Mickey?" Loni motioned to slow the pace.

"That's right." Mickey shortened his stride. "I was unable to redeploy into a tactical theater of operations." Mickey clenched his teeth.

"Still sitting sour in your gut, honey?"

"Loni, I had been meritoriously awarded the Purple Heart, and the Bronze Star with V for valor."

"I know, I remember." Loni stopped and mimicked reading from a scroll. "'For his selfless action in treating the wounded under fire, Mickey Peronne is awarded this special award.'" Loni's smile soured. "Apparently, being a wounded hero has an expiration date."

"Even with my limp," Mickey tapped his leg, "I have been a health care provider here in the Family Practice Clinic. That should count for *something.*"

"Don't sell yourself short, Mickey. You also took on the additional duty of chief of the Hospital Emergency Response Team. Honey, General Framingham knows this. I mean, you're his chief consultant on the medical management of chemical casualties, for heaven's sake."

Mickey nodded curtly. "Unfortunately, coming up short seems to be a trend with me today." He gave a weak smile and took his wife's arm in his own as they continued their quickstep across the grounds.

Passing briefly back through the first-floor mezzanine of the clinic building, Loni and Mickey Peronne ran into Mickey's medical colleague and own personal physician, Dr. Christiansted. Stoking newly founded resentment, Loni nevertheless smiled pleasantly, accepting the cheek kisses from Prentice. Her gaze drifted from the pair.

"Hi, Mickey." Prentice poked Mickey's shoulder. "I've really been aiming to talk to you. I submitted my evaluation of your orthopedic findings to the medical board."

"Yes, I know, Prentice." Mickey frowned.

"I'm judging that they didn't accept my recommendation that you were fit for duty with modification of responsibilities?"

"No, they just gave me the boot." Mickey gave Prentice a forced smile, but then shot a downward gaze to his colleague's left boot. If he had x-ray vision, Mickey would be able to see inside the leather of that combat boot to a foot without the lateral two toes which had been lost to a foot joint cancer. Five years ago, the medical evaluation board found that Prentice, despite his bird foot, was fit for duty and quite retainable for further military service as an orthopedic physician. But, last week, as Prentice Christiansted's own personal physician, Mickey had to break the news that the foot cancer had returned.

"I guess we aren't exactly the army's poster children, are we, Mickey?"

"I guess that depends on the poster."

"How about the poster that says, 'Uncle Sam Wants You.' You know the one. It sits at every—"

"—recruiting station in the world," Mickey finished. "Did you get the command surgeon's position at the Army Recruiting Command?"

"I did, Mickey."

"Isn't that in Kentucky now?"

"Fort Knox."

"Wait. The on-post hospital there at Fort Knox has an outreach program with University of Louisville medical school's cancer research center."

"So I hear, Mickey."

"What does Bridgette think about you all up and moving to—"

"She hasn't said," Prentice cut across Mickey.

"She's the general's handpicked chief of staff. If she is about to give up her dream job to—"

"The truth is I haven't told her. And, Mickey, I'd appreciate that you and Loni hold tight to this information. I'll know when the time is right to share."

"Prentice, I can't help but feel that strategically you are going about this in the wrong way." Mickey looked at Loni and knew she agreed. "But we will keep silent."

Loni looked at one man then the other. They were the epitome of contrast. Whereas Mickey was youthful even in distress, Prentice had deep forehead lines and weathered crow's-feet at the corners of his eyes. In her mind she saw the parallels in their careers. They were so different in many ways. Yet, as medical mishaps they were virtually twins. She was glad when the men shook hands in farewell. It seemed that a cloud of sadness always hovered over the pale, almost fragile Prentice Christiansted.

✠ ✠ ✠

It wasn't much longer until Mickey and Loni arrived across the installation at the European Medical Command Headquarters building. Mickey sat his wife down in the foyer while he negotiated the grand staircase spiraling high above them.

Show no weakness in the presence of weakness. Therefore, amble up the stairs instead of taking the elevator. Mickey groaned with each step. *Call me crazy,* Mickey grunted, *but I can't shake this feeling that as my supervisors, the colonel and the general are cooking something up on my behalf.*

The sounds of Loni's nervous first-floor foot taps became more distant as the thought of leadership plotting grew louder in Mickey's head. *Maybe I should have said something to Loni before I left. Maybe it would have reduced the tension that I know she's feeling. Maybe she'll stop twirling her hair with her finger.* Mickey stopped, turned, and started to retrace his steps when he caught a distant cellphone chime followed by Loni's murmuring. *Well, it's too late now. Loni is now caught up in other distractions.* Mickey turned and finished his final ascent. By now, Loni was several floors below, such that even the faint echoes of her foot taps were silenced.

9

Morell and the Message

European Command (EUCOM)
Stuttgart, Germany

"Cold water to the face, slaps to the face, pinching the skin ... nothing seems to work." The airman stared at his sleep-deprived face in the restroom mirror. *This is not what I signed up for.*

Airman Morell was on his fourth straight uneventful graveyard rotation at the US Army's European Command Headquarters. This lonely night shift had started just like every other one during this overseas deployment. It was a continuous battle with boredom.

"Sorry, Morell." Sergeant Cathy came out of the restroom stall still adjusting his uniform. "Staring at an ugly face in the mirror doesn't change the fact that it is still ugly when you leave."

"Does this duty get any easier over time, Sergeant?"

"I could lie and tell you yes," Sergeant Cathy chortled as he washed his hands at the sink. "Yes, it does ... in a pig's eye."

"Why do they keep me on nights, Sergeant?"

"They? Who is they?"

"Whoever does the scheduling."

"Morell, I do the scheduling."

"And you placed me on four straight stretches of night shifts."

"I place myself on straight night shifts too."

"That's right, Sergeant, you do. Why do that to either of us?"

"Here's the thing." Sergeant Cathy grabbed a paper towel and leaned back against the sink while drying his hands. "Military events of great significance require a certain amount of shock and awe."

"I haven't seen either in the past four weeks, Sergeant."

"What do you read when you're on night shift?"

"I dunno … comics … magazines laying around." Airman Morell folded his arms. "You're not suggesting I should read one of those thick novels?"

"Morell, I know you're not a thick novel–reading type. However, I do notice that you have a knack for history."

"Yes, my family runs deep in military history."

"I notice that the comics you read are those related to history subjects like military, war, combat, knights, Templars, and such."

"I guess me being in the military is just a way of playing the military games I always did as a kid."

"I was the same." Sergeant Cathy smiled. "I would get up at three in the morning and attack the bedroom windows of my fellow neighborhood play-mates." Sergeant Cathy threw the paper towel in the bin. "Have you figured out why I placed us both on night shift?"

"No, Sergeant."

"Surprise attacks in the wee hours," the sergeant winked. "They always work best when the enemy strikes fast and early. When they do, Airman Morell, I want to be the one receiving the message."

"Are you expecting an attack?"

"Always … and never. Lately it seems everything I have had to handle has been a false alarm. That's why I brought you on shift."

"You think I could be good at picking up a real threat?"

"With some training, maybe." Sergeant Cathy headed for the door, opened it, and paused. "First you need to leave home behind—then it'll be easier to stay awake."

"I guess I came on this deployment for the wrong reason."

"Many of you guys from the Gulf Coast arrive here for the same wrong reason."

"Really?" Airman Morell furrowed his brow.

"Look back in that mirror again, Morell. Take a walk. Think about things. Don't come back until you figure out where you need to be and why." Sergeant Cathy proceeded out the door.

Airman Morell watched the door swing to-and-fro until it became still. He leaned on the sink and stared, really stared into his own eyes. "Why are you here? How can I possibly leave home behind?"

As an activated reservist, Morell had come here alone while his wife, little girl, and infant son remained at home in Mississippi at the air force base which had been slammed by last season's unexpected freak hurricane. *Thank God we were all on vacation.* The gale force winds had sent ocean-side structures deep into the base housing area of the air force garrison situated strategically along the Gulf Coast of the United States. *Every day was full of more duty assignments as a trash and garbage recycler.* Home life had almost returned back to the routine. Then an assignment came open for a Special Operations airman to perform full-time duty in Germany.

I had a choice between being a street sweeper or a tactical operator. Imagine! The intrigue! The danger! He rubbed his hands roughly over his face. *The delusion. The disappoint-*

ment. Reality proved to be very different than his anticipations. On the graveyard shift of Special Operations there hadn't been a whole lot of cloak or dagger.

Airman Morell meandered outdoors to the picnic table and stared for hours at the lights on the flight line. *Great expectations, see where that gets you?* He scoffed then looked at his watch. It was late. He needed to return to his workstation. As he dragged his feet to his desk, he saw the little red light flash and heard the phone buzz. He sprinted to the phone.

"Strategic Operations. This is Airman Morell." Morell swallowed hard. "Sir, could you say again—slower and clearer." Morell snatched up a pen and jotted furiously.

10

Slumber Interrupted

European Command (EUCOM)
Stuttgart, Germany

Airman Morell slammed the phone down on its receiver, his heart pounding loudly in his ears. He had to take deep breaths to get control of himself. He couldn't believe what just happened. *This is big, very big.* What he did in the next few minutes would make a huge difference to all those Special Operations agents in the field. *This is my first big event to report. I can't screw this up.* Morell shot a glance to the shift sergeant. *When in doubt, ask.* Airman Morell walked hurriedly over to the shift leader's desk.

"Sergeant Cathy, I got a hit on my line."

"Yeah, I saw." Sergeant Cathy wiped his eyes, stood, and stretched.

"This is it. This is what we talked about. There seems to be something big brewing. I want to make sure I report this correctly."

"Big for you?"

"What do you mean?"

"You're new to Tactical Operations, right?"

"Yes, I have only been—"

"So, you haven't seen a lot of things come through."

"No, Sergeant Cathy. You know that."

"So, I ask again … big or big for you?"

"I'm not so sure now."

"All you green guys get excited. Quick to run it up the chain. Before you know it, everyone else is worked up, and in the end it turns out to be nothing." Sergeant Cathy scoffed. "Then someone asks the question, 'Which shift leader is responsible for this garbage?' You see, Airman Morell. I don't want that situation to be mine."

"You haven't heard what the event is, Sergeant."

"Don't have to," Sergeant Cathy snuffled. "It's usually nothing."

"Well, what should I do?"

"Tell you what. Let's make a teaching session out of this. Let's write up the SITREP together and see what you've got for the situation report." The sergeant

38

yawned and twisted his torso until his spine yielded a satisfactory popping sound. He sighed. "If it's big, I'll let you know."

"Sure."

"You being green and all, you may not realize it, but reporting a situation is as important as the event itself."

"No, Sergeant, I knew that. That's why I came over here to you. I wanted to ensure that it is done correctly." Morell watched as Sergeant Cathy pulled out a fat notebook and flipped over several plastic-sleeved pages.

"Ah yes, here it is." Sergeant Cathy sat down.

"What does that page say?"

"Well, it says here ... " Sergeant Cathy underlined with his finger as he read, "'The report is as important as the event.'"

"Yes, Sergeant."

"So now you know that I know what I'm talking about."

"Sergeant Cathy, those stripes you wear tell me that you know what you're talking about."

"Enough with the bootlicking, Airman."

"I was just making an observation."

"So was I." The sergeant coughed. "It says here ... " Sergeant Cathy followed with his finger, "'the report must be filed timely.'"

"Aren't we losing a little time here ... right now?"

"Now see? That's what I'm talking about. You want to get it out fast, and we haven't even determined if this is a worthy event to report."

"Sergeant Cathy, I feel pretty sure if I tell you what it is, you will agree that—"

"Fine. Here's the form. Jot down there on that line the nature of the event. Take your time. Make sure you check your spelling." Sergeant Cathy glanced over at the coffee pot. "I'll be back in a minute." The sergeant shook his head, mumbling, "Young folks ... so quick to get riled up."

When he returned with the coffee, Airman Morell had already returned to his station. Sergeant Cathy started to pull the coffee mug to his lips as he read Morell's completed SITREP. The sound of a coffee cup crashing on the floor preceded the shout across the room.

"Morell! Get your Strategic Operations airman's hindquarters over here! Right now!"

11

Stirring the Poles

European Command (EUCOM)

Stuttgart, Germany

"Sergeant Cathy?" Standing at Sergeant Cathy's desk, Airman Morell stared at his clenched fingers. On the floor was a shattered coffee cup in a pool of splattered coffee like a Rorschach test. "You don't look so well." In front of him was an enormously stressed shift leader. In the wake of the excitement, Morell couldn't focus on his job—all because of that urgent, flashing panel light that had heralded a ring from the NATO priority line. "This is big, right, Sergeant Cathy?" Morell stood; his stomach knotted.

"I can only imagine the stir this is going to cause upstream when it reaches General Bloomfield's desk." Sergeant Cathy stared at the red hotline phone labeled *EUCOM Commander.*

Morell followed Cathy's eyes. "Are you going to use the bat phone?"

"I'm picturing the grimace on the face of General Bloomfield when I brief him on this. He has this nasty habit of going ballistic and bouncing off the walls." Sergeant Cathy leveled his eyes. "Okay, Morell, tell me *exactly* what you heard."

"But, Sergeant, I wrote everything down just like you asked me—"

"Pull up a chair. Tell me word for word. Now."

"About two hours ago in southwestern Poland, a batch of weapons-grade chemicals from a former World War II chemical munitions site was uncovered."

"This alone is ominous, Morell … but there's more, right?"

"Yes, Sergeant." Morell scooted his chair forward. "Something more than just lost chemical weapons was found on-site." Morell swallowed dryly. "On-site personnel indicated that if what had just been found landed into the wrong hands, it could threaten the safety of the entire world."

"Regarding falling into the wrong hands, he used the exact words, 'could threaten the safety of the entire world.' Right?"

"Yes, Sergeant."

"No embellishment on your part?" The sergeant pointed his finger at the airman.

"Negative."

"Did this person ever tell you what, specifically, had been found?"

"Negative, Sergeant."

"Did you ask?"

"I did." Morell leaned forward. "He told me that he did not have secure communications on his end."

"You told him that we had high side operations here, right?"

"Affirmative, I did," Morell shook his head. "He seemed to be worried that his inability to have communications scrambled on his end could compromise the data."

"This is the reporting individual?" Sergeant Cathy pointed to a name on the SITREP.

"Yes, Sergeant Cathy. That's the name, rank, and title he gave. He called himself the chemical recovery site officer."

"And this is what he kept repeating?" Cathy traced the words on the paper.

"Yes, Sergeant." Airman Morell stood. "Over and over he kept repeating, 'Holy Jesus, are you getting this? Confirm. Confirm. I say again, are you getting this?'"

12

Of Stars and Eagles

European Command (EUCOM)
Stuttgart, Germany

Still working hard to control his rapid breathing, Airman Morell briskly looked down at his watch and then at the strategic alert roster. Now that Sergeant Cathy had called General Bloomfield, the sergeant was picking up stray ceramic shards while dabbing at the splashes of spilled coffee from the side of his desk.

"Who is next on the call list?" Sergeant Cathy shouted.

"It says European Medical Command Headquarters."

"That would be General Framingham," Sergeant Cathy barked. "If you feel comfortable talking to a general, I need to go bandage up my hand before I bleed to death."

"Sergeant Cathy, I've never...."

"Okay, give me a minute. I'll be right there." The sergeant groaned. "If we are going to get you to do this *well*, we need to see to it that you do it *right*. It might be better to start you on bird colonels. For the most part, they are a nicer bunch."

After Sergeant Cathy, with bandaged hand, notified the medical general, he pointed to the colonel's name ranking third on the list.

"Colonel Bridgette Christiansted. She is the medical commander's chief of staff, while serving as director of the European branch of the army's Medical Research Command. She is just down the hall from General Framingham. Both are co-located just ten blocks down the street. If you fold up your SITREP into a paper airplane, with a good throw, you could land that puppy right on her desk." Cathy laughed as he pulled up a chair and sat down at Morell's workstation, then listened as Airman Morell reported the facts to Colonel Christiansted as he knew them.

"That was good, Airman," Sergeant Cathy nodded. "Remember, when you don't have the information, just say so by saying 'negative knowledge.' If they press you for more information, indicate that you will specifically request that information from future report submissions."

"I'm nervous speaking to high-ranking officers."

"They put their pants on one leg at a time, just like you, Airman."

"That's an image I don't need to have in my head, Sergeant."

"Actually, you do. People are just people. Everyone has someone they answer to. These folks have got to get the wheels turning in their fields of expertise. They have folks they have to call. All we are doing is getting the ball rolling."

"Roger, Sergeant."

"So, who is next on the list?"

"It says the Mobile Emergency Medical Response Team. There is no name."

"There is no name because the teams change names, depending on who gets the mission. The MERT is a deployed hospital asset under EUCOM control. Your call will go to a message node that will, no doubt, hold this information if the team is out doing field operations or some military medical research in the desert."

"Who do we ask for?"

"I don't have a name, but the important thing for you to know is that you're calling two hours ahead to Southwest Asia and the Middle East. Leave your message with the officer in charge." Sergeant Cathy watched as Morell gave a more confident report.

"I have one last name on my list, Sergeant."

"You've got this, Airman." The sergeant slapped Morell on the shoulder and stood up. "I'm going to find me a sturdier coffee cup. Let me know how it goes with this last notification."

"Roger." Morell again checked the time on his watch. The fourth, and last, number on his list would be a stateside call late into the evening hours. This always brought a pang of anxiety to him and, he could guess, to the poor soul on duty at the receiving end. He punched in the number, remembering what his boss had always said: *Bad news never gets better over time.* He formulated his words as he heard the rings and waited for the eventual click at the far end when the operations duty officer would inevitably answer with an irritated tone. He remembered what his Grandpa Freddy always said: *No good deed ever goes unpunished.*

13

Fired or Fried

European Medical Command

Heidelberg, Germany

*C*annons to the left and cannons to the right, so "rode the six hundred" on "into the valley of Death."

Mickey walked the long hall leading to the commanding general's office. Along the way, his eyes perused the door plaques identifying the types of work being done in the various third-floor rooms. *There's the office door of the army's Medical Research Command's European Satellite Office. When they need me to act in the role of the European consultant on military medical history to the Office of the Army Surgeon General, the key magically appears in my hand. Not a one of my professional colleagues has duty responsibilities which interface on three different echelons. Yet all of them are out there and I am in here making the slow jaunt to the professional gallows.*

Passing another set of office doors, Mickey heard raised voices. Inside that room, standing squarely centered, Prentice's wife, the female Colonel Christiansted—the European medical commander's chief of staff—was verbally raining blows on the cowering staff of military researchers. Her eye caught Mickey as he paused in the hallway outside the door.

"Hey, sorry you had to see that." Bridgette pasted a forced smile. "Prentice mentioned he was looking to close a loop with you."

"Loop closed, Bridgette." Mickey searched her face for a hidden agenda. "On the way here, actually."

"Well, good … good … " Bridgette licked her lips. "I take it you're not here to see me."

"No, my business is down the hall with your boss, General Framingham."

"Well, you probably shouldn't keep him waiting." Bridgette winced, shifting uncomfortably. "Unless of course you're early. We could chat."

"Not this time, Bridgette." Mickey could feel the turmoil behind her eyes. *Bridgette doesn't know about the return of the cancer in Prentice's foot. She wants an update but knows I can't divulge. When will Prentice break the news? When is the right time? There are some things in life that do not get easier with the passing of time. Where will Prentice find the*

44

words to ease his wife's shock? Where will I? "Maybe next time on your dime." Mickey strode away fast without a backward glance.

Mickey's mind raced as he arrived at the European Medical Command's rank-heavy hallway. *I could have an immediate release, delayed release, reduction in responsibility, loss of rank, loss of status, or a stop-loss action with retention for continued active service.* A few deep breaths later, he stood at the threshold of the general's door. Mickey sucked in a shivering breath. General Framingham's booming voice could be easily heard. *Why is it that generals never sound happy?*

After being granted entrance into the general's suite, Mickey now found himself in the presence of, and confronted by, his two immediate superiors—the ruddy-faced Colonel Birdsong and the cigar-chewing General Framingham. Mickey entered the office and held his salute until both officers returned the courtesy.

"Don't bother to relax, Mickey," said the colonel. "We have a developing situation that is going to impact your ability to perform your present mission."

"Respectfully, sir, I really don't have a mission anymore. I was on the way from your office to receive the—" Mickey found himself staring at Colonel Birdsong's hand, indicating silence.

"There's more to tell." The colonel glanced at his watch. "However, we're still waiting for an expert who should have already been here."

After many moments of the general's cigar-chewing, Colonel Birdsong continued. "The folks at EUCOM are reporting a major find in Poland. Mickey, we will need your expertise out in the field. I sense that you will be minimally supported, at first, at least until we can get more pieces out on the playing field for you."

"But, sir, I am trying to tell you—"

"You'll be working with forward ground operations as the lead torch element. Can you slide yourself back into a command surgeon mode?"

"Yes, Colonel, I can always take solo lead on a forward mission but—"

"But me no buts, Mickey. Can you execute forward operations given limited operations support and guided by sketchy intelligence at best?"

"How limited and just how sketchy, sir?"

"I don't rightly know. That is what the missing person is supposed to tell us." Everyone's gaze turned to the empty, open doorway, then back at each other.

"Sir, if we're waiting for Colonel Christiansted, I just passed her mentoring some—"

"Mentoring?" The general laughed. "Is that what her technique is called?" He plucked some cigar tidbits from his tongue. "We're not waiting for Bridgette."

"Roger, sir. If I may ... in my best estimation of the mission, it seems that what you initially need is a speed bump." Colonel Birdsong scowled but General Framingham laughed agreeably.

"I told you Hutson," the general pointed with his cigar, "this boy's quick."

"Respectfully, sirs, as the speed bump, you need for me to link up with this intelligence source at a later time to see what level of medical, historical, or medical history operations can then be executed." Before Colonel Birdsong could answer, a knock on the door was given entrance privileges by General Framingham. The general's voice had a clearly different authoritative tone to it as he spoke in a resounding baritone.

"Dr. Peronne, we truly need you for this mission tasking." Mickey opened his mouth to reply but heard a feminine voice behind him speak.

"Happy to support the mission, sir." Dr. Loni Peronne carried herself like the quintessential professional that she was. She directed her continuing commentary to both the general and colonel as if her husband was not even in the room. "Gentlemen, I am not spun up on any mission-specific intelligence relative to EUCOM's discovery in Poland right now, but I can tell you what support DIA can offer in the European theater of operations."

Mickey shot his wife a *Did you know this all along?* kind of look. Shaking her head, *No*, she pointed to her cellphone. She looked squarely at Mickey.

"Dr. Peronne," said Loni, "it looks like we are still connected to that digitally camouflaged umbilical cord, compliments of the US Army."

"She's right, Mickey." Colonel Birdsong smiled broadly. "The medical board ruling is sidelined. You're being given another opportunity to succeed."

"Sir, I ... " Mickey stammered, thinking only of the boot camp response to the demands of unrelenting push-ups from the drill master." He mumbled, "Thank you, sir, may I have another?"

"Did you say something, Mickey?" Colonel Birdsong asked.

"Uh, no sir, I was just wondering if I was going have another ... never mind, I think I already have enough." Sorting through his jumbled response as a reinstated active-duty army physician, Mickey looked at his feet which had just been thrust back into the fire without the courtesy of at least being provided a frying pan. A puzzled Colonel Birdsong stared, beet-faced, as he ciphered through the cryptic nature of Mickey's response.

Meanwhile, General Framingham, cigar in mouth, rendered a full-belly chortle. "You've been had, Colonel Birdsong!"

No, General, Mickey thought as he cupped his face with his icy hands, *it's me who's been had.*

14

Morell Confounded

European Command (EUCOM)
Stuttgart, Germany

*N*o good deed ever goes unpunished. Yeah. Here goes.
As the phone continued to ring to the United States, Airman Morell began thinking about Grandpa Freddy who loved to speak that phrase. As a kid, Morell used to spend hours in the barber shop listening to Grandpa Freddy talk about the greatness of his father, Dr. Theodor Morell. Morell grew up understanding that his great-grandfather had originally coined that phrase in the family. *There was a good reason he had coined it.*

Dr. Theodor Morell had all the training in the world to do *good* but was sorely limited in his ability to use it. As the phone kept ringing in the current day, Morell's mind went back to Grandpa Freddy telling his father's story.

✠ ✠ ✠

Dr. Morell had done all he could for his patient, the elderly chancellor, but it just didn't seem to matter. The man seemed to want more and more at a time when the doctor had less and less to give.

Dr. Morell sat at his rolltop desk. He drummed on his desk pad as his neck craned in a methodical search. The shelves situated above the desk held an antique mantel clock radio. Its grooves were filled with dust. On either side of the radio was a personal medical pharmacy. The doctor pushed aside bottles and vials of medicine into a jagged formation. His eyes read across the labels on the half-turned assorted glassware and then roamed around his workspace as if hoping to find an answer there among the tools of his trade.

On the left side of the shelf, closer to him, sat the medicinal chemical belladonna next to its cousin, atropine. On the far-right side of the radio, all in a row, sat the potassium bromide, caffeine, testosterone, and cocaine. There were more bottles and vials stacked behind, peering through the not-so-neatly aligned files. He perused through them before turning his search downward.

On the surface of his desk, almost in the center and acting like a paper-weight, was an open vial of enzymes and vitamins which were always good to treat those things that generally ail people. A stack of three medical reference books acted as a coaster for a cup-sized ceramic pharmacist's mortar and pestle branded with the heraldic crest of an eagle. Cigar ashes, not just crushed medicines, caked the bulbous end of the well-worn pestle. Unfulfilled, he pushed himself away from the desk to search new areas.

The fronts of the desk's drawers were in various degrees of closure. In the lower drawers of the desk, medical syringes with affixed needles of variable sizes and shapes poked out at odd angles. His search continued. The large drawer on the lower right held a bottle of whiskey which was, of course, only used for medicinal purposes. He rubbed his eyes and blinked hard, willing an answer to come to him.

Dr. Morell had once been told that an unkempt, messy desk was a sign of genius. Being both a physician and a medicinal chemist, he was an example of all that and more. His medical training came from France and Germany. His actual medical degree was French, but his medical practice had always been among the Germans. Additional study in medicinal chemistry accentuated the essence of his brilliance. Dr. Morell had all this education to provide his patients with the best medical care, and yet the old doctor sat roadblocked with the medical issues at hand. It appeared that brilliance alone didn't seem to hold the answer to the medical management of his one and only patient, the old chancellor of Germany.

Most physicians have a troublesome patient who causes them hours upon hours of professional concern and grief. Dr. Morell was no different. He was currently managing the old gentleman's case of irritable bowel syndrome which seemed to occupy both of them constantly. The doctor was hoping that a medical concoction of intestinal bacteria, enzymes, and vitamins might prove to be the potential cure-all.

The chancellor had certainly become very disturbed as of late—always worried about having a sexually transmitted disease. Presently, however, he seemed to be obsessed with more than his sexual health. He was becoming increasingly concerned about the total amount of time he had yet to live. Already at the midpoint in his fifties, he looked ahead into the next two decades and wondered how much of them he was going to be able to enjoy. So much so that he started making changes in his environment right away.

He had begun denying the good doctor, as he did with anyone who had personal contact with him, the pleasure of lighting up any cigar or cigarette in his presence. The chancellor felt that tobacco smoke might negatively affect the health of his lungs. Ruminating on this, Dr. Morell smiled. He remembered the location of the lost item. Reaching to his face, he pulled a chewed matchstick from his teeth.

After multiple strikes to get a spark, Dr. Morell's face lit up against the fiery end of a glowing cigar. *Smoking bad for the lungs? Could anything be more ridiculous?*

15

Into the Fire

European Medical Command
Heidelberg, Germany

*I*t's difficult to squeeze more onto a plate already full. Loni's mind was clicking and ratcheting, trying to configure how to approach this new duty.

Back at the first-floor lobby, while Loni waited for Mickey to descend, she sat deep in thought, intensely tracing the curves of the cuticles on her nail beds. She reviewed all that was just added to her DIA plate. First and foremost, she had to deal with this leaning tower affair. *Now, thanks to what General Framingham and Colonel Birdsong revealed, I'm designated as lead intelligence agent for an operation to investigate an extremely bizarre find in a chemical weapons site in Poland.* Both these recent events topped her previous main mission termed the Missing Art Project, a long-running investigation engaging remote viewing techniques to locate two pieces of missing European/Middle Eastern art. *Why do things have to be so complicated?* Before the answer arrived, Loni heard Mickey's distinctive footfalls increase in volume. She turned toward that staccato sound only to see him silently slip into the men's restroom. She noted a marked paleness in his color which wasn't there before the meeting upstairs. She took another deep breath and waited for the bathroom door to again open.

It appeared to Loni that Mickey's trip to the men's room seemed so much longer than the entire time she spent sitting on the front steps at the entrance of the main hospital building earlier that morning. When Mickey finally approached, she stood up and squared off in front of him.

"You *okay*?" Loni searched his face. "I'm asking because you don't look okay. *Okay*?" Loni reached up to brush away droplets of sink water which tenaciously clung to Mickey's eyebrows. He caught her hand curtly at first, but then eased into a more familiar, gentle grip.

"Easy, honey." His voice had a trace of a quiver. "Don't you mean to ask me how I feel about being posted out as cannon fodder?"

"Mickey, I am long past that. You accepted that mission eons ago. What concerns me is that my husband has just been handpicked to do some sort of medical historical task that no one here has the background to do. I don't even have all the mission intelligence yet and I have no doubt it's dangerous. So you see, my dear, I have all the seeds planted to grow a new batch of gray hairs. The worst of it is I, personally, am going to be centrally directing your life based upon data from scanty sources." Loni's voice broke as her eyes began welling up with tears. "So, Mickey, are we going to waste time parrying with the obvious or are you going to tell me if you are *okay*?" Loni reached under both of his arms, holding him like there was no tomorrow. Deep inside she knew maybe there wouldn't be. Her ear pressed against his chest, and she could feel, as well as hear, his voice. It wasn't as soothing as she wanted it to be. She felt that she was embracing a statue.

"First of all, let's get on the same sheet of music, Loni. It's not a mission *I* have been given. It is a mission *we* have been given. Although you will later get the notification from DIA channels, I am here to tell you we have been tasked to execute a search-and-seize mission where I am the chess piece, and you are the chess master. The DIA is playing God with me and frankly, I don't like it." With every word spoken, Mickey's body grew even more tense. Loni released her hug and pushed back. She positioned herself within his personal space, yet far enough to let him see that he was not the only one suffering.

"This is not about DIA having the lead, is it, Mickey? It's about me, your wife, being in the lead. This may be uncharted waters for you in your professional world. For me it is the worst possible scenario."

"Loni, I...." Mickey trailed off, picking at his chin aimlessly.

"Think about it, Mickey. If you have to go headfirst into the lion's jaws, wouldn't you rather it was at the order of someone who cared if you were hungry, cared if you were warm and dry, cared if the approaching shadow of the night brings comfort instead of harm to you? Wouldn't you rather that it be me, who has your very best interest at heart, calling the shots? I would hope that if I wasn't the one assigned this lead, that you would be the one shoe-pounding on the desk demanding it."

"I'm not so sure about that. There will come times that, as the chess master, you'll have to make sacrifices for the betterment of mission success. Right?"

"Right."

"Well then, Loni, be prepared to execute for God and country over 'for richer and poorer, in sickness and in death.'"

"Health."

"What?"

"It's health. The words are 'in health' not 'in death.'"

"Hmmm." Mickey flicked at the whisker debris he had collected on his fingertips. Coupled with a thousand-yard stare through Loni, Mickey bit the inside of his lip.

"It goes like this," Loni inched closer, "'for richer or poorer, in sickness and in health, for as long as we both shall live.'"

"Well, ma'am, I hope you're right. It's just that I am not so sure ... especially about the *living* part."

"What do you want me to say to that?" Loni eyes again welled.

"I'm sorry, Loni." Mickey exhaled and softened his tone. "It's tough being me right now. Also, it's time for the up-brief. I was asked to come get you for the mission briefing." Mickey pasted on a magazine smile. "Dr. Peronne," he bowed slightly, "if you will please kindly follow me to the ERMC Operations cell, Chief of Staff Bridgette Christiansted and G3 Operations Chief Luis Toro-Calderon have requested an audience with us."

Loni couldn't suppress the small grin pushing up the corners of her mouth. "Kiss me," she said, taking his hand, but after only a few steps, Loni pulled her husband's arm and stopped him dead in his tracks. "Kiss me, Mickey." With gentle firmness, she spun him around until they were nose-to-nose.

"Loni, we don't have time for this."

"Well then, how about we just make time. Kiss me."

"Loni ... "

"I'm not going anywhere until you kiss me." Not waiting for him to move, Loni closed the gap, kissing him hard and purposefully. When Mickey tried pulling away she continued to hold him until he held her kiss willingly. Only then did Loni release him.

"Mickey, you still have the leverage to say no to this," Loni whispered.

"So do you."

"I know."

"I know you know."

"Why do we do this, Mickey? Is it patriotism or just a death wish?"

"Heads or tails?" Mickey started to reach for something in his pocket. Loni stopped his hand with hers.

"Some days it's just a coin toss, isn't it?"

"More than you know, Loni."

"Tell me, Mickey, before I arrived in the room, did Colonel Birdsong or the general say when DIA would give me the particulars?"

"They said nothing about it. I believe neither knew." Suddenly Mickey grinned boyishly. "That being the case, they gave me some unexpected latitude."

"Latitude?"

"That's right, there is an upside. They gave me the keys."

"The keys? What keys?"

"You know ... *the keys*." Mickey freed his pinned hand from hers, waving an imaginary dangling keyring.

"No way. Not *the keys*."

"Oh yes, ma'am. Believe it. General said I could use his helicopter ride. Who's the man?"

"A man with helicopter keys?"

"Roger."

"Come on, *Mr. Man*. Let's go on to the mission brief."

"Hey, Loni, who knows? Before this is all over, you also may be given latitude, altitude, and a helicopter ride of your own. But until then ... who's the man?"

"I can't believe you got the keys." Loni pinched Mickey's arm as they went into the operations wing. "Well, I hope you have airsick pills."

"Why do you think I went to the bathroom, Loni? Just the thought of flying makes me want to...."

16

Morell Than You Know

Dyhernfurth, Poland
1930s

Why can't answers to my questions float to the top of my brain and arrange themselves in a simple, cohesive manner? Dr. Morell tapped his pen against the side of his glass of iced tea. He watched as the ice cubes floated to the surface of the liquid, aligning themselves in such a manner as to resemble human skin cells. It was more than just a difficult patient that contributed to the down-spirited doldrums that faced the doctor.

Dr. Morell was caught in a sticky situation. He had the mission to heal the chancellor in such a way as to obtain immortality. *I need to do this quietly.* Despite his current research at the Tegernsee laboratory, Dr. Morell was smart enough to realize that his current personal, medical, and scientific knowledge was not enough to find the answers to immortality. He needed to be able to access current medical research. The problem was that he needed to do it before any of his peers and colleagues caught wind of his prowling.

It is possible that Karl might be of help? However, Dr. Morell knew he had to be careful just how much information he leaked out to Dr. Karl Brandt in search of the chancellor's quest for immortality. *It would not do for Karl, the mere physician, to accidentally arrive at the solution before me. If this happens, it could be fatal to my career or even to me myself. Coming in second will not be seen well in the eyes of the chancellor. I need the answers and I need them now.* From his secret office in Poland, Dr. Morell's eyes looked west to the burgeoning field of scientific medical research.

He knew that in the border region of the Alsace, which now again belonged to the Germans instead of the troublesome French, Dr. Albrecht Kossel at the University of Strasbourg had just won the Nobel Prize in Physiological Medicine for cell tissue studies. A while back, another colleague, Dr. Friedrich Miescher, a physician-scientist, had found a protein that could be separated from the nucleus of living cells. In the rolling hills of south Germany near the town of Tubingen,

53

in the state of Baden-Wuerttemberg, there was also talk at a local university that a supramolecular spiral protein might hold certain codes which could link into heredity and immortality. Dr. Morell's face squinted in pain as he realized just how close the world was to achieving the answers that he was seeking.

People had heard murmurings of such things for as long as he could remember. A Moravian monk, Gregor Johann Mendel, made some obscure scientific studies in predicting the color of garden peas in Brno, Silesia, in the last century. *What if these medical researchers in this field of nuclear protein chemistry could synthesize and make copies from the codes and sequences? Could this create a whole new cell exactly the same as Mendel could predict?* The realization of immortality was very close, too close, right now in the hands of the enemy Allies warring against the Germans and their growing Nazi state.

Dr. Morell knew that more recently, the Brits and Americans had made some significant headway in nuclear chemistry beyond the level achieved by his medical researcher colleagues. Unfortunately, the tension for war would prevent him from getting his hands on that information. His only hope was that his fellow medicinal chemists and physician research scientists at the University of Strasbourg would have recent data on current studies, or even updates on the international front. Within hours, couriers could have that information brought to him.

Hurriedly, Dr. Morell picked up the receiver and dialed the phone to contact the research lab at Strasbourg. He held his breath as the lab phone rang without end. *Why aren't they answering?* His imagination began to race. *Are they busy shouting from the tops of their lungs because they have the answers I need?* The last thing Dr. Morell wanted to hear was an excited voice trying to speak into the phone, overwhelmed with the sounds of clamoring and cheering in the background. The increased pressing of the phone receiver against his head made him feel yet another aspect of pain and discomfort. The phone rang incessantly without a prayer of an answer.

Finally, he let out a sigh. There was going to be no first-place finish for him today. He kissed the lips of defeat, admitting to himself that the answers he was seeking were now already known and being celebrated at the far end where the laboratory phone rang endlessly. Soon his boss and sole patient, the chancellor of Germany, would find out that Dr. Morell, the chancellery's lead staff physician, had miserably failed. *This will not end well for me.*

Just as Dr. Morell started to hang up the phone, his motion was stopped by an audible click and squawking, tin voice. He cautiously returned the phone to his reddened ear. From the earpiece, he heard no background sounds of joy nor screaming sounds of jubilation at the distant lab. There was no celebration, only the steady, lifeless voice of a lab scientist stating again and again in dreadful monotone, "Hallo, Cell Research Laboratory, is someone there? Hallo? Hallo?" Dr. Morell smiled, cleared his throat, and began to speak to the lonely scientist with a voice projecting all his importance as the personal physician to Adolph Hitler, chancellor of all of Germany.

17

Spinning Up

European Medical Command

Heidelberg, Germany

Current Day

*P*ieces of me pulled left ... pieces pulled right. Now DIA is pulling the biggest chunk of me—that which manages the life of the one person I love dearest. Loni twisted her hands in her lap while carefully scoping the walls of the briefing room. *I've got to keep it together ... or at least look like I'm keeping it together.* Loni swallowed dryly, surveying the room. The digital screens on the wall and desktops were filled with battle rhythms, charts, graphs, and mission trackers. In this room she sat with the European Medical Command chief of staff, Colonel Bridgette Christiansted on her left; to her right sat a very anxious Mickey trying, she knew, to look more confident than he really was. Loni hung on to each word briefed by Luis Toro-Calderon, the G3 Operations officer, as he locked her in his gaze.

"There are things we know with a moderate level of confidence and things we outright don't know." Luis nodded toward Loni. "What we do know is that the DIA will be shunting information to you, ma'am. There is a confidential transmission to be received any time now." Loni nodded back to Luis, knowingly.

As they waited for this information, Bridgette, undergoing some cerebral lobe wrestling, leaned in toward Loni and whispered, "There are a couple pieces of data which we do have but we aren't sure of the value, Loni. It could be totally unrelated and totally meaningless." Bridgette took a breath. "Honestly, we would appreciate any insights you have on it."

"Sure, happy to help if I can. What are they?" Loni whispered.

"There was a bizarre murder at a leaning tower in Niles, Illinois. Also, I am told that Jean Dalton is in country—"

Mickey's pen snapped, flinging the ink cartridge across the room. "Jean Dalton! The same fellow from the army's Institute of Chemical Defense?"

"Mickey," patting her husband's arm gently, Loni spoke softly, "I believe Bridgette was talking to me."

"Yes, ma'am, I was," Bridgette confirmed, shooting Mickey a disapproving glare. Mickey stared down at the broken pen casings in his hands.

"This is so interesting, Bridgette," said Loni. "Jean Dalton—head of Security Forces at one of the army's leading research facilities stateside—finds the time to prowl around Europe. He must be investigating, researching, or coordinating something classified. After all, he is … how do we say this kindly? He is … "

" … the absolute personification of unbridled vulgarity expressing itself forcefully," blurted Mickey as Loni and Bridgette rocked back in their seats while Luis's jaw dropped.

"Well, Mickey," scoffed Bridgette, "tell us what you really think—"

"He is a beast with robot eyes," Mickey cut across her. "A cold, callous, unfeeling monster. He is truly a despicable person who sees little beauty in anything except the taste and smell of fear. He revels in its ambience." He paused for a breath, almost panting. The three other occupants in the room looked at him in frank bewilderment. Rarely had anyone ever seen Mickey Peronne so graphically explicit about the character of another human being.

"Subjectively, you are most likely correct, Mickey." Loni's steady voice returned control of the conversation quietly, but firmly. "Objectively, he is—in reality—Jean Geoffrey, high school dropout and army enlistee cook and dog handler."

Bridgette flipped open the file on the table in front of her and read aloud, "He appeared first as Jean Dalton on his GED. He seems to like the ambiguity of his first name. In English-speaking countries, people call him Jean. In the other countries, the pronunciation of his name morphs to John. For some reason he kept his former last name as his new middle name. Dalton attempted both military airborne and ranger schools but just like in high school, as you noted, Loni, he washed out. He somehow finagled a high school diploma thus promoting his ability to matriculate at Virginia Military Institute where he graduated *cum laude* and received a commission." She paused for a moment, then continued gruffly, "Hmmm, VMI … smart *and* dangerous."

"Yes, Bridgette, plenty smart but plenty stupid too," Loni added. "Dalton entered active service at Fort Hood and wasn't there long before he was accused of sexually harassing the females in his platoon."

"Were the accusations substantiated?"

"No, for some reason all the accusers dropped the allegations." Loni took a piece of the broken pen barrel from Mickey's hand to draw a large question mark in the air. "Although later, there were unsubstantiated rumors that he continued to stalk others at Fort Hood before he finally shipped off to his next assignment."

"Oh yes, I see here he had follow-on military assignments first at Fort Sam Houston, where he was acquitted of stealing, and then later at Fort Leavenworth. At the latter, as a captain, he was dismissed from service due to some issues involving unacceptable behavior?"

"The army should have been done with him at that time," said Loni. "However, for some reason, the director of the Chemical Casualty Care Division of the Institute of Chemical Defense—Dr. Joachim Wunschmann, also called Yogi—picked him to be his chief of Security Forces. Since he had lost his military rank,

Dr. Wunschmann frocked Dalton with a campus rank that gave him leverage to go and be in places where he had no business."

"Like ogling females at the pet park, skulking along hiking trails, and also camping out at the gymnasium for ladies' aerobics night," said Mickey. "Loni, he stalked you for weeks until he learned of your connection to me."

"That could never be outright proven. Anyway, I always had Domino with me. He wouldn't, or couldn't, lay a hand on me over her indefatigable Dalmatian umbrella of protection."

"I don't need a judge to render a final court decision for me to know the truth," growled Mickey, as his hands gripped open and closed.

"Let it go, honey. I have." Loni spoke softly while Mickey replied with a low-pitched grunt of long-standing discontent. Firmly eyeing Mickey, Loni resumed cautiously, "As I was saying, Bridgette, DIA intelligence confirms your medical channels data. I have recently been briefed that Dalton is at Lake Tegernsee in the German Alps."

"That is a resort area," said Brigette, marking a note on her file. "Why there? Why now?"

Before Loni could answer Bridgette's query, a knock on the door was answered by Luis. Loni sat nervously as she watched the DIA folder being passed with signatures from the messenger directly to her. She signed quickly, broke the seal, spent a few moments reviewing the data, and then pivoted her gaze to the faces around the table.

"Apparently, historical chemical weapons weren't the only things found at the site." Loni took a deep breath. "There was evidence of biological weaponry as well. Also, even more disturbing, something else was found that exceeded the expertise of Chemical Corps personnel on-site." She consulted the file and continued, "In order to fully evaluate these additional findings, army assets have been earmarked by EUCOM from a Medical Special Operations element now on-site in the Middle East and from the Medical Research Institute in Maryland. Of course, the lead element is already in Germany," she nodded toward Mickey, "and is to be sent to Poland on the first bird out."

✠ ✠ ✠

Sitting back out in the foyer, Loni was glad the operations briefing spin-up was over. The Operations Section was an overwhelming, information-rich environment. Loni was pleased she could provide the European Medical Command the additional intelligence and guidance they needed to have.

Unbeknownst to them, there was still more information in those portfolio pages that she could not share with them—things she already knew involving the murder at the Leaning Tower of Niles. It was very possible that the three army elements from Maryland, the Middle East, and Germany might all stumble onto something far greater than that which involved chemical and biological weaponry. All in all, Loni knew that the answers to everything on her plate seemed to lie east of Germany, right across the border in Poland.

Loni's gaze caught motion and she focused on the silhouette of her husband as he returned from the drinking fountain, wiping his moistened handkerchief across his face.

"I have a bone to pick with you," said Mickey, looking straight into the eyes of his wife.

"Sorry, honey, it'll have to wait. I need to ask you about the murder."

"What murder? Who's been murdered?"

"Were you not just in the briefing room with me when Bridgette said that she had two things she wanted to run past me? Number one, there was a bizarre murder at the Leaning Tower of Niles, and number two, that Jean Dalton—"

"I can't believe you knew that scum bucket was here in Europe and you never told me."

"I will tell you what you would tell me to do in this situation: 'Take a deep breath in, get over it, let the bad air out.'"

"Yes, but—"

"Mickey, I love you, but I need you not to be my husband at this moment in time. Right now, I need you to be that academician with your brilliant historical knowledge database. I need to discuss the murder with you."

"Roger." Mickey puckered his lips into a scowl and nodded affirmatively. Even if he was a wincing husband, he had the wherewithal to be the professional she needed him to be. Mickey listened astutely as Loni laid out the particulars of the DIA case.

"Father Judas Lenz, the tower keeper, was hanged, midline eviscerated from neck to pubes, and left to die dangling from a rope tied to the banister of the railing at the Leaning Tower of Niles."

"The tower keeper Lenz went by the name Father Judas?"

"Yes, Mickey, he did. So?"

"One version of history says that Judas Iscariot—the beloved disciple of Jesus Christ—after betraying his master, was found hung from a tree with his bowels and entrails hanging from him."

"Wow. What are the other versions?"

"They vary. Some say that due to his guilt and treachery, he had succumbed to gluttony and was run over by a chariot till his guts spewed from his body. Another version comes from the Lost Book of Barnabas. It says that his betrayal was a ploy. In reality, Judas looked so much like Jesus that it was Judas who went to crucifixion which then set up the faux miracle of Jesus returning to the living three days later. The point is, a hanging death of a man named Judas which involves entrails and evisceration has a theological connection to it in one way or another."

"What would you say if I told you that the DNA of the victim, Judas, was about two thousand years old?"

"Seriously?" Mickey laughed out loud. Loni's face remained carved in stone. "Well … I'd say that you need to get a new test, new testing equipment, a recalibration of that equipment, a new tester, a new tester off drugs and alcohol, or all the above."

"My data says the data was reproducible and indeed reproduced. However, I will get back to you on the DNA piece. Labs can make errors. Thank you for the insights on the Judas death. I can start to feel my way on this one."

"Can we talk about your concealing from me the European presence of Jean Dalton?"

"Mickey, stand down. Let it go, please. Again, let me tell you what you always tell me in these kinds of situations: 'You just didn't have need-to-know.'"

"When will I have a need to know, Loni?"

"You'll know it when you know."

18

Waking America

European Command (EUCOM)
Stuttgart, Germany

Holding the phone to his ear, Airman Morell felt the same emotions as his great-grandfather must have felt as he too was serenaded by an endless series of telephone rings. He wondered why the duty officer in Maryland hadn't returned from his permissible five-minute break.

While being a direct descendant of one of the most famous of all Nazi physicians, Airman Morell further understood the irony of his being an American fighting man stationed in Germany. Sometimes he wondered why that fact alone never prevented him from getting a security clearance in the field of military intelligence. "I guess I'm lucky," said the airman as the phone ringing ended with a click.

"Army Medical Research Command, Edgewood Arsenal, Emergency Operations, Master Sergeant Hawkins speaking."

"Master Sergeant, this is Airman Morell calling from Emergency Operations at EUCOM. Is the duty officer there?"

"I am the staff duty officer tonight, Airman," the master sergeant groused. "What information does EUCOM have for us?"

"I have a hard copy of a message to be sent to your station involving a chemical site finding in Poland."

"Are you sure you have the correct command, Airman?" Master Sergeant scoffed and continued, "We are a research command."

"Roger, Master Sergeant. The hard copy message has a specific recipient intended."

"Are you telling me that you have a message there at EUCOM point targeted to a specific individual within this research command?"

"Affirmative."

"Well, Airman, who is this superhero from army research destined to save the day out there in Europe?"

"The message is to go to the deputy chief at the Chemical Casualty Care Division."

"A schoolteacher at the CCCD schoolhouse? That's interesting. Is there a name associated with the message?"

"No, Master Sergeant, only the job title."

"I see. So now your work ends and mine begins. I have to find the name attached to that title," Master Sergeant Hawkins huffed. "When is this message destined to arrive?"

"It's being transmitted to you on the high side. Please send confirmation of receipt, Master Sergeant."

"Wouldn't the schoolteacher getting the message be sufficient?"

"No, Master Sergeant, that wouldn't be—"

"I'm jerking your chain, Airman." Master Sergeant hissed a laugh. "You'll get your confirmation once I have received the message." The master sergeant cleared his throat. "So, if there is nothing else you need to share, Airman, I need to finish some urgent personal business. None? Research Command, out." The phone clicked.

Morell sighed and felt closure as he finally, successfully, passed on the message about what had been found in Brzeg Dolny, Poland. *Could what the master sergeant said be true? A schoolteacher at the schoolhouse? Eh, no matter. Who am I to judge anyway? Once that message gets read by the superhero schoolteacher in Maryland, the answer to the Polish question might lead to more questions and lots of homework for the other people and teams contacted tonight.* As he relinquished the phone receiver to its bracket, he imagined the numerous fluorescent lights flickering on in Maryland's operations center as the duty day began.

However, elsewhere in the United States, a distant air force base family housing unit remained dark and quiet. Morell's wife and their two children slept quietly, not knowing that their beloved but sleep-deprived night shift airman had begun a chain of events which committed leading military expertise to investigate a historic question posed by the long-dead Chancellor Adolph Hitler himself.

19

The Commander's Ride

European Medical Command
Heidelberg, Germany

In the lobby of the general's building, Mickey grabbed his go bag, then clipped on his utility vest and ran his hands over the gear affixed to the upper body harness known as the LBE, load bearing equipment, knowing by feel alone that everything he needed was present and accounted for. His hand paused momentarily over his tactical light recalling his hobbit lore and the Phial of Galadriel. He then left the building and hopped into the noisy Blackhawk nesting on the helipad at Nachrichten Kaserne. This bird was the exclusive property of General Framingham himself. For better or for worse, after a necessary refueling stop, Mickey had his wife's DIA directive and the general's blessing to take this helicopter across Germany and into Wroclaw, Poland, the Silesia region's largest city. There, rotary blades would be exchanged for a set of rented wheels on the ground.

"Chief, what is our flight plan?" Mickey asked the pilot, Chandra Lamar, though he had a hunch. He pulled his map from his near-empty knapsack. He compared his route to the one marked on Chief Lamar's trip map.

"Sir, we will be cutting across southern Bavaria and then northern Czech to get to Wroclaw."

"Let's follow the contour of Germany above Czech, Chief. There are some towns I'd like to see from the air."

"Roger." Chief Lamar rolled up her map and pointed the bird east.

Staring out of the open side of the helicopter at the southern Rhine Valley down below, Mickey mulled over the commander's note given to him by the curt German secretary and the remarkable DIA briefing that Loni had recently given. If it wasn't for that commander's note, he would have been planning a flight west over miles and miles of Atlantic Ocean waves instead of flying east over the verdant fields of Bavaria. Either way he had to fight the rising nausea of airsickness.

All in all, Mickey hated the whole *note* thing because notes rarely contained good news. For Mickey, notes were always instructions on how to do things he really never wanted to do, or written proof that he was in trouble. When it came to notes, Mickey's parents were notorious. His father, the draconian martinet US Army Infantry colonel shockingly turned Chaplain Franklin Peeples Peronne, would leave him notes on the bathroom mirror in their Ann Street mansion—*Cut the grass today*; *Dress up for dinner tonight*; *Sweep out the garage*; or all of the above. Of all the chores, Mickey always liked anything that involved the garage. It became his personal refuge.

"Sir, that's Schloss Seehof. How do you like that fountain?"

"I see it, Chief. Reminds me of the one back home, only it's a hundred times bigger."

Flying over Bamberg and its beautiful castles toward what used to be Eastern Europe, Mickey's mind trailed off again to his family's Ann Street home, complete with fenced-in patio, water fountain, and double garage. The Peronne family home was a 1917 block house which had an abundance of hidey-holes where he used to sit and imagine that he was his favorite animal. Mickey loved pretending. One day he'd be a bear drinking water from an upward bubbling artesian well at Smoke Hole Cavern; the next day, a member of the family from *The Swiss Family Robinson* as they were stranded in a beach cave; or sometimes just himself playing army with his best friends Mike Winnabe and Mike's girlfriend Zelda Anne Ward. They lived just blocks away on Julia and Market Streets, respectively. When Mike lost his family, he actually lived with the Peronnes until he graduated and joined the army. Ironically, Zell, who always played the combat medic in their games, never joined the military. But, her nuisance little sister, Bridgette, who was never allowed to play army with the gang, became an important army officer.

Although he was deep in thought for an eternity, it wasn't all that long until his eyes began panning the jagged terrain within the eastern border of southeastern Germany—a place the Germans themselves liked to call Saxon Switzerland.

"Sir, there's Mödlareuth."

"Roger. I see the remnants of the wall there. Bring us down lower."

"There are the gun emplacements, and no man's land."

"Roger. The wall runs right through the middle of town. Of the thousand miles of wall that used to separate the two Germanys, this is all that is left, Chief."

"Roger. We're in former East Germany now, sir."

Mickey let his mind recap everything he knew and everything he didn't know about this mission. *Thank God I have what information the DIA has available. But I wonder just how much Loni herself still doesn't know.*

There was much information that she *did* share and that was disconcerting enough. However, he knew Loni. Just like in the case of Dalton, she was holding something back. There may have been more to Father Judas's murder that needed his insight, but it looked like Loni was struggling with that piece of data herself. All in all, it was still possible there were nuances of this mission that he still did not know, all based upon some person's perception of *need-to-know*. If his life was being put on the line, more information was always better than less. Mickey's logic was etched in stone. No matter the source of the information, he had a burning *need to know.*

In the white noise of the chopper's blades, Mickey puzzled over the importance of this recently mandated physician assignment. *What exactly is my mission? Is it to investigate something medical or historical at a recently discovered chemical-warfare site?* Time and again Chemical Corps personnel easily handled the cleanup operations at old chemical sites. Even if it was a confirmed biowarfare operation at the Polish chemical site, Chemical Corps folks still had the skill and training to contain and decontaminate it. This he knew for sure, since having been a chemical officer before he pinned on the Medical Corps caduceus after medical school graduation.

There is no doubt a hidden agenda that someone senses but is unwilling to fully share. Loni had briefed them that just seven days ago, northwest of Wroclaw, the largest cache of 1914–1918 Great War munitions had been unearthed by eager land developers looking to expand the Polish earthenware and pottery industry. *That's why they're bringing in Suzanne Coletrane. She is perfect for the job.* It was Suzanne who had replaced Mickey as chief of operations last year when Loni and Mickey decided not to retire, but instead to leave Maryland and take the overseas assignment to Germany. Standing five foot eleven, with a record for rarely pulling punches, Suzanne was formidable. *How could she not be?* Mickey mused. She was the product of the six-foot five Colonel Maximilian Niles, who was legendarily famous for his raging Max Attacks, and the colonel's Korean bride, a lady small in stature but tough enough to handle a crusty old division chief of staff. Mrs. Niles's daughter, Suzanne, only favored her mother in character strength. Her version of Max Attacks earned her the nickname Viking Witch. However, when the chips were down and the mission needed a strong leader, her name rose to the top of everyone's dance card.

This chemical find in Brzeg Dolny also engendered a request for the Special Operations talents of physician-scientist, Lieutenant Colonel Russell C. Lange, whose name was already surging through the European Command's Mobile Emergency Medical Response Team's cyber channels. The DIA and their European-based lead agent, Loni, both knew that Russell was everything one would expect of a Special Operations spook.

The DIA knew that the bonus of mobilizing Mickey, which even General Framingham had not fully appreciated, was that he was a published historian of military medicine as well as knowledgeable in Christian theology, although without theological portfolio. Loni knew that, if needed, this additional expertise would lend itself to significant service as well.

"Sir," Chief Lamar pointed, "there's Bautzen."

"I see it. No city in Germany has more towers per city block. Chief, are we almost there? My stomach cramp is just curious."

"Roger, sir. That's Poland on the horizon."

Flying over the former Eastern Bloc landscape, it seemed as if the color dial had lost function. Whereas the German state of Bavaria was filled with the pattern of blue and white diamonds and colorful cities bubbling in hues of golden yellow, burnt orange, and a plush verdant, the border crossing into the former east went colorless. It seemed that the demilitarized zone of the former Inner German wall had the ability to suck the color directly from the rosy cheeks of life. Cities grew gray, frowning upward with dingy black slate roofs. Concrete structures rarely had enough paint to cover the spattering of dirt on the roadside walls of buildings. Credit nevertheless must be given to the people of former East Germany who, with colorless materials, still managed to express their inherent taste through the clever arrangements of tiles which formed charming, eye-pleasing shapes albeit in alternating shades of black, white, and gray.

Mickey and his stomach were most grateful when the chopper skids finally touched down in Poland. In the Stare Miasto, the city center of Wroclaw, he exchanged steel skids for vulcanized rubber tires, complements of a local rent-a-car company.

Mickey started the engine and pulled out of the parking lot. He smiled to himself. *Loni would have been proud that I made it this far without having to use my entire complement of airsickness pills.*

But his grin faded when, not very long afterward, on a rough Polish road, Mickey hit a mega pothole mimicking a moon crater. Both his car and stomach heaved, groaned, and then never seemed to run the same thereafter. Nevertheless, with air travel in the rearview mirror, Mickey hoped from here on out to travel as nature intended—in a car. Mickey caught a glimpse of the helicopter as it buzzed overhead back to its home station. Wondering where he would be sleeping tonight, if at all, Mickey began humming the Ann and Nancy Wilson song *Alone*. Meanwhile he drove, rattling and sputtering, with heart into the westward-sinking sun.

20

No Guts, No Gory

Tactical Operations Center
Edgewood Arsenal, Maryland

Having just received the alert message from Airman Morell in Europe, Master Sergeant Hawkins, the night shift operations officer at the Tactical Operations Center, fidgeted at his desk with one hand pressing on his belly while the other wiggled his pen. All the while, his guts sheepshanked.

"Are you sure, Filmore?" Master Sergeant Hawkins shifted. "Check your clerk's list again."

"Yes, Master Sergeant, you asked for CCCD, right?"

"Right. I want to find a schoolteacher at the Chemical Casualty Care Division schoolhouse, Specialist Filmore. You know … I'm looking for a four foot ten, thin, frail, gray-haired librarian-type with an apple on her desk."

"Sorry, Master Sergeant, no dice. The only name that hit against the information you provided is one each: army issue, olive drab shade of green, Suzanne Coletrane, colonel, medical corps."

"Check again. There has to be a mistake." Hawkins swallowed hard.

"I take it she's not the meager schoolmarm you were hoping to find."

"Not even close, Specialist."

"She's not under five foot?"

"She's over six in combat boots."

"No apple on the desk?"

"I heard she has a hand grenade on her secretary's desk with a queue ticket numbered one pinched between the grenade and the pin. The note on the grenade says, 'Take a number and have a seat.'"

"What's wrong with that?"

"You have to pull the pin to get the number, Filmore." The master sergeant clenched his gut and a little groan escaped his lips.

"Are you okay, Master Sergeant?"

"Am I okay?" Master Sergeant's constipation issues were not going to get any better with his intestines currently doing early morning calisthenics. "Let me

66

ask you something. Do the names Killer Coletrane, Headmistress Little School of Horrors, or Death from Above ring any bells?"

"Wait," said the clerk. "Is she the one that—"

"Yes, that's her." Beads of sweat now decorated Master Sergeant's brow.

"And because of her, students were known to—"

"Without a doubt."

"Master Sergeant, I heard about her but thought she was an urban legend."

"No, she's real." Master Sergeant Hawkins fidgeted. "I've just never had the pleasure—luckily—till now."

"Do you still want the antacid for your stomach, Master Sergeant?"

"Go look in the cabinet and see if there is a large bottle of arsenic on the shelf."

"How do you spell that?" The specialist wiggled his pencil.

"Never mind, Filmore." Master Sergeant scoffed. "Get back to the morning reports." Hawkins picked up and then hung up the phone a couple of times. The task of awakening the colonel would be distasteful. His experience had always been painful when dealing with sleepy upper-level field-grade officers. This full-bull colonel was amazingly caustic during daylight on a good day. *This is not going to be pleasant.*

Master Sergeant Hawkins was a senior sergeant and seasoned in the ways of high-ranking officers. He had the wherewithal to tame the wild beast—that is, if his ulcers and bowels would hold up. It was very early in the morning on the East Coast. He positioned the notification roster, dialed the number, and as expected, heard the raspy, gruff voice of the awakened devil incarnate, the Viking Witch—Colonel Doctor Suzanne Niles Coletrane. The knot, which masqueraded as his colon, painfully tightened another notch.

21

Chaucer and the Tale

Schloss Tegernsee
Tegernsee, Germany

"Track Colonel Suzanne Coletrane," the squawking voice on the telephone commanded. "When she moves, you become her shadow." The listener's metallic eyes combed over the majestic German Alps from the windows of Schloss Tegernsee while he blew wood chips from the grooves of his pocketknife. Like the listener, this castle was not what it seemed to be from its rustic exterior. The building looked medieval from the outside, but there was sheer modern scientific technology bursting its seams from within.

Captain Jean Dalton shook the fresh wood-chip shavings off his shoes. He was showcased to be a professional Security Force element but, in reality he was no more than just a thug with a borrowed rank—and he knew it.

Dalton wasn't a big African American man—he stood five foot five but, like a fire hydrant, he was solidly built. He demonstrated an athletic musculature which always brought sports into the conversation, but his forte was history. Dalton had a keen appreciation for the subtleties of war tactics. Inasmuch, he could mentally recreate a holograph of any battlefield despite the number of moving parts. It was as if he had a bird's-eye view of every major historical battle ever fought, along with a full capacity of what could, should, and would be done at battle's end. At the Virginia Military Institute, Dalton saw himself as the modern version of the brilliant General Thomas-Alexandre Dumas riding alongside Jean-Baptiste Bessières and the Iron Marshal Louis-Nicolas Davout. Napoleon Bonaparte's successes were indisputably attributed to these great battlefield leaders. Unfortunately, few shared Dalton's vision of himself—they saw no war genius, only hired muscle.

The breathtaking beauty captured by Jean Dalton's eyes stirred something within him. He could no longer remember what it was like to enjoy pure, unmolested beauty just for beauty's sake. Thinking how Hannibal's armies marched with elephants over those Alps, he shaped the trunk of the whittled creature. Dalton's ears perked as more information came through the phone resting against his left ear.

68

"From the information we have gathered," the voice said, "you need to go on to the Rheinland-Pfalz region of the western part of Germany. We know that Suzanne will be arriving by fixed-wing airplane close to midnight at Ramstein Air Base and then will go by helicopter into Poland. I need you there seeing what she sees and learning what information is availed to her. Keep your ears focused to anything involving *leaning towers*. If this comes about, get back to me as quickly as you can. You are my eyes and ears, *Chaucer*, don't let me down."

Dalton liked it when the boss called him Chaucer. Being based upon the British spelling of his middle name, Geoffrey, his codename felt so very eloquent and refined. For a split second in time, Dalton felt he could be held in high esteem merely by his name alone. This was brief indeed. The famous, historic author Geoffrey Chaucer's specialty was the writing of literary tales whereas the infamous, modern Dalton's version of Chaucer was to quite literally apply a tail to unsuspecting targets.

Dalton didn't really mind providing security over science geeks here in Bavaria. As a lot, they were a very passive bunch and always completely consumed by their work. Like the flock of sheep to a sheepherder, most of the time they took care of themselves. Some nights, when Dalton found it difficult to sleep, he would stroll through the castle checking on the quieter graveyard-shift workers. He wondered how they could keep themselves awake as the incessant blinking panel lights from their machines would only serve to tug him into the world of sleep. On these nights, pine aardvarks and frilled iguanas would wiggle free from their wooden encasements, thanks to the dexterity of his skilled bladework. Dalton would carve furiously—dark hands, light wood, and silver blade moving in syncopation. He often asked himself why he was here. Most definitely it was the intrigue. If truth be told, Dalton never really wanted to be contemptible. All he ever wanted to do was visit battlefields and carve wood like his grandfather. *Geoffrey's Wood Works* read the sign that hung over the front door of his grandfather's craft shop. He wished that it read, *Jean Dalton's Wood Works*.

On this very quiet night, after getting his new orders from the boss, Dalton found himself in the office of one of the more peaceful labs. It was nice because there was a fish tank filled with a handsome variety of tropical fish. Staring mindlessly through his refection to the fish in the tank, he sat in an overstuffed chair, while setting his pocketknife and carving on the chair's arm. Dalton's head began its final descent downward as the dream world overtook his consciousness. He started drifting into his favorite dream of a faraway place.

✠ ✠ ✠

The people seemed to know him. They called out to him by his first name—it sounded like they were calling him *John*. He gazed down at his roughened, chapped hands covered with the crevices and calluses of a dedicated builder, carpenter, and woodworker. He looked around at the lack of trees in the area and saw stone nearby. He was a master of both.

He bore the bruises from rubbing chiseled rock surfaces and the splinters from the frayed ends of freshly cut trees. The hard work shaped his powerful arms into skilled appendages. Whether he worked in wood or stone, he loved his job which was more than most of the folks around him. In his village, most of the people lived their lives doing what the generation before them had done. Miller's children were millers. Shepherd's children were sheep herders. He could always see the sadness in their faces—the ones who were forsaking their own heart's desire to live out their father's hopes and dreams. John was different. He had no living father. The day that a certain Temple Mount priest was found murdered at the tabernacle, John had lost forever the love and mentorship that only his father could have given. As he worked, John remembered when he was a boy, he often left his chores and slipped away with his dog to do what he wanted to do instead of what was required of him.

He used to go to his favorite place where he and Smarl could be alone. He was drawn by the bubbling sound of nearby water. To the local folks it was nothing but a little stream. However, to him it was a vibrant reflection of yesterday while simultaneously a window into the future. It was a place where fantasy met reality. At his stream, he could be John the sailor one day and John the traveling merchant the next.

One special day when John went to the stream he wanted to be a Holy Essene. He channeled the water into a little lake and then practiced the ritual bathing he had witnessed the holy men do on many occasions. The water was said to wash away the impurities of the body and soul—he watched it splash over his young, strong limbs. After bathing, John felt closer to his God and the memory of his slain father. As it would happen, on that day it appeared that the stream itself had grabbed a tree branch and forced it down the channel into his ritual bathing spot. The hapless branch jutted into the air above the surface of the water. As Smarl barked, John's gaze was fixed on that waving tree branch. Yes, it was indeed a branch—a piece of wood from the part of some tree. However, in its present association with the stream, it was much more. This branch was uniquely blessed with its own special character. A careful inspection of it revealed an oddity in the shape. Because of its curvature, this branch formed a virtual hand whose fingers continuously skimmed the water's surface. As such, it became a floating basket, filled with an abundance of magical treasures. John remembered having noticed it before, farther upstream. He recalled that this branch had always captured items that were, in essence, a piece of untold history. Whatever was cast in or lost from the village became a resident of this floating basket. His mother's favorite plain rust-colored scarf once floated down from a trader's market in the local casbah, coming to rest within the gnarled fingers of this very branch. It had evolved into a game; to guess each day what prize the river basket might have snagged. This day, in his bathing spot—the new home of the branch—he spied his catch. His heart lifted. The spastic jerking of a fish thudded against the thickest part of the branch. It was time to leave John the Holy Essene and become John the fisherman.

John saw that in the fish's mouth was a weighted hook from which it could not escape. It appeared that, with the aid of the unique branch, for the first time the river had given him and his family the potential for a rather exceptional fish dinner. His mother would be overjoyed. With great haste, he waded out into the stream and with a firm tug, he freed the fish. But the fishhook string had also wrapped around the wood and thus he dislodged the tree branch in a muddy cloud. Feeling his heart stop, John watched his favorite tree branch shoot quickly downstream.

Wildly splashing, John the fisherman turned into John the sprinter. He raced along the bank, forgetting and forsaking his recently acquired fish prey in a determined rescue attempt to save his branch. He reached the nearby curve in the river and saw that the branch was spiraling in a shallow water eddy. God granting him a bit more strength, he hoped to retrieve his old wooden friend from the clutches of the swift, swirling waters. John jumped into the stream and waded to where the floating branch spun. Out of breath, he lifted the soggy wooden branch. Holding it tightly, he steadied his feet in the moving stream. Although he had lost his fish, John was not going to lose his wooden friend twice. His breathing slowed, and his eyes began a deeper scrutiny of the branch that he reverently cradled in his hands. He marveled at what he saw.

The branch had been so long in the river that the water had shaped the wood in ways no man could. Waist deep in river water while Smarl barked at him from the riverbank, John stood awestruck at the way Mother Nature had meticulously carved and shaped the wood's surface. She had instilled a beauty into the branch beyond his ability to describe. In this captured moment, John understood the power of the waters. He knew that he had to be just like the river, a shaper of wood. Amidst the lapping of the water against his legs as he worked his way to the bank, he could hear the voice of his mother saying, *Be careful what you want, John, you just may get it.*

22

Undesired Post

Schloss Tegernsee
Tegernsee, Germany

"I have rounds to make … doorknobs to rattle … I need to check the security of—" he mumbled. Wearily, Jean Dalton lifted his head off his chest, but the monitor beeps and clicks never forced his eyes to open. He heard modern-day voices murmuring around him in an unintelligible drone. Even the humming of the fish tank filter rendered a sense of monotony. There was absolutely no evidence of urgency, and so Dalton deduced that he could return to his respite.

✠ ✠ ✠

John's youth had passed into manhood and on into the workshop of a master craftsman. John the craftsman stared down at a piece upon which he had spent months working. Probably it was one of his finest works, but there was no joy, no sense of pride. In fact, looking at this eloquent work made John's gut cringe.

Made all of wood, the flogging post was a three-foot tall, hour-glass shaped structure—broad at its extremes and tapered slender at its middle. All told, it sported the width of a middle-aged sycamore tree. Along its sculpted flanks, divots and caves were beautifully carved out to produce recessed pockets for storage. The top surface was the oddest feature about it. By request, it was designed to be concave—a giant bowl reaching a hand width at its greatest depth. As unique as this artisan piece was, it was but a wooden twin to the stone version he began several months ago.

He was forced to create this wooden sculpture because the Roman governor could no longer wait for the marble replacement of the existing flogging post. Although John had worked diligently, he had not yet completed the marble post. He was thus directed to provide a wooden understudy, a replica flogging post to substitute until the final marble masterpiece could be finished.

John always preferred the working of wood to that of chiseling on stone.

The rate of completion was quicker as would be the inevitable payment for services. Masonry and sculpturing paid much more, but the time between payments drastically lagged. This flogging post project had further drawbacks in that the specifications were so very precise. As a result, John now possessed two almost completed posts, both rejected because of a failure to meet the requirements.

The Romans were always extreme in their perfection and therefore exacting in their product expectation. John looked at his third attempt. *Why do they have to be so extravagant in their cruelty? Couldn't an ordinary flogging post with attached iron rings be sufficient for their needs? No, not for them.* The Roman governor wanted beauty as well as functionality. Stone was more durable than wood, but that piece was more than two months from completion.

Whether wood or stone, why does it matter? Either way, I am cursed. Because of John's skill in both masonry and woodworking, he was the chosen one to bring these atrocities into the world. It seemed that all his hard work to make himself a diversely, multiskilled craftsman of wood and stone was the very basis for his selection as the artisan of choice. *History will never see me as a great artist, but as a twice-condemned scourge of functional art.* Even now he could hear the cracking of the flesh-eating whips upon the backs of the poor wretches chained here, where he laid his hands. He cupped his rough hands—he could see the blood of the oppressed leaking between his fingers forming a crimson pool within his palms. No matter how many times he went to the river with the Holy Essenes to wash himself, the blood always seemed to be there. *God forgive me because I can never forgive myself.* There was no way to rid the blood or to silence the cacophony of terrible screams in his dreams at night.

✠ ✠ ✠

The symphonic dirge snapped Dalton from sleep and into the blinking lights and mechanical beeping around him. Eye to eye with the indifferent stare of an aquarium guppy, he massaged the sweat from his palms. If nightmares indeed provided the tincture of insanity needed for sane functioning within the waking world, then he was set for a lifetime. Dalton picked up his carving and continued shaping the wood.

"What do you all think?" Dalton said to the fish. "Enough rest for the night?" The lack of dissension among the numerous aquarium residents convinced him he was right.

23

Yawn in Time

Route to Dyhernfurth
Brzeg Dolny, Poland

"Kill me now," grumbled Mickey amidst the Polish rental car's clinking and clanking. "Never mind, I'm already dead."

Just eighteen miles northwest of Wroclaw, in what had now become the worst rental car he had ever had, Mickey's ride heaved and groaned into the Polish town of Brzeg Dolny. The city flag, red with a left-to-right descending diagonal swath decorated by three red poppies, let him know he had arrived. He passed the city's small arch and continued past its famous present-day chemical factory, Rokita, equivalent to anything in the Maryland/DC chemical research triangle. Where he wanted to go now was the former World War II chemical factory site called Dyhernfurth, built when the town was occupied by Nazi Germany. Polish police along the way directed him, using English in response to his badly broken German questions and his poorly pronounced Polish greeting, *"Dzień dobry."*

As he approached the final drive into the excavation site, Mickey had to engage serpentine maneuvers, weaving between large dozers, graders, and haulers. He was really surprised that here in Poland there were such a pro-portionately large number of earthmovers titled with the English logo, Lucky Industries.

Quick movement in front of him drew his eyes off the machinery and onto the narrow passage ahead. Locked side by side, a pale blue Russian sedan and a red German mini car simultaneously shot between a dump truck and a heavily loaded work van. They were heading straight for him.

"Mary, sweet Mary, Mother of God, please help me in this my hour of need...."

He could not veer to either side. Mickey sucked in a deep breath, clenched tightly on the steering wheel, locked his elbows in full extension, and thrust his body painfully rearward against the seat. At the last possible moment, the sedan backed off allowing itself to be overtaken by the mini car which brushed the dust off Mickey's front bumper. Mickey blew out his breath in relief and

74

shuddered into the bizarre realization that somehow, outside his control, he'd just cheated death.

"What in hell's kitchen was that? The Polish version of chicken!?"

He looked into the rearview mirror. There was no sign of the idiot drivers, which was good for them. He didn't know whether to vent anger or rejoice for life. As it turned out, he had time for neither. He had arrived at his destination. Mickey was more than ready to finally swerve into a small parking place, thus ending any further possibility of vehicular death. As his rental car halted, it backfired loudly then shivered fitfully into an uneasy silence. While Mickey wiped the sweat from his palms on his trouser legs, a rather stocky-built chemical officer dressed in an American soldier's uniform strode to the driver's side window.

"Fancy driving, dude. You about done showboating?"

"Looked like you needed the entertainment."

"Where'd you get the rental, Polish Rent-a-Wreck?" The officer slapped his hand on the roof of the car and leaned over to speak to Mickey through the window. "No matter. Glad you medical pukes decided to show your ugly mugs around here. Give you a chance to meet the real talent." The chemical officer's verbal jousting was framed with a playful grin. His ruddy face was firm and tense, but friendly. He was clearly an army officer, but if he were dressed instead in the uniform of New York's finest, he could fit the motif of any baton-twirling Irish cop. His big, athletic neck sat squarely on mammoth shoulders depicting a demeanor of confidence. Mickey mopped the sweat from his brow with a sweep and placed his left forearm on the car's window ledge.

"Don't get your hopes up, Chemo, talent's still on the way. I am just the dazzling pace car for the advance party." Mickey watched as the chemical officer scanned his face for clues. "What's up with the Chemical Corps anyway? Are you all too lazy to do your own investigation these days?"

"Or could it just be that the subject matter is a wee bit too important, else you guys wouldn't have called the Medical Corps cavalry?" Mickey tapped the fingers of his right hand on the steering wheel for a moment and then stopped. Then he leaned back and, folding his arms across his chest, Mickey locked the officer's gaze eye to eye.

"In other words, Chemo, how is it that I can help you flailing bugs and gas guys anyway?" Mickey watched the searching expression on the chemical officer's face transform in a widening smile.

"Come on, Doc," the officer winked, "you're not going to baffle me with the *army's biggest lie* routine, are you?"

"Sure, why not? I came here to help."

"Well then, allow me to retort with the same lack of candor. Thank you, sir. I'm so very glad you're here." The officer stepped back from the car door and stood up straight. "Lieutenant Colonel Ronald Talbot at your service." The man burst into a sincere laugh. Talbot's softening features let Mickey know that, indeed, medical expertise was something that was needed here onsite, and it would be sincerely appreciated. In response, Mickey decided to ratchet down the intensity and begin probing for answers. He grabbed his LBE vest, opened the car door, and stepped out.

"So, Talbot, did you contract this American construction equipment for your planned *on-site* operations?" Mickey strapped on his LBE as he surveyed the area more closely.

"No sir, Doc. They were part of the original problem. Apparently, Lucky Industries wasn't as lucky as its name would imply."

"Frankly, it looks like Lucky Industries took action on a venture which came out of the wrong end of the Good Idea Pig."

"Roger that, sir. Lucky bowled into a cache of underground chemical munitions in storage. From what I gathered from the locals," Talbot stopped and motioned to a group of people standing nearby, "the American foreman wasn't in any big hurry to report the incident. Evidently, he thought he had hit a gas pipeline. If the locals hadn't engaged the police, I don't think we would be here now."

"Yes, but we are," said Mickey.

"That's the foreman," Talbot snarled, "the one with rolled-up sleeves and yellow hard hat over there, the one leaning over the bed of that gator talking to the locals. Let me tell you, Doc, he's truly a piece of work."

"What's the ongoing issue? It still looks heated over there," said Mickey, noticing a strange-looking woman with a distorted, twisted face conversing with to the foreman. "Were these civilians exposed to chemicals, Talbot?"

"As of this date-time group, there are no chemical casualties documented here, civilian or otherwise."

"Well then, is it anger or just a case of genetic disfigurement in that hyperanimated bird-faced woman?"

"Don't read into this, Doc. That could have been facial damage from something else long ago. Some of these Polish folks have been through absolute hell."

"No matter, Talbot, look at her. Her issue is not being addressed by the foreman and she knows it. Look now, she's pulling that scarf back over her face. She's received his message. She's now wondering if he has received hers."

"Yes, I see. I agree," said Talbot. "She's done with him."

"You know, I can't hear them from here, but I'll bet a dollar to a doughnut that yellow hard hat is only relaying the party line—he is not the man in charge. Look at her, Talbot—she's reading his face. She's got his number. She knows he's just a weenie in a yellow beanie. However, now that her face is mostly covered, I can't tell if her expression is one of frustration, disgust, or just frank sadness."

"Don't know, Doc, but I can see it through those sunglasses—those eyes are glaring. You are correct about one thing, though. He certainly is not the big cheese, not here, not today, and there's only two people in China who don't know it."

"So, Talbot, I see the blue-collared stiffs. Where are the corporate geeks?"

"Sir?"

"You know, paper pushers and bean counters. Are there any pencil-necked, white-collared industry executives on-site?"

"Yellow hard hat over there told me that a corporation representative out of the Baltimore home office has taken the company jet and is flying it over the big pond now."

"Just now, a transatlantic flight? A week later? Amelia Earhart could have been here and back by now. Lucky Industries is certainly rolling the dice ... "

" ... and posturing for some unlucky litigation, wouldn't you say, Doc?"

"Roger that. You know, I'm betting that the delay is due to a mega-meeting of the corporation legal beagles."

"Well, I know that if I was the CEO, I'd be absolutely sure I had my legal ducks in order before I had to take a public platform."

"Who is the CEO, Talbot?"

"Don't really know. I suppose it might be some Polish immigrant who made it big in the USA."

"In other words, you really don't know."

"No, sir."

"Well, whoever he is, he will certainly have to convince the world that Lucky Industries had no idea of the potential of hitting chemical munitions here despite the local history. Lucky Industries really should have done their homework."

Having chemical warfare background in their career portfolios, both officers knew the history of the area. The Polish town of Wroclaw was situated adjacent to Dyhernfurth, the site of one of Adolf Hitler's largest chemical gas munitions factories. Whatever the failure was for not initiating chemical warfare in World War II, the tons and tons of Nazi chemical munitions which were produced had to be stored somewhere. That somewhere was here. Being able to converse on the intricacies and subtleties of chemical warfare history well outside the halls of medicine was a trait of Mickey's that quickly endeared him to Talbot.

"That is going to be a major smoke-and-mirror production that I wouldn't want to miss," chuckled Talbot.

"Lucky Industries will have to do more than just an entertaining sideshow," said Mickey. "They'll have to engage a hard sell to the Polish public that Lucky Industries was totally unaware of the history of the area."

"Frankly, Doc, I think that Lucky knew and was really more concerned with keeping to a time schedule and the propping up of another Polish pottery store—don't you?"

"Ah yes, it always boils down to the bottom line—the almighty dollar."

"That would be the euro, Doc."

"Indeed, in this part of the world, it certainly would."

"In Lucky's defense, why would anyone think that any chemicals still remained after the Russian's economic rape of the area? Remember, at the end of the war the Soviets dismantled the entire Nazi chemical munitions factory, brick by brick, and railed it back to Mother Russia. This chemical factory became the seed of the Soviet Chemical Weapons Program."

"Good point." Mickey nodded. "Since all this occurred behind the Iron Curtain, the occupation forces in western Europe were pretty much kept in the dark as to the extent of the program. Escaped Nazi scientists employed by the

USA in the post-Hitler era were probably the first to shed light as to the massiveness of the Russian theft."

"Operation Paperclip?"

"Indeed. There still may be horrors yet to be discovered."

Tight lipped, Talbot nodded his agreement.

"Bottom line," Mickey counted on his fingers, "two things: number one, chemo. Lucky Industries had the responsibility of finding out the history of this area before breaking any ground; and number two, there is not a single thing that I'm seeing here in my medical lane."

"Whoa, hold your horses there, Doc, you haven't seen it all yet. Everything is not as it seems. Follow me." Talbot led the way through American, Polish, and German military types toward an excavation site which revealed some recent commercial diggings. Mickey's mind played out a dozen scenarios as to what his physician-scientist historian role could be in all this. After ten minutes of walking, Mickey poked the bear.

"Medical documents … "

"Sir?"

"You Chemical Corps guys found war-era medical papers that shed light on something not chemical, biological, or nuclear?"

"Patience, Doc. One picture is worth a thousand words."

"The word count is up to 999, Talbot. Show me the picture already!" Before Mickey could issue another demand, they had rounded the corner, and his eyes sucked in a blackness so deep that he couldn't breathe.

Mickey saw what the two Qumran shepherds must have seen as they peered into the black hole of the hillside which held the Dead Sea Scrolls. This gaping hole was similar only in that it held potential treasure.

"Amazing isn't it, Doc? Kind of like what that English fellow saw when he first saw King Tut's tomb."

"Howard Carter," mused Mickey.

"Yeah, that's the fellow. Some kind of fossil digger, he was."

"Archeologist, Talbot. He was an archeologist."

Mickey knew, like Carter, he was on the threshold of a living, breathing, time capsule.

Directly in front of Mickey was the frame of a building littered with broken tiled flooring. Nothing else vertical remained of the building that once stood there. Positioned in the near left-hand corner of this foundation appeared to be an open cellar door. From the corners of the gaping, mouth-like entrance ran hoses connected to fans, cables, and cords—the stage had been prepped for a further investigation. Thinking about his current track record of failure, Mickey became worried. Regarding Howard Carter, Mickey knew the rest of the story. Besides discovering King Tut, Carter also had to deal with the untimely demise of his tomb-raiding entourage. Mickey glanced at Talbot with a look that clearly asked, *We aren't going down there, are we?* Certainly an underground room which had been sitting idly for the past sixty years wasn't an ideal area for a casual jaunt.

Immediately, an image appeared in Mickey's head. The words *Curse of the Pharaohs* and *Death shall come on swift wings to him who disturbs the peace of the King* were imprinted quite clearly in the forefront of his mind. If his brief knowledge of Egyptology didn't belie him, Mickey remembered that many of the tomb raiders died horrible deaths. However, before him wasn't a tomb, or at least, he didn't think so. The only chance of a curse would be in the more tangible form of a booby trap laid by the departing scientists. Although unlikely, it could be possible. Mickey remembered yet another gaping hole in the earth and some idiocy in the desert. A Chemical Corps captain, an engineer lieutenant, and himself were three fools who had investigated a gaping bunker at Objective Armstrong in the Iraqi desert in 1991. They found an unexploded ordnance with a trip pin inside a briefcase. But for the grace of God, he should be stone-cold dead now. However, that was the past. Today he wasn't dead. Nevertheless, he was still stone-cold.

24

A Mystery Beneath

Dyhernfurth chemical site
Brzeg Dolny, Poland

"A tomb's curse does not differentiate between those that raid or those that record." Mickey felt the sweat trickle down from his armpits. Safely separated from Howard Carter and his tomb raiders by both time and space lent no justifications as to why Mickey's pits and palms were bathed in copious sweat. Wiping his hands on his combat uniform trousers, Mickey's thoughts turned to the death of Lord Carnarvon from Howard Carter's team and its relation to the present place and time.

If he remembered correctly, seven of Carter's team members died mysteriously and they all had one thing in common. They were all tomb raiders of sacred places, and each had touched Tutankhamun's sarcophagus. Mickey doubted seriously that there would be any Egyptian mummy here in Poland, but there still could be unseen dangers.

He recalled that a later investigation of the King Tut deaths cited the tiny bacteria Staphylococcus and Pseudomonas as culprits along with the fungus Aspergillus. Most definitely this constituted biological germ warfare even way back then. If that wasn't bad enough, the Egyptians tacked on some elements of poison chemicals as well. History documented there was evidence of toxic gases in King Tut's tomb, even though all were of trace amounts. *The air that sustains us can also kill us. Howard Carter and his band of tomb raiders bear witness to that very fact.* Mickey's face reflected the sarcasm of his thinking until Talbot's voice again brought him back to himself.

"What we have here, Doc, is the reason we brought you."

"Tell me that you don't have a mummy."

"Sir?"

"A mummy, Talbot, tell me that there isn't a sarcophagus here that German General Rommel brought to hide in Poland."

"No, sir. To my knowledge there is no mummy. Did you really think this was a crypt?"

"Not important. What were you about to say?"

"Honest, Doc, it's not a tomb. However, what we do have for you down that entrance is a World War II–era chemical munitions laboratory."

"Talbot, you certainly don't need my expertise in a chemical munitions factory laboratory. Tell me this isn't the reason I was summoned. Tell me that—"

"Patience, sir. There's more to the story."

"For your sake, there had better be. Right now, I'm pretty sure I could get off with justifiable homicide."

"Are you always this intense, Doc?"

"This is my friendly side, Talbot."

"Fine." Talbot forced a laugh, a hard swallow, and an audible clearing of his throat. "The Russians, for whatever reason, pillaged and plundered from the ground up. They destroyed everything above the foundation level. However, they didn't bother to pull up the floorboards and tiles to check beneath. What we found was why you have been called, sir."

"You found a room that has some unexplainable medical paraphernalia, right?"

"We found a room, but we aren't clear how many more are down there."

"When will you know, Talbot?"

"We won't know for sure until the special investigation team arrives."

"Which team is that?"

"Some guys from downrange."

"Downrange from Iraq, Afghanistan, Kuwait, Kosovo, Romania, or the former Russian state of Georgia?"

"All the above, probably."

"Hmmm." Mickey began thinking about Russell's mission downrange in Iraq. Russell had teamed up with a Mobile Emergency Medical Response Team to test out ground-penetrating radar for trapped bunker casualties or bodies. "Was there anything said about ground-penetrating radar?"

"Roger, Doc."

"How many teams?"

"Negative knowledge, sir."

"What equipment?"

"Negative knowledge, sir."

"What *do* you know?"

"I … uh…." Talbot's hand went to his mouth pensively. He began to speak again, but then paused. Not a word escaped.

"Bottom line up front, Talbot: you have no clue how deep this shaft goes or how many other underground storages are here."

"Not until the desert team—"

"Yeah, yeah, so what have we got, Chemo?" Mickey blurted impatiently.

"Ummm…." Talbot stalled, clearing his throat.

"So this is it? I'm the worm dangling on the fishing hook." Mickey pulled a face, detesting the thought that within minutes he was going to be rummaging around, alone, in a dimly lit, dank cellar that the Nazis abandoned ages ago.

Mickey found himself in a paradox. As much as his curiosity had reached painful levels, he dreaded the thought of the plunge beneath the surface.

Mickey undid his cuffs, took up the slack in each sleeve, and then clasped each cuff tightly. He knew that not a thing was going to help prepare him, or anyone, for the task which lay ahead. *I'm stalling.* To his knowledge there was no Egyptian sarcophagus or Dead Sea Scroll wrapped with future fame in the abyss to his front. His feet were lead. This hole in the ground was one for which a working knowledge of chemistry or chemical warfare would not lend the needed fix. Instead, it needed him as a physician-scientist historian, and right now. *What could be in that darkness that needs my expertise? Why won't anyone tell me?*

Talbot cleared his throat again.

Worm or no worm … time to take the plunge.

25

Dust on Death

Dyhernfurth chemical site
Brzeg Dolny, Poland

F.E.A.R. stands for: Forget Everything And Roar ... or is it Retreat?

Biting at the cuticles of his left thumb, Mickey nodded to the wide-eyed, toxically eager Talbot, and crossed himself—the race was on. Piercing through the last remaining roving cohorts of masked and unmasked chemical detection teams, Polish scientists, and an occasional, curious scraggly dog, Mickey eyed his destination. Quickly they closed the distance to the very edge of the gaping hole in the floor.

"Stay on my wing, Doc. Here is when the fun begins." Talbot exuded an obnoxious level of excitement highlighted with a widening boyish grin. Mickey stiffened as he slid into the porcelain tile-framed abyss. His heart pounded in his throat.

As he passed through the hole in the floor, an instant temperature change from the outside ambiance to the inside shadows shocked his skin, turning it to goose flesh. The musty stench of neglect blasted his nostrils, filling his eyes with water. *Death shall come on swift wings to him who disturbs the peace of the King.* Mickey wasn't sure whether the environment or the mantra in his mind had initiated the irrepressible shudder sweeping over him. It took many steps to shake off the heebie-jeebies.

It seemed like they were walking forever, and then, at the far end of the fifty-foot square room, Talbot stopped at arm's length from a dead-end wall with his arms outstretched, looking crucified. Silently, he pivoted 180 degrees and looked straight at Mickey. Mickey stared blankly at Talbot's shadow, a mural of crucifixion.

"I'm failing to make the connection here, Chemo," Mickey choked out as dust swirled around them. Smiling, Talbot twisted ninety degrees to his right and pushed upon the corner of the far wall while dust danced vulgarly about his feet. A crease appeared in the wall and an invisible portal hinged backward into an even deeper blackness. *I thought the entryway to this place was shocking enough, but this.... I am in the very bowels of Satan.*

"In there, Doc. *That* is why you are here, and *this* is where I leave off. Let me know if you need anything. I am at your service." Without waiting a millisecond after the last word left his mouth, the thick-limbed chemical officer strode off as if having accepted the baton pass from an unseen sprinter in a relay race. Since further conversing with another breathing entity was not an option, Mickey looked toward the dark doorway—to the task in front of him. His tongue cleaved to the roof of his mouth as he unclipped his tactical flashlight. He slid his thumb down the barrel until he felt the switch. Seconds later a cone of white light pierced the darkness, changing swiftly to a new beam a moment later. *Red red, keeps night ahead. I must conserve my night vision.*

Mickey went through the portal, down several series of steps, always moving toward a large, dimly-lit area somewhere far to his front. Finally, he stepped into the room at the end of his journey. He could feel it. *Here's the payoff.*

In front of him, and to each side, stood rows and rows and more rows of shelved munitions poised in a dusty military formation. Any wine connoisseur would be proud to have a cellar filled with such an array of dusty bottles. *These are no cabernet sauvignons. These are metal tube containers of misery, pain, and death.* Mickey changed the beam color again. *Blue blue, brings lines to view. This should make reading easier.* Ciphering the markings on each round, Mickey noticed the telltale cruciform signs indicating that these were bombs filled with war chemicals. Closing one eye while briefly switching to a white beam with light diffuser, Mickey used his open eye to engage color. He saw the yellow cross of sulfur mustard blister agent and the blue cross of choking gas. He groaned as he remembered the millions of gas casualties which were wrought from the first employment of gas warfare on Thursday, April 22, 1915 in the small city of Flanders, Belgium.

Now on green beam, Mickey cautiously crept past rows and rows of munitions. *Green green, I can't be seen.* His eyes saw different versions of chemical gas shells which he knew were mainly World War I stocks. *I hope World War I is the end of this stockpile. Then again, if it was, I wouldn't be here.* When, finally, the initial rows and stacks of the World War I stocks had finished, Mickey caught a glimpse of something that made his stomach sour. He switched back to blue beam.

His eyes now began fixing on shelves of munitions with a new marking. *It wasn't enough to have skin blistering and lung choking agents, was it?* Cradled in these newer bomb racks were nerve agents which came about after World War I. *It seems like the Nazis had all the known flavors of the time.* He saw TABUN, called *GA*, and SARIN symbolized as *GB*, and almost incomprehensible, there on a rack by itself perched SOMAN, *GD*. They were all products of Dr. Gerhard Schrader's post-World War I chemistry lab. Mickey continued to look, bomb by bomb, as if his life depended upon it. As far as his skilled eyes could see, all were still just chemical bombs.

"There is still nothing here that a chemo can't manage," Mickey said aloud. His voice hit the echoless dead air. As he passed endless racks and shelving, the air became increasingly stifling. Farther on his trek through the dungeon, lit only by strange porthole lighting, the second rows of racks came to an end. In an opening before him, Mickey saw the semblance of a chemical laboratory. Then his eyes landed on the unexpected. Words escaped his lips, his jaw refused to close. "My Jesus, God Almighty, and Holy Mother Mary, it can't be. It just can't be.... "

26

More Than Meets the Eye

Dyhernfurth chemical site
Brzeg Dolny, Poland

White, white, away the night. Using white light, Mickey scanned fervently from side to side and top to bottom, but he couldn't drink in the wealth of information quickly enough. On the dusty floor he saw where some footprints stopped abruptly. *Here's where Talbot stopped.* To Mickey's front were longitudinal files of chemical islands upon which basic biomedical studies could be done. There were what looked to be benchtop incubators and many, many large processing areas for living tissue.

Immediately he knew both by its design and the secrecy of its placement that this was not solely a chemical or biological munitions laboratory. Evidently the group of highly trained Nazi scientists working here went well beyond the scope of the Dyhernfurth chemical warfare mission. *But what was that mission? The clues have to be here.*

Mickey's mind shot back to Loni's DIA briefing. *How much of what lies before me is in the sealed folder that was handed to her in the briefing room? Is this the data that I had no need to know? Is this tied into the murder and evisceration of Father Judas in the United States? Is this why the loathsome Captain Dalton is prowling the byways of Europe? Hmmm, a little advance warning would have been nice.*

Mickey's eyes continued to dart about as he shook his head to clear it and then moistened his lips. *This is big ... too big. This needs to be carefully and methodically managed. Thank goodness Suzanne and Russell are on their way.* Mickey took in a deep breath to think. The operational tempo of this mission was about to go into overdrive.

"What was it that Loni had said about the DNA of Father Judas?" Mickey whispered to himself. "Was it one thousand or two thousand years old? If it was one thousand, then there might be an explanation here if there was, perhaps, a decimal point error and one thousand was actually one hundred. That would place the DNA in the early 1900s when biomedical research was being done by Nobel laureate Dr. Kossel in Strasbourg. And then there were also Drs. Miescher and Morell who were studying medical biochemistry at that time.

"But why was DNA being age tested on-scene at a murder site anyway?" Mickey poised his whispered question to the silence that engulfed him. "Did someone expect to find carbon-dated material disproportionately old? If so, who and why?"

As the white beam darted, Mickey's eyes searched the dusty lair for an administrative area which might give some meaningful insights. He knew what it should be like but was still taken aback when he actually saw it. Mickey blinked hard. What he saw along the left wall was a row of desks, each with their own private library, phone, chemical pharmacy, and work area. It was an odd arrangement for the era. Pharmacy items as well as medicinal and atypical chemicals were present. Here was where the porthole light came from, so with a snap to his LBE, Mickey retired his tactical flashlight. *Thankfully I won't have to face Shelob in this dark place ... though there are things here just as murderous and malicious, if not more so.* He turned his thoughts away from gigantic literary spiders and back to the task at hand.

"This just doesn't fit the time. If this level of science was known, why was the world not informed?" he asked himself. "Was it held in check by the tight-lipped secrecy of the Third Reich?"

Nazi Germany had its own manifests and lists of who had a need-to-know. As evidenced in front of him, it might have been that these folks here had the knowledge and only Adolph Hitler himself had the need-to-know.

On one rolltop desk, Mickey found what seemed to be a physician-scientist's workstation. The telltale sign was the general disarray of the clinical notes on the surface of the desk. Many papers bore the stamped symbol of a snake on a pole.

"Hmmm ... the Staff of Asclepius ... medical, not chemical."

Mickey didn't have to read German to understand the stick-figure drawing annotated with numerical fractions at the joints. His own clinical shorthand depicted the neurologic evaluation of deep-tendon reflexes in the same way. Tap the knee here and record the level of kick there on a stick figure.

"Some things never change."

On the shelves above the desk, huddled on either side of the dust-covered radio, were numerous pharmaceutical vials, equally dressed in dusty shrouds. Among them he saw kalium and natrium which he knew were potassium and sodium respectively. On the desk was a mortar and pestle imprinted on the side with an eagle holding a Nazi swastika. He opened drawers and saw syringes, bottles of whiskey, boxes of matches, and a German red wine. Mickey smiled. It was then he noticed the stack of hand-typed cover sheets displaying Nazi logos along with the words *Flusszigeuner* and *Unsterblichkeit durch Medizinische Forschung* repeated across them.

Mickey was not fluent in anything but restaurant German—he could handle a menu and talk to the wait staff. However, he *had* been in Germany long enough to recognize something about rivers and immortality.

"What is this? Is this whole thing a chemical-medical experiment on a biocontamination of Europe's major rivers?" Hitler certainly had his favorite methods when it came to persecution. Contamination of the water supply of undesirables, such as the hated pariah-rich groups of Poles, Slavs, Gypsies, and Jews, certainly wasn't beneath the Third Reich. Pivoting from desk to desk to compare papers and notes, he saw that rivers, immortality, and medical research seemed to be the common theme of this hidden laboratory.

"But what does it mean?"

The last interesting find that Mickey made was a series of distribution lists of concentration camps. The location names: Ravensbrück, Sachsenhausen, Neuengamme, Natzweiler-Struthof, Spandau Prison, and Buchenwald appeared almost every time on the various lists, either singly or in cohorts of pairs or triads. There was one pattern that struck with great regularity. No matter which paper he read, the approving signature on the bottom of every document belonged to the same physician-scientist—Dr. Theodor Morell.

Mickey scanned his mind to find a commonality. It suddenly became clear. He wasn't just dealing with rivers and immortality. He was dealing with something much more grandiose and esoteric. *I need Russell....*

Dr. Russell Lange's vast and specific knowledge of World War II history and of military medicine would help Mickey make sense of these surging thoughts and these mysterious clues. Russell was the ideal military medical historical resource when the chips were down. Then something else crossed his mind. *Suzanne Coletrane.* Mickey pulled up with a lurch.

Even now, as he held these museum treasures in his hands, he realized that the DIA wheel of mission execution had Dr. Suzanne Coletrane on her way here. He knew the sequence of her deployment: Aberdeen Proving Ground—secret stateside military airport—Ramstein, Germany.

I need to catch her before she connects out of Ramstein. She is very close to one of the concentration camps on the list. She can serve more efficiently in France than here in Poland.

Mickey tapped several stacks of papers into a manageable ream and shoved it into the front of his uniform trousers. Under the cover of his jacket, the ream disappeared into anonymity. The seventy-year-old German red wine nestled into his right cargo pants pocket.

Led by a bouncing white spotlight, Mickey darted past the rows of munitions and out of the laboratory, up the several landings, through ghastly rooms filled with dusty grim reapers, and into the sunlight. Once on the surface he caught sight of Talbot who was directing the miscellaneous excavation operations. Like a vexed junkyard dog, Mickey barked to the chemical officer as they walked back to Mickey's car.

"Seal off this laboratory until we can get an army Medical Research Team from Heidelberg to do a careful study. They shouldn't be far behind me."

"What did you find, Doc?" Talbot's eyes bounced between Mickey and the path back to the car. "More than meets the eye, huh?"

"More than meets the eye, Chemo. *Much more* than meets the eye. Keep me in the loop if anything else turns up before the Medical Research Team arrives.

After that, we'll keep all of this in medical channels. I say again, keep this in *medical*, not *chemical* channels. Thanks, Talbot."

"Will that be all, your majesty?"

"I did say 'thanks.'" Mickey paused in his walk, looked down at the ground for a moment and then lifted his eyes back up to the grinning Talbot. "Yes, there is one more thing." Mickey resumed his pace. "Do you know anything about immortality research and a river people?"

"I dunno." Talbot scratched his head through his black beret. "Maybe ... folks who like to fish ... who like to stay physically fit ... forever, I guess ... I really don't know."

Mickey stared at him. *Fishing for fitness; now there's a multi-neuron, upper brain–level response.* "Real genius," he muttered.

"Snake Oil Willy," interrupted Talbot.

"What?"

"You asked me for the name," said Talbot. "So, I got you the name."

"What name?"

"The CEO of Lucky Industries."

"You are telling me that the executive officer of a large international company goes by the name Snake Oil Willy. You cannot be remotely serious."

"So it seems. Anyway, the yellow hat foreman on-site here calls him Snake Oil Willy." Talbot smiled. "No matter, Doc, I know his real name. It's Wilhelm Wunschmann."

"Wilhelm Wunschmann?"

"Yes, sir."

"Can't be."

"I'm pretty sure that's what I was told."

"It cannot be Wilhelm Wunschmann." Mickey blew into his fist.

"Why? What's up, Doc? This guy's a friend of yours?"

"He's nobody's friend anymore. He's recently dead."

"What?"

"Presently, he is without life. He is no more. He's dead."

"How can he be dead?"

"Physiologically, his brain fails and his breathing stops, then—"

"I got that part."

"Well then, what part of *dead* don't you get?"

"Relative to CEOs, and head of industrial land developing companies, pretty much all of it."

"Talbot, forget what I said about keeping this info in medical channels." Slowing his stroll, Mickey took his keys and beeped to unlock his car. "Keep the info tighter than that. When Dr. Russell Lange gets here, tell him to only talk to me, no one else. If Dr. Suzanne Coletrane should contact you or arrive first, tell her only to talk to me. If something comes up before anyone arrives, talk only to me."

"Anything else, sir?" Talbot held open the car door.

"Yes, hold the current info close to your chest. Don't report an update to anyone right now. No one, Talbot. Not Dr. Lange. Not Dr. Coletrane. Not the DIA. Not even General Bloomfield. Not a living soul. Give me your full attention, Talbot. For at least seventy-two hours, keep this tight on the high side."

Remembering that the papers from the lab were still in his trousers, Mickey reached down, retrieved them, and then, while leaning into the open door, shoved them into his knapsack wedged between the seats. Talbot watched this paper shuffle with great dismay.

"What's the ... ?"

"High side, Talbot," reinforced Mickey, as he removed his utility vest and thrust it into the bag on top of the papers.

"Actually, that looked kind of on the down-low to me."

"You're killing me." Mickey sighed with exasperation and offered no more explanation as he hopped in, buckled his seat belt, and pulled away. As he paused the car before turning out of the excavation site, in his rearview mirror Mickey could see Talbot scratching his head through his beret again. He could imagine what the chemo was thinking: "Dead CEOs, crotch pot papers, and a high side ride. So much juicy data to run up the flagpole but I have to keep quiet. Useless medical pukes! God love 'em."

Mickey chuckled for a moment, pulled the wine from his pocket and stashed it in his knapsack before turning his wheels northwest toward the town of Cottbus, Germany. If his hunch was right, he needed to be in Berlin as a launching pad for the concentration camp sites at Sachsenhausen and Ravensbrück. *Too bad, anything from Spandau Prison is long gone.* Quickly, Mickey did a systems check. He was already very tired, quite cranky, and the German megalopolis of Berlin was hours and hours away. He punched hard on the pedal of his rent-a-wreck. With a groan and a lurch, for better or for worse, in sickness or in death, he was on his way.

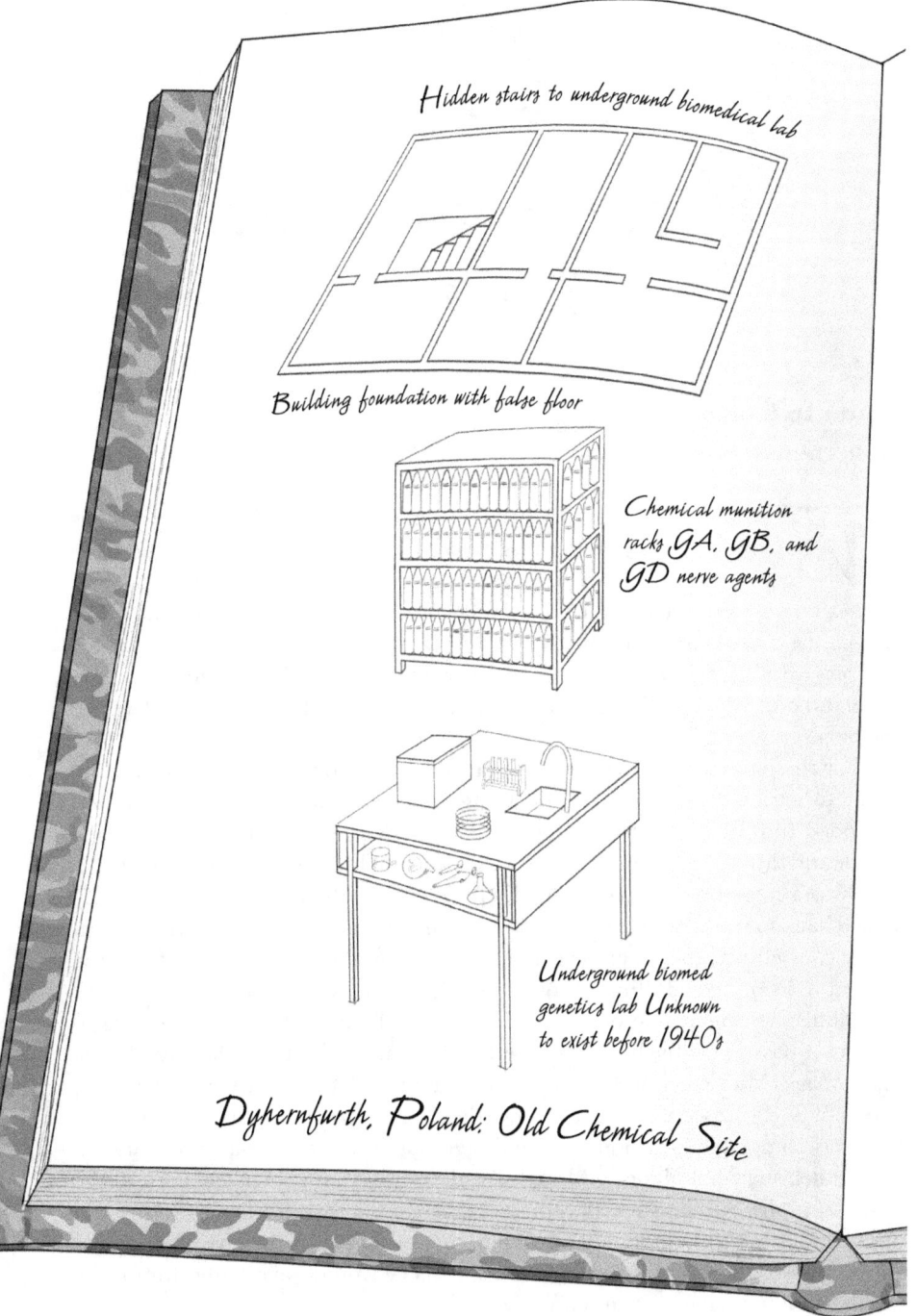

Hidden stairs to underground biomedical lab

Building foundation with false floor

Chemical munition racks *GA*, *GB*, and *GD* nerve agents

Underground biomed genetics lab Unknown to exist before 1940s

Dyhernfurth, Poland: Old Chemical Site

27

Possum and the Posse

Route to Cottbus
Western marches of Poland

Why aren't they here when I need them? Thoughts racing hundreds of miles an hour, Mickey knew that he badly needed Russell's input. *I also have to get to Suzanne.* He was split in his priorities. *Who do I reach first? Where is Suzanne right now?* Violating European law and using his cellular phone while driving, he dialed first one, then the other, but neither picked up. *Probably in a dead zone for cellular output.* The miles went by but not quickly enough. This part of Poland had very small roads and every town along it looked exactly like the one he just passed.

For the longest time, Mickey was on the two-lane road back to Germany alone. Occasionally, he saw an oncoming Russian sedan or a mini car which reminded him of the earlier game of chicken. Mickey scanned his rearview mirror and saw yet another red mini car gaining on him. Ahead, driving toward him, was a huge transfer truck which entirely filled the opposite lane. Mickey looked back to see how much ground the mini car gained, but there was no sign of any car behind him. Then he caught a movement in his periphery. It was the dratted red mini car pulling up on his driver's side. The idiot driver was now straddling the center lane between Mickey and the oncoming truck, trying to execute a pass. Reactively, Mickey jerked his car to the far-right edge of the road. *Moron.* Mickey glanced over to give a dirty look to the driver. The driver, a man of Slavic descent, never acknowledged Mickey's attempt at glaring. This Slav was completely oblivious to the dangerous situation he had precipitated. With quick snapshot glances, Mickey sized up the character of the man in the other car. The Slav possessed very short, cropped, dark hair, olive skin, and dark eyes. He had a short beard which cupped his chin. It gave him a very austere look. Under a different situation, Mickey would have found him to be totally without menace, even scholarly.

The oncoming truck blared its horn.

"I see," said Mickey, "the rules of the road today in Poland are that there are no rules on the roads today in Poland—and probably every day. That truck's going to get a new red hood ornament any second."

The red car squeaked past in the nick of time and sped off ahead, leaving Mickey grumbling to himself as the miles ticked by all too slowly.

☩ ☩ ☩

Farther down the road Mickey saw the same little red mini car sitting astride what looked like the snapped-off portion of a wooden highway signpost for Bolesławiec. *I wonder how you say "I told you so" in Polish.*

But before Mickey could gloat, compassion swallowed his anger. From his vantage point, the driver appeared to be seated with his head forward on the steering wheel. The physician in Mickey was rising to the surface as he began to slow down to investigate the extent of injury to life and limb. There was no sign of movement.

Keep going, said Loni's voice inside his head, promoting his well-being. Mickey's foot reached toward the accelerator.

Good Samaritan laws are universal, Doctor, another voice said. *Despite any danger to yourself, you have the skills to help this guy.* His foot reached for the brake.

This guy was an accident waiting to happen, Loni's voice urged. Mickey's foot moved right toward the accelerator. His foot hovered over both pedals …

What if he dies and you could have saved him?

What if you try to save him and he dies anyway?

What if you try to save him and he lives?

What if this is a set up for a robbery?

"What if it's not?" Mickey said aloud as he pulled over and stopped.

Leaving the car in neutral and the engine idling, he engaged the emergency brakes. Mickey's gut cringed, but he knew in his heart that this was the right thing to do. He hurried over to the mini car and wrenched the car door open. The driver was motionless with his head forward against the steering wheel. Mickey reached across the unconscious driver to release the seat belt and tilt the chair backward. An elbow caught Mickey in the mouth and sent him reeling backward into the dirt.

The driver quickly overcame the unsuspecting Mickey. In his head, Mickey heard Loni's voice saying, *I told you so.* Within seconds Mickey watched the Slav posture over him, brandishing a handgun. While Mickey's hands held pressure to his bleeding nose and mouth, he looked down the business end of a revolver.

Thirty yards away, an evening bus screeched to a stop. The opportunistic gunman tucked his weapon into his pants and under his jacket. As the people disembarked from the bus, they saw Mickey and rushed over to him thinking he was the casualty from the mini car. The gunman quietly eased backward through the pressing crowd, hopped into Mickey's idling rental, and drove away with a plume of smoke dancing to the rhythm of misfiring spark plugs.

"That's my car!" Mickey shouted over the group of locals who kept trying to push him back and wipe the blood from his face. The car disappeared into the horizon. Lying back, Mickey groaned. The precious papers were inside the rumbling piece of wheeled, rental crap.

He pulled himself up and gently extracted himself from the crowd. He looked at the broken signpost. Bolesławiec *is a short drive, or a moderate walk, away. It's the center of the Polish pottery industry—usually heavily frequented by Americans. Maybe someone there can help.* His legs burned from scurrying down and up the secret laboratory's steps and from the recent scuffling. Besides that, because of his reverse flop, his backside also smarted. Most injured, however, was his pride.

Even as he was unclipping the man's seatbelt, Mickey remembered he had thought it was certainly odd that there were no the keys in the ignition. *For crying out loud, the engine wasn't even running.* The scenario cycled over and over in his head, and he felt more and more the complete jackass. He had been successfully carjacked by a Polish possum. *Could anything be more humiliating?* The only satisfaction that Mickey could gain was that the broken seat spring of the hijacked car was probably connected to a critical piece of the engine. The carjacker could be broken down, for real this time, just up ahead on the road. However, Mickey wasn't sure if meeting up with a hostile force in the dusky evening was something he really wanted to face at this time. He hoped the carjacker didn't stumble upon the knapsack and arbitrarily toss out the critical contents while looking for money or food. Mickey picked up his walking pace, wishing that the Polish rent-a-wreck would blow up the carjacker and leave only the important lab papers intact ... *and winged monkeys might fly out your butt,* Suzanne would chime in if she were there. But, she wasn't; there were no monkeys, and his phone charger was hanging out of the cigarette lighter in the car. *Life really sucks right now.*

Mickey's limping saunter eventually carried him into the city limits of Bolesławiec. His ears pricked at the sound of English being spoken by a group of women. A group of American ladies stepped out of the doorway of a frequented blue-and-white hued Polish pottery shop, Ceramika. Arms filled with weighted sacks, they were all heading toward their vehicle for the return trip back home to, presumably, Germany. Mickey hobbled toward them shouting in English, but the blasting horn of an oncoming commercial transfer truck drowned his attempt. The noisy ladies were totally unaware of their surroundings and caught up in a game of besting each other relative to their shopping prowess. The eighteen-wheeler whizzed past, sending a cloud of dust at the four ladies and forcing them to stop in place.

"You!" Mickey panted. "You are Americans!" The women circled their wagons and drew in closer to one other. Mickey imagined that they saw a bloody-faced Igor look-alike staggering toward them out of the dust.

One voice from the group rose above the murmurs, "Yes, who's asking?"

"I know it doesn't look like it, but I'm Doctor—"

"Peronne. You're Dr. Peronne."

"He's Dr. Peronne."

"What are you doing here, Dr. Peronne?"

"What happened to you?"

"What happened to him?"

"Are you okay?"

"He doesn't look okay."

"He's Dr. Peronne, my doctor from Heidelberg." Feeling overwhelmingly relieved, Mickey dropped to one knee and allowed the four ladies to encircle and swarm him with their overflowing kindness and concern.

"I need your help. I need to get to Berlin. I was going to Berlin. There was a car accident … but it wasn't an accident. He was playing possum … I was carjacked. I'm okay—does anyone have a hanky? Can you get me to Berlin?" *I'm blubbering.*

The ladies backed away to a modest distance and again huddled together. After a significant group debate, imbued with elaborate gesticulations, Mickey could tell that a decision had been reached. *They won't help me.* Mickey braced himself for the verdict. Before the group leader could verbalize her regrets, from the nearby gasoline station Mickey heard a familiar sputtering and whipped his head around toward the sound.

The rent-a-wreck. It heaved and choked by, stirring up the dust cloud which had just settled from the eighteen-wheeler. Mickey watched its progress with sharp eyes. *It's heading away from Berlin to the border town of Gorlitz.* There was no indication that the driver saw him. Mickey re-engaged the group's spokeswoman before she could start speaking.

"Never mind—can you take me with you in the direction of that car?"

The ladies again huddled.

"Ladies, please," Mickey urged, as the sounds of the sputtering faded into the distance. One head craned from the group, looked around, but dived back into the roadside consortium. For what seemed to be infinity, but actually was a mere minute or two, a thumbs-up came from the group. Mickey was soon comfortably seated in a puttering minibus amidst boxes, bags, and a million questions. Mickey rubbed his tired eyes. *We'll never catch him like this.*

As they drove, Mickey began looking for signs indicating that the German border was ahead—the duplicity of the German and Polish languages on the printed street signs was usually the first indicator. Until then, he let the background conversation in the minibus drone into a sleepy silence while his mind reviewed the facts of the day as he best understood them. Smugly, he concluded, there was no way that what was happening now was any part of the DIA scenario that Loni had briefed. He had been assaulted and robbed. To top it off, the string of his failings had now reached a new country where he didn't even have any personal transportation. *Where are the keys to the helicopter when you really need them?*

28

It's a Gas, Gas, Gas

Route to Gorlitz
Western Marches of Poland

"I was crowned with a smack to my head … " Silently moving his lips, Mickey searched for the lyrics. " … but it's all right, I'm Jumping Jack Flash."

Mickey leaned back against his seat and massaged the bridge of his nose. The image of a panel truck with multiple knobs and faucets kept spinning through his mind. It was three o'clock in the morning and his analytical mind just couldn't maintain sleep. *What I wouldn't give to have studied those Nazi papers just a bit longer.* Mickey knew that Dr. Morell's distribution lists from the underground laboratory were specific to locations where medical, chemical, and biological experimentations were done on concentration camp inmates. *What is that elusive link between the camps and the underground bunker lab?* He was betting that hidden within those documents in his knapsack was evidence supporting the presence of a freezer or incubation truck to preserve human tissue while in transit. *There has to be.* The camps were certain to have the prototype of the refrigeration truck, possibly in the guise of a refurbished gas van with emplaced flow valves and knobs.

"What's a gas van?" one of the American shopping ladies asked.

"What?"

"You said, 'gas van,' Dr. Peronne. I clearly heard you say the words 'gas' and then 'van.' Don't say you didn't."

Mickey noticed that besides the driver behind the steering wheel, only this traveler was awake, although a bit groggy. He grunted as he reached forward, grabbing the metal frame of her seat back while pulling himself closer to her. He watched the drowsiness in her eyes clear as he repositioned himself for better conversation. After all, no use waking up all the sleeping ladies on the minibus just because he was perseverating on Nazi gas vans.

"Just before World War II," Mickey began, in a poor attempt of a whisper, "when Hitler arrived at the decision that he needed an inexpensive, highly efficient means to execute people en masse, he first looked to World War I history and arrived at the gas van."

"What a horrible thought," said the traveler with a shudder. "Why did Hitler choose a gas van?"

"By accident really." Mickey shook his head slowly. "The motorized World War I ambulances deployed by the US Army Ambulance Service had the ever-present problem of sufficiently warming the freezing casualty during winter warfare along the western front in France."

"Wasn't Ernest Hemingway an ambulance driver in World War I?"

"Ernest Hemingway? Yes, I think so … maybe not … I don't know…. Anyway, the point is that as true winter approached and the ambient temperatures dropped below freezing, motorized ambulance drivers like Hemingway, and whomever else, took suitable tubing, connected it to the vehicle's exhaust pipe, and routed the warm exhaust gases so as to transfer the heat from the motor into the patient cabin. This resulted in a pleasantly warmed-up cabin and a toasty casualty."

"Isn't that bad for you? Carbon dioxide can kill you, can't it?"

"Monoxide, not dioxide. The presence of only one oxygen attached to one carbon—and yes, carbon monoxide can kill a person through asphyxiation."

"Asphyxiation … is that the same as suffocation?"

"Well, in a sense. Overall, the end point is the same."

"Hemingway was apparently a better writer than an ambulance driver, it seems," said the traveler.

"Yes, probably so. Needless to say, some casualties arrived worse off, or even dead, due to carbon monoxide poisoning. The gases from the ambulance tail pipe were sucked deep into the lungs of the wounded soldiers, causing destruction of lung tissue which resulted in death. While attempting to warm up a cold casualty, a warm corpse was often produced."

"It appears that no good deed goes unpunished, Dr. Peronne."

"I believe that, more than you know," Mickey said, rubbing the bridge of his aching nose.

"However," continued the woman, "what does that have to do with the gas van?"

"That was exactly my question, Ms. Monardi."

"It's *Min-ee-ar-tee* … but you were close."

"Sorry, Ms. Miniarti," said Mickey. "To answer the question you just posed, several years ago I went to the United States Holocaust Memorial Museum in Washington, DC. In the research library on the second floor, the library staff guided my research in the Nazi methodology of human extermination."

"You're talking about killing all those folks in the concentration camps to make room for more poor unfortunates, aren't you?"

"Yes, before there were extermination camps, there was an extermination van. The gas van appeared early in Nazi history, being used primarily on the Russian front."

"Those poor Russians."

"Russians, Poles, Czechs, Gypsies, Jews, and many, many more. Prisoner interrogation vans were rolled into areas where the Nazis needed to conduct mobile intelligence operations. When the gestapo inquisition was finished, hoses coming from the tail pipe of the truck's running engines were distally attached to specially designed ports on the side of the vehicle and Haber's law of gases did the rest. Not a shot had to be fired nor any ammunition wasted."

"Sounds dreadful."

"It was. However, over time, the Nazis began to realize that just like bullets, motor fuel itself was a precious commodity. As a failed experiment, the gas van lost favor as a killing machine.

"Wake up, ladies and gent," a commanding voice from the front of the minibus shouted. "Everybody, get out your passports."

Mickey reached through his shirt, toward the small leather pouch slung across his chest and resting against his ribcage. *For Christ's sake, really?* In all his preparations to get out the door, he never double-checked that his passport was in his sling. *I've got my military ID, though, thank God.* His ID and some political schmoozing had gotten him over many borders in the past. Mickey drew in a deep breath and tried to look nonmenacing.

Passing through the gate in the wee hours worked greatly in favor of the weary travelers. The border guards looked at the military identification card and passed it between themselves. With an authoritative nod, they returned it along with the short stack of tourist passports. Nonetheless, Dr. Peronne's presence with the shopping group raised few eyebrows of interest at the border crossing.

"Nazi experiments on helpless camp prisoners were held in secret," said Mickey, returning his ID card into his pocket. "No one knew and so no one could rush to help."

"That's beyond horrible. How … can anyone … in their heart and mind—"

"Isn't that … " Mickey spotted a familiar prey in the form of a smoking tail pipe ahead.

"Yes, Dr. Peronne, it is," the driver responded. Apparently, the carjacker was limited by the quality of the car he stole.

"Don't lose him!"

"Haven't lost him over the past hour and a half," the driver retorted with a hint of injured pride. "However, I think he's reached his destination. He's exiting up ahead toward Bautzen."

Mickey went through the list in his head. Bautzen would be no more than a delay. The concentration camps where chemical experimentation took place were: Neuengamme near Hamburg; Sachsenhausen near Berlin; Ravensbrück, just north of Berlin at Oranienburg; Buchenwald near Weimar; and Natzweiler-Struthof near Strasbourg, France. Bautzen was none of these. It did, however, have a prison whose library might save him some travel, but even that was a stretch.

Maybe, after getting back the papers, I can get another rental car in Bautzen. Then I can begin covering all of the camps and their archival records except for Natzweiler-Struthof. Suzanne will be a better asset employed there than back at Brzeg Dolny. If he was right about the concentration camp link, immortality via medical research and River People might be more than met the eye. The thought of Suzanne being in transit to the wrong end point rushed back into his mind. The sun had long disappeared from the sky even before he had left Poland. If not delayed, she had probably touched down in the darkness of the Palatine Forest and Ramstein Air Force Base as both hands of the clock stretched absolutely northward.

The aching in Mickey's left leg had worsened from the increasing stress of traveling. From head to toe, he felt physically abused. The only parts of him that didn't ache were his hair and fingernails. His escape from the carjacker five hours ago had now created his unpredicted arrival into Bautzen, the city of a thousand towers. It was four o'clock in the morning and there was a new hint of light in the German sky. *It is amazing how the nights are so short this time of year in Germany.*

In less than an hour his beautiful Loni would be sliding out of bed to pull down the *Rollläden*, the rolling shades covering the windows and balcony doors. He recalled how much he enjoyed watching her feminine frame move through her backlit nightgown. In her morning rituals, Loni would start on the east side of the house to block out the morning sun and keep the house cool. Before returning to bed she would go over to the western rooms adjoined with the patio and balconies, turn off the night-lights, pull up the rolling window shades, and open the sliding glass door. This would allow the shaded cool morning air to ventilate from the west, inward. The last step in this morning ablution would be to gently pull the dog blanket, printed with bright Dalmatians in varied action poses, over the head of Domino. Nothing was allowed to disturb Loni's idolized polka dot baby girl, not even cool air. At this time, and only this time, Mickey would receive his morning kiss. Once Domino was tucked in, she would walk around to her side of the bed and slide her body between the sheets, next to him. Today, it would be Domino instead of him who would receive the last bit of Loni's morning attention. *Lucky pup.*

29

Beauties and the Beasts

Esso service station
Bautzen, Germany

"**M**ake a move only when there is a tactical advantage to be gained, ladies," whispered Mickey coarsely as the minibus slowly closed the distance on the carjacker. "Sun Tzu said that in his *Art of War.*" Hence, with great stealth, the minibus followed Mickey's Polish rental car into an all-night Esso station. The minibus switched to parking lights as it crept to an over-watch position near a phone booth. Mickey sucked in a deep breath; he prepared himself for the confrontation that would soon ensue. The minibus rolled to a stop. He wished his leg pain would abate. At the far end of the distant gas-pump island was the completely quiet Polish rent-a-wreck. Mickey watched as the carjacker went into the station, heading for the food counter. He plucked at his eyebrows as he wondered just how this needed to play out.

"What do you want me to do now, Dr. Peronne?" the driver blurted in an uncomfortably loud whisper.

"Drop me off and please go on. I've got it from here."

"Ladies?" Totally ignoring Mickey, the driver twisted in her seat to face the other passengers.

"No way are we leaving him," said Molly Miniarti.

"I'm in," said Cyndi Labelle Framingham.

"Me too," said Maggie Colquitt.

Margie Bloomfield, the other general's wife, sitting behind the steering wheel, squared off her shoulders and with a sense of quiet authority looked straight at Mickey and said, "I guess that makes four against one—what do we do now?"

"Ladies, I am dealing with a dangerous carjacker, and I don't know *what else.* There are some classified documents involved and he has a gun. You ladies don't really have a dog in the fight here. I beg you, for everyone's sake and for safety,

100

drop me off and go home. If you're not going home, at least find a place far from here before stopping. It may get ugly."

"Dr. Peronne," Margie Bloomfield started, "allow me to introduce you to the European District Veterans of Foreign Wars Ladies Auxiliary Executive Council. For years we have hosted social gatherings, posted supplies for troops, sponsored patriotic activities, and wondered just how much difference we really made. Right now we do have a dog in the fight, Dr. Peronne, and that dog is you. So, sit and stay."

"Great! Now I'm a dog. Well then, ladies, follow my lead and watch out around any fire hydrants."

Quickly overruling Mickey, it was unanimously decided that he would not be allowed to leave the minibus as he was well-known to the carjacker.

"What we need is a two-fold attack." Margie Bloomfield began sketching out a diagram, speaking with great authority. "We'll call it Operation Beauty and the Beast."

"I don't want to be a beast," whined Molly.

"You don't have to be. Maggie and Molly, you're Team Beauty. Put your youthful charms into high gear and go into the station—find some way to delay the carjacker while he eats."

"We could spend time teaching him not to eat like a pig." Molly glanced at the stand-up table where their quarry stood, scarfing down schnecken after schnecken. The growing debris collected on his chin hair. "That should take about an hour."

"Cyndi Labelle, you and I are Team Beast. Our job will be to sneak quietly over to the car and steal back Dr. Peronne's bag. Hopefully, the carjacker will never notice that it's gone. Even if he does, maybe the importance of it will escape him."

"What about me?" Mickey probed.

"Do what doctors do worst."

"And that is?"

"Be patient." Margie signaled for silence.

Dejected, Mickey watched from the driver's seat of the parked minivan as the two teams split up to execute their mission. Maggie and Molly's delay tactics successfully kept the carjacker, as well as two other station attendants, well occupied with their award-winning performance. Meanwhile, Margie and Cyndi Labelle as Team Beast slipped in and around the vehicle, stealthily snatching the knapsack. Mickey craned far forward to get a better view at the theft in progress. A loud, blaring honk resounded across the asphalt.

Immediately all eyes were on Team Beast and the carjacked vehicle. Mickey threw the minivan doors open and ran toward Cyndi Labelle who was carrying the knapsack. The carjacker glanced as Mickey corralled Cyndi Labelle and her knapsack; then to the car where Margie was poised over the handgun on passenger seat; and finally, back to Maggie and Molly, whispering loudly to the two gas station attendants and pointing to him. The carjacker darted out the station door toward the car. In an instant he seemed to realize that he would never get to his weapon before it was fanned in his direction. He turned back toward the station, but the attendants were advancing on him. He turned toward the wood line and hightailed it over the small fence, then dashed onward into the trees beyond.

One of the station attendants followed the carjacker over the fence. The ladies and Mickey converged on the minivan and happily exchanged accolades—until Mickey opened the knapsack.

"They're gone!" he cried. Mickey ran back to the car and rifled through every compartment imaginable but came up empty. The carjacker was gone, the car keys were gone, and so were the secret papers. The brief happiness of a successfully executed Operation Beauty and the Beast evaporated in the growing light of the disappearing Bautzen night. Mickey folded his hands above his head then walked in circles aimlessly. *At this point, rock bottom would be an upward glance.* The only thing that made it worse was the apologetic gesturing and shrugs of the winded, empty-handed station attendant as he returned from the wood line.

"What do we do now?" Molly asked, frowning.

"I'm not sure," Mickey groused. After a brief deliberation, it was decided that the minivan four plus Mickey would go to a nearby lodging to rest. It had been a harrowing night. They glanced around for a clue as to which way to go. All signs seemed to lead to the city center and the town's largest hotel. They proceeded in a stunned silence. In ten minutes, the minivan turned into the sleep Mecca at the city center.

After getting beyond all the ladies' hugs and goodnights at the checkout desk, and after negotiating check-in using his international driver's license, Mickey took the elevator to his room on the first floor—which in Europe meant the second floor, the first floor being what they call floor zero.

Mickey got to his room and threw his pilfered knapsack on the bed. At least most of his personal travel items and the LBE, although well rummaged through and tousled, appeared to be present. The drapes of the room were pulled open and there, framed by his oval window, was one of the thousand towers of Bautzen. He gawked at the image and began to think that either his room was crooked, or the window leaned because the white tower framed within the oval windowpane was most definitely slanting to his right. He picked up his room phone and dialed the reception desk.

"May I help you, Dr. Peronne?" a female voice with a German accent answered.

"There appears to be a leaning tower outside my window, in front of the hotel."

"Of course, Dr. Peronne, it is the Realm Tower which is very old and famous."

"Why is it outside *my* window?" grumbled Mickey, annoyed at being subjected to such an imperfection.

"Actually, the hotel is outside the tower's window. The tower has been here for a very long time. The brochure in your room should tell you all about it." Mickey's eyes fixed on the date, 1492, noting that this tower was built about the time that Genoese Christopher Columbus sailed from the Andalusia region of Spain, following existing Templar sailing routes toward the Americas.

"Unfortunately, Dr. Peronne, our tower has been falling ever since it was built."

"Right. Thank you. Could you please see that it doesn't fall before I have had an opportunity to rest?"

"Very well, sir," she chuckled. "I will personally see to it. Have a good rest."

Mickey concluded that serendipitously, the decision to engage the use of his hotel preferred member card had placed him next to this historic icon. *I wonder if this has anything to do with Loni's murder case....* It was too late to spend energy in that direction. He needed sleep, and badly, but he had one thing to do first.

Leaning Tower of Bautzen

View from my hotel window

30

Viking and the Visible

Ramstein Military Air Terminal
Ramstein, Germany

"Oh my!" Dr. Suzanne Coletrane gasped. "It's Ungnyeo the bear-woman meets the Kraken."

In a nearby plate glass window, Suzanne stared back at a haggard reflection of an airline traveler in a combat military uniform, complete with LBE. *This version is a hideous semblance of my usual self.* Normally, to the naked eye, she was the confident image of her father, with just a whisper in her eyes and cheekbones of her Korean mother. However, today Suzanne's tussled golden locks, bloodshot green eyes, and pallid complexion were a truly washed-out version of both. *Am I even awake?* Suzanne sidled over to a water fountain and alternated drinking with splashing water on her face.

"Are you okay, lady?" a child's voice resonated.

"Do I not look okay?" Looking down into the child's upturned face, Suzanne flashed back to images of her own reflection.

"Are you done with the fountain?"

"I don't think you're going to be able to reach up here to drink, little one."

"I don't need a drink." The little girl turned around and pointed. "I just need to get enough water in this cup to give to Lacy and Scooby."

"Are they your invisible friends?" Suzanne looked around. "Because I don't see anyone."

"You can see them over there." The little girl motioned farther on. "They're in those crates. They are dogs that my mommy rescued from Romania."

"Lacy and Scooby don't sound like Romanian names."

"They actually don't have names."

"That's too bad. It's nice of you to give them names, though." Suzanne filled the cup for the girl and returned it. "It's very late, you probably should get the water to the dogs so you and your folks can travel on."

"I told Mommy you'd be nice."

"Your mother didn't think … never mind, little one." Suzanne waved at the lady sitting next to a stacked set of pet carriers. She then looked back to the little girl. "Safe travels … and remember, never talk to strangers."

Not in her usual crisp military manner, Suzanne sluggishly turned and proceeded down the terminal. It was five in the morning here in Europe. Suzanne could not recover from the daze she felt by the chain of events which took her from her warm, comfortable quarters overlooking the Chesapeake Bay to this beautiful landscape near the Eifel region of western Germany. Ramstein bordered places where Suzanne had many wonderful memories as a youngster. The gruesome look-alike face that peered back from the reflective glass didn't seem to share those pleasant memories.

Heels thudded loudly through the terminal, and she wondered why she was brought from America for German chemical munitions which were found in Poland. *Mickey is here. That means that both Chemical Corps and Medical Corps assets are already in-country. Maybe the rumors are true about him getting the boot from the active service. If so, then there's no research-trained Institute of Chemical Defense asset in-country. Hmmm … it's still strange.*

Suzanne's instructions from EUCOM were straightforward: Get to Brzeg Dolny and support overseas operations. *Am I really the best person for the job? Mickey would certainly be anyone's first choice. Russell would be the next-best choice. I wonder where he is. Somewhere in the Middle East, I think. Well, I guess that leaves me, the third-best choice.*

She had undergone this deployment drill in practice many times before. This, however, was the first time that her deployment recall drill had exceeded a mere arrival at the secret mobile port of call in the United States. In past drills, she usually went back home from the undisclosed airstrip. She had always wondered what she missed beyond the air force hook-up for the trip over the Atlantic Ocean. With a chiming cellphone inside her backpack, she passed like a ghoul through the graveyard passenger terminal in Ramstein. *Guess I'm going to find out.*

31

The Witch and the Coletrane

Hotel
Bautzen, Germany

Another leaning tower? Seriously? Mickey tilted his head. *What are the chances? After I rest, I'll go talk to the tower keeper. Maybe I can access some of the archives. Perhaps there's a connection between this leaning tower and that one in Illinois.* All in all, Mickey had to acknowledge that despite the bumps and bruises of the night-long adventure, Jesus had brought him here safely. Although many doors had been shut in his path, God had left him a window with a view, albeit slightly tilted.

Sitting on the bed, Mickey pulled out his cell phone, plugged it in, and engaged Suzanne's number. It was almost five o'clock local time. She would well be in-country. The number rang and rang unanswered. Mickey feared that something ill had befallen her—either she was badly delayed en route or, having arrived, something detestable had happened to her. Neither option was a pleasant thought. The image of the carjacker's face jumped to mind as he redialed, and the phone continued to ring unendingly. He closed his flip-phone and fell back on the bed, his mind bogged down. He felt his body grow heavy, sleep urging him onward, then his cell phone went off.

"Though I had doubts, Mickey," the voice was gruff but friendly, "I'm glad to see you're still in the game."

"Where else would I be?"

"I heard something about a broken-down old war horse put out to pasture."

"Still not pulling any punches, are you, Suzanne?"

"Mickey," he heard the raspy voice say, "get to the friggin' point. Wha'cha got?"

"What happened to your voice? Is it still on United States time?"

"No—it's on a later flight, I guess. It'll probably arrive about the time I'm ready to depart."

"So, I guess I have the pleasure of your company for the next couple of months, eh?" Mickey chided.

"Mickey, I'm tired. I have been in a strap-hanger seat on a cargo flight for as long as I can remember. So, cut the crap. Save it for a late-night television show reminiscence if, and when, we ever retire. Right now, I am on the chalk line for a helicopter doing nap-of-the-earth in a few hours—you know, that terrain-hugging, stomach-clenching flying that I *love* so much. What is it that you need me to do?"

"Suzanne, I need you to redirect your verbal hostile fire." Mickey hated the Viking Witch demeanor of Suzanne when she slid into the dark side. Conversely, it was a source of amusement when she raked some unfortunate recipient, six-guns blazing. "I'm not the enemy."

"Really? It's sad to know I am rousted out of my comfy quarters stateside and standing here, jet-lagged, at Ramstein because you are one of the good guys."

"But I am. Just listen and take notes, okay? This is a redirect from the instructions from EUCOM and Loni."

"I'm all ears. Tired, but all ears."

"Good. There's a lot of information that I can't provide on this unsecure line, but the bottom line is that I need you to go to the Natzweiler-Struthof Concentration Camp site west-southwest of the Alsatian town of Strasbourg in France."

"I know it. The French call it Natzwiller. Holy mackerel, Mick, that's a complete one-eighty. What's going on? What can you tell me?"

"Go to Natzweiler and find anything having to do with fish."

"Are you saying *fish* or *fiche*?"

"Yes."

"Yes, what?"

"Yes, ma'am."

"Okay…. " Suzanne slurred. *It seems that vague is in vogue.* "Fine. I got your back on this one, Mickey, but I'm going to need a whole lot more G2 information and military intelligence if you expect me to succeed at this mission. Am I on track guessing you are on the way to some other camps throughout Germany?"

"Yes, ma'am." *She's very quick on the uptake.* He continued, "But right now I have a date with a falling icon." There was silence on the other end. "Did you hear me, Suzanne?"

"Indeed I did, and I hope you fare better than I did with Douglas. Out." She immediately dropped off.

Pulling tight his lower lip, Mickey replayed the closing dialogue. *Maybe she didn't get it. I should have said leaning icon.* Regardless, he felt that the *falling icon* jab at her ex-husband, Douglas Coletrane, was completely unnecessary and that he really couldn't totally agree with her. Douglas, for the most part, was a good guy. The reality was that when it came to Douglas, Mickey rode the fence.

Tired of the mental gymnastics, Mickey collapsed backward onto his pillow-top mattress and drifted off into a fitful sleep filled with vivid dreaming.

☩ ☩ ☩

Mickey was in a yellow castle and somehow he knew it was filled with many scientific laboratories. As he walked the halls he noticed that the walls changed from a pale-yellow plaster, to gray sweaty bricks, to a rack of dusty wine bottles. He stopped to pull one of the eye-level wine bottles from the rack. As he reached for it, he noticed that it wasn't a wine bottle at all. It was a mortar shell with chemical markings. They all were. Before he could tilt the munition to read the inscription, a hand grabbed him and pulled him through the rack into a small, dark office. Mickey stood draped in a cloud, dusting himself off.

In the center of the room, lit only by a single hanging lamp, sat a well-dressed, bespectacled man with a trimmed goatee. Oddly, the man sat facing to the left and not in a working position toward the rolltop desk near him. The desk was in general disarray, weighted down by clinical notes, typed papers with Nazi insignias, ominous bottles, a dusty mantel radio, and a well-worn mortar and pestle.

The man was deep in thought. He kept rocking back on his swivel chair, his eyes fixed on the ceiling. Clenched in the man's teeth was a big cigar, emanating puffs of smoke rising into the air. All the while, he kept blindly tapping cigar ashes into the mortar on the desk—half the ashes went into the bowl while the other half fell into a growing heap beside it.

Then the face of the goateed Nazi morphed into a dark-skinned Slavic man with a cup of thick, black hair on his chin. The man spun his chair so that he faced Mickey. In his hands the Slav held the papers of the secret laboratory and a German Mauser automatic pistol. He pointed it at Mickey. Mickey looked straight back in attempted fearlessness. He gasped. The Slav was gone. Instead, there were the soft curves of the face which could only belong to Loni. In one hand she was holding the Nazi papers and in the other hand she held the DIA portfolio. She spoke, saying again and again, "I don't understand this DNA data, Mickey. What's up with it?"

32

Hello Goodbye

Ramstein Military Air Terminal
Ramstein, Germany

*I*f someone was to walk in right now and offer a thousand-dollar bill to the most fatigued person in this terminal, I would say, "Roll me over and slip the bill into my back pocket." Suzanne's fingernails raked the pale skin of her forehead. Unlike Mickey, Suzanne's day was just beginning. She had no more energy than he probably did but somewhere east, she figured, he was getting some shut-eye. Instead of sleeping on a flight, she was facing an unfortunate delay.

She wanted to get on the road to France before exhaustion had a chance to dig in its heels, but according to the air terminal information pamphlets, the base's rental car service would not be opening until at least eight o'clock. She now had three hours to review her notes on the significant places involving chemical war gases here in Europe. Again, she was at a disadvantage.

The didactics of teaching the technical aspects of the medical management of chemical casualties was something she was trained to do, not something she aspired to do. With significant effort and elbow grease, she made her subject blocks of teaching seem second nature. Nothing could be further from the truth. In reality, what she had worked so hard to achieve, her teaching colleagues—Mickey Peronne and Russell Lange—did exceptionally better and quite effortlessly.

In all circles, these three physician-scientists were recognized as the army's medical research A-Team. However, Russell and Mickey actually loved what they did. Suzanne did not. It was Russell and Mickey who really delved into every meaningless nuance and intricacy of history. This is why they, and not she, were selected to be history consultants to flag-ranked general officers and commanders, which in turn had earned them inclusion in the Medical Corps Order of Military Medical Merit. *You can keep your O2M3.* If the truth be told, Suzanne hated history—especially her own. The way her life played out always seemed to be a mockery of her intended plan. Her marriage to Douglas was a perfect example.

Well, like it or not, I'm in Germany now. Next up, France. She wanted to catch three hours of sleep but that wasn't about to happen. Instead, the subject of military medical history and the medical management of chemical casualties had to be her study focus until she could negotiate the long drive into the Alsace. Suzanne smiled as she remembered Alsatian wines and the delicious delicacy of rooster in wine—*coq au vin* Riesling. She hoped time would permit a chance to enjoy these treasured fruits of France. She readjusted her notes and tried to focus on the details of Natzweiler-Struthof. It had been in high school with Russell when she was last there at Natzweiler-Struthof ... *and probably an even longer time if it was my choice to go back.*

Suzanne grimaced, remembering the year after the rainy school field trip at Natzweiler-Struthof, when Russell departed Europe. The water that fell did not come from the sky but from her eyes. She had no hope of ever seeing him again. Hearing that Russell was caught up in some community intrigue, her father had one of his famous Max Attacks and saw to it that Russell's entire family was sent back to the US. At the thought of losing her first love, she pleaded with her mother to help, but Colonel Max had decreed it, reported it up the chain, and that was that. Loni's father, the commanding general, signed the paper that cinched it. Not even at sporting events could Russell and her meet since high schools in Athens, Georgia, didn't have away games in Mannheim, Germany. *God, I hate history.*

It was dark. She folded the notes in her lap and closed her eyes. Suzanne dreaded the thought of going to places that led back to thoughts of Russell. He was now only a whisper of the love which had once warmed her lips. Soon she would be on the road again. Maybe during the pending drive, she would forget all the ill that sabotaged her relationship with Russell. And maybe winged monkeys would fly out her butt. *At least if that happens it would be a historical note worth remembering.*

33

The Drive South

Route to the Alsace
Rheinland-Pfalz, Germany

*R*ude, *crude, and generally unacceptable, was I.* Suzanne winced as she again mentally replayed her phone conversation with Mickey. *Maybe he wasn't happy hearing from me, but I enjoyed talking to him earlier this morning.* Reviewing Mickey's instructions to visit at the only remaining Nazi concentration camp in France, Natzweiler-Struthof, Suzanne pointed her rental car south. Having engaged the German autobahn, she soon trundled into the Alsace region of France and soaked in her surroundings taking careful note how pretty the scenery truly was. It was unfortunate that these spectacular panoramas were just inevitable milestones leading her to a somber end point.

Suzanne loved the German autobahns. Unlike anything in the continental US, she could put pedal to the metal and hurl to any destination in half the time. Today, she chose not to do so. In her rearview mirror, her eye caught the enlarging shape of mint-green 2CV duck car. *Well, that's different. A European car declining to pass.* With her occasional rear-mirror glances, she could see that the driver was very dark-skinned and of stark African heritage. She noticed that he was nicely dressed with his suave suit, complete with shirt and tie ensemble. *Hmmm, looks like a preoccupied businessman thinking about today's market fluctuations.* She considered that he could be an American GI because in her experience, most Black people she had encountered in Germany were from the United States. However, if this was the case, he would most likely be in uniform. If he was an American, he could be one of the many civilian support staff either in contracted labor or education support. Suzanne grew weary of this guessing game and just concluded he was an employee of the Department of Defense Dependents Schools, affectionately known as DoDDs.

The acronym DoDDs pulled her mind back to her years in overseas schools where she met Loni and Russell. Loni was younger and probably two grades behind Russell and herself. Suzanne smiled as she recalled Loni telling her that it was in high school when she and Mickey first met. Interestingly, Mickey never responded when Suzanne had asked him how long he and Loni had been married; not to mention the circumstances surrounding his meeting Loni. He would hedge a bit and almost always comment, "not long enough" to the question of how long and, "under installation arrest" when asked how he and Loni first encountered one another. Suzanne knew that Mickey felt fortunate to have won the undying favor of a celebrity's daughter.

Loni's mother was a famous French child actress, and her father was none other than the ultimate celebrity in US Army circles, General Monty Meriwether. Having a commanding general for a father might be great for the rest of the world, but it always seemed to Suzanne that Loni would have just preferred to forget it. Suzanne liked to think about Mickey and Loni—it meant that she didn't have to think about Russell and her.

Hey, I don't have time for this. Suzanne felt her tires hit the rumble strips at the road's shoulders. Noticing now the heaviness in her lids, Suzanne quickly rolled down her window. After stretching into a yawn, she rubbed the back of her neck. *Maybe I should drop back next to the duck car and strike up a conversation. I need to do something to keep myself awake.* Suzanne glanced up at the rearview mirror. *Unless he's behind that transfer truck, I guess I've lost that opportunity.* Suzanne scanned her mirrors. *Nope, I see nothing but a giant truck. He probably exited.* Suzanne's breath quickened, as in her forward vision, she spotted a roadside rest stop. Engaging her blinker, she eased onto an exit ramp, feeling the transfer truck blast past her in a gust of wind. Surveying a mostly empty rest stop, she maneuvered to the first open parking spot, parked, cut off the engine, and then leaned back closing her eyes. *I should probably roll up my window. Sure, maybe in a minute.* As Suzanne's breathing gradually slowed, a mint-green duck car slowly passed behind, eased over to a far parking spot, and with a mild shudder, shut off its engine.

34

Natzweiler-Struthof

Rest stop on the route to concentration camp

France

A *place actually exists where humanness is consciously and meticulously extracted from* *humanity.* Suzanne awakened with clammy hands and a forehead beaded in sweat. *I hate that dream of being in an extermination camp and yet, with every bit of energy I can muster, I will soon place myself in one.* Suzanne started up her car, pulled out of the rest stop, and continued toward that place of nightmares past and present. It wasn't very long before she left the autobahn to access the less linear secondary roads. Rounding sharp curves, Suzanne gripped the steering wheel tightly. After traveling an hour of winding roads southwest of Strasbourg, Suzanne arrived at the Struthof camp. It was nestled just uphill from the main Natzweiler cantonment area.

This multi-camp complex was notorious for being the only Nazi concentration camp in France. Its subcamps ranged far in every direction—places well known to American servicemen serving in Darmstadt, Coleman Barracks, Mannheim, Heidelberg, and Frankfurt. Natzweiler had provided human cadavers, supposedly from camp volunteers, for those studying medicine at Strasbourg University. It was also one of five locations where chemical war gases in the category of pulmonary and dermatological vesicant agents were used on unfortunate and unwilling inmate volunteers. The definition of camp volunteer was quite nebulous as coercion could never be ruled out during the war crime trials at Nuremburg after the war.

Suzanne pulled into the cantonment area where she had arranged to meet the camp archivist who came up from Strasbourg University nearby. She expected to see a dumpy, disheveled bookworm of a man but was quite surprised to see a rather pleasant young lady who not only possessed the data but, more importantly, the confident ability to articulate it in English. After a few hours of intense dialogue, Suzanne had an abundance of information. Leaving the archivist to her other responsibilities, Suzanne climbed the hill to sit at the foot of the memorial just as she had so many years before as a teen with Russell. She needed to synthesize the data and organize her thoughts before she called Mickey to tell him what she learned. *What better place to discuss major events from the past than at the place where those first steps were gathered?*

35

Mouse and the Owl

Hotel

Bautzen, Germany

"Stop ringing already! See? I've pressed the stupid button on the stupid phone … but it just keeps ringing!" A still mostly dressed Mickey squirmed fitfully on his bed and covered his head with a pillow.

It was many hours, and many troubled dreams later, when Mickey awoke to his phone again ringing. This time he answered.

"Mickey," said Suzanne, "you aren't going to believe this."

"What? Who?" Placing his booted feet on the floor, Mickey now sat at the bedside and struggled into coherency.

"Mickey, pay attention!"

"What is it, Suzanne?" Mickey stood and began pacing the floor of his hotel bedroom. His head was pounded rhythmically with the sound of hammering coming from the street below.

"Get this, Natzweiler-Struthof was a feeding station for significant human study in the fields of anatomy—"

"I know that, Suzanne. What else?"

"Shut up and listen, that's what else."

"Okay, okay. No need to get Viking on me." Mickey ran his hand through his hair still trying to roust himself into alertness. "Go on, sorry. Jeez."

"As I was saying, Mickey, for years Strasbourg University, just thirty miles down the hill, has been involved in huge scientific strides in anatomy, cellular biology, nuclear chemistry, molecular synthesis, and supramolecule synthesis."

"Say what?" Mickey strained to hear Suzanne over the noise coming from outside. He eased toward his window. The sound grew.

"Mickey are you getting what I'm saying?"

"Speak up, Suzanne, some moron here is hammering in the street." Mickey raised the decibel of his voice volume and continued, "Lots of medical universities are doing that, Suzanne—come on, you know that."

"We're talking about Nobel Prizes in chemistry and physiological medicine."

"Well, that is big," said Mickey, "but I remember Russell saying that just last year there was—"

"Break. Break. Mickey. I am talking about the year 1910."

"Whoa."

"Exactly. Much of the groundwork for these Nobel Prizes was done in the late 1800s and early 1900s. The Nobel Prize in physiological medicine was in 1910. Amazing, huh?"

"Amazing? Suzanne, that's incredible! That would mean that profound physiologic knowledge in cell and molecular biology, including DNA technology, had been mastered by medicinal chemists in—"

"Mickey, it means that an early understanding of DNA existed so that concentration camp prisoners could be tested. My first brief scan of the camp's records surfaced this. However, discussing this with a Strasbourg University expert confirmed my research as well as providing me much more substance."

"Great, tap into expertise with substance," said Mickey vacantly as he stared out his window. The sun was visible high in the sky, and because the tower right outside his window was leaning, he could see its shadow. His eyes followed the shadow to the base of the tower where he saw the source of all the hammering. He squinted to see the wooden frame upon which the man was hammering. *Why is something so relatively frail so loud?* The tanned workman in blue overalls barely glanced at the numerous people in the pedestrian zone entrance to the marketplace. His skin glistened with perspiration as the afternoon sun baked.

"That's not what I said, Mickey." Suzanne groused. "Listen to me. There's so much more information to brief."

"Give me a second." Mickey threw the phone on the bed. With Suzanne's voice squawking into empty space, Mickey shouted out the window and tried signaling to the man below. The workman had trouble localizing Mickey's voice as it echoed off the nearby buildings—he kept turning his head back and forth and his long black ponytail swung in response.

"Hey, up here!"

The man looked up and called back, "*Hallo!*"

"You!" Mickey noted the freshly shaven face had a hint of recognition, and it wasn't pleasant. *"Warten Sie bitte!"* Mickey yelled with urgency. "Wait!" *I need a closer look at this guy.*

"No problem." The man smiled, calmly waved, and shouted upward in clear English. "I wait."

"Suzanne, I'm tracking with your research," Mickey blurted into the phone "Back-brief me after you have confirmed your leads with the experts there. Right now, I gotta go." As Mickey was slamming his flip-phone shut, he heard a very disgruntled Suzanne on the other end of the call verbalizing her irritation in French, German, and whatever other foreign curse words came to mind.

✠ ✠ ✠

In just his combat uniform trousers, boots, and light tan T-shirt, Mickey shot out the door, down the stairs, out the hotel entrance, and across the cobblestones to the man working at the base of the leaning tower.

"Don't I know you?" Mickey asked through labored breaths.

"*Ich weiss nicht.* I don't know." The workman switched from German to English with ease. "Do you?" he said with a lingering accent. "Where is it you think we met?" Not making full eye contact, the workman spoke with a pleasant smile and continued to work carefully on what Mickey saw was a bowed, framed picture. Briefly, the thought passed in Mickey's analytical head that a picture frame bowed in such a manner would curl away from a wall. Instead, this framed picture, like a piece of abstract wall art, would curve out in a most peculiar manner. The thought passed as quickly as it arrived.

Mickey grabbed the screwdriver from the workman's hand and pushed the startled German against the side of the tower. "You know quite well where we met, you carjacker!"

The workman, now ruffled, pushed back saying, "Back off, GI Joe, you need to get your facts straight and then get some manners."

"I … uh …." Mickey recoiled in horror. *There is no way the guy's short hair could have blossomed into ponytailed, shoulder-length hair in just a few hours.* Mickey stood confused and embarrassed. "I'm sorry, Mister … I … uh … thought … I…."

"Herr Lenz. I am Herr Matthias Lenz." The man grabbed back the tool from Mickey's hand, picked up his bowed picture frame, and headed toward the door of the leaning tower. "Frankly, I am not happy to meet you," Matthias said scowling.

"Really, Herr Lenz, I am sorry." Mickey blew through pursed lips. "It's just that yesterday I had a bad experience on the road from Poland which—"

"The road from Poland?" Matthias stopped in the doorway, slowly turning. "Did you say Poland?" The muscles in Matthias's face relaxed. "Well then, please come with me." He motioned inside the tower. "I think I can clear things up for you."

"How can you do that?" Mickey's forehead furrowed. "You don't know the particulars."

"Yes, but I think I know the source of your confusion."

"The answers are in there?" Mickey pointed to the tower door.

"I believe so." Matthias smiled. "If I'm wrong you have lost nothing but a few minutes." Matthias shrugged. "The choice is yours."

"Fine. Give a second." Mickey waved his hand toward an upper room of the hotel. "I'm stepping into this tower for a few minutes," he shouted at the empty window. "Have the guys come get me in about ten or fifteen minutes. Thanks, Moose." He then took a deep breath and followed Matthias into the tower.

Once the tower door closed, Matthias paused thoughtfully then spoke pleasantly. "Before I begin, could you answer me a quick question?"

"Sure. I guess so," Mickey responded haltingly.

"Why were you in Poland?" Matthias asked pointedly.

"This is your attempt at clearing up confusion?"

"An American in Poland? There must have been a reason."

"I am not free to answer that, Herr Lenz." Mickey fidgeted.

"You are if you want my help to clarify things."

"Tell me." Mickey widened his stance. "How can you, a street workman, help me with that?"

"What if the workman is more than he seems?" Matthias thrust out his chin. "I happen to keep this tower."

"Keep the tower?" Mickey repeated slowly. "Wait, Herr Lenz. You're the tower keeper." *A Lenz and a leaning tower?*

"I just said that."

"You want to know why I was sent to Poland?" Mickey noted the head nod. "Okay. I'll tell you but, in the name of clarification, but I'll be asking some questions myself."

"Go ahead. I have nothing to hide."

"Good, Herr Lenz." Mickey sucked in a deep breath. "Be advised that I was sent to investigate an area of concern near Wroclaw." Mickey studied the pondering face.

"Possibly, Brzeg Dolny? Please, call me Matthias ... and you are ... "

" ... embarrassed beyond words," Mickey felt his face flush, realizing not once had he introduced himself. *Could I behave any worse?*

"Forget it, GI Joe. What's your name?"

"First of all, GI Joe was an army pigeon."

"Are you thinking that I mistook you for an animal bird?"

"No, of course not." Mickey coughed. "Just call me Doc."

"Duck? Matthias puzzled. "Like an animal bird?"

"No, not *duck* ... Doc."

"Sorry, I misunderstood, Mr. Doc."

"No, just *Doc*," Mickey extended his hand.

"Doc," Matthias clasped the hand firmly. "I think maybe, after all, it is nice to meet you."

"I'm truly sorry for my lapse in manners. It might be better if I move to a different city in a different country."

"Maybe Brzeg Dolny, Poland?"

"No, not at all." Mickey's eyes narrowed. "Tell me about this leaning tower, Matthias. It's very interesting."

"Yes, Doc, I've always thought so."

"Would you allow me access to your library archives? I need some information."

"Of course you do." Matthias grinned. "I knew you would be coming to see me when Dyhernfurth was found at Brzeg Dolny."

"How do you know about Dyhernfurth? I didn't know about it myself until ... and, hey, I wasn't *coming* to see you."

"Come now, Doc," said Matthias. "All roads lead to my tower." Matthias surveyed Mickey's stunned face. "Please, there is much more I need to ask you before you can ask me questions. There is much more here than meets the eye."

More than meets the eye? Have I just been had? Mickey's instant replay shot back to the day before, when he heard those exact words from Talbot. His fists clenched. *Talbot knew that the biomedical lab situated in that dark hole was far more than any chemo was trained to handle. Could it be that Matthias Lenz has the same depth of knowledge? Does he have more? Matthias said that all paths lead to this leaning tower. Does that include a carjacking path? Was Talbot in on it? No, of course not. Was there a conspiracy involving the wives of key military officers? No. Not a chance. It doesn't make sense. Keep your cool, Mickey. Maintain a poker face.*

"So, Matthias, did your eyes see what happened to me on the road from Brzeg Dolny, Matthias?" Mickey synthesized every facial movement.

"No, Doc, not at all ... but I can certainly guess. You probably think someone accosted you, don't you?"

"That's a mild interpretation of assault, battery, and theft, wouldn't you say?" Mickey felt the blood boiling up his neck. *Acquire composure ... poker face ... acquire composure.*

"We will return to that later. Please understand that *we* needed you to come here to Bautzen." Matthias smiled. "Consider that the nature of the invitation had to be one that—how do you Americans say it?—one that could not be refused."

"'We'? Who is 'we'?" Mickey licked moisture back into his lips. "You mean to say that everything was orchestrated for me to come here? That's impossible."

"You think so, Doc? Come. I believe we can convince you otherwise."

"Cut me some slack, Matthias, and stop with the 'we' ... or at least tell me who the 'we' is. Have you a mouse hidden in your pocket? Who is the other part of 'we'?"

"Come, Doc, up the stairs to my quarters on the second landing of the tower." Mathias climbed ahead with Mickey closely in tow. "This and many other of your questions will be answered. I promise. Besides, do you have an owl with you who will eat my mouse?"

"Owl? Mouse? What are you talking about?" Mickey wanted to just turn around, head down the steps, and out the door but he was hooked. He just couldn't leave. "Herr Lenz, just tell me who ... who ... ?"

"Ah, the owl returns," laughed the tower keeper as they arrived at his room. "I must now protect my little mouse!" Matthias walked over and opened one of the two window drapes. Light shot into the room.

The room looked very comfortable. *This would be a nightmare for a drunk on the street looking for a corner to pee in.* The round walls were all concave as were the framed pictures which hung on them. *Oh ... he was curving a frame in preparation for its hanging.* Across from the door, Lenz hung the picture on the northern wall. It was a framed and matted picture of the Last Supper. Mickey remembered seeing da Vinci's *The Last Supper* at a church, Santa Maria delle Grazie, in Milan. This version was not it. This unfamiliar rendering looked to be Byzantine or Greek Orthodox in its origin. Mickey couldn't fix on where the original painting resided although he knew he had seen it before. As his mind filtered through the endless churches and art galleries he had visited, he crossed the round room to better scrutinize the picture. Along the bottom of the frame was an inscription of the Templar Knight's Creed: *Not unto us, O Lord, Not unto us, but unto thy name give glory.*

In his periphery, he glimpsed a shot of the oval window at his hotel across the street. Almost to give comic relief, on a small table below the picture of the Last Supper was a normally framed, modern-day photo of the Leaning Tower of Pisa.

The computer-generated picture had three Matthiases doing the famous tourist's pose of trying to hold the tower upright. As Mickey turned to Matthias to make a comment, he saw two Matthiases standing side by side. The second Matthias was stroking his hair-cupped chin, training a gun on Mickey.

36

And Lenz Makes Three

Leaning tower of Bautzen
Bautzen, Germany

"Well, of the five reasons to be facing the business end of a gun," Mickey swallowed dryly, noticing now that the second drape in the room was now fully pulled back, "I'd say murder is off the table."

"Is it?" The man with the hair-cupped chin shrugged.

"Yes, I'm still breathing." Mickey steeled himself. "That leaves kidnapping, hostage taking, leveraging, or robbing…. Wait a minute. You've already robbed me. I guess that only leaves three."

"Allow me to introduce you to my brother, Thaddeusz," Matthias said. "It seems you have already met and probably now realize that he also is a Lenz."

Waving the barrel of the gun in a downward motion, Thaddeusz motioned for Mickey to sit down.

I've been had. Mickey shook his head slowly, watching as Matthias sat down in the chair across from him. Mickey's mind went quickly to work. *A German Mauser—not the same gun from the carjacking site, but from my dream. How can that be? I'm not clairvoyant.* There was much that he wanted to say, but right now there was still much more he wanted to know. Not a sound violated the room as the three men carefully scoped each other. Finally, Matthias spoke.

"Doc, I need to know what you learned from the chemical laboratory in Brzeg Dolny. Was there anything said about *Fluss Menschen*?"

"*Fluss Menschen*? Nazis citing the river people?" Mickey tilted his head. "Well then, quid pro quo?"

"What?" Matthias shot a glance at Thaddeusz then back to Mickey.

"Look. I will tell you things, only if you begin to tell me."

"Okay. I guess that's fair," said Matthias sighing. "The intent of all of this is for a friendly exchange of information."

"Friendly? Then is the Mauser really necessary? There are two, or maybe three, of you and only one of me. Anyway, I have just one simple question to ask."

"Okay, Doc." Matthias nodded to his brother and Thaddeusz grudgingly put the gun away.

"Two is one too many to handle the likes of you," Thaddeusz snarled.

"Was it your intent to kill me or are you all just in the habit of carjacking?"

"That's two questions," growled Thaddeusz.

"Good God, no," blustered Matthias almost apologetically. "Thaddeusz's sole mission was to ensure that you felt obligated to come to Bautzen quickly. The carjacking accomplished that."

"You mean we were following my car here because it was leading me to you? Don't tell me the shopping ladies were in on this."

"Ahh, the lovely ladies," sneered Thaddeusz. "Not very skilled drivers, were they? There were times I felt I would have to drive in reverse for them to keep steady onward to Bautzen."

"So, you two succeeded in bringing me from Poland. Why am I here?"

"You are here because you have knowledge of the Nazi papers," said Matthias. "The desire you demonstrated to secure the secrecy of the papers told us much about you. This desire is the same as ours, but maybe not for the same reason. We brought you here to find out that reason. What did you think when you found the Nazi papers, Doc?"

"The Nazi papers?" Mickey chewed on the inside of his lip, picturing Thaddeusz rifling through his knapsack.

"Doc?"

"I believed that Hitler stumbled upon something when his physician-scientist delved into very focused medical research."

"Exactly, Doc. It is that something that needs to be protected. That something is so very important, mankind would be—"

"Was *Fluss Menschen* or *Flussleute* mentioned in any document or paperwork found in the laboratory?" Thaddeusz interrupted.

"You should know. You have the papers."

"Those were *all* the papers?" Thaddeusz probed.

"I left no others like those behind."

"Was the word *Fluss*—"

"No. Not the words '*Fluss Menschen*' or '*Flussleute*' but the word *Flusszigeuner* did appear quite frequently in the documents I saw. Who are these River People?"

"He knows nothing, Matthias. He's useless." Thaddeusz's grim face leered at Mickey. "Can we still shoot him?"

"Thaddeusz…." Matthias patted his brother's arm then turned to Mickey. "That's a hard question to answer, Doc. We are the River People or rather, the River Gypsies. But there were many more."

"More rivers or more Gypsies?"

"Which is your connection, Doc? Is it through Operation Paperclip and its repurposing of Nazis?"

"Paperclip? That was a long time ago. No, I have no connection, never did. Any of the Nazi scientists who were secretly hired to work in US military research labs under the protection of Operation Paperclip have now probably all retired or died, or both. Why? Does this involve the River People or River Gypsies?"

"Yes, it does. Your government has worked hard to access the River People. You work for your government, no?"

"Yes, as a doctor, scientist, and educator."

"But you are an acknowledged military medical historian of the Order of Military Medical Merit."

"Yes, Herr Lenz. If you know all this about me then you must know that I am not a professionally trained historian. I am without portfolio, sir. How is it you know so much about me?"

"Sometimes we learn things of greater value without the formal training. Sometimes we learn things of greatest value because our hearts thirst for the knowledge. We need to know the things that drive your thirst, Doc. It is our job to know everything about you, even the degrees you display on goatskins."

"Sheepskins."

"Sheepskins? What's wrong with using the goat? After all, the skin of the goat when properly tanned—"

"Enough with the animal skin diatribe, Matthias," Mickey said. "If you know as much as you say you do, then you know that the US military has only rarely utilized me in this historical capacity. There are many other military historians with significant credentials who are much more adept and qualified."

"These other historians are likely not physician-scientists as well."

"No, that is quite true."

"You are *Unikat*."

"Unique?" said Mickey, recalling the *Unikat* stamp on only select pieces of high-end Polish pottery. "I never really thought myself to be—"

"What do you know of Lucky Industries?" Thaddeusz cut across.

"It's a strange story, Thaddeusz. Why don't you guys start answering some questions instead of just asking them?"

"You want a story? You want a *story*?"

"Yes, Thaddeusz," Mickey goaded, "I do."

"Well, I have a good story for you. I think you will like this story, Dr. Peronne. Like you, it is about a physician-scientist. His name was Theodor. He was a brilliant man who became enslaved by a tyrannical patient. The patient held him in check, using Theodor's ego as his Achilles' heel. This patient, a chancellor of a rising powerful state, was very ill and he gave Theodor all the leeway to personal greatness. Along the way the chancellor would get the product that he sought—immortality. The physician-scientist—"

"—was Professor Doctor Theodor Morell," Mickey nodded emphatically. "That would mean the chancellor was Adolph Hitler himself, yes?"

"Exactly," Thaddeusz and Matthias said simultaneously.

"Der Führer was known by this and many other names here in the fatherland," continued Thaddeusz. "Obsession with his immortality consumed him.

It is said that he began the research in order to clone parts of his own body as a medical reserve so that he would always have enough organs in waiting, should he develop a disease in any that lived within him."

"This would explain the recurring references to *Unsterblichkeit durch Medizinische Forschung* in the laboratory. What exactly does it mean?"

"This means 'immortality through medical research,' Doc," Matthias said. "Dyhernfurth's chemical laboratories provided the equipment for the studies to begin. The problem was that testing had to be done on human subjects."

"I see the rationale. Where would have been a better place for Dr. Morell to practice biomedical cloning techniques than in the biological and chemical proving grounds of selected concentration camps?"

"Unfortunately, for those upon whom the experiments were done, no other concentration camps could serve better. Under the *Nacht und Nebel*, or 'Foggy Night' authorization, any person, for any reason, could be removed by the Nazis from the face of the earth without question."

"If you know all this, why did you need me to come to this leaning tower?"

"I believe you already know that answer."

"I'm not sure that I do, but I have a hunch." Mickey raked his teeth over his lower lip. "I know of two leaning towers and two keepers named Lenz."

"We'll leave it there, Doc," said Matthias. "However, I sense that your hunch is correct."

"Why does this tower lean?"

"That, Doc, is the correct hunch. The answer I give you now is the same answer Dr. Morell received many years ago when he sought what you now seek. This tower was built to lean."

"How?" Mickey puzzled. "Why?"

"The tower falls because of the use of loose filling layers in the original construction." Matthias gestured. "This, along with the weight of the added baroque hood, is responsible for the northwest lean. Today it leans a full meter plus forty-four."

"Is that the amount the tower leaned when Morell asked the question?"

"He is smart. Isn't he, Thaddeusz? No, Doc, in the last fifty years since Morell died, it has fallen more. Is your hunch still correct?"

"It is. This tower is falling. I must call my colleague."

"All in good time, Doc, rest assured, we have time."

"How does *Flussleute*, *Fluss Menschen*, or *Flusszigeuner* fit in?"

"For that answer, Doc, I am afraid you must see yourself back to Poland. You must go with Thaddeusz since the places that he must take you are better known to him than me."

"Is it really necessary for me to return to Poland?" Looking at Thaddeusz, Mickey shifted uncomfortably. "After all, I have taken great time and effort to leave."

"It is very necessary. Anyway, the parts of Poland that you must now visit are different than you saw earlier."

"Parts? There is more than one place I must go?"

"Enough questions. Know that you go now to get the answers to questions you have yet to ask."

"So, I am being rushed back to Poland to get answers to questions I don't even have?"

"Yes. You must hurry."

"Why couldn't you have just politely asked me to come to Bautzen?"

"Would you have rushed to come to see me had Thaddeusz not stolen your car?" Matthias nodded to his brother and Thaddeusz tossed Mickey's keys back to him.

"Will you also give me back the papers?"

"We will and more."

"More?"

"Yes, more."

"Like what?"

"Do you know anything regarding the lost Second Book of Benjamin, Doc?"

"I know there are many lost books which were, for one reason or another, not included in the Bible as it exists today. Some of these books reside among the apocryphal and others among the pseudepigraphal. Many books were found in Qumran, in the Holy Land, such as the Dead Sea Scrolls. I know the Book of Isaiah was found there. I think that it was the oldest known copy to have been uncovered. However, I have never heard of the Second Book of Benjamin, and the fact that it was lost means nothing to me."

"Good, apparently no one else has heard of it as well. If God is willing, nobody will ever know it because we were charged to keep it secret. It must remain lost."

"'We'—you two?"

"Ahh, the mouse again. No, I do not have a mouse in my pocket. I mean the collective *we*."

"Tell me about the picture at the Leaning Tower of Pisa in Italy. It has three of you. Where is Lenz number three?"

Silence stretched around the round room and circled back to Mickey, his eyes searching the faces of the other two men.

"Why all the secrecy for something which I now believe I know the answer?"

"Can you now keep the secret, Doc?"

"Yes, of course."

"Then we have something in common."

"I get it, Matthias. I can also remain silent and say nothing about Judas." Mickey looked at Matthias and Thaddeusz. Neither moved, blinked, nor flinched. *Maybe my data is inundated with DIA inaccuracies. However, Judas Lenz and leaning towers cannot be a coincidence. Whatever. I'll table it ... for now.*

After a long stare down, Matthias again spoke.

"Thaddeusz will explain much more to you as you two drive the seven hours back to Poland."

"What?" Mickey frowned at the thought. "It doesn't take seven hours to go back to Poland."

"True enough, if you were going back to where you had been. However, Poland is a big country. You must now go to a place I know you have never been, Doc."

"But my rental won't last another seven hours."

"Of course not. That is why you and Thaddeusz will go in his car."

"Your car is as good as dead," Thaddeusz interjected. "Leave it here. We will collect it later … if there is anything left to collect."

"Why don't we all go?" Mickey looked at Matthias.

"I would really like to go, but for me and my mouse, our work is here," said Matthias. "Anyway, we decided that it is really best that only Thaddeusz goes back to Poland with you. You will understand more when you arrive."

"'We'—that would be you and Thaddeusz? I certainly had no say-so in this pairing."

"'We' would be us, yes."

"At least I now know who the 'we' is."

"Good, now 'we,' that would be us, will see that you meet the Owl."

"Who?"

"Exactly!" Matthias laughed. "Exactly."

37

Friend and Foes

Battalion aid station
Middle East Operations area

Insanity is doing the same thing repeatedly over again yet expecting a different outcome. Russell Lange shifted on his aching knees. *I told higher headquarters not to use my Mobile Emergency Medical Response Team in support of forward tactical medical operations.* Russell's MERT found itself supporting a forward battalion medical station. *I'm a strategic asset. This is the third time I have been repurposed and the third time that repurposing me has gone sideways.*

Despite careful planning and preparation for the US Army military mission in Iraq, the Sunni insurgents overran the battalion aid station. They brought the surviving soldiers into a huddled mass in the center of the medical aid station tent. The Muslim leader was grazed and wounded, but he strolled by each of the dejected, kneeling soldiers and forced off their headgear so he could gaze unencumbered upon their unprotected heads and faces.

The rage within him was accentuated by the whipping snap of wind-flapped tenting. He stalked back and forth looking at each of them. He sheathed and unsheathed his scimitar repeatedly, causing its metallic glint to reflect in the eyes of Russell and the other the soldier captives. Abruptly, he stopped his pacing. He snatched the protective collar of the last soldier, jerking the head and neck back forcefully. The Saracen leader sucked his breath, then hissed through his teeth, spitting venom with each spoken word.

"I choose the absence of fear. It might be that this one longs for death." Moments passed as he stood above Russell, pausing and glaring deeply into his eyes.

Russell's haunting dark eyes were set against the dark, smooth skin of his face. His body's musculature shaped a look very akin to Captain America meets kung-fu master. He always apologized for accidentally hurting anyone with his swift, unpredictable movements. Too many times to count, he had accompanied such apologies with the statement, *When I hurt someone, I want them to know that it was no accident.*

128

Each man in the tent remained motionless. After several seconds the lead insurgent broke away, glaring back from a short distance. Russell involuntarily released an exhalation and dropped his look downward only for a moment. It was all the justification needed. His next memory was blurred as his face caught the full impact of cold steel to his temple. His wrists bound behind him; Russell hit the desert floor face first. The dust that kicked up in his nostrils changed to smoke as his reality shifted into another world … one free from the pungent odor and taste of his own blood.

✠ ✠ ✠

The fragrance that filled Russell's nose was not of earth, but of a harsh smoldering waft which drifted up from a once raging fire. He was sitting and staring at his image reflected in a water bucket set between his feet. He felt that degree of satisfaction which Roman warriors have after successfully completing a mission. He saw that his face, which once reflected youthfulness, now reflected the residual harshness of countless battles. He looked haggard. The only remnant evidence of his youth lay in the shiny, sparkling glimmer reflected in his eyes from the water. He knew he still had the strength to endure at least one more of the hardships which undoubtedly lay ahead for the legion. A comrade walked by mumbling an unsolicited commentary about Russell's scraggly appearance. The comrade laughed loudly, calling out to Russell, " … Legionnaire Tiberius Julius, sir."

In the smoky, ground-hugging haze, Russell saw bowmen walking along the riverbank to provide the appropriate level of security. They saluted respectfully as they passed his locale. Russell realized that he, as Tiberius Julius in this place and time, was the absolute authority of this Roman outpost guarding against the wild Germanic tribes. His mind wandered back to times and places where life held more for him than being on point for Rome in a job that nobody wanted, in a place that no one wanted to be, to do what no one wanted to do, at a time when nobody wanted to be there. Worst of all, this job epitomized the dread of every deployed soldier—that he would most likely die far away from his family, where no one knew him or loved him. This was his rightful baggage; a burden he had accepted when he made the decision to become a soldier some forty years before.

His reflection vibrated in the water bucket, and the memories of many long trips replayed in Tiberius's mind. He had spent a lifetime in the Roman Army. His personal life was interrupted time and again by the demands of his chosen military profession. He had a woman once, a beautiful young Jew, with flowing dark hair. The touch of her hands on his brought him to a dimension of pleasure that nothing could rival. The long marches home always seemed endless as he knew she would be there for him. She patiently and faithfully waited for him despite the increasing number of foreign-based military campaigns he endured. *What soldier could ask for more?*

Tiberius remembered the upwelling feeling of pride for the son she eventually bore him. Now he could barely remember the sensation of the tiny hand which gripped his calloused fingers. The time with the boy and his mother seemed to be only a blink in his lifetime as the fortunes of soldiering took him farther and farther away to where he sat now on the frontier outpost in eastern Gaul known as Silesia. This journey began at Temple Mount in the walled city of Jerusalem, built on Mount Moriah where the Jewish god oversaw Solomon building the greatest temple ever made. It was the most civilized jewel of the Eastern Roman Empire.

On that departing day so long ago, Tiberius found that this fortressed city was, indeed, a world all unto itself. Its personality was rivaled by none in either intensity or romance. It appeared that the interface of so many cultures and religions fanned the flames of fervor thus leading to celebrations one week, crucifixions the next. He and his legion were swept up in a wave of frantic festivity. The music played loudly. Day and night people danced in the streets ensconced within the stony arms of Jerusalem. In these shadows, Tiberius and his Syrian Roman archers laughed and toasted each other knowing that tomorrow they could all be dead.

In the middle of all this gaiety, there was another stark realization that they all shared. They would never be again assigned here in their homeland. Every song, every drink, every walk, every tear within Jerusalem would be the last. Tiberius and his men hoped against hope to be positioned nearby, perhaps assigned duty in Dalmatia, Macedonia, or even Sicilia—close to home would be better than never being able to see home again.

The stinging in Tiberius's eyes was as intolerable now as it had always been with all the other fires, whether in remote campsites or on some distant, smoldering battlefield. He rubbed at his eyes as the smoke continued to waft up along the edge of the quietly flowing waters. In the distance, the sound of archers pacing up and down the stream faded away into a new rather oppressive grinding-like reverberation.

✠ ✠ ✠

The crunching of desert sand hovered in Russell's ear. Over this sound he heard a snarling voice which fueled the pain of an already all-consuming headache. The taste of blood rushed in.

"This one," the voice said. "This one will make the choice for all." Russell felt himself being hoisted up by his body armor into a kneeling position, the binding on his hands cut free. Wobbly, he looked down to see what the Muslim had placed into his hand. It was an American 9 mm pistol with the hammer cocked.

"Destiny," spat the Muslim. "It is all in your hand. Kill a pig and your own pig's life is saved. Refuse and all lives belong to me." Using both his hands to steady himself into an upright position, Russell placed the cocked pistol on the ground. With a heave, he propelled himself to an unsteady stance, pausing briefly to pick up the revolver before finally arriving at a full standing position. At full height, Russell was at least four inches taller than the Muslim. The Muslim stood back, scimitar unsheathed. All eyes, Muslim and infidel, were on Russell.

With his free hand, Russell unsnapped his throat-and-collar armor, letting it fall onto the sand. The sand glinted golden and brown on his dark skin and stuck to the stubble of his usually smooth, shaven head. He rubbed the side of his bleeding face which was imprinted with the broadside of the Saracen blade. A clear channel of flesh could be felt as it sliced downward through the black war grit on Russell's face. Looking at the bloody debris on his fingers, Russell knew his only advantage was a verbal gambit. *In chess, the worst outcome would be loss of maneuver pieces. Here, I'm gambling with lives, everyone's life.* Sucking in a deep breath, Russell spoke slowly, methodically, almost trance-like. "The first of the five Islamic Pillars of faith requires that one acknowledges that there is only one god, Allah, and Mohammed is his prophet." The jawline musculature of the Muslim warrior clenched.

"The second of the Islamic Pillars requires that a believer must pray five times a day in the direction of Holy Mecca." Shifting sounds could be heard from the remaining kneeled Americans as they slowly joined the Muslim leader's consternation. Russell continued, undaunted, pulling apart the closures and metal snaps of his body armor revealing his sweaty, crumpled combat uniform and a body just as strong as the armor which protected it.

"The third pillar requires that the believer must not eat during daylight hours during the holy month of Ramadan." The Muslim's scimitar which was once held threateningly now propped up the disbelieving man.

"The fourth pillar states that the believer must participate in the giving of alms to the poor and downtrodden." In the tent, all heads turned, fixing squarely on Russell whose voice captivated every ear—friend or foe.

38

Saving Face

Battalion aid station
Middle East Operations area

"The fifth and final Pillar of Islam states that the believer, you Mullah," continued Russell, "must participate in haj, the pilgrimage to Holy Mecca, at least one time in your life. Have you done so? I am guessing that as combatants, you, or even I, may never have that opportunity as our tomorrows are never a certainty."

"How do you know these things?" The Muslim's voice quavered as his spoke. "Do you practice Islam?"

Never making eye contact with the Muslim, Russell squared his shoulders and kept the revolver in his hand pointing straight downward. He cleared his throat.

"It doesn't matter what I know or what I am. Would you treat me any differently? The issue is that you don't see me as a man. You see me only as an infidel, a person unfaithful to God and Islam. I never said that I was Islamic, nor did I say I wasn't. Yet I am hoping the last of the one hundred twenty-four thousand prophets will forgive us both as I play the hand you have given to me. So Mullah, I'm asking you now, whom of these servants of God do you think deserves to die first?"

The thought of the pending execution brought a look of conflict to the hardened face of the Muslim. It was further compounded by the squatting down of Russell's troops who were now captives of the words of the American. Russell's eyes scanned over the Muslims and then over his fellow beleaguered American soldiers whose widened eyes met his sequentially in turn.

"Maybe, it should be this one—a senior medic who carried in a wounded Muslim soldier. Did you happen to ask the wounded whether his god answers to the name Jehovah or Allah? Inside the aid station tent flap, does it really matter?" The medic shook his head slowly.

"Maybe it should be this one—a nurse whose crime it was to triage and treat according to wound severity. You chose that Saracen over this American, didn't

132

you? Did you ask your patient if the tables were turned, would he save *your* life?" The nurse shut her eyes, tightly squeezing tears onto both cheeks.

"Mullah, if anyone deserves to die first here, the selection is quite easy. It should be the one responsible for placing these soldiers in this dilemma. It is me." The Muslim's face contorted as he saw his power play slowly dissolve before the eyes of every warrior.

"I am the one to be held accountable. These soldiers are all here for one reason—to support me in my quest to save—not take—lives. This is their only crime, Mullah." Russell raised the gun slowly, the barrel turned inward, toward his body until it rested against his left, and already throbbing, bloodied temple. Outside, the wind blustered, and dust swirled at the lower edge of the tent flap. All eyes were on Russell.

Russell clenched his jaw and felt the crackle of sand in his mouth. He squeezed his eyelids closed as if this could reduce the pain of what was about to happen.

"My Jesus forgives assassins," he said. "I hope that he will find it in himself to forgive me this transgression." The hammer fell, *click*. No instantaneous muzzle flash or bang. Nothing was heard, save the explosion of dead silence.

Just then, another voice broke in. This voice was not harsh or snake-like, it was a harmonious voice that Russell once fondly remembered but right now could not place.

"Did you think he would kill the others to save his life? As I told you, Nabil, my son, Dr. Russell Lange does not fear death, for he has already given up any hope of life once his foot hits the battlefield." All Muslims now stood and bowed respectfully in the direction of the only voice speaking in the tent.

"Let me now answer for everyone the question hanging in the air. No, he is not Muslim or a follower of Islam. He does, however, possess a heart that holds the spirit of the Five Pillars by which Muslims live, fight, and die. I should know. I was there when he first learned them. I was his mentor and his teacher—I was his Mullah." The new voice moved closer to just behind Russell's ear. It belonged to Asaad Baghbah, a chemical engineer in the Jordanian Army.

"How was it phrased to me, Russell, so many years ago when we studied chemical warfare at the US Army's Chemical School?" Asaad placed his hand on Russell's shoulder. "You said, 'The ones who die in battle are the ones who cling everlastingly to life. On the battlefield, I have no hope of living, nor should you.' Is that not what you said to me, d'Albret's father?" Asaad smiled, having used that Arabic term of respectful endearment.

Not a facial tremor, not a quiver from the bloodied lip, but a single, unemotional tear cut a clean line down Russell's gritty face—not from fear, not from relief, but only from comrade recognition. Russell knew the voice and the man who brandished the words. Only one person ever used that Arabic nickname for him. The voice belonged Asaad Baghbah al Bethany—the engineer turned museum curator, working in Istanbul, Turkey.

A sound of the rustling of clothing brought into Russell's view the familiar, kind-faced man, tall in stature, but thick, stocky, and powerfully built for war. In the man's hand was a polished jewel-topped walking stick that greatly supported his authority as well as his weight. Asaad gently reached and took the pistol that Russell's hand was resistant to release.

"Hello, sponsor," the Palestinian spoke in a respectful and kind manner. "I trust you have been better."

"It's good to see you," said Russell, bouncing his gaze to and from Nabil. "Your ill-tempered son is a lot bigger now than in the pictures I remember."

"Yes, he is. However, a holy war complicates past friendships."

"And present friendships too, Asaad." Russell pointed to the handgun. "Why am I alive? Did that weapon misfire?"

"It's my pistol. I emptied the chambered round before I gave it to Nabil."

"You knew what he would do with it. Didn't you?"

"What do you think, Russell? He is my son."

"What if he had re-cocked it?"

"Let's dwell on happier things." Asaad passed the weapon back to Nabil. "Do you remember the Arabic phrase that I taught you?"

"*Sahid-nee ah Sahid-dek,*" said Russell.

"Do you still remember what it means?"

"You help me, and I will help you."

"I have helped you, Russell. Now I need you to help me."

"Look at me, Asaad." Russell raised his war-stained palms upward. "Do I look like I'm in position to help anyone, much less you?

"Why would I ask you if you weren't?"

39

Farewells and Good Nights

Battalion aid station
Middle East Operations area

A hand on a scimitar ... hand on a pistol ... now a hand rests on me. Russell felt Asaad's grip on his arm. *From minute to minute this tempo has shifted.*

There was little Arab hospitality in welcoming the American soldiers—that is, until Asaad took command of the situation. He gently superimposed a father's will over his fiery-tempered son, Nabil, and took the reins of the situation at hand.

In great privacy, Asaad led Russell out of the tent. "I need you to do something for me that I cannot do for myself," he whispered.

"What could that be, Asaad?"

"I need you to see that this is delivered." Asaad pulled out a small felt box and placed it in Russell's hand."

"A simple delivery?" Russell scoffed. "Is this another of your tests?"

"The name inside the box links to a person from which right now I must remain separate in time and place."

"Is it the box or what's in the box that needs to be delivered?"

"You will see what is in the box once you open it to retrieve the name. It might be better just to send the box with its contents.

"Will possession of this box be dangerous to the deliverer, that is, me?"

"I doubt that you will be the deliverer as the place it needs to travel is far and the time it needs to get there is soon."

"Can't you post this yourself, Asaad? It seems easy enough."

"No, if I could, I would have already done so." Asaad sighed deeply. "This needed to have been sent out weeks ago, but an opportunity never arose."

"If you hadn't met me here, how would this have been delivered?"

"Sahid-nee ah Sahid-dek." Asaad gripped Russell's arm. "Although war tends to make simple tasks much more difficult, sometimes it presents strange unex-

pected opportunities." Russell listened as Asaad explained that when he had answered the call of the jihad, which commanded all Muslims to fight the enemies of Islam, he was unable to commit wholeheartedly.

"Even as I came to the aid of my Muslim brothers, I knew I could not take your life," he told Russell. "There is much about Christianity, a religion of peace, which makes me reevaluate my Islamic faith."

"And yet you gave your son a weapon that could have killed me and others as well." Russell frowned.

"My pistol was the price for your freedom," said Asaad. "As I told you, it was I who ensured that a round was not chambered. It was by this test of wills that you could save face in front of the warriors and be spared from death."

Russell placed his open hand over his heart, tapping his chest in the Arab way of expressing gratitude.

"I know you, Russell." Asaad's voice quietened. "I would have regretted seeing you executed if the scenario played out any differently."

Clutching the felt box, Russell listened in silence as Asaad spoke. Both knew that all in all, the kindnesses of the past were now repaid in full.

"Should we meet again, and if Allah deems it necessary, neither of us should expect mercy."

Russell accepted the promise and followed his soldiers into the night. Russell looked back at the now shadowy outline of his friend.

"*Sahid-nee*, d'Albret's father," the outline spoke.

From the lessening shadow of the growing morning, Russell replied, "*Ah Sahid-dek*, Nabil's father." Russell stepped away musing. Besides Suzanne, not many ever knew of d'Albret, not even his own immediate family. Russell studied the box in his hand. *Some secrets need to remain secrets, at least for now.*

He followed the other soldiers onward to the ambulance exchange point. Once there, US assets could be contacted to carry the survivors back to safety. The dead were permitted to be taken as well.

When Russell arrived back at the brigade surgeon's field office, he had a message waiting for him. It was arranged so that only he could decode the original message.

Atypical Chemicals found in Dyhernfurth, Poland. Break. Dr. Mickey Peronne mobilized from European Medical Command, Heidelberg. Break. Dr. Suzanne Coletrane mobilized from the Institute of Chemical Defense, Maryland. Break. Dr. Russell Lange to mobilize to MK Romanian Air Base—further instructions awaiting there. Nothing follows.

Within hours Russell had his wounds dressed, his gear on, and was boarding a flight headed to Europe. He sighed deeply. *Next stop, Constanţa, Romania.*

40

Fish, Flowers, and Falling Towers

Boulangerie
Strasbourg, France

"Americans eat ... but Europeans *dine*." Suzanne sniffed the air. *Europeans just get it. Busy Americans never will.*

Sitting at an outdoor café, Suzanne basked in the ambiance of the food, drink, and scenery all seemed a little more pleasant. Her phone rang as she finished the last of her flask of wine. Setting her glass down next to the remnants of her meal of Alsatian cheese on a baguette and a variety of Dijon mustards, she picked up her phone hopefully. *Maybe it's Russell.* She saw the number. *Nope.*

"Hello, Mickey, you sound less harried."

"Suzanne, I'm sorry about popping smoke abruptly on our last couple of communications checks. I really had to leave."

"It is what it is." Suzanne tried to shake the disappointment out of her voice. "Are you okay, Mickey?"

"I think so," he faltered. He was braced for the dragon fire, which was sure to come, but surprisingly, her voice was demure. "I will know more once I get to Pyrzyce, Poland."

"Did you say, 'pirate's eye'?"

"No, but it certainly sounds like that, doesn't it? It is a town in northwest Poland."

"Mickey, there is no concentration camp there. Can you tell me why you need to go there?"

"Negative knowledge. I can't tell you what I don't know—"

"And yet you go ... "

"Yeah, Suzanne. This is my cross to bear. Tell me about the research you did at the concentration camp."

"Sure. I was so amazed at the connection between Natzweiler-Struthof concentration camp, and the studies done simultaneously at the University of Strasbourg."

"I got that. Many of the scientific gains had occurred well outside the spectrum of the Nazi era; however, it was reasonable to assume that strides made prior were facilitated by the inmate population of the camp."

"Yes, Mickey, even advances made afterward could certainly have been influenced by the camp's chemical weapons medical research."

"That's very true, Suzanne." Mickey nodded. "Was there more?"

"Yes, I also wanted to tell you about the Nobel Prize-winning work from Albrecht Kossel and Jean-Marie Lehn. Their work was influenced by Dr. Albert Schweitzer."

"No kidding … more Nobel Prize winners."

"More importantly, Mickey, Dr. Schweitzer was a member of a Knights Templar organization called the Order of Saint Lazarus of Jerusalem. I'm not sure what that means but I think it is probably important."

"Roger that, Suzanne. I certainly agree. As a Templar, in addition to his professional obligations, he would have had the responsibility to help Christians at risk, protect the holy shrines, and safeguard the holy relics."

"Okay. We all know Dr. Schweitzer went to Africa as a missionary. What does this have to do with inmates, cell studies, and Nazi experimentation with chemical war gases in Europe?"

"Sometimes we can help at-risk populations by what we do for them strategically rather than tactically."

"What do you mean, Mickey?"

"Oskar Schindler helped people at the tactical level by saving a list of people in his corner of the world. That was noble but didn't address the bigger strategic picture. It didn't stop the process. It is likely that your two Nobel laureates, based on influences from Schweitzer, used their knowledge to address the issues of medical biochemistry on a grander scale, strategically."

"How?"

"Consider the strategy of harnessing the DNA molecule. The strategic impact would be global, Suzanne."

"Well, I agree that intervention on a strategic level would eventually stop the process of using camp inmates as guinea pigs. Unfortunately, that would be of no immediate help to the people in the concentration camp."

"True, but depending on what the scientists learned, they could apply a solution to help millions of people instead of hundreds of people."

"What is the overarching issue here? Is it the process or the end point that we are looking to find?"

"That, Suzanne, is what we don't yet know. The overarching process seems to be linked to things I can't discuss on an open communication venue. The end point can be so grand that it has worldwide implications."

"Good God, Mickey. What have we gotten ourselves into?" Suzanne tugged at the straps of her LBE. "I thought this was just supposed to be about chemical war munitions."

"I know, right? Things here are not what they seem. Suzanne, please do something for me. Go to England. Travel first to King's Lynn in the east and then on to Bristol in the west on the Welsh border. Initiate discussions with the Brits regarding falling towers. Find out the basis for their lean. Then call and update Russell. You may have a better connection on reaching him than do I presently. Tell Russell that he must go to the four falling towers in Italy at Burano, Venice, Bologna, and Pisa. Fill him in on everything you know—especially that our probing is not only about concentration camp victims, at least not entirely."

"Roger. Can do easy."

"Tell Russell that we begin searching for leaning towers with a discovery mind-set of global proportions."

"Okay. What, specifically, are we looking to find?"

"At the falling towers, you must both look for fish."

"I take it we are talking about more than just an animal."

"Correct, Suzanne. You two must find that fish wherever it hides from you."

"Fish? Can you be more specific?"

"No. You'll know it when you see it, Suzanne. I promise you. Keep in mind that a rose by any name is still a rose. This is critical."

"*Romeo and Juliet*, Mickey? Fish, flowers, and falling towers? Do you realize how absolutely bizarre you sound? Are you sure you're okay?"

"Never said I was, Suzanne." Mickey cleared his throat. "Even as I replay the poetry in my own head, I can't think of any better way to say things. At present, I don't have high-side secure communications capability. Do you at least hear and understand my words? Are, at the very least, my searching instructions clear?"

"Crystal."

"Really, Suzanne, I need to know."

"Crystal, Mickey, crystal. I'm not a shavetail lieutenant."

"Good, I'm glad you're not." Mickey let out a big sigh. "Please relay this info to Russell."

"So, you want me to sound like a lunatic too?"

"Don't worry, Russell is used to it."

"Hey, I—"

"Sorry, Suzanne, save it for Oprah. Right now, I've got other fish to fry."

"So it seems." She paused. "Are you still planning to head to the other concentration camps, Mickey?"

"Yes, I probably will eventually, but not right now. I must first keep an appointment with an owl."

"Will you stop it with the animals already? Who do you think you are, Ace Ventura?"

"Speaking of Ace Ventura, Suzanne, I have a question for you. What has a big red nose and lives in a test tube?"

"This is no time for riddles and jokes, Mickey."

"I never said it was a joke. Make sure you pass this question on to Russell as well." The phone clicked and the connection ended.

Mentally replaying the conversation, Suzanne paid her check and strolled over to her car. Instead of driving across Germany to Poland, she now had to make the next flight to London. She had to get to the closest airport. Obliviously passing townsfolk and tourists, she lined up the events that had to play out. Once the sequence made sense, she nodded to herself in affirmation. As she rounded the corner of the boulangerie, she noticed a solitary, calico cat who sat methodically licking its paw on the front doorstep of the bakery. She thought about Tobermory, her cat of exceptional confidence and poise, and wondered if he was faring well at their Maryland quarters on Plumb Point Loop. Usually the neighbors were good about taking in Toby when she had urgent missions. Hopefully they stepped up for him without having been given notice.

Suzanne had a gut feeling that thus far in her career, this was the most significant mission she had been given and it was one she hoped not to screw up. *But there are so many ways this can go wrong. Why does Mickey have so much faith in me? Why can't I have the confidence of the literary Tobermory—Saki's brilliant, talking cat?* Suzanne pointed her car out of France and toward Germany. Quietly, a green 2CV duck car pulled out right behind her.

41

Of Distress, Determination, and Destinations

Route to Berlin
Bautzen, Germany

"The adventure lies not in the destination, but in the journey, right?" Then Mickey mumbled, "Who am I kidding?"

"Why is everything that comes out of an American's mouth either a billboard or a bumper sticker?" Thaddeusz sulked behind the steering wheel, directing the car out of Bautzen.

"What is the plan here, Thaddeusz?"

"Why do you care, Doc?"

"I just want to know that it is the straightest, quickest route."

"Well, if you must know." Thaddeusz motioned to a road map. "The plan is to head north to Berlin, and then due northeast on the A-11 to cross the German-Polish border."

"That would take us to northwest Poland ... " Mickey traced his finger on the map, "and then ... ?" He looked expectantly at Thaddeusz.

"And then to the southernmost outskirts of the city of Szczecin. From there, we leave the autobahn and head southeast, on lesser roads, to get to the city of Pyrzyce."

"Final destination?"

"The Baszta Sowia, a leaning tower in western Poland." Thaddeusz sneered, "Fear not. It'll be eye-opening for you."

This seven-hour trip is going to be painful. Mickey grimaced. *If I live long enough, I need to understand who this character is they call the Owl. Is the Owl an oracle? If yes, how is the Owl connected to leaning towers?*

✠ ✠ ✠

Russell was preparing to rocket east to west, from shore to shore, in Italy through Burano, Venice, Bologna, and Pisa. The question that still needed an answer was why he was hopscotching from leaning tower to leaning tower asking about fish that weren't really fish. *Maybe Mickey will eventually clue me in.*

Russell's flight arrived into the Mihail Kogalniceanu Air Base in Romania where he switched over to a C12 aircraft headed for Aviano Air Base in Italy. He made his connection quickly.

"American, no?" a ground crew asked.

"American, yes." Russell nodded. The MK Air Base ground crew quickly escorted him over to the Red Room—for the distinguished visitors—at the civilian side of the airfield. He remembered being here just last year in support of a mission across the way on the military side of the airfield.

✠ ✠ ✠

The Red Room for distinguished visitors was plush in mahogany, red velvet, and huge red oriental rugs. *Either I'm in a bordello or a finely designed physician's office.* Russell chuckled as he chose a comfortable-looking chair and settled in.

As a chiropractic physician working in Medical Operations, Russell had little opportunity to do direct patient management. After he had finished a two-year tour of duty at the Institute of Chemical Defense, his patient-encounter rate was eight per month. Russell knew at that point that he needed to step into something more clinically oriented so that he could maintain his level of manual skills. The last thing he wanted were hands of stone. Cracking his own stiff neck didn't provide his hands the hours and hours of manual medicine contact time he truly needed. As a result, he had jumped at an assignment to Romania, hoping it might provide some downtime and some more clinical opportunities.

Russell massaged the muscles in his hands as he sat, taking in the Red Room. With his back to a wall sporting a huge Romanian flag, he was looking directly across at a row of digital world clocks displaying times from Los Angeles to Tokyo. On the wall to his right were two actual clocks labeled *Germany* and *Romania*. *This makes sense*, he mused.

At the moment, the US Army was beginning to stretch its reach eastward, dabbling in joint-training exercises with the former Eastern Bloc countries of Georgia, Poland, Bulgaria, and Romania. Plans had long been set to do exercises based out of MK Air Base—the former top gun fighter training locale for Romanian ace pilots.

Can't have training without medical support. What was needed was a medical clinic to support US Army training operations in the region. The army wanted someone who had the credentials and the experience to stand up a medical clinic from scratch. Of the names that were discussed, Mickey Peronne, Suzanne Coletrane, and Russell Lange were in the top five selections.

Russell looked at the clock labeled *Germany* and thought about Mickey. *Having a professional skillset in both traditional and manual medicine, as an osteopathic physician, Mickey was the number one choice. Too bad that an ongoing medical evaluation board took his name off the list.*

He stared across at the digital display clock for America's East Coast. *Suzanne didn't have the manual medical skills needed and without equivalent colleagues in the workplace, she was one-deep at ICD.* His eyes tracked back to the clock labeled *Romania*. *That left only me to be assigned.* As a combined asset with the other incoming medical staff, Russell and his manual medical skills got the nod for the slot at MK Air Base.

With Russell at the helm, this combination of medical professionals was viable to support medical mission. *In reality, I was truly the best choice.* Russell's forte was medical plans and operations. He designed and implemented the nuts and bolts of a medical support system which spanned four medical stations positioned throughout three training areas in two countries.

The most unusual aspect for Russell was the fact that although he had SPOOC training, it never came into play at MK Air Base, where the Ukrainian border and the Black Sea were close, and the Soviet state of Georgia was a stone's throw away. He had thought for sure that what he learned at SPOOC—the Special Operations Officer Course—in Alabama would be an asset in this mission. During his time there the Chinese and Russian attachés visited the forward air base. They wanted to see the specifics and intricacies of the health clinic operations where the Joint Task Force East Command surgeon and chief physician was a Special Operations guru. They were not mollified after meeting the army's premier medical "spook."

✠ ✠ ✠

It wasn't all that long of a wait for Russell until the MK Air Base customs officer came through to recertify the papers and passports of the travelers who were on their way to Aviano, Italy.

"Passenger Russell Lange?" a voice to Russell's right came from the door ajar. The woman was tall and thin, with Italian-like features akin to the people from the region.

"For you," Russell winked, "I'll be whoever you need me to be."

"Follow me, please." With minimal prompting, the female airport officer was proud and quick to tell Russell what he already knew about the country—about how Romanian heritage and language spans directly from Rome.

"Indeed," Russell offered, "Romania is an island of romance language in a sea of Slavic nations." Just across the border, in the Ukraine and Bulgaria, Russell knew how the language, and even the alphabet, changed dramatically. The Cyrillic alphabet rendered virtually every American illiterate. Thank God for Andrea, the Bulgarian linguist who faithfully and competently served as the interface between the Bulgarian medical people and Russell whenever Bulgaria became his mission. Russell began to dwell on the memories of being taught

Bulgarian cuisine by Andrea. However, the shuffle of feet in the Red Room meant that memories had to give way to present-day priorities.

"I trust you will have a pleasant flight." The airport officer smiled as she placed Russell to the front of the boarding line.

Passengers began lining up to board the C12 plane to Aviano. In preparation for his walk back out on the tarmac, Russell stuffed his beret into one LBE pouch and pulled his orders out of another. His follow-on orders directed his footsteps onward to four major Italian cities.

His heart ached as he knew he wouldn't have time to go into Romania's capital city, Bucharest, to have dinner. He recalled a time when he and his dear Romanian colleague, Dr. Mihail Dancescu, whom he nicknamed Danno, had once enjoyed a remarkable meal: tantalizingly spiced meat stuffed in grape leaves served with a chilled Moldavian Romanian Chardonnay which rivaled the best that western Europe had to offer.

Russell left the terminal for the windy tarmac. He realized that he would also have to forego his traditional hop over to Bulgaria where he would normally enjoy the wonderful cheese dishes of the region. He looked longingly in the direction of the neighboring country. *So close, and yet so far away!* No country in the west could come close to the flavor explosion that a Bulgarian meal could provide—all done with the clever application of the right kind, quality, and quantity of a carefully shredded dusting of cheese on every plate. *It won't be long before the culinary secrets of the former Eastern Bloc will be unlocked by the travelers of the world. But, until then, the lines will be short and the people friendly.* Russell smiled to himself. Only the infrequent moments he could capture with Suzanne were better than the still-secret joys of this region's cuisine. *Every minute with Trane is like imbibed velvet. I'd love to bring her here someday.*

It was eight o'clock and light still remained in the evening sky over Aviano Air Base when Russell's plane pried a screech from the sleeping military runway. It was too late to get to the leaning tower of Burano, but Russell needed to get within striking distance tonight. *I have to go the long way to Cavallino-Treporti … no time to rest.* He procured a rental car and invested two hours of travel time that evening so as to execute a late arrival by water taxi into the island city of Burano. Overwhelmed with fatigue, Russell knew that a visit to the church and its leaning tower would definitely have to wait until morning.

While the water taxi hummed toward Burano, Russell's thoughts went back to Romania and an adventurous trip to Snagov, right outside Bucharest. *It was a dark, dreary, rainy day. The dripping fog over Snagov Lake sat like a damp shawl over our heads and shoulders. It's a good thing that Danno was there.*

Danno, the young and brilliant Romanian flight surgeon. Danno, a master of Italian, English, Spanish, and, of course, Romanian, overcame the language barrier and helped Russell charter a water ferry across to another lonely, cloud-blanketed island where dwelled an Orthodox monastery. *Then again*, Russell thought as the current water taxi rocked him to and from the world of reality and dreams, *what language* doesn't *Danno know?* He remembered that once they were inside the monastery chapel near the midpoint of the nave, and Danno pointed out a four-foot-long grave marking etched in the floor panel. There heralded the final resting place of the revered Vlad Tepes. Danno explained how Vlad was known to the world as Vlad the Impaler because of his intolerance toward criminals, enemies of Romania, and enemies of Christendom. To the knowledgeable remainder, Vlad was also known as Dracula. Russell had puzzled at the short stature of this world icon until he learned from Danno that Vlad had been beheaded before his burial. Even now, at the thought, Russell felt a lurch in his gut, just as he had back then.

The water taxi to Burano arrived and began the jerky, staccato docking process. Russell looked around his immediate seating area to ensure he had all his gear collected—a painful process because physical exhaustion separated his mind from his body. His sluggish memory recalled that it would be many years, if ever, before Vlad Dracula's head could be returned and reunited with his body. Russell stared at the shores of Burano. *How much longer before my mind will have a reunion with my rumbling, stumbling, bumbling body?*

For the longest time, Russell stood at the entrance to the off-loading gangplank. He looked at the narrow ramp, felt the wobbliness in his legs, glanced at the cold dark waters of the lagoon, and then locked his gaze back at the clanking ramp. *I can't stand here forever. Even if I fall, a side trip overboard into the water would be progress toward a night of rest, albeit a damp rest.* Upon his fatigue, he supplanted a tenuously determined game face. He drew in the deepest of breaths, balanced the best he could against the rocking of the boat, and forged ahead, forcing his shaky limbs over the water and onto the shores of Burano, Italy. Without any sound of a thunderous splash, the night swallowed a tired, and gratefully dry, Russell into its darkened folds.

42

Peeling Layers

Route to Pyrzyce
Northwestern marches of Poland

Mickey strummed his fingers on the passenger-side glass of Thaddeusz's vehicle. In the front window's reflection, Mickey could see that Thaddeusz was grinding his teeth while squeezing hard at the steering wheel. *Has Matthias set me up to be murdered by his discontented brother?* Mickey remembered Thaddeusz's glare back at the carjacking site. *Thaddeusz certainly had intent, but not opportunity.* The miles leading to Pyrzyce clicked by in total silence until Mickey spoke.

"Why did Matthias stay behind?" Mickey wasn't really sure if he had survived a good cop, bad cop routine, or if he was now coupled with a fanatic like West Virginia's Mothman of the mid-1960s. Thaddeusz certainly wasn't Matthias and right now Mickey sorely wished he was with the other, less grumpy, brother.

"Why don't you ask the question you really want to ask?" Thaddeusz growled.

"Okay, I will." Mickey sucked in a deep breath. "Why is it that I have to go to Poland with you?"

"Don't you feel better speaking your mind?"

"I'd feel better if you'd just answer the question," replied Mickey, shooting him an unpleasant scowl.

"You know, Doctor, I wouldn't have killed you unless I had to do so."

"Then your God must forgive murderers and assassins."

"As must yours." Thaddeusz thrust out his jaw. "Be careful of your accusations when the cloth that you wear on your body represents years of war and endless killings."

"I'm a doctor of medicine."

"So, you bury your mistakes? Does that make you any less the murderer?"

"Look, Thaddeusz, we have several more hours together. Can we start again?" Mickey pasted on a magazine smile. "Hello, my name is Doc. It's nice to meet you ... or at least, it's rather interesting to meet you."

146

"It's not necessary for us to know or even like each other. All we need to do is better understand the mission."

"What is the mission?"

"Listen, for a change, then you tell me."

Thaddeusz recited with a reverence Mickey thought incapable of such a man, "Chapter two. Verses nine and ten: 'Mountains and towers cast no shadow upon the three in the height of the day. Only a jutting mountain or leaning tower can reveal the light at the height of day. In the shadows of the leaning towers and jutting stones secrets lie. It has always been.'" Thaddeusz sat solemnly afterward wanting, and needing, no response.

"Nice."

"That's all you gather from these words? 'Nice'—that's it?" Thaddeusz scoffed. "Matthias was certainly wrong about you. He thought you would under-stand that which is revealed by—"

"—the Lost Books of Benjamin?"

"Yes, Doc, specifically from the Second Book of Benjamin."

"When were they written?"

"After the crucifixion of Christ. We River Gypsies took it upon ourselves to secure and protect a great secret. We did this because we were guided in the spirit of our Lord. In the Second Book of Benjamin is the guidance which allows us to unravel a great secret."

"You have recited two verses from a single chapter," said Mickey. "I'm sorry to be the one to tell you but a couple of verses from a chapter does not a mission make."

"True enough. Each chapter provides greater clarification. When all of the chapters have been collected, the story is fully known."

"Where are the other chapters?" Mickey asked.

"The Owl will tell you more."

"Who is the Owl?"

"Right now, you are." Thaddeusz smiled at his own words.

Mickey closed his eyes and shook his head, then continued, "Okay, Thad-deusz, for argument's sake, let's assume that verses written in the first century give guidance to hide a great secret. Can we agree that the secret lies among the leaning towers and the jutting stone?"

"Yes, we can agree," Thaddeusz nodded. "Those who are charged with the secret must then hide the secret where only those who know where to look may find it. In chapter two, verses nine and ten, the Second Book of Benjamin tells them to hide the secret among leaning towers and jutting rocks."

"The choice then is to use the leaning towers which were built in the first century," said Mickey.

"Yes, and many were used. But over time, many leaning towers, which in reality are falling towers, fell." Thaddeusz gestured. "They no longer met the criteria to hide the secret."

"What if a leaning tower couldn't be found? You can't just go pushing on a tower so as to make it lean."

"True enough," Thaddeusz nodded. "But what if leaning towers were initially built with the expressed purpose of falling?"

"Okay. What would be the advantage?"

"Well then," said Thaddeusz, "those who were charged with the secret, like us River People, transients, or Gypsies, could place the secret in the leaning tower."

"Right from the get-go."

"'Get-go'?"

"Onset ... from the beginning," Mickey explained.

"Can we just speak English?"

"I will try, Thaddeusz. The problem is that I speak American."

"Continue, American."

"So, you River People or transients probably couldn't build a leaning tower because you dealt only with fish." Mickey twisted his lips.

"Agreed."

"I know of no indications that Gypsies were prolific in building with stone."

"Agreed, Doc."

"However, Thaddeusz, stoneworkers and masons of the era could build a tower ... but ... " Mickey trailed off into silence.

"But what?"

"I was just thinking. If I were a mason, I would not be inclined to build a falling tower. It would go against everything I was taught or believed."

"What if the mason possessed a higher belief?"

"A belief higher than the quality of his work? I can't imagine ... unless ... "

"Yes, you see it now, don't you?"

"I do, Thaddeusz. We are not talking about just a mason."

"No, Doc. We're not."

"We are talking about a mason who serves Him. We are discussing the beliefs of a Christian mason."

"You surprise me. You are very bright, for an American. Maybe Matthias *was* right about you."

"Enough, Thaddeusz, play nice. I am on to something here."

Thaddeusz glared but remained silent.

"Well, I thought I was on to something here." Mickey pulled on his fingers until they popped. "Thaddeusz, tell me about the Christian masons."

"What is there to tell? For Lord Jesus, contrary to their training and tutelage, they would build a tower to fall."

"How does flawed masonry specifically link with chapters of the Second Book of Benjamin? The mason would have to—"

"Enough about masons!" Thaddeusz clapped the steering wheel. "Why are you so blind?"

"One minute I am the bright American, now I am—"

"—traveling down the wrong trail."

"Christian masons would build a tower to fall, yes?"

"Yes, Doc."

"Christian masons would place a chapter of the Second Book of Benjamin in this flawed tower, yes?"

"Yes."

"What happens next?" Mickey's eyes darted side to side.

"Would Christian masons stay at the leaning tower to guard the chapter, Doc?"

"No, Thaddeusz, they wouldn't. A rose by any other name is still a rose. A mason by any other name, even a Christian mason, is still a mason."

"Yes."

"He would go on to build as masons do." Mickey tapped on his knee.

"Yes."

"Who would secure the secret?" Mickey's tapping increased in tempo. "Who would move it in the face of danger? Who would have the freedom to move the secret to the leaning towers?"

"Not a mason." Thaddeusz stared straight ahead.

"Correct, not masons. They are those obligated to work in a fixed geography."

"Yes, Doc."

"Since masons are builders—linked to the earth by wood, metal, and stone—what must be considered is some kind of armed traveler."

"Correct again," said Thaddeusz.

"Traveling soldiers of a religious order would have the strength and power of protection," Mickey leaned forward, "not to mention the church-sanctioned wherewithal, to move with holy documents unencumbered and with ultimate freedom."

"Yes, they would."

"It sounds like we are talking about soldier-monks." Mickey clapped.

"Yes … finally a glimmer."

"Templar Knights, if you will. The securing of the secret at the leaning tower would have to be the charge of the tower keeper who could be a monk or a soldier-monk." Mickey collapsed back in his seat. "The Templars would be responsible for moving the secrets from leaning tower to leaning tower." Stone-faced, Thaddeusz listened to these words from Mickey.

"All true. All true," Thaddeusz conceded. "However, in the situation of a sudden onset of danger, an underlap of communication between the soldier-monks and the tower-keeping monks could, in fact, exist. In such a circumstance, the tower keepers would be left to provide a level of security for which they weren't trained. This could endanger the security of the secret … "

"Unless the tower keepers secretly are trained as soldier-monks as well," Mickey finished. Thaddeusz suppressed a growing smile.

"Oh my God! Chevaliers! You and Matthias are tower-keeping Templars!" Mickey held his hand up for a high five. Thaddeusz stared blankly, leaving Mickey's hand locked in awkward extension. Thaddeusz continued to drive. Slapping his own palm, Mickey withdrew his hand.

"There is one problem with this theory, Thaddeusz."

"What problem is that?"

"The timeline is wrong. Templar Knights did not come into existence until the late eleventh century. Much of what we discussed occurred in the early centuries after Christ ascended."

"What is the problem?" Thaddeusz flared his nostrils. "You said a rose called by any other name is still a rose."

"Are you saying Templar-like entities existed in the early centuries after Christ?"

"Maybe. After all, you are the one who called them 'Templars.' I did not. In the early centuries, followers were led by the apostles. Remember, Paul was a warrior evangelist. Later, the early church created dedicated individuals to be monks and tower keepers in consonance with the words of the Second Book of Benjamin. In time, some became soldier-monks. Ultimately, in the eleventh century these soldier-monks became temple knights. They were still a rose, but just with another name."

43

Of Knights and Plights

Route to Pyrzyce
Northwestern marches of Poland

*"Y*ou are a Templar Knight, Thaddeusz."
"Yes. Is it so hard to believe?"
"A modern-day Templar."
"Yes."

"Why didn't you tell me you were a Templar Knight?"

"First, because I don't like Americans. They come into Europe and act like they own our home. Second, I don't like you. You are the armed representation of a nation which vomits death in the name of freedom. Third, I ask you the same question. You did not offer that information to me either."

"Oh, but Thaddeusz, I am not a Templar Knight of your caliber. Within the US Army Chemical Corps, I am vested into the Order of the Dragon. Internationally, I am only vested with a humble knowledge of the lineage of knights in the Order of the Ermine. My father was a knight of the Ermine Order of Brittany. I am but a humble companion of that order."

"You know of knightly ways."

"That is because I am a Templar Knight within the order of the USA. I had hoped for advancement into leadership within the Grand Priory but ... suffice it to say that I am an American Templar who is only on the fringe of the greatness of the international order. Maybe one day ... "

"Maybe not today ... but the new sun rising always brings hope to the companion who yearns to be knighted within the World Templar Organization."

"You're right, Thaddeusz." *There's more to this guy than a grizzly rough exterior— at least I hope so.* Mickey listened quietly as Thaddeusz spoke in a voice that for once was sincerely kind.

"There is a time and place for information to be known and shared among our order of knights. Basically, we have two obstacles. First, you are not a knight or a companion of our order. Second, it is unclear just how much information to share."

Mickey smiled his response. He accepted the secrecy of the moment and looked beyond the driver to the scenery in the distance. The signs for Berlin had come and gone. The sun was high in the western sky as they headed northeast toward the Polish border. Mickey continued to think out loud with conversational guidance from the international Templar. He felt the barrier between the two of them, although each was standing tall, slightly beginning to drop.

"I can now understand why leaning towers exist, Thaddeusz. I get that the fish and the River People are deeply intertwined. Beyond this, I'm still struggling. Nothing connects. Can you help me?"

"No, I can't. This is why we must go visit the Owl."

"The Owl?"

"Answers lie there that don't lie here. Until then, however, I give you this chapter from my brother, Matthias. It comes from the leaning tower there at Bautzen." Thaddeusz handed Mickey a one-page document in a sealed plastic sleeve on top of the stack of familiar papers. "All the papers that you discovered from the underground lab in Poland are there as well."

CHAPTER 2

1) It is when the sun is highest in the sky that the light provided by the Father is the most that can be achieved in the day.

2) John was dual skilled like the sun above which at its greatest height casts twice more shadows from the numerous rocks rather than the few trees.

3) The trees were young because they were few. The people took from the earth faster than the new trees could grow.

4) The stones were plentiful but for a mason to work stone takes time. A wise craftsman will choose stone over wood. The wisest of all craftsmen works with both.

5) Who will then see the bleeding soul of wood within the heart of stone? Only in the height of the sun or moon when the light which falls casts no shadows and all can be seen within the rivers, even the fish that dwell within. If you approach with an open heart and humble soul, you will better visualize the wishes of the Father.

6) The keepers of the secret will be those who can know it and speak not even a whisper in the darkest ebb of nightfall.

7) The stone that was made when the sun stood tall was followed by two that were flawed. John kept the flawed as does our Lord for there is always hope as long as there is life.

8) A stony cloak shades not the light from the wood. Beneath the cloak the light burns bright in the one, not the three.

9) Mountains and towers cast no shadow upon the three in the height of the day. Only a jutting mountain or leaning tower can reveal the light at the height of day.

10) In the shadows of the leaning towers and jutting stones secrets lie. It has always been.

"Thank you and Matthias for trusting me with this." Mickey tapped the chapter. "And for returning these," he added, holding up the lab papers.

"Do not thank me. I have trusted you with nothing. It was not my choice to trust you. I am only doing that which was asked of me."

"Well then, if you are in the mindset of doing what others ask of you, then please tell me of your brother, Judas Lenz."

"I have no brother Judas Lenz. I know of no priest named Judas Lenz. I do know of a Judas ... a Judas Iscariot whose treachery cost us the living presence of our Lord and Savior."

"I never said he was a priest, Thaddeusz."

"Yes, you did."

"No, I didn't."

"Well, I must have heard the title from somewhere."

"Maybe you did, Thaddeusz. In the Book of Barnabas, the biblical Judas took the place of Jesus on the cross so that our Savior would not be crucified."

"Are you saying that Jesus was not crucified?"

"No, never." Mickey shook his finger. "Barnabas wanted only to demonstrate that Judas had remorse. Nothing at the time would prevent the Jews from recommending Jesus's death. Nothing could stop the Romans from executing Jesus."

"The Book of Barnabas is not one of the sixty-six books of the Bible."

"Correct, Thaddeusz. Neither is the Gospel according to Philip or the Gospel according to Mary Magdalene. However, in their own way, they provide partial insights, glimpses if you will, into our Lord."

"Maybe so, but Judas *was* a traitor."

"Yes, he was, Thaddeusz. However, think. What if his initial intent was not traitorous? Would you agree that a man as insightful as our Lord Christ would be shrewd enough not to pick a despicable scoundrel to be an apostle?"

"Christ didn't pick him."

"Okay, you're correct, Thaddeusz. Christ selected the apostles by following the will of the Father." Mickey sucked in a deep breath. "The question remains. How can we explain the selection of Judas as an apostle with traitorous behavior tendencies?"

Thaddeusz tapped his thumbs on the steering wheel for a moment then looked at Mickey blankly.

"Thaddeusz," Mickey continued, "consider that Judas's intent was not traitorous, but instead he was the keeper of a very great secret."

"I'm listening, Doc."

"Consider that perhaps Judas had knowledge of something extremely powerful that could free the Jews from the Romans as it freed them from the Egyptians. Consider if Judas had established an agreement with Messianic Jews that he could convince Jesus to wield that power. What if Judas whispered this to Jesus at the time the Jews took him at Gethsemane? What if Judas was again sent to Jesus on Thursday night, to the cistern pit on Mount Zion, to convince him to take the power unto himself, become a warrior king, and overthrow the yoke of Roman oppression?"

"Riding on a donkey on Palm Sunday, Jesus clearly demonstrated he was a lamb … not a lion."

"Yes, Thaddeusz, Judas's non-traitorous hopes would fall short since he did not fully understand that Jesus's death by crucifixion would have greater effects than any show of force."

"Jesus's refusal of Judas's wishes would have sealed his own fate and the countdown to crucifixion would have begun."

"Yes, Thaddeusz."

"What about Judas?"

"Judas would have been seen as a failure, unable to complete his mission, and would have been scourged by every Christ-follower at the time. It could have led Judas to suicide."

"I see that, Doc."

"But don't you agree that it is difficult for a man to hang *and* eviscerate himself in a suicidal act?"

"It would be. Many scholars see this as a contradiction between Matthew and Luke."

"Maybe, but not impossible," Mickey countered.

"Are you saying that any of this is an alternate reality?"

"I'm not saying that any of this is true. I do believe, however, that all information regarding Jesus Christ our Savior must be considered. Wouldn't you agree?"

"You have given me much to consider."

"I have one more thing of which to inform you, Thaddeusz. Judas was indeed found hung and his bowels were spilled upon the ground."

"Yes, I know. The Bible says it was so."

Mickey leaned over, securing the documents for the journey. "I'm not talking about the Bible, now Thaddeusz. I am talking about a report from CNN."

44

Viking and the Liking

Route to airport
Karlsruhe, Germany

What mysteries do these leaning towers in England hold? Suzanne tried to relax her vice grip on the steering wheel but found it impossible to do so. *History would tell me, if only I knew. It's too bad I hate history.* Both Suzanne and a shadowy person in a duck car departed from the Alsace. Both arrived in Karlsruhe, Germany, in time to catch the evening six o'clock flight to London. Sitting in the airport, she checked off her list. Most importantly, on a quick call, she was able to pass on Mickey's instructions to Russell. *I hope he is making more sense of it than I am.* Suzanne frowned. By the time Suzanne landed at London Stansted Airport, and then negotiated the awkward reverse highway and vehicle driving to King's Lynn, she felt virtually trashed. It was only nine at night and the sun was still reasonably above the horizon as she approached the strip of northern coastline where Greyfriars Tower hailed. In her mind she imagined it to be a cold, lonely stone structure much akin to lighthouses she had known. *What on earth does Mickey want me to find? How does the maze of fish, flowers, and falling towers fit into all this intrigue?*

She arrived at King's Lynn as the sun painted the port-side town burnt orange, heralding the coming of nightfall. *It's too late to get over to the Greyfriars church square.* Her eyes kept darting up to her rearview mirror. She had the sneaking suspicion that she was being followed. *I hope I'm just imagining it.* Even then, a shadow passed in her peripheral vision. Her training in basic field operations at West Point Academy was a very long time ago. When Russell was a spook at Fort Benning, she was allowed to sit in on some of the training classes when she was doing internal medicine work at the local Martin Army Community Hospital. At times like this, it was his voice in her head saying, *Don't move till you know.* Suzanne was pretty sure it was nothing, but she knew, nevertheless, that she needed to remain watchful. Soon she would cross the Great Ouse River

155

and safely check in to an east-bank hotel in King's Lynn. *I'll investigate Greyfriars in the morning … and check to see if I have one shadow or two.*

✠ ✠ ✠

In northwestern Poland, Mickey and Thaddeusz wearily pulled into the tree-lined streets of Pyrzyce. Thaddeusz ensured that a meeting with the Owl would take place later that night at the city center.

✠ ✠ ✠

In Burano, Italy, a fatigue-laden Russell worked hard at physically balancing himself on his stroll from the water taxi. Sleeping is generally a pleasant thought to most anyone but a spook. Heavy-lidded, Russell fought to keep his wits about him as he negotiated the narrow streets of Burano. *Food, I need food. Sustenance first, then slumber.*

Russell spotted a small sidewalk café whose flickering neon sign indicated that it had not closed for the night. Like a homing pigeon, Russell shot for an open chair, its back to the wall, facing the sidewalk. Once seated, Russell scanned every dark corner. Satisfied that no cloaked dagger lurked, Russell perused the menu card, rubbed his eyes, then again perused. *I'm looking and I'm liking, but is this for real? Don't move till we know. Certainly, Lady Luck hasn't followed me from Romania to Burano.* Craning his neck to better read the lit sign on the wall, Russell nodded and smiled. *If I'm dreaming, don't wake me … at least not for a few minutes longer.* Tilting his nose skyward, Russell sniffed at the aroma that drifted from the café's open door. It looked like he would be partaking of spiced meat stuffed in grape leaves served with a chilled Moldavian Romanian Chardonnay after all.

45

The Virgin and the Captain

Greyfriars Tower Plaza
Kings Lynn, England

*T*he *leaning tower of Lynn … a leaning tower in England. Go figure.* From the south, along the manicured walkway, Suzanne approached the Greyfriars Tower biting the inside of her cheek and wringing her hands nervously. The morning sun cast her tall shadow toward the Greyfriars Square Library. It was quite embarrassing that as highly trained as she was, she couldn't get over the feeling that she was missing the obvious. The glaring truth was that, until last night, she had been aware of just one leaning tower in the world and that was in Pisa. Russell's voice in her head said, *Look at the bright side, Trane, your knowledge just doubled.* When it came to her, he was always that annoying optimist. Maybe that's why she loved him. He was everything she was not. *Why didn't Mickey send Russell here? Maybe the whole English leaning towers scenario is a bad gamble for mission success and it's better if I take the fall. They are probably rocketing through the clues they need at their assigned destinations. Not me.*

Although Suzanne coveted greatness, she had failed in her attempt to branch Special Operations, failed in her marriage to Douglas, and now was entertaining a prelude to a pending failure to find the fish in the first of her two assigned English cities. *I may fail; however, no one can say that I didn't do my homework.*

Suzanne learned that King's Lynn was more than just a quaint and lovely English port town which boasted a millennium of proud history. Its streets were filled with people visiting the home of the seafarer Vancouver who discovered the far northwest of the United States. Additionally, the Grey Friar Nicholas of Lynn lived and died here. The fact that European clergy from England had a presence in the Americas a century before Columbus arrived gave strength to Mickey's claim that Templars had made critical visitations in the New World following their disgraceful disappearance from Europe in the early fourteenth century. The Greyfriar monks of King's Lynn had even established a lighthouse in the tower of their church.

Even as Suzanne had driven through its streets looking for her leaning tower, the fervor surrounding seafood industries bustled at nearby aromatic markets and restaurants. It was like driving in a storybook, and with every turn she was subjected to imbibe a thousand years' worth of history in a single glance. For the average person, this might be a thrill. For Suzanne Coletrane, exposure to this abundance of history was like drinking salt water from a fire hose.

Oh, how I hate history. The fact that she was a skilled teacher of history made her choke on the irony. For her, military history and military medical history were the pinnacles of the worst versions of this source of malcontent. While Mickey, Russell, and she were permanently stationed at Aberdeen Proving Ground, or even when on temporary duty missions to remote sites, the guys used to bore her to tears with historical dialogues, discussions, and discourses, arguing fervently into the wee hours. *Why didn't I at least pay attention to their historical jousting and bantering?* Instead, she would long be in bed with ear plugs ignoring their voices which could still be heard debating some obscure point of history.

"A little pain then might have saved me so much pain now. Why couldn't I have just buckled down and—"

"Dr. Coletrane, if I might be so bold … " a pleasant alto voice behind her interrupted her shameless self-flagellation. Suzanne turned to make eye contact with a very mousey-looking man.

"I'm the Virgin." He received a blank stare. "The librarian from the Greyfriars Square Library. We spoke earlier."

"Oh, yes, Mr. More, thank you for seeing me. Did you just say 'virgin'?"

"Indeed. Please, call me Jude—a bit less formal and straight away, don't you think, Dr. Coletrane?"

"As you wish, Jude."

"A mite easier as it rolls off the tongue, don't you think? How is it that I can best help you, Doctor?"

"I am here to find some fish?" She looked quizzically at Jude, hoping he understood her.

"Oh dear, if you will forgive the metaphor, although quite appropriate in this case, I do believe you have the right church but the wrong pew. That is to say, Dr. Coletrane, the town of King's Lynn will certainly provide you all the seafood that your heart could desire, but here at the Greyfriars Tower, I'm afraid just a spot of tea and some biscuits in the research room would be the best I could muster."

"Could you possibly walk me through the leaning tower and let me see if I find the substance I seek, Jude?"

"I'm sorry, Dr. Coletrane, but as I said on the phone, you caught me today as I am headed to the local Barclay's Bank for a financial transaction, then out of town with my brother. I'm afraid we have a commitment tomorrow for discussions on the mainland."

"Let me be candid, Jude. I am in a position where there is some significant data to be found here and I really don't know the right questions to ask. Can you start by giving me some general history of the Greyfriars?"

"Dr. Coletrane, I sincerely have to get to the Barclay's. I really would like to help you, honestly, however—"

"Then do so, Virgin, and stop wasting the time neither of us have." Suzanne's voice shifted into Viking mode. "My two colleagues and I have stumbled upon some crucial information tied in with atypical chemical munitions that were found in Poland. One colleague has just left Bautzen, Germany, and is headed for something that sounds like *pirate's eye*, which is probably some lost buccaneer cove in Poland or something. The other has been pulled from Special Operations in the desert to go to Burano, Italy. I now know that human lab studies were done in Natzweiler, France, and somehow involved in the mix are some book-shelving Templars helping Christians at risk. Toss in a fish or two; add a dollop of confusion; three jiggers of restless, sleepless nights; my calico cat who might be destitute; and you have what is standing in front of you, Jude. I am a woman on the edge—pushing the envelope on time and what I need to know is divided between here and Bristol. You are my only hope, Jude. So, start somewhere—anywhere. Tell me why gray versus black, or even white; why some friars have made a tower of significance; or why I need to locate a fish. Start explaining *something*. Virgin, this is very, very important!"

"Dr. Coletrane, please!" Jude looked at her with startled, wide eyes. "You ask much, and I don't know quite where to start. I must say I have to agree with your assistant who said you could be very persuasive—"

"Assistant? What assistant? I have no assistant."

"A Black fellow—funny, I can't remember his name," said Jude, baring his teeth in a tight-lipped grimace and jerked his eyebrows and chin in an awkward fashion.

"Mr. More, I'm not sure what you're putting in your Earl Grey tea these days, but other than the colleagues of whom I just spoke, I have no other compatriots and definitely no assistants. What is it that this alleged assistant of mine asked of you?" Suzanne looked directly at the Virgin's face whose lips went pale and silent, giving rise to a mild quiver. *Holy Shih Tzu and shitake pasta!* Suzanne realized all too late that, yet again, she missed the obvious. She pursed her lips tightly and shoved her thumbs inside her LBE with a jerk.

"Allow me," a man's husky voice from behind her broke the awkward silence. "I asked our good friend Mr. More here to tell me what you were researching in England and France, when you should be investigating bunkers in Poland."

Without turning around, Suzanne said, "How's the world's oldest captain? It's still captain, even though the bars you wear are recycled military gear, right?"

"It's nice to see you too, sweetheart."

Suzanne turned around to see Jean Dalton standing behind her, his .45-caliber pistol drawn with the safety disengaged.

"That would be Colonel Doctor sweetheart to you, Captain. What's with the gun? Feeling a little sexually inadequate these days?" Suzanne's question resonated more with disgust than fear.

This is one man, and Saki would agree, whose life could definitely be improved by a horrific and tragic death. Talk about a case of inmates holding the prison keys. How does he manage to be at the right place at the right time? Some men are born bastards but you, Dalton, are one hundred percent a self-made man.

46

Banking for Kicks

Greyfriars Tower Plaza
Kings Lynn, England

"Put away the gun, Dalton ... or if you're planning to shoot, at least release the safety."

"Nice try, Doctor." Never shifting his gaze, Dalton smiled. He knew that if Blythe—the head of the Institute of Chemical Defense—had not given him a job all those years ago then he would most likely be peddling popsicles in Tunisia. Today Dalton was peddling again. It didn't look, however, as if Suzanne was interested in buying. "The old man seems to think you are working off a different agenda. Tell me it ain't so, darling."

"What I am doing is not even remotely any business of yours, Dalton. As for Colonel Blythe, if he has an issue with my agenda, he needs to take it up the chain and talk to Dr. Wunschmann, and if that isn't enough, he can just—"

"Why aren't you in Dyhernfurth, Colonel?" Dalton raised his voice with tempo as he tried to increase his intimidation factor. "The boss sent you to Poland."

"The same reason you aren't in hell, Captain. It's the right place for you, but it just wasn't the right time to go!"

"Careful, ma'am, your mouth isn't bulletproof."

"Neither is yours." Without waiting for the next retort, Suzanne kicked directly into the barrel of the weapon, automatically engaging its safety. Dalton tried to react, but before he could, a half-full sack of coins smacked the side of his head. He crumpled down to the ground, unconscious.

Suzanne and Jude looked up at the same moment. As their eyes met, Jude queried, "Is he dead?"

"I hope so, Virgin." She felt his carotid. "No such luck. When he wakes up, he'll probably wish he was. Anyway, nice shot, kiddo!" Suzanne cast around for the gun, retrieved it, and tucked it into the waistband at the small of her back.

"Oh my, it'd be quite messy if, perchance, I'd killed him." Virgin checked the inside pockets of his coat. Satisfied that everything was where it should be, he exhaled. "Seems only fitting, though, that this sack of sterling, which was given to me by the church square librarians, should go to this kind of use."

"How's that, Virgin?" Suzanne asked, still trying to fully catch her breath.

"These quid were donations to the Greyfriars Tower to be used in its best interest."

"And that would be?"

"Well, Dr. Coletrane, part of the donations collected are required to be used to pay the dustman to clean up the grounds of all the unwanted, discarded rubbish."

"You are right on the money there, no pun intended. Call it dust or garbage, it still links with Dalton by any web search engine," said Suzanne, rubbing the tightness out of her cramping right hip. "My friend Russell taught me that move as a defense against less reputable types and home security salesmen. I never thought I would ever use it. Thank God it went to this slimeball. Thank you for the cash deposit, by the way."

"You're most welcome, Doctor. There are advantages to an English pound actually weighing a pound." Jude More patted the bottom side of his cash bag.

"Frankly, Jude, I really didn't anticipate any help from you."

"I'm sorry, Dr. Coletrane, Captain Dalton said he would see to it that something ill would befall my brother and me if I didn't cooperate."

"For the record, his title of captain is a campus rank. He isn't in any way worthy to wear the rank though he has done so longer than probably any military officer alive or dead since Christ was a corporal." Suzanne snickered and audibly snorted at her own attempt at humor.

"Don't worry, Dr. Coletrane," Jude monotoned, "we'll just have the authorities from the constabulary on the adjacent block come and haul away the disreputable captain … I mean Mister … oh, dear …."

"I believe the title you're looking to find is *Deutsch-bag*."

"Yes, I imagine so. Our authorities will secure Mr. D. Bag Dalton until the Air Police from the Mildenhall or Lakenheath US Air Bases can retrieve him."

The Virgin seemed very flustered regarding the whole matter. Suzanne, however, kept pondering the implication of Dalton's involvement. *How best to explain this to Colonel Blythe?* She was uncertain. Blythe must have been really worried if he sent a goon to babysit her. This was peculiar because he never worried about her mission execution in the past. *Did Dalton just play the situation his way or is he responding to someone else's direct order? Either way, how many more goons from ICD are just over the horizon—or behind my shoulder for that matter? How much do I need to tell Mickey? Well, first things first. I need to probe this kettle of fish.*

"What I need now is that tour of your leaning tower, Jude."

"And so you shall receive it, my good doctor." The Virgin smiled, paused, and kneeled to the ground. He picked up a small wooden object.

"What is this?"

"Looks kind of like a dog. Therefore, I would say that is a Jean Dalton carving of an elephant. It probably fell out of his pocket." Suzanne took the carving and shoved it into her cargo pocket.

"You really don't like the fellow, do you?"

"Not even a frog hair … "

"I never realized that American frogs had hair," mused the Virgin as he took Suzanne's elbow and led her, still slightly limping, to the north side of the tower. There he unlocked a wooden door. Once inside, his voice rang with pride as he espoused the greatness of his leaning tower. The Virgin was in his element.

"Dr. Coletrane, this tower was built by Franciscan Friars who were girded in gray, floor-length robes accentuated with a black hood. They were called Grey Friars. In conjunction with Knights Templar and masons, who were friends of the Templars, the purpose of the tower gained an additional slant, no humor intended," smiled Jude.

Suzanne smiled back at the Virgin and slyly winked. "Absolutely no humor taken, Virgin."

Jude nodded, pulled at his collar, then cleared his throat. "Alluvial clay, used by wool sorters, was placed in great quantities into the foundation of the church and the tower. This, in conjunction with the silt, and the loss of the church walls as supports, all led to the eventual lean."

"What evidence do you have of the use of alluvial clay, Virgin?"

"Please, ma'am, the Grey Friars were quite famous for their friar's wool. The alluvial clay was heavily used in the wool sorting industry."

"You know, in the medical management of chemical casualties, alluvial clay is often used as a field expedient decontamination source for sulfur mustard victims. It absorbs the chemical poison quick and slick. Its consistency is quite soft. But I am struggling to understand why something so malleable would be used as a building foundation? That is an engineering idiocy."

"Really?" the Virgin mused. "I think it rather brilliant."

"Brilliant, are you daft? A tower built on such a foundation is doomed to lean and fall. Why would anyone build a tower to fall?"

"Why indeed?" Jude More, with great care and reverence, reached into his coat pocket and then handed Suzanne a very old-looking document laminated in plastic.

CHAPTER 9

1) By the time the sun sets, only a memory of the light remains. Although work can be done, the need to rest now outweighs the need to grow in brightness.

2) At the end of the day, John had produced thrice times twice. The needs of the multitudes now ruled his personal need and his personal light dwindled to naught.

3) John's stone need not falter as its place is to sequester and protect, giving it greater purpose than that of the wood.

4) The stone itself holds no glory. Forever having the enduring stone pales to the wood which holds within it a gift from the Father. Let those with eyes which are enlightened with the spirit see.

5) Stony fingers clasp tightly a wooden core. Bathed in darkness for none to see until the time when shadows reveal.

6) The sealed tomb within the stone reflects the secret kept. The guardians will pass their charge to generation upon generation until nature's mountains and man's towers fall.

7) The three that once stood together will only be brought into sameness when their seals are broken and the secret revealed. There will be no question unanswered and no fact unknown.

8) One stony cloak gives a hint of what will be, by providing man with what was, and will never again be.

9) At sunset the leaning tower possesses either the longest shadow or none. Such is the soul of the wicked who sees with his eyes and understands for naught.

10) At the end of the day, we rest our heads for our work is done. Not one deed of our good works gains us entrance to the Father. Only if we possess the light through the Lamb will we stand without shadow before God the Father.

Eyeing the plasticized document, Suzanne asked, "What is this, Jude?"

"Dr. Coletrane, you ask but I believe you already know. It is your fish. That is a part of a book of instructions written to the guardians of a great secret. This tower was built to fall."

"How is this gibberish my fish and, more importantly, as I asked before, why would any person build a tower to purposely fall?" She passed the document back to him.

"The fish is a symbol which is imprinted on every chapter heading. This is chapter nine. Verse six is the charge I, and those like me, have been given since the beginning of Christianity."

"You're a Brit, Jude. Speak English."

"It probably won't help. I speak English and you understand American."

Suzanne nodded her head in mutual affirmation. "Two great nations separated by a common language."

"Dr. Coletrane, did you not see the carved symbol of the fish on the west wall arch?" As he spoke, Jude transferred it back to his inner coat pocket. "Did you not see the weathervane on the rooftop whose shape epitomizes a fish? You may not know it yet, but this paper is the very fish which you seek. Let's go to Bristol and meet Justice James. You will better understand, and I will explain much on the way." Jude escorted Suzanne out of the tower and back toward her car.

"So, Virgin, is that a title or a way of life?"

"Please, Doctor, it would be best if the journey of that conversation became a path less traveled."

"Ah, I see. It's a way of life." Suzanne broke into a melodic laugh. In the distance, Dalton's moans could be heard as the bobbies took him into temporary custody. Suzanne continued to chuckle as she recalled the excellent bank shot to the temple which knocked Dalton into submission. She reigned herself in. *Time to drive into the British sunset with Dalton's pistol, my jujitsu, and a punch-packing Virgin. You know, life just doesn't get much better than this.*

47

The Church Mouse

Hotel
Burano, Italy

*M*an! Russell shook his head as he dropped his gear. *What was I thinking?* He flopped onto the bed in the hotel room. *There are a hundred dangerous reasons why I shouldn't have pushed myself to Burano in the wee hours. It's a bold move to gain access to a city which has no roadway connection to mainland Italy when fully conscious, let alone in the condition I am now.* He passed out immediately.

However, validation of his risky choice arose with the dawn.

The smell of *bussolai buranelli* wafted into his window from the pastry shops on the island. This provided a metaphysical aroma of therapeutic healing that he knew Douglas Coletrane could, and would, professionally endorse. Russell still felt somewhat disoriented by the steady tug of fatigue from the activities of the last twenty-four hours. However, after a delicious *bussolai* Italian doughnut washed down by a double cappuccino, he concluded that he had made the best possible decision.

It was eight o'clock and the Venetian waters rippled off the beautiful little island. The morning sun stirred up the vivid purples, pinks, and blues of the brightly painted rainbow row of houses along the canals. *The island's church has a leaning tower and is the first of four that Suzanne said Mickey wanted investigated.* However, at this time, Russell felt that the chance of the church and its leaning tower being open to the public was quite slim. As he strolled into the opening of a wide piazza, he could see the broad side of a church situated on the far side of the square. He pondered what he would do if, indeed, this destination was securely closed.

Pointing to the church's leaning belltower, Russell approached one of the lace artisans on the piazza to gain better information. Comfortably sitting at her kiosk, she was executing her art flawlessly just like those who engaged the trade since the early 1500s. It was good that he met her as she could best give him directions to the lace museum there on the Baldassare Galuppi Square. The museum, of course, was inconsequential to Russell. Unlike his artist mother, Russell wouldn't know a fine lace shift from Shinola. However, it confirmed that the Church of San Martino Vescovo, the destination of this morning's stroll, was indeed the very church which occupied the same square and was sitting next to his leaning tower of interest.

When Russell arrived at the church's entrance, his worst fear was realized. *The church doors are securely locked.* Russell huffed. *It was a long shot, but then again, what else could I do?*

"Of all the rotten luck," Russell said. "Want a seat at church and can't buy a way in. Lord Jesus, I need some help here."

"Did you come to pray?" said a voice in English, sporting a heavy Italian accent. "I ask because many visitors just come to view Tiepolo's piece, *The Crucifixion*, that he made in 1723."

"I know the piece. It was his first major church commission. Wasn't it? I guess I had forgotten it was here." Russell's knowledge of art and earnest love for Italy produced a smile on the face of the Italian.

The man was shorter than Russell and his skin was deeply tanned. He was vested in a guayabera shirt which, as far as Russell knew, was not typically Italian. His hair was black and full, with streaks of gray at the temples. His face was stern, but kind, and Russell felt no threat, so he continued to converse.

"I came to speak to the church master or keeper of the leaning tower here in Burano," said Russell.

"What would you say to the church master or tower keeper?" the Italian asked.

"Well ... " Russell paused for a minute to think through his response. *This is going to sound insane.* "I would say that I am in search of fish where leaning towers fall." Russell braced for the startled response as the Italian searched his face.

"Please, be so kind as to walk with me," said the Italian, never blinking. "I might have something that satisfies like a *bussolai buranelli*."

"That would be hard to imagine. Nothing satisfies like a *bussolai buranelli*," Russell said chuckling.

"So, you are knowledgeable both in our art and our local cuisine? Maybe you already know what I have to share with you." From his pocket the man produced some keys and unlocked the great doors of the church. Russell followed the Italian like a hungry dog hoping for a piping handout. The man spoke as he walked across the brown and white diamond flooring, his voice and steps echoed within the nave of the church.

"Your journey for this information has long been anticipated."

"You know what I am searching for?"

"I know that when the seekers of the fish come, they often do not know fully what they ask."

"I believe that this is quite true of me, Mister ... "

"I am Simeone. I am the Church Mouse here and I am responsible for protecting the holy site and its holy relics. The painting is one of the treasures that many seek. The tower and its lean rarely attract visitors. It makes me sad." They had reached a door in the back of the church upon which his name appeared in shiny glass inlay.

"Well, Simeone Giovanni Giordano, you have guessed correctly. I *am* on a quest to find something that my mind does not see clearly. How is it that you know what I seek?"

"Mister … I'm sorry, if you said your name, I do not recall it."

"Russell Lange, Dr. Russell Lange."

"I am sorry. Not mister, but Dr. Russell Lange, please sit here in my office. I have to tell you a story that will help you understand about the things you seek. Do you have time?"

"My time is yours."

"I venture to guess that Venice itself is also on your agenda today."

"It is."

"There are lost books which tell about a man named John."

"Like your name?"

"Yes, I guess it's like my name. In Italian Giovanni is like John. Unlike me, the John I have to tell you about was a skilled artisan. He worked wood and stone. His hands created great things and terrible things. John's skill was put to use by the Romans. He was commissioned to make a flogging post of stone which would be beautiful, functional, and terrible. The specifics of the stone flogging post were so exact that John was left with several imperfect versions before producing the final product."

Glancing around the office, Russell continued to listen. On the bulletin board next to where he sat, his eyes caught a solitary paper amidst an abundance of announcements and bulletins. It was titled with two words: Chapter Five. *Huh, wonder if that's the end of a short book or early in the story of a long novel.* From what he could ascertain, the way the text flowed, the book had to be short. It certainly wouldn't be a best seller. *What does a biblical artisan named John have to do with fish, flowers, and chemicals found in Poland? Is this all just a waste of time?* It was quite possible that Simeone was telling the right story to the wrong person or vice versa. He decided to give Simeone a bit more time before excusing himself and venturing onward into Venice.

48

Of Potatoes and Fish

Leaning tower of Burano
Burano, Italy

"To make a long story longer … " Simeone paused to scan Russell's face. He hoped that this vessel, in the trustworthy shape of Dr. Russell Lange, had the capacity to hold and fully understand the vital information which must be given to those who appropriately seek the fish. Simeone took a deep breath and continued. "John the mason and woodworker realized that he could not meet the deadline and instead provided the Roman governor a suitable alternative. That is, the same specifications in a flogging post but all in wood instead of stone as was initially requested. The Roman governor accepted this as a temporary fix until such time that the final stone version was complete."

"This flogging post made of freshly cut wood was the one the Romans used when beating Jesus Christ, wasn't it?"

"Yes. It was used only once and then replaced with the final stone version."

"What happened to the wooden flogging post?"

"Knowing that it had the potential to be a relic and worshipped in association to a potential messiah, the Romans had it taken away and burned."

"Who burned it?"

"A Roman unit from Syria which was in the process of deploying to the frontier. The unit was given the post and the mission for its destruction."

"They didn't do it, did they?"

"No, Dr. Lange, the legionnaire who was in charge of these Syrian archers secretly took the post back to John and asked him to hide it in a place where no Roman could bring harm to it. Tiberius, the legionnaire, received from John a substitute post which he took to the frontier and burned so that none knew of the deception."

Russell's hand drifted subconsciously to the healing wound on his face from

Nabil's blade knocking him to the desert floor. Tracing it gingerly, he pursed his lips and asked, "Why would a Roman do that?"

"Why indeed?" Simeone echoed musingly. For many moments he searched the contours of Russell's face. "Some alleged it was the love of a father for his dead son."

Russell's dark eyebrows raised a few notches. "A dead son who had been crucified?"

"Possibly."

"I don't understand. Are you saying that a Roman was the father of Jesus?" Russell asked.

"Some say it is so."

"Scientifically speaking, without a father, Jesus would have only half the human chromosomes needed to live as a human entity."

"Yes, Dr. Lange. Science claims that humans with the incorrect number of chromosomes are very visibly abnormal."

"This is true. However, doesn't this muck up the whole religious idea of a virgin birth? Mary cannot be a virgin if her son has a biological father, Simeone."

"Prophecy dictates that Mary, superintended by the Holy Spirit, had to be a virgin and pregnant."

"How can a woman become pregnant and still be a virgin?"

"AI—"

"Alien intelligence?"

"What?"

"AI, alien intelligence. Some people postulate that—"

"Dr. Lange, I was speaking about AI—artificial insemination."

"Artificial insemination, an ancient idea? That's a stretch," said Russell. "You're not purporting that artificial insemination existed in the first century. I hardly think so."

"As it exists now, I would have to agree. However, consider a first-century version."

"What do you mean?"

"Potatoes."

"Potatoes don't inseminate."

"Potatoes are known to be the earliest form of birth control."

"I thought we were talking about promoting pregnancy, not preventing it. Wait a minute … oh my God, I see it!" Russell exclaimed.

"Yes, now you understand!"

"Yes, I do. If the very potato which has been carved to be used as a cervical diaphragm—a form of contraception—was instead used as a semen reservoir and then placed like a diaphragm against a dilated cervix, it would seal and virtually guarantee pregnancy."

"Indeed, a virgin could then become pregnant having never been penetrated by a man in a sexual act."

"Why would a Roman soldier, or any man for that matter, defer to this type of pregnancy rather than the way nature intended?"

"Superintended and guided by the Holy Spirit, one could speculate that maybe the Roman was wounded so that he couldn't have sexual intercourse."

"Maybe his sexual desires demanded external ejaculations to achieve a heightened level of erotic pleasure...."

"Or maybe," said Simeone, "the hand of God guided him, if it was him, in this manner so that the miracle of a virgin giving birth was secured as was prophesied."

"So, science and religion *can* walk hand in hand?"

"As a possibility, it seems so, now doesn't it?"

"I don't know that I am comfortable with Christ's genetic lineage being from Rome. What if the Roman was not the biological father, but just the patron?"

"Then the father could still be Joseph via the direction of the Holy Spirit and thus, the Hebrew lineage would be conserved." Simeone tapped his temple. "But don't forget, Mary's family line also was based within the lineage of King David." Simeone rocked back and clapped his hands. "All things are possible with the Holy Spirit. Man seeks for explanations and many times, like a child, cannot understand the explanation when given."

"Going back to John," redirected Russell, "what did John do with the actual wooden flogging post?"

"John took the freshly carved, singly used, bloodied and battered flogging post and placed it in a stone shell of the same shape but slightly larger in size."

"Ingenious," exhorted Russell. "This essentially creates a sarcophagus which would tightly seal the one greatest source of Jesus Christ's physical body and blood."

"Yes, Dr. Lange, the only true Holy Grail. All other versions pale in comparison."

"Incredible."

"John, being guided by the Holy Spirit, took two more of the failed stones and hollowed them out as well. He then placed wooden flogging posts within them. To prevent confusion, only upon one did he carve an identifying mark. He carved upon both the wood and the stone a symbol constructed of overlapping curved lines representing a fish."

"Simeone, is this the fish you think I am seeking—is this the fish you are planning to give me?"

"No and no, Doctor. I cannot give you what I myself do not have. I am telling you a story to help you better understand what you seek. May I continue?"

"Forgive me. Please continue."

"With the help of the Fish People, followers of Christ, some or all sarcophagi were buried in the bowels of the Temple of Solomon protected only by the Staff of Moses and the Rod of Aaron, collectively known today as the Rods of Power. You may know this location today as Temple Mount in the old city of Jerusalem. After that, there is indication of them being moved to outer locations."

"Where would those be?"

"Dr. Lange, tell me what you know of the lost books."

"Weren't they books which were prevented from entering the Bible and were found at Qumran on the Dead Sea and somewhere in Egypt as well?"

"Yes and no. They were books that, for one reason or another, were not placed in the Bible. The Second Book of Benjamin was never intended to go into the Bible. It was written for the sole purpose of providing instructions on how to hide—in plain sight—the secrets which God wanted kept."

"In 'plain sight'?"

"In places where everyone could see, but only a few would know the significance—"

"Enter, leaning towers," interjected Russell.

"Yes, the leaning towers, with the help of masons, were intentionally built to mark the location of—"

"—the sites for the three stone sarcophagi grails."

"No, Dr. Lange, I said that I could not give you what I do not have. The falling towers mark the location of the Second Book of Benjamin."

"You have the Second Book of Benjamin?" asked Russell.

"I have a portion of it."

"How many towers are there and how many Books of Benjamin are there?"

"Eight, I think."

"Eight books or eight towers?"

"Three books and at least eight towers. In the First Book of Benjamin, much is discussed about visions, songs, poems, and God's plan for Benjamin's life. The Second Book of Benjamin was written with a different intent."

"What was the intent?"

"To hide and protect. Inasmuch, it was written and reproduced only once. The original of the Second Book of Benjamin was bound and held in secret. The copy, a version of the first, was unbound and distributed."

"In plain sight."

"There is no greater secret than the one that everyone sees, but only a few know. Isn't that a little like the discipline known as medicine?"

"Hmmm, maybe." Russell stroked his chin musingly. "I'm not sure I understand."

"How do you Americans say it? You may not be able to see the forest for the trees."

"Then tell me more about it."

"There is only one Second Book of Benjamin and, as I said, it has been transcribed only once."

"Where is the original?"

"The location of the original is unknown to me. The transcribed copy lies within the leaning towers."

"All leaning towers?"

"No. There are many towers and only the tower keeper of each tower knows if they hold a fish."

"Fish?"

"Yes, each of the chapters has a fish symbol inscribed upon them like the one carved into the true Holy Grail. In the old days, the fish were kept on fiche, and this confounded the matter a bit further. I remember one time when—"

"Which chapter resides here?" Russell interrupted.

"You should know—you were looking at it earlier."

"I don't understand."

"Yes, you do. I saw your eyes scan it as we chatted earlier."

Russell stared around the room, puzzled.

Simeone pulled down a document in a plastic sleeve from the cork bulletin board and handed Russell the fifth chapter of the Second Book of Benjamin.

Russell mouthed the words, "In plain sight."

CHAPTER 5

1) It was upon the eaves of John's house that the rain water fell quickly; for there is nothing to hold back the flooding energy.

2) John's father, a priest, guided him in the footpath of his own. But when the light left John's eyes, he had produced three great works which left him cursed among all men.

3) The wood he created began in innocence and in the end was bathed by the blood of the innocent. Can then a curse truly be a curse?

4) The wood uncased by stone is vulnerable to those who have ill will as their guide. The sealed wood will preserve in time that which will serve as hope for all of mankind.

5) The uncarved stone reflects the hope of the buyer. The final sculpture, though sterile in its existence, serves to encase the hopes and dreams of believers. It is the charge of the guardians to protect these hopes and dreams.

6) The guardians will grow, peak, and fade but will never lose their purpose. Only by substance the stone endures longer.

7) The flawed stones began short of the light. Over time, they too protected and served our master. Although apart when the light fails, their purpose reveals that the wicked shall have been led astray.

8) The rocky shroud thrice made in the alpha and twice undone over time. At omega, the third stands like a tower testament to the love of our God and by His son we are made worthy.

9) A tower that leans either has no shadow in the morning or the longest shadow of the day. The ones who follow the shadow for guidance live lives that are lost in the morning or lost at the end of days.

10) Learning from the light is weakest at the dawn and dusk of our lives. Initially we learn by seeing. At midday we learn most with our eyes closed and our hearts open.

"Is this the haphazard manner in which sacred documents are revered and protected by select tower keepers?" Russell chastised.

"I can think of no better way. Can you?"

"I could have easily stolen it when you weren't looking."

"But you didn't."

"But I could have."

"Did the words hold that much meaning for you when you glanced at them earlier?"

"Actually, no they didn't, Simeone."

"Didn't you deduce that its value was limited since it was easily accessed?"

"I did think it had limited value to me," Russell conceded.

"Do these words *now* hold meaning to you?"

"Honestly—no. The flow of the text is poor, and the individual verses hold little meaning."

"Would they have held meaning for you outside of the church had you read it upon the wall?"

"Probably not," Russell replied as he stashed the paper away.

"Then I guess their security was never in question."

Russell knew that Simeone was correct. He remembered that in his junior year in high school, his mother had handled a similar situation with great wisdom.

✠ ✠ ✠

Daphne Deloris—DiDi—Lange received about 130 framed art pieces in wooden crates for a joint art-philatelic display to be held in Athens, Georgia, at the University of Georgia Coliseum. She never dreamed that the crating for the numerous William-Adolphe Bouguereau art pieces and the Albert Coyette stamp collection would become a problem, but they did. Because of a local labor dispute, a ground maintenance crew disagreement blossomed into a quasi-strike. All the empty art crates were left for days in the open breezeways of the coliseum. The manpower, time, and fuel to remove these crates were behemoth. Russell watched his mother's brilliance in action.

DiDi neatly stacked every crate against an unsecured portion of the loading dock area. Then on each one she placed a tag upon which she wrote a monetary value. When done, she left for the evening. In the morning when she returned, all the crates had been pilfered. By advertising the alleged value of a given object, she accomplished her desired outcome.

✠ ✠ ✠

Russell surmised that Simeone had done what DiDi had, but in reverse. Realizing now the incredible value of the document in his hand, Russell offered to return the chapter back to Simeone, but the Church Mouse refused. "Hold on to it and return it to me after we come back from the Church of San Giorgio dei Greci in Venice. There is still more for you to learn."

Russell sighed. "Can we at least get a coffee on the way?"

He knew that his sharpest mentality was sorely needed, but fatigue played combat volleyball with his attempts at maintaining a focused attention. This day, he feared, would be longer than the hour hand's shadow on the church clock.

49

Son of the Right Hand

Route to Venice
Burano, Italy

"Water as roads … water as streets … water as alleys … " Russell gazed across the expanse of water. "No place in the world has this reality for everyday life except Venice."

"All other attempts … " Simeone drew in a deep breath then audibly exhaled a sound which connoted failure.

"Yes?"

"That is all. Only in Venice." Simeone smiled then thumped Russell on the back congenially. "Come, you must be hungry."

After a pleasant lunch, they took the water taxi from Burano and found themselves arriving in Venice, very early in the afternoon, at the San Zacoana docking station. From the landing, they strolled along with the Canal di San Marco on their right as they passed the Palace Dandolo and the church Santa Maria della Visitazione on the waterfront. A quick left turn into the narrow Calle di Pieta led to some twists and turns, then under some arching homes and gardens, until finally the bridge at the Calle del Magazen stood in front of them.

Russell loved the way that the most beautiful streets of Venice are all waterways. A gondola stroked by which carried a pair of people back toward the Canal di San Marco. Russell surmised correctly that a quick gondola ride would have streamlined their morning walk, but without the ambulation through back alleys and byways, the journey would have been much less satisfying. They would have missed the pleasant sidewalk cafes, tiny glass figurines, carnival masks, and a variety of lace shops intertwined with the unending litany of Venetian history that formed a basis of much of the life that people live today. When Russell and Simeone arrived at the second bridge, the view stopped Russell dead in his tracks. *Italy is truly a postcard in living motion.*

Simeone didn't lead him across the bridge over the canal. Instead, he made an immediate left along a narrow walk following the signs to a Greek museum—Istituto Ellenico di Venezia. Russell stood in front of the museum and saw, to his right, the courtyard of a Greek Orthodox church complex. The church itself stood to the far left and the campanile tower leaned over the canal off to the far right.

San Giorgio dei Greci had a sign on the front door indicating that it was closed to visitors today from one to two-thirty.

"Shouldn't we have arrived when Saint George of the Greeks Church was open?" Russell asked, almost accusingly.

"It *is* open," commented Simeone.

"Not according to this posted schedule." Russell traced his finger in a line under the printed times.

"The church has its schedule and I have mine. I also happen to have these," said Simeone brandishing a ring of rustic-looking skeleton keys.

"You are the key master for this church and this leaning tower as well?"

"Can you name anyone better suited?"

"Who can?" Russell smiled, conceding he had been bested. "You said there was more for me to learn in this church. What would that be?"

"There is a painting inside. I think you know of it, but it isn't what you think."

Special Greek Orthodox services were being held as the pair quietly passed into the rear of the church. Russell noted that the church and the service had some unusual aspects compared to what he was used to seeing. First, there was no congregational seating—not a single pew, not a single chair. The membership stood quietly in the nave of the church surrounded by a cornucopia of Byzantine masterpieces. Second, there were four priests, each wearing distinctively different religious garbs as they chanted and sang within a cloud of incense. Third, during the Holy Communion, a symbolic gold right hand was held for the congregation to kiss and revere. *It's so beautiful ... why does this service have to be held under lock and key?*

As the lines of the congregation processed to the front of the nave, Simeone led Russell around the Holy Communion to the center door that led to the back office. Simeone pointed to a painting resting midpoint above the crosspiece of the office door as he plunged through the propped saloon doors. Russell paused only momentarily, noting the details of this rendition of the Last Supper. His mother's profession had given Russell a tremendous appreciation for life's details via unparalleled exposure to art of all kinds. Russell loved paintings and sculptures in particular and could appreciate them deeply. Some people, like Suzanne, could precisely recall written words with great ease; others, like Russell, had great spatial aptitude. He could study art in his memory long after the lights were out. Under his breath, Russell softly thanked Mickey for having assigned him to two consecutive churches with a remarkable art presence.

Upon arriving to the rear office and shutting out the last of the sounds of the Holy Communion, Simeone looked straight into Russell's eyes and asked, "What did you think of the painting?"

"There were many paintings, all very beautiful and rich in religious history."

"The art of the Greeks stirs the soul. Would you agree?"

"The art, the perfect acoustics, the incense, the lighting—the seven lamps across the front and the three that split the nave—this ambiance bathes my spirit and stirs my soul more than I have words to describe."

"So, you can appreciate it?" Simeone pointed.

"Very much so. It seems only fitting that Byzantine-style paintings decorate a Greek Orthodox Church."

"What of the painting above the center office door?"

"It appeared to be of the Last Supper, though a version I have never seen."

"True, agreed. It is different. Is that all you saw?"

Russell closed his eyes and pulled the image into his mental visual field, his eyes darting under his lids. "I see a round, not rectangular, table with the Twelve Apostles in various conversations. Christ is clearly at the center of the table and the apex of symmetry in the painting."

"An interesting construct since a round table has no center seating. What did you see on the table?"

"I see a person, maybe a man or a woman, next to Christ's right hand, collapsed on the table. I see numerous decanters but only one goblet and one cup—neither in the reach of Christ."

"Intriguing, don't you think?"

"Also … " with his eyes still closed, Russell continued, "there are three large bowls on the table. I don't know what, if anything, was in the bowls. Wait … wait … I do see something. I see fish. By God, I see one fish in each pot."

"Excellent. These were the original Fish People."

"Being followers of Christ makes them all Fish People?"

"Yes, Dr. Lange, it does. The fish in the bowls also symbolically correlates well with a grail in a sarcophagus."

"I see that, Simeone."

"What brackets the body of the picture?"

"The edges of the bench have a high backing, almost like towers."

"Did you see the leaning tower?"

"I see a tower which leans toward Christ—arguably on the left-hand side of Christ, but most definitely on the right-hand side of Christ."

"Now for the most critical question, Dr. Lange. If you had to attribute a name to the leaning tower on the right-hand side of Jesus Christ, what would it be? Remember that Jesus was Hebrew and in the lineage of David, not Greek."

After a long silence, with a trace of defeat in his voice, Russell opened his eyes and yielded, "I honestly have no idea."

"You would name it Benjamin. Benjamin in Hebrew means 'Son of the Right Hand.' As emphasis, Jesus himself, in the painting, has his right hand raised. Isn't it reasonable that the Second Book of Benjamin and the towers which are falling have a timeless correlation beset by Christ himself?"

"One might think so."

"Many did think so and as such, they gave selfless service to God."

"The Fish People."

"Of course, but the soldiers of Christ who said, *'Nōn nōbis, Domine, nōn nōbis, sed nōminī tuō dā glōriam.'* What of them?"

"Knights Templar?"

"You know this saying of the Templar Knights, Doctor?"

"I should."

"Because of your studies?"

"Because of my pledge to be a Poor Companion of Christ and of the Temple of Solomon. I am a knight of the United States National Templar Order."

"I thought so." Simeone grabbed both of Russell's arms and gave them a strong, firm shake. *"Egli è un soldato e il cavaliere di Cristo."*

"Yes, I am a soldier and Knight of Christ," Russell smiled warmly. "Simeone, we must go back. I have a long drive ahead, first to Bologna and then onward to Pisa."

"No, you don't."

"I don't?"

"We do. I will go with you, Sir Russell. I will introduce you to the tower keepers in these cities. I know them quite well."

"I would like that very much."

Simeone smiled and escorted Russell back through the last of the church-goers receiving Holy Communion. They exited the side door and into a courtyard with a well. Simeone went over to the metal-gated, steel-barred door at the base of the leaning tower while Russell peered into the mouth of the well. Simeone motioned for Russell to come over; he wanted to show him the symbol of the fish which had been chiseled into the archway. Since Russell did not receive a subsequent invitation to climb the white tower, he meandered back to the twisted tree which sat along the sidewall in the courtyard. He waited patiently as Simeone retrieved the fish from somewhere within the tower. Simeone was back in a flash.

"Here is the fish that this leaning tower has guarded." Simeone handed him a laminated single-page document.

CHAPTER 8

1) As the sun arches late across the evening sky, its light starts to lessen and fade with each moment that it moves.

2) Since man strives to live life without regrets, John's skilled hands sought purpose in accepting the blood of the Lamb.

3) John's wooden post cries at the lashes upon our Lord. Let those that flick the whip shudder at the power of the wood over the stone.

4) The stone serves long as a lonely sentinel. When combined with the blood of the Lamb, it becomes a beacon in the darkness fourfold.

5) The stone as a mantle takes more of the mason's time and skill and so arrives later. Although thinner, it carries a greater depth. In the failing light, it grows ever stronger in purpose.

6) On the deathbed, the sins of man are purged with confession. Not so with the secret of the stone. Even beyond death, the seal must remain closed.

7) The seals of the paired guardians will be broken and within will be found the soft bark. The evil will be bested because in fulfilling their own desires, the will of God has been exercised.

8) One stony cloak holds the blood of the lamb which will give life that is not sanctioned in the light but instead hides deeply within the changing shadows.

9) The long shadow of a leaning tower can fade in the late of day. The short shadow lengthens as the sun sets.

10) Our flesh is weak and fails with time. Only His light sustains us. He is our stony mantle and the flesh and blood within are what we use to divert from the shadow and find our way to Him, our Father.

"This has meaning to you, Simeone?"

"Meaning and answers comes with time, Russell."

Russell ran the back of his fingers of one hand across his cheek and sighed. "Unfortunately," he replied, "I have very little of either."

50

The Wisdom of
the Three

"I cannot do this anymore, I just can't," the voice said. Out of the blackness, Mickey awakened to the sound of sincere, heartbreaking sobbing.

It was dark and Mickey's head was spinning in fatigue. He knew the voice but couldn't imagine why it would be in such distress. Mickey lifted up his weary frame, reached over and turned on the bedside lamp. Standing there beside the bed in her blue blazer, white button-down blouse, and plaid skirt was his precious wife, Loni.

"What are you doing here?" Mickey asked.

With tears of frustration streaming down her face she affirmed, "I just got back the set of corrections on my dissertation from the fifth, and final, graduate committee member, Dr. Boca-Alehauser." Loni paused long enough for Mickey to take a deep breath and posture for what he knew would be bad news.

Gritting his teeth through a veil of sleepiness, Mickey asked, "What did the good doctor have to say … again?"

"The changes he recommended have brought me back full circle to square one," Loni blubbered. "That means that the last four months of intensive revisions and rewrites were for naught. There is no possible way I could feel any lower right now. Honestly, Mickey, what good is it to have this burning desire for excellence when I am constantly reminded by my mentors just how mediocre I am? Has my reference of value become that skewed?"

Gruffly scratching his sleepy head like a caveman searching for the antelope on the seventh slope, Mickey tried to muster a well-thought-out and concise reply. Time evidently expired on him though, because before he could utter a word, Loni continued her tirade.

"Mickey, I am at the point that I don't even care if I ever finish this education doctorate. For all I care, Nova University can just take it back. After all, I already have a master of arts from the University of Pennsylvania, an Ivy League school, thank you very much. Anyway, how many people can say that they worked in the highly desired fellowship at the Cape Cod Autism Research Center with Dr. Lori Williams? That should count for something, eh?"

181

Mickey pulled back the bed covers, exposing his naked legs. Sliding the tired limbs over the rough sheets, he planted his long, muscular legs on the cool, concrete floor. *No more sleep tonight. Now is the time for unabashed eloquence.* Mickey cleared his throat and began the verbal medicine that his beleaguered Loni so needed to hear. Her sobs softened as he spoke. "Loni, for many years now, as my beloved wife, I have had the pleasure to witness your life, your works, and your tireless efforts. As such, one would think that I would instantaneously have the correct words for you. However, as I search for those words, they evade me. The only voice in my head belongs to a familiar, French-accented woman—"

"I'm sorry—are you saying that my mother is the voice in your head?" Loni wiped the tears from her eyes and raised her eyebrows skeptically at Mickey.

"Well, yes. Apparently, at this moment, she is."

"You are insinuating that she has the answer to my dissertation dilemma? If that is the case, I could have cut out the middleman and just called her directly."

"That I can't say. What I can say, with certainty, is that I recall your mom talking to someone and giving guidance to resolve a situation much like yours now."

"To whom is she talking and what is she saying, Mickey?"

"As strange as it sounds, it appears that what I am hearing is a conversation between your mother and sister."

"Mother and Jillian? Brace yourself. I'm not sure I want to hear any dialogue between those two. It often brought me to tears to see the disrespectful clash of those two strong wills."

"Cool your jets, Loni. The tone is quiet and instructive. Your mom is recalling an event at her Parisian dance school when she was just a girl."

"Dance school? We were talking about a doctoral dissertation. Mickey, I hardly think that a conversation between Jillian and Mom about dance could—"

"Quiet, Loni, these are your mom's words, not mine. Listen." Mickey's voice took on a parental tone quite uncommon for him. Accessing his best recall, he continued, "She's quoting some thoughts from Martha Graham."

"Martha Graham, the first lady of dance. The artist who danced for presidents in the White House?"

"The exact one."

"Mom certainly knows how to reference the best. What is she saying? That is, what piece of Martha Graham's wisdom does Mom have for Jillian?"

"She reminds us that each of us has an absolutely unique gift to the world."

"Mickey, isn't that rather obvious? I don't need Mom or Martha Graham to tell me this."

"Loni …."

"Okay. Zipped. I'm listening."

"The vision expressed by your work is possessed only by you, a person who exists as a unique entity since before the beginning of time. You were known to

Him before you were created within your mother's womb. So saith the Lord in Jeramiah. Because of this uniqueness, what you express in your work is unequivocally unique. If you surrender to this doubt placed in you by others, your work will cease to exist. It will never again exist through any other medium and it will be lost. The world will never have it."

"Mother and Martha said this?"

"I'm extracting the meaning from what your mother is telling your sister. I am paraphrasing the best I can."

"You're doing fine, it's just that … "

"Loni…."

"Zip." Loni mimicked locking her lips closed and throwing the key away.

"Your mom is telling Jillian—and you, by proxy—that it is not your business to determine how good, how valuable, or how comparable your vision is."

"Okay."

"It is your business only to keep your creative channel open. You do not even have to believe in yourself or your work. You have to keep yourself open and be keenly aware to the creative urges that motivate you."

"How can I keep my creativity alive when committee members make me believe that what I have produced has no value? There is no way to please them—or myself."

"No one who creates is ever pleased, Loni. Creation by definition is a constant voyage into the unknown. Do you think Michelangelo looked at his sculpted masterpiece, *David*, and said, 'This is perfect'? I am sure he saw minute flaws only his eyes could find which are absolutely invisible to the world."

"Am I then doomed to a life absent of any professional satisfaction?"

"Funny you should say that, Loni. That was exactly Jillian's response."

"What did Mother say?"

"She shared Martha Graham's wisdom that an artist's life was a life filled with a queer divine dissatisfaction, a blessed unrest that keeps them in a never-ending forced march—"

"—which makes those who create more alive than all the rest. Yes, I remember the snippet, Mickey. She said as much to me, more times than I can count. I see it now. It was hidden in plain sight. It took three *M*s to make me see it, but I see it now."

"The tape company?"

"No, silly. Three *M*s: Mom, Martha, and Mickey."

"Well three *M*s or not, I believe you've got the gist."

"Thanks, Mickey. I love you." Loni brightened into a smile. Mickey lifted the bed covers and patted the mattress next to him.

"Honey, come on, undress, lay down, and relax. Dissertation papers with corrections are on the credenza, right?"

"Yes."

"Scissors are in the top drawer along with the tape and a stapler?"

"Right."

"You rest while I sort through your work. I'll read some of the critiques, do some cutting and taping, and give you a version that encompasses the changes without altering your basic ideas as I know them. You can peruse them in the morning and solidify the final revision. Loni, your dissertation is a stone's throw away from being done. I promise."

"You are going to do all that right now?"

"Well sure. Why not?"

"Well, for one thing you're in your tiger-striped manties."

"Manties?" Mickey laughed every time she made this clothing reference.

"And since you don't have your manssiere ... " she paused, twisting her lips and mocking deep, contemplative thought. He smiled at her name for his genuine leather Italian holster-like armpit purse. Loni continued, " ... maybe the revisions can wait a bit."

"I thought you were upset?"

"I am ... I was."

"But not now?"

"*Well* ... " she stretched the sounds of the word, "maybe not *so* ...."

Loni ceased the coy behavior—the sly sensual look on her face gave rise to horror and distress.

"Duck! Duck! Duck!"

Mickey recoiled in fear but it was too late, he felt the impact on his left shoulder, a firm shake rocked his body, his visual field blackened, and Loni's face faded from view.

Leaning Tower of Pyrzyce:
Baxta Sowia — The Owl Tower

51

Bird Faced

Baszta Sowia plaza
Pyrzyce, Poland

"Doc ... Doc ... Doc," repeated Thaddeusz as he firmly held both of Mickey's shoulders and vigorously shook him. "Come on, wake up. It's time."

"Time for what?" Mickey tightened his focus. "You're not Loni."

"Come. We must go see the Owl. The sun will soon rise."

"Where's Loni?"

"Who?"

"My wife, where is she?"

"I have no idea where your wife is." Thaddeusz shrugged. "We're in Poland, Doc."

"I assume Martha Graham and the Owl aren't here either."

"Who?"

"Exactly," Mickey murmured, rubbing the sleep from his eyes.

Mickey's mind had to reset from the vivid hallucination that marred the past memory in his dream and reorient himself to the living nightmare he had been enduring since his arrival in Poland two days ago. When they arrived in Pyrzyce, south of Szczecin, it had been too late for Mickey to make the immediate connection with the Owl. So the pair of weary travelers succumbed to their fatigue and slept in the car along a road within the walls of the old city. Mickey was on the verge of physical exhaustion despite the forty winks he just caught.

In the waning night, the Baszta Sowia, the leaning tower in Pyrzyce, was the first thing on the docket, the very first thing. It was three o'clock in the morning and the sun was still soundly sleeping.

Having heard about the Owl for so long, Mickey had created a myriad of images of how this character could present itself. *Maybe the Owl came from one of the many Pomeranian misfits which historically found Pyrzyce a haven? If yes, then the Owl could be from the lineage of one of the Knights Templar who sought refuge here after their fall from grace.*

Thaddeusz was very anxious and very concerned that they weren't able to

186

make the visit when they had first approached the city. Mickey knew that the fact that he was bordering on exhaustion was of little consequence to Thaddeusz based on his constant refrain of "You can rest when you're dead."

Highway 3 approached Pyrzyce from the north and was the main thorough-fare to the center rotary which circled, auspiciously, just in front of the old city wall. A beautiful circular water fountain was spewing arches of vibrantly colored water into the cool night air. The town's inhabitants were nowhere to be seen on the benches which surrounded the water fountain. Thaddeusz exited the rotary on the road that had served as the city entrance between the two towers. Imme-diately after passing the leaning tower, Thaddeusz took a hard right and parked the car along the inside of the wall and near the foot of the tower.

Mickey glanced at the tower's backward lean into the city. It appeared that at one time it was an integral part of the city wall. The Baszta Sowia's life began by being connected via an archway with its twin tower which was now conspic-uous by its absence. The twin bastion fell hundreds of years before. Now leaning, the Baszta Sowia, or "Tower of the Owl," stood alone.

In true military fashion, Mickey surveyed his surroundings. On the wall across the way someone had spray painted the phrase, *Rise with the Fallen*. Mickey pondered the phrase as he looked at the base of the falling tower. On the inside of the city wall was mounted a blue plaque lettered in white which said, *ul Szkolna*. Mickey guessed it named the pavement upon which he would soon plant his full weight. He stepped out of the parked car and gazed up at tower doors on the equivalence of a second and third story.

"How do we gain entrance to a tower which has no ground-floor access?"

"Carefully." Thaddeusz cloaked a smile.

The pair skirted the inner city's wall until they found a recessed stone stairway which proceeded to a catwalk along the top of the wall. From there, they came to a camouflaged stone door and entered the tower at the level of the second floor. The second-floor room was small but beautifully lit. Not a hint of light had escaped into the night.

In the room, in a high-backed chair, sat a living caricature of a woman of undeterminable age. Against her left knee leaned a long walking stick carved with vines and flowers which, while delicate, also exuded strength. Around her shoulders she wore a cream-colored cloak fixed at the neck with a tunic. On the tunic was a black cross. Her hand seemed to be a claw which clasped the tunic front securely in place.

The Owl wore a thin veil that bridged her nose and obscured everything except a haunting pair of eyes. Her very large, round eyes were deeply set on a tiny face, far too small to possess eyes so large. The irises of her enormous eyes were so large that scarcely any whites could be seen. Mickey noticed that though her head moved, her eyes within the sockets never seemed to do so. In every mental variation of what he had concocted, Mickey never imagined the Owl to be anything close to the woman who sat in the high-backed chair before him. As the two men walked into her presence, the Owl stirred only slightly. Nonetheless, the sound of brushing feathers echoed within the acoustics of the tower's room.

Thaddeusz spoke to the Owl in a Pomeranian dialect of the Polish language. She responded to him in the same tongue but then reverted to heavily accented English.

"I smell fear, Thaddeusz. Who comes into my presence and harbors such fear?"

"If I am fearful, it lies not with this place or you," said Mickey. "My only fear is that I would be most unworthy to be here, now in your presence."

"He speaks eloquently and with a proven heart, Thaddeusz. You can learn much from this one." Redirecting her comments in Mickey's direction, she continued, "Don't worry, it is not you from which the fear emanates."

Taken aback, Thaddeusz mumbled something to her in a strange language. She stopped him cold with fingers raised.

Looking directly at Mickey she continued, "Tell me who you are and why is it that you have come here."

"My name is Mickey Peronne and—"

"You are Philip."

"Excuse me?"

"Did I stammer?"

"Why would you think that my name is Philip? Everyone who knows me calls me Mickey or Doc."

"I do not know you. To me Mickey is a mouse and Doc is a dwarf. This is not a fantasy tower, and you are not a cartoon. To me you are Philip. That is all."

"Well, ma'am, you are correct in some respect, I am *a Philip*—Michael Philip Peronne. Most just call me Mickey."

Nodding, she continued as if she never heard him, "Philip was an apostle."

"Yes, ma'am. I believe my parents knew that when they named me."

"Thaddeus was an apostle too." Thaddeusz groaned but the Owl continued, "Tell me, Philip, what do you know about my tower?"

"Honestly, it really will be easier if you just call me Mickey."

"If you insist … tell me, *Mickey*, what do you know about my tower?"

"I know that it is one of two that I must visit in Poland. I know that I have been on a great mission to find answers and I have learned all roads lead to you. I don't know why. I don't know who you are, how you got here, or how is it that you are destined to help me. I only know that our paths are destined to cross. By which name might I call you?"

"Again."

"I'm sorry." Mickey searched her face.

"You should have said 'I only know that our paths are destined to cross again.'"

"We have met before?"

"Do you wish for me to restate the obvious? If this is the case it will be a very long night with the value greatly diminished."

"Maybe it's fatigue … "

"Maybe not." The Owl peered at Mickey's puzzled face and then released the clip which allowed the veil to fall from her face. "Most people refer to me as the Owl. Few call me Szkolna anymore; but you call me what you like. Even though we have met before, this shall be our official beginning."

"It's you." Mickey's eyes scrolled from upper-left to lower-left as he frantically searched the logic side of his brain. "You were at Dyhernfurth, weren't you?"

"As were you, Mickey."

"I saw you from afar," said Mickey remembering her from the chemical site at the start of his journey. "You were talking with the yellow hard hat fellow—you were the bird-fa...." Mickey's face went beet red.

"There are meetings and there are *meetings*, Mickey. Because of that encounter, you stand before me today ... again."

"What were you doing there, Miss Owl—Madam Owl?—Owl—please, Lord, just let me shut up now...."

"Transportation."

"Pardon?"

"I was awaiting transportation."

"Yes." Mickey's eyes moved from side to side as he continued to access his memory. "The red mini car?"

"No, that was Thaddeusz. The blue sedan came for me."

"Why were you there? It must have been important since you shun the daylight, I'm guessing."

"All in good time. You know of John and his work through the writings of the Second Book of Benjamin, yes?"

"I know that the Second Book of Benjamin has many chapters which are hidden in falling towers not unlike this. I know that the chapter which was held at the leaning tower in Bautzen mentions twice the name John."

"Give me your hands," the Owl said, reaching out to Mickey. "I will take you on a journey to the first century where John lives."

Inside, Mickey braced. He wasn't sure if it was the thought of another trip or the touch of the bird-faced woman that sent a surge of panic into his lower bowel. Either way, Mickey knew that after this journey, nothing for the two of them would ever be the same again.

Szkolna Gora:
The Owl

52

Where Blood Flows

Baszta Sowia
Pyrzyce, Poland

Who are you, Mickey Philip Peronne? With an eyebrow raised, the Owl looked deeply into Mickey's face as if to ferret out some hidden truth. Mickey never flinched. Having no reservations, the Owl spoke. "Know this, Mickey—John created a flogging post which was the one greatest relic of our Lord because it was the largest known reservoir of our Savior's blood." The Owl's small frame gave an involuntary shudder which did not escape Mickey's attention.

"'Take and drink this, this is my blood,'" Mickey quoted. "The Savior said that in the cenacle, the upper room in Jerusalem and the site of the Last Supper." With his finger, Mickey mimicked drilling a hole in his palm. "There are many that say there are traces of blood on a slew of holy relics."

"I cannot say that the claims are unfounded. The crown of thorns—in the church in the center of Paris—shrouds, veils, nails, cross, and spear tip all were touched by the blood of Christ. However, because of the cruelty of the Roman soldiers, the flogging post made of freshly cut wood absorbed the flesh and blood of our Lord in a quality and quantity unknown by other relics. None of them even come close to compare."

"Did John know the significance of the blood-drenched wood?" Mickey asked.

"No, probably not. John was guided by our God to preserve and protect the blood of our Lord for all time. It was his mission, given to him after the purification of Christ at the River Jordan."

"Are you saying that this is the same John who baptized Christ in the Jordan River?"

"I say no such thing. John the Baptist would have already been dead. He was beheaded prior to the flogging of Christ. Nevertheless, the Lost Books of Benjamin account that the bloodied flogging post was returned to a man named John who originally made it."

"I don't understand. John made the flogging post but died before the flog-

191

ging took place. Then after Christ was flogged and crucified, the post was returned to the man named John who had made the post?"

"Yes."

"Forgive me, but that doesn't even make sense."

"Think with your heart … not your brain. What would you do, Mickey, if you were given back a flogging post that had been made by John?"

"I would accept the flogging post stained with the blood of our Savior in the name of John."

"Of course you would. Your heart would lead you in that direction. Would it be important for you to credit yourself at that time?"

"No, I don't think so. My brain might give out my name, but my heart would definitely give out the name John. I see now."

"'Not unto me, Lord, but unto thy name give glory.' Right, Mickey?"

"Right, but, Templars did not exist back in the first century."

"True, but the code of the Templar rests in the teachings of Christ. A rose is a rose. Following the teachings of Christ makes one a Christian. Executing these teachings as a soldier makes one a Templar."

"A rose is a rose *is* a rose."

"It is only right that a second humble man acted in the name of John. He was there to receive the holy relic and preserve the Savior's blood forever."

"In resin … a substance where human tissue can be preserved for all time," mused Mickey.

"John protected the porous wood with a nonporous sarcophagus. He then further provided security by creating two exact imitations."

"A pair of stone and wood decoys. Where did these faux sarcophagi go?"

"There are things we know and things we don't know," said the Owl.

"What *do* we know?"

"We know that the sarcophagi were hidden in Jerusalem on Temple Mount in the ruins of the Temple of Solomon and rested there until another structure was built upon the ruins."

"That's where an order of holy knights built their church, thereby giving them their name—Knights Templar," recalled Mickey.

"Yes, with the help of these holy knights, one sarcophagus went from Tunis in North Africa; to the island of Malta in the Mediterranean; to Marseille, France; to Paris, France; and through the trail of Jehanne's tears at Vermandois before arriving in Belgium at Ieper in Flanders Fields. There are some that say that the gas attack of April 1915 was an attempt to retrieve the sarcophagus in Ieper."

"Are you implying that the defense of Ieper was in defense of the sarcophagus?"

"There are people who think so. There is a street in the town marked for the Templars. Unlike you, the way of war is something in which I am not schooled. However, this I do know—there have been many factions searching for the sarcophagi, and for many reasons. In the late 1800s, research science gave a new reason."

"What reason would that be?"

"As a physician and scientist, I think you know that answer better than me, Mickey. We will defer that conversation until later."

"What if later doesn't come?"

"Then it is, what it is, as He wills it. As I was saying, we know that another of the three sarcophagi went to England by way of Ethiopia in Africa; the Spanish island of Majorca; Tomar, Portugal; Mont-Saint-Michel, France; New Castle, England; Edinburgh, Scotland; and finally, to Haltwhistle, one of the border towns along Hadrian's Wall. Some suspect that the planned invasion of England by the Nazis was to get to that sarcophagus."

"This would mean that both world wars had common themes. Both had German aggressors. Both had major plans to capture places where the sarcophagi lay."

"How did the Germans know of the surreptitious locations of the sarcophagi and why were the Germans so very interested in finding them?" the Owl posed.

"That was my question before," said Mickey.

"As it was in Dyhernfurth when you were there with the thick-limbed army soldier … and my previous answer stands. God will reveal in His own time, not ours."

"I didn't know of sarcophagi at the time."

"Really? Hmmm. Yet, I saw your respect and felt that you understood the significance of the place as if it was a—"

"—tomb. Yes, it felt like being at the site of a tomb. Again and again King Tut's tomb raced in my head."

"Yes, a tomb but at another place and time, Mickey."

"'Time and tides wait for no man.'"

"From the play *Everyman*?"

"Yes, ma'am."

"In the play, only Good Deeds provided salvation for Everyman. Do you believe this?" the Owl queried amidst the increasing sound of ruffling feathers.

"We can't earn our way into heaven with good deeds. Only Christ is the way of salvation."

"You espouse much knowledge, Mickey."

"I know enough to know that I know nothing. I am still learning."

"A person who is wise enough to know that they have much to learn will, in turn, learn more—and so you shall." The Owl continued, "The third of the three sarcophagi moved from Jerusalem to Palermo, Sicily, and then on through Pisa, Italy; Milan, Italy; Vienna, Austria; Brno, Czech Republic; Prague, Czech Republic; and then to somewhere in Silesia, now along the German-Polish border region."

"It is not known where?"

"It is known but not exactly. The Second Book of Benjamin provides the specifics."

"Which sarcophagus was soaked in blood?"

"All of them, it is said."

"All of them? How can that be? I don't understand."

"Some think that the decoys were soaked with the blood of a lamb. There are others who say that the blood of Magdalene or Judas Iscariot was placed on the decoys. Some say the decoys received one of each. This is something I do not know."

"I ask again. Which one was the true sarcophagus?"

"Again, as I said before, the specifics lie within the Second Book of Benjamin."

"I have the chapter from Bautzen. My colleague, Dr. Suzanne Coletrane, is seeking the chapters from England. While my other colleague, Dr. Russell Lange, is seeking the chapters from Italy. Do you have chapters for me here in Poland?"

"I do." The Owl released the clasp, allowing the shawl to drop back off her shoulders. A parchment in protective plastic was in her lap; she immediately handed it to Mickey. "I have chapter six."

CHAPTER 6

1) Harnessing our energy allows us to grow in spirit as we grow in years. Let us gain in light as the light gains throughout the morning.

2) Though John listened to his father as the Lord commanded, he also listened to the voice within guiding him and his hand to a different work.

3) John's metal on wood and stone shaped his destiny. Early works may not perceive the Lord's intent. Patience and prayer will bring peace to the developing masterpiece.

4) The beauty of the polished stone masks its true functionality. That is good, for those with eyes will only see the beauty.

5) Who will see the stone as a guardian and not just a stone? The light of the indwelling spirit granted by the Father reveals the stone for what it truly is.

6) As we walk in the early light we may not see the stone for we are not searching. If we find it within us to seek it out, we will quickly join ranks of the guardians themselves.

7) In the beginning we are all stones that are flawed and can't find our purpose. The Master's hand shapes and polishes the rock so that we can arrive at the one true purpose that the Lord has intended.

8) The making of the cloak was guided by the heart of man while the stone stood finished by his hands. The greater of the deed cannot be known until the secret is revealed.

9) The shadow of the leaning tower either shortens or lengthens as the day progresses. The secret lies in the direction the tower leans.

10) As time passes we see and learn more by avoiding the shadow and moving into His light.

53

When Leaning
Towers Fall

Baszta Sowia
Pyrzyce, Poland

A litany of meaningless words. Waving the chapter in his hand, Mickey exhaled through clenched teeth. "Forgive me if I seem … disrespectful, but this verbiage does not … lend itself to understanding," Mickey spoke. "Meaning neither flows through it or from it. If anything, it creates more confusion than understanding—at least to me."

Nodding toward Mickey, the Owl clipped the veil back into place so only her eyes were visible. Then, using the walking stick to steady her, the Owl rose from her seat and took two slivers of meat from a plate resting on a table beside her left hand. Mickey could see she was not a tall woman, somewhat petite, but nevertheless strangely empowered. He glimpsed clothing layered beneath her cloak; it seemed in contrast to her starkly plain outward appearance.

"Not everything can be fathomed at first glance, Mickey. Some things require time. Take me, for instance. I was born along the Vistula River and was raised among the Romani people; you probably know them by the term *Gypsy* and your opinion of them is probably as the rest of the world," she scowled. "Contrary to what most think, we are not thieves and ne'er-do-wells. We are a people who, from the East, brought new light into dark times. We hold to a cultural standard different from that which surrounds us. Because we are different, we are feared, and yes, even hated. My parents were killed outside Torun when I was just a child. Hitler hunted us to gain information and then he tried to extinguish us. I think that as a war-fighter, you know this."

Mickey watched as she walked over to a drape which he now discovered covered a recess in the tower wall. On the left of the recess was a picture of the Last Supper—yet another version he had never seen. On the right was a portrait of a Teutonic Knight with the subscript: *Krzyżacki*.

Without turning around, the Owl said, "Crossbearers. The title of the picture upon which you gaze refers to the knights of our Lord, *Crossbearers*. They were defenders of Christianity and in the paternal lineage to the Maid of Lorraine." The Owl parted the cobalt blue drapes, sliding them back against the corners of the wall's indentations. Perched within the niche were two medium-sized, snow-white owls. Their feathers shuffled and Mickey understood that this was the sound which plagued him from the onset of the visit.

"Mickey, please to meet Trzesniowski and Lagowski. From these and all their relatives before them, the Baszta Sowia—the Owl Tower—received its name."

"I thought you were the Owl of this tower."

"As I warned before, not everything can be understood at first glance," said the Owl. "I am who God wants me to be, as are you Mickey. You now have two chapters of the Second Book of Benjamin. Two chapters which give information to the location of the prize for which the kaiser-led Germans, as well as the Nazis, past and present, have made a focused search. Soon you will understand the concept that *when* leaning towers fall is far, far more important than *where* they fall."

"I don't understand."

"Not all towers that lean are actually falling."

"Okay."

"Those that are falling have a purpose greater than those that just lean."

"I see."

"You don't see, do you, Mickey?"

"No, not really. Sorry, I'm just tired. I'm sure that eventually I will."

"Read with your heart for understanding and know that God has brought you into our lives to do His will."

"And what would that be, Szkolna?"

"A glance at my two feathered friends here should tell you. As a child, I was starving while living within the Stalag prison camp. They cared for me when no one else did. They brought a starving outcast food when fellow humans did not. They did for me as God would expect from the least of his creations. As I grew, I cared for them. Now I care for their offspring. You should be no different. May the love, knowledge, and conviction of the apostles always be with you." Looking now at Thaddeusz she said, "Thaddeusz, as a Knight of Christ, see that Torun gives Mickey its secret and then return him to Matthias. Our work here is almost done."

Thaddeusz nodded the acceptance of his mission.

"Mickey, though at the time you did not know it, I knew you before you knew me. I watched you and looked upon your face. In it I saw respect, kindness, and the inner light that one possesses when he serves others. Therefore, I knew that you were the one that God had sent. It was I who sent Thaddeusz to lead you to Bautzen and the leaning tower there. All that has happened to you until this point has been a result of what we needed from you. That which happens beyond your return to Bautzen is out of our hands and out of our control. We will all be at the mercy of God and His knight, Sir Dr. Michael Philip Peronne. Serve our Lord well and give him the glory, Mickey."

"I know these words. Are you charging me a knight's task?"

"God has already done that. I am charging you with a task as a companion of our order."

"But I am already a companion of an order——"

"Yes, but not of an order of international Templars. Now you may be acknowledged as a companion who walks in the light of Christ. Don't worry. It is acceptable, for now, that you have not yet made the personal commitment to be an international Christian knight. However, a lack of personal commitment will not be acceptable on our next meeting." With that said, using the stick to assist her, the Owl closed herself behind the drapes within the recesses of the tower wall. Mickey felt a soft touch on his shoulders. Thaddeusz's voice broke the silence with a gentleness and respect Mickey did not think possible.

"It is daylight now and the Owl retires. Our work is done here, Doc. We must go back to Bautzen by way of Torun, Poland. The roads are small and the distance far. We have traveled much, and our bodies and minds are fatigued; I fear for our safety. Please, let's go now."

Surprising himself at his need to have closure, Mickey genuflected, kissed the back of his fingers, closed them into a fist, and then blew the kiss softly toward the closed drapes.

"Take me away, Thaddeusz. I hope that I have what it takes to understand and fulfill this mission."

"As I see you now, through the eyes of the Owl, my initial fears are allayed. I believe now that you are the one God has sent."

"Is this the fear the Owl sensed in you when we first entered?"

"Yes."

"She believed that I was the one answer to her prayers. You feared not."

"Yes."

"Are we friends now, Thaddeusz?"

"No, you have not earned my friendship. However, you do have a budding respect. At present I can now say that among disgusting American soldiers, I dislike you least." Thaddeusz smiled and winked.

"Well now, I guess that's progress."

54

A Square Peg

Route to Torun
Northern marches of Poland

*T*he more *information received*, Mickey frowned, *the squarer the peg*. After several hours of driving, the blazing morning sun lessened its intense barrage on the eyes of the knights. They sliced a bit more easily through the flat Polish countryside heading for Torun. In these lands lay the history of the Teutonic Knights who carried the hopes of the Templars until such time as Napoleon officially forced them underground into places as distant as the Valley of the Lorraine in France.

"I understand so much, Thaddeusz, but it doesn't fit into a round hole."

"What are you saying, Doc?"

"I just cannot see the connection between the events which transpired in biblical times to the present situation."

"It would help greatly if you could tell me what you need to make the connection clear."

"I wish I could. The problem is I don't have enough mastery to tell you the places where connection fails. It's like medical school. I feel like I am trying to fill a row of thimbles with water from a fire hose."

"Does it help having these two chapters of the Second Book of Benjamin?"

Mickey looked at the two chapters and read back through their words. *Square peg. Round hole.* "Connections to understanding may be here but, honestly, I cannot see them."

"Would it help to know that there are at least ten chapters in the Second Book of Benjamin?"

"To me, that only means that I have a maximum potential for twenty percent understanding."

"Well then, after visiting Krzywa Wieża, the leaning tower in Torun, we could be at thirty percent clarity in the quest for understanding."

"Simple mathematics tells me that thirty multiplied by zero understanding gives me a great big goose egg."

"Indeed, maybe so, but we will be in Torun soon. There will be no time for geese or their eggs."

"You're right, Thaddeusz. Time is a scarce commodity. I must be optimistic and focused."

"What specific insights do you think these chapters need to provide you?"

"I would like to understand why the flogging post drenched in the blood of Christ has to be caught up in such intrigue. Is it to create value by becoming a sought-after relic?"

"Maybe, Doc, but the creation of a relic allows us to remain physically connected to Christ."

"In this case the post had no value until it became soaked in blood. It is Christ's blood that is the relic. Its greatest power is as a symbol."

"True," agreed Thaddeusz, "the physical blood of Christ does not promise physical immortality, power, or wealth. It only promises spiritual salvation."

"So why preserve the blood of Christ unless there is some use for it in future time, Thaddeusz?"

"I don't think early Christians thought about practical or potential uses for Christ's blood. I believe they just wanted to have a part of Him, any part or relic. After all, He emphasized that very fact when He served the apostles wine during the Last Supper. 'Drink this—my blood—in remembrance of me.'"

"Correct. That would mean that only minds which desire a perceived advantage would then search for the blood as a physical entity."

"The question that connects the past with the present is this, Doc: Why would seeking to obtain the blood of Christ drive the kaiser in World War I and Hitler in World War II to the brink of European decimation?"

"Well, Thaddeusz, obviously both the kaiser and Hitler were men engaged in military operations. Perhaps they believed Christ's physical blood to be a source of infinite power—a military weapon of sorts. To be guaranteed victory on the battlefield, they would stop at nothing to get it."

"Where did they get such a notion?"

"Probably from the Templar Knights, Thaddeusz. Remember that in many of the crusader battles, the physical cross of Christ was carried into the fight."

"The physical cross would have traces of the blood of Christ. It didn't matter to the kaiser and Hitler that crusader armies, bolstered with Templars, were defeated even in the presence of the physical cross?"

"Not at all." Mickey shook his head. "Their own egos would compensate for what they imagined were poor battlefield strategies employed by crusaders and Templars."

"So, once the kaiser and Hitler obtained the blood of Christ, they would need a remote place where it could be protected."

"Yes. Silesia would indeed be the perfect place."

"Absolutely, Doc. England warned Hitler not to go into Silesia. Yet Germany marched into Poland and into Silesia on the first of September 1939, thus starting World War II. Hitler's need for Silesia was something very specific and very urgent."

"Okay, I grant you that specifically, Silesia has a really great forest for hiding things, but without the blood in hand, there is absolutely no urgency. No, Thaddeusz, there has to be more that Silesia offered."

"Silesia offered wealth. Besides containing a remote forest, there existed vast mineral deposits which were raw materials for chemicals."

"Then *there* is your reason that Dyhernfurth's chemical munitions factory and Nazi chemical research center was embedded in Silesia," said Mickey.

"All you would then need is to capture and ship the sarcophagus to Silesia where it could be secured in anonymity and quietly studied by Nazi physicians and scientists."

"That's just what happened in the secret laboratory, under the operation code names *Flusszigeuner* and *Unsterblichkeit durch Medizinische Forschung*." Mickey recalled. "Those are the stamps for *river gypsies* and *immortality via medical research* I saw on the papers that I took from the underground lab."

"Not necessarily, Doc. Although this is a scary bedtime story for little children, it means nothing unless that secret laboratory could actually process the contents of a sarcophagus. Did you see evidence that the sarcophagus or Christ's blood were processed, or even capable of being processed, at that site?"

"I saw a slew of incubators ... but you're hinting at much more than maintaining a tissue bank for replacement cells for the Führer. You're broaching the science of tissue culturing and cloning of blood cells. Thaddeusz, that technology didn't exist in the era of Nazi Germany."

"Really? I believe you know differently. Just because the world wasn't aware of the existence of such technology doesn't mean that a select few, like Dr. Morell, didn't have the ability to study and process the blood of Christ."

Without warning, Thaddeusz braked the car suddenly, throwing Mickey into a forward-and-backward jolt. He looked to the road in front of them. For a moment, he saw a dog's tail pass quickly off to his right. He cocked his head to better scrutinize the animal when he realized that it wasn't a dog at all. The broad, flat cranium and piercing eyes led to a darkly tapered snout. Although it was rather large, the animal was clearly a gray fox. Confirmation came seconds later as another fox, possibly a vixen, passed less aggressively—and seemingly more annoyed with the car—than the first animal. Mickey pondered how identically the foxes looked. His mind returned back to cloning.

They did not encounter any more foxes. However, the number of stork nests seen along the five-hour drive was staggering. It seemed that every town along their route was blessed with at least one of the rather massive nests built on an elevated structure about thirty feet off the ground. Beyond foxes, storks, and conversations on culturing and cloning, the pair pulled into the northwest corner of Torun and a short while later, the old city center finally appeared on their left.

"We are here," said Thaddeusz proudly. "Torun is the home of our Teutonic Knights, keepers of great secrets, who some believe were in the bloodline of the Maid of Lorraine."

"How does the leaning tower figure into all of this?"

"The leaning tower in the town played only a tangential part. Its stone and mortar could do nothing to save the flailing reputations of the disgraced Teutonic Knights. That is something that the knights would have to do for themselves, and they did. They executed missions far away from their home here in Poland. Among Christian knights, Teutonic Knights became unique just like the Krzywa Wieża, which was shaped unlike all other leaning towers. It was built square."

"A square peg?"

"What?"

"It's not important. Please continue, Thaddeusz."

"The square Krzywa Wieża, a city tower since the fourteenth century, is most notable because of the severity of its imposing lean."

"Bad engineering?"

"Maybe, Doc. Some said that poor soil sedimentation was the source of a weakened foundation which caused the lean. Although slanted, its functionality never lessened. In its years, the tower has been used for the imprisonment of wayward women, a smith for guns and weapons, a domicile for forlorn travelers, and the beating heart of Torun's historical societies."

"It serves a purpose today?"

"Of course. Today, besides being a noisy pub and quaint souvenir shop, it is my home, and I am its keeper. Therein resides the fish which lured an unworthy seeker from the Rhine Valley of Germany."

"So it seems." Mickey tapped his chest.

After entering the walls of the ancient city, the pair veered right until a round tower marked the corner for the ensuing right-hand turn. Down the long one-way street they proceeded, passing many businesses and shops. There was one, Pod Atlantem, which particularly caught Mickey's eye for two reasons: first, it had the ambience like a coffee shop he frequented during his time in medical school; and second, in its doorway stood a stunning, casually dressed town girl whose height and shape would be the envy of most any women's athletic team. Frowning, she tapped one foot vigorously. *She seems distraught ...*

In Mickey's periphery, as they passed her, he saw her leave the shadow of the doorframe and pivot around the corner of the charming coffee shop. The pair drove one more block to exit the arch of the south gate of the town. At the last possible moment, Thaddeusz engaged his right-turn signal and turned down a ridiculously narrow street which hugged the inner aspect of the south city wall. Directly ahead, leaning inward from the wall, sat the square tower, Krzywa Wieża. Thaddeusz pulled up to the entrance ramp of the tower which lead to the second-floor entrance.

Hopping from the car, Thaddeusz blurted, "I will retrieve the fish and then, before journeying farther, we'll stop for some bread and drink."

"We'll toast to our ability to create our own miracle of understanding," said Mickey.

"To good health and success!" Thaddeusz held high an imaginary wine-filled goblet.

"Wouldn't that be *Unsterblichkeit*?"

"Yes, Doc, if good health led to immortality."

"Doesn't it?"

"I don't know. Possibly. Think about it while I am gone. Anyway, you should know. You're the physician."

Watching Thaddeusz round the corner, Mickey sat in the car thinking aloud.

"What diet of the River People would lead to immortality?" he mused. He repeated the question several times while aimlessly doodling on the gathering condensation on the window. All of a sudden, his eyes grew clear and sharply focused. Moistening the tip of his finger, he created a sketch on the glass. Mickey announced the answer to the only one present in the car. "Of course, of course, fish. Obvious, yet not. There are fish and then there are *fish*. Not all fish are created equal. Methinks we now have a connection with *Unsterblichkeit durch Medizinische Forschung*—immortality through medical research—and *Flusszigeuer*—river gypsies. Only, ladies and gentlemen, we may be sixty years too late."

Leaning Tower of Torun: Torun, Poland

55

Of Girls and Ghouls

Krzywa Wieża parking area
Torun, Poland

Better late than never.

Feeling a little happier after his revelation that fish meant much more than just fish, Mickey altered his focus from within and began observing the people in the surrounding streets and alleys near this portion of the city wall.

In the distance, behind him and to his right, stood that same young lady previously seen at the corner coffee shop. Inexplicably, she increasingly demanded his full attention. Now getting a better look at her, he surmised she was in her late twenties. She was dressed casually so he ruled out a businesswoman in the midst of her routine workday. She stood on the church corner, turning her head from side to side, looking up and down the cobblestone alley. She was obviously waiting for something or someone—a ride, a friend, a lunch date. Her watch, he gathered, was rotated to the inside of her left wrist as she habitually rotated it inward and upward giving it a quick glance. This was usually followed by a quick tapping of a foot, a glance in both directions, and a sigh. Seeing this repeated sequence of movements triggered a strong memory.

✠ ✠ ✠

Loni waited patiently for ninety minutes, while Mickey waited outside a closed Albert's Confectionaries in Athens, Ohio. Mickey kept thinking, *Where is she? Did she see that Albert's was closed and leave? If she left, where did she go?* Then, after about two hours, it dawned on Mickey. He knew where she was, and he hoped that she still would be there. Hoofing it around the corner and through the center of the city, Mickey negotiated four city blocks and arrived at Another Fool's Café, panting. Framed within the propped-open door sat a single small round table and a seated Loni Meriwether looking directly at him.

Out of his mouth flew the words, "I'm not late—I'm not late."

Loni extended her left arm, exposing the watch face on her inner wrist, lifted it to her face and smiled. Striding to the table, Mickey pulled out the seat directly across from her and sat down hard as the waitress quickly brought him a half tonic water and half fruit juice spritzer with a twist of orange that Loni had ordered hours before. Never diverting his eyes off Loni, Mickey feigned a smile to the waitress.

"How long have you been here?" Mickey asked, cringing at the many ticks which had left the clock.

"Almost two hours."

"Didn't you wonder where I was?"

"No, I figured you would be en route or possibly at Albert's."

"Albert's is closed."

"I know, so I couldn't be sure you would be there."

"Can you forgive me?"

"For what? For *not* being late? For forgetting which restaurant we decided to meet at?" Loni smiled and the room brightened.

"Tell me the truth, Loni," Mickey exhaled. "How much longer would you have waited?"

"Until you arrived."

Her words shot arrows into his ears and straight down into his soul. *I couldn't ask for more.* Mickey's eyes welled up as he reached across the table, cupped her face, and then took her hand in his. He kissed both her eyelids and then lightly kissed her sweet lips. At that moment, he knew she was a woman for all time.

✠ ✠ ✠

A car noisily rolled by, splashing a mud puddle, and snapping Mickey back to the present. In the passing car there was a heated debate occurring between the driver, a man roughly in his late twenties, and the tall girl who had been impatiently waiting in the alley. Mickey assumed this conversation wasn't in any fashion close to the dialogue he had had in Athens, Ohio almost eighteen years ago.

As the car passed, Mickey noticed two men moving into the shadows on the balcony of the tower. Mickey stepped out from the passenger's seat to get a better look. Once outside, he saw nothing. *It must have been shifting shadows or my overactive imagination.* Clearly there was no living body nestled within the darker regions of the crannies which framed the tower ... at least none that he could now see. He started to turn away when the peripheral movement again returned. A chill moved up his spine. He hopped back in the car, closed the passenger door, and secured the door locks. As his eyes panned up from the now locked door latch to the passenger window, he saw the face of a person. The face was so large and so close that it obliterated the view of the city behind it. He jolted back in horror, involuntarily bringing his arm upward to shield his face. When he peeked over his arm, the face in the window was gone. In the distance, Mickey noticed another figure moving toward him. His heartbeat pulsed in his neck.

Returning from the leaning tower in a steady stride was Thaddeusz. His retrieval of the fish was relatively quick, and after a couple of spins through the dreary, colorless, city streets, they were comfortably parked in front of the coffee shop where the tall girl once stood. From the outside, the shop was as dingy as the other business fronts along both sides of the same street. However, having a coat check and notable flawless colorful décor, this coffee shop was truly an enigma. Neither the prolonged wait to be seated nor the comedic rousting of a drunken guest could shake Mickey's mind from the bizarre encounter at the leaning tower.

After the drunken lush had been less than pleasantly escorted from the establishment, the waitress, wiping her hands on a dish towel, guided the pair to a secluded front room overlooking the street where Copernicus had once lived.

Trance-like, Mickey sat stirring his mocha latte cappuccino. After a minute he placed the spoon on the table, narrowing his gaze on Thaddeusz. "Tell me, when you came to the car, did you happen to see anyone standing near my window?"

"A man?"

"Yes," said Mickey.

"Dirty and shabby in his dress?"

"Yes."

"Old and decrepit?"

"Yes."

"Possibly a workman, artisan, or maybe even a mason."

"Yes, yes, yes!" Mickey was overjoyed in this validation.

"No," said Thaddeusz. "I didn't."

"No?"

"No."

"Hmmm," Mickey furrowed his brow while scratching at a dimple in the table. His eyes never left Thaddeusz. "If you did not see the person you described—"

"I answered you honestly," Thaddeusz interrupted. "I did not see the man."

"Then how did you know what he looked like? In fact, how did you know he was a man?"

"Dr. Peronne, he could have been one of two men. You saw one of the two brothers of Krzywa Wieża."

"Who are they?"

"Were," Thaddeusz enunciated.

"Outside the car," replied Mickey.

"Not 'where,' Doc. I said 'were.'"

"'Were' as in *were*wolf?"

"No, I don't think so." Thaddeusz shook his head solemnly.

Mickey sat speechless. He replayed the dialogue in his head, then attempted another thrust in this verbal fencing. "Who are the brothers?"

"Were—who *were* the brothers?"

"Excuse me. Who *were* the brothers of Krzywa Wieża?"

"Their name is not known, but they live in the tower with me," admitted Thaddeusz.

"Are they ghosts?"

"Yes, most likely. At least I hope so or I am due a lot of rent," Thaddeusz snickered, stirring his coffee.

"And you're okay with this?"

"What choice do I have? They were there first."

56

A Tower Squared

Coffee shop

Torun, Poland

"Who are they, these ghosts?" Mickey asked.

"It is said that they were the masons who were charged to build the tower. They were brothers who were publicly devoid of brotherly love and had no respect for one another. Although they were greatly skilled in their art, their hearts were harder than the stone which they were so adept at crafting. Egocentric, they refused to talk to one another in the building process and so the tower that resulted leans."

"What about the sand and the weakening of the foundation?" Mickey asked.

"Perhaps it was done to spite the other?"

"Was it?"

"No, Doc. They agreed that it was to be done in this manner."

"They agreed? That's hard to do if they aren't speaking one to the other."

"There are communications and then there are *communications*."

"What are you saying?"

"I am saying what I am saying. I am here to tell you that the tower they built was an agreement between two brothers and the tower was intended to fall."

"Why?"

"It is easier for a fish to jump from a place where the bottom can be seen below him."

"Thaddeusz, what are you saying?"

"Doc, the fish you seek has jumped into your hands from a tower which falls. The face you saw has been waiting for you for many centuries. What more is there to say?"

"I need another drink. This time, triple the alcohol."

"Being drunk doesn't lend itself to better understanding."

"Being sober doesn't seem to be doing the trick either, Thaddeusz. Besides, the more I drink, the more you might start to make sense."

"If that is the case, I am glad I brought this from the car." Thaddeusz placed a bottle of red wine on the table. "It's German."

"That came from the laboratory," Mickey scowled. "You took it when you stole my car."

"Oh please, such harsh words between friends? Besides, it was just one of many things I took," he smiled smugly.

Mickey ignored the second comment and replied, "So, now we're friends?"

"I'll know if you offer to share a drink. It looks to be quite old."

"Not as old as the fish."

"That's true. You know, maybe I should be drinking the wine alone without you." Thaddeusz reached for the bottle.

"Why is that?" Mickey pulled the bottle closer to his side of the table.

"Doc, everyone knows that white wine serves best with fish." He placed a paper, facedown, on the table.

Mickey pulled the document toward himself. "Too bad you weren't this charming on our last adventure in Poland."

"Too bad you're an American. I guess some things can't be changed."

"Too bad you have to shut up and pour us each a glass of wine," said Mickey, sliding the bottle across the table.

"Yes indeed … too bad. Only an American would drink red wine with fish."

Both men laughed. Smiling, Mickey flipped the paper over.

"Chapter ten."

"It is the will of the Owl, Doc. I am obligated."

Mickey read silently as he sipped the wine Thaddeusz passed him.

When the waitress put the previously ordered beef goulash on the table, Thaddeusz engaged her in conversation. Mickey supposed they were talking about the discharging of the drunk, disorderly guest, but he let their talk flow over him as he tried to decipher what he was reading.

CHAPTER 10

1) This is why the Father takes our Lord now rather than later. The brightest light can give the longest shadow.

2) When the Father takes, the Father gives. It is through that taking that the gift becomes available for the people.

3) This ultimate symbol of the Father's giving must, like the wood, be made, hidden, and protected for all time. That within us holds the key to unlock the gift. But, we must see with our hearts and not our eyes. Those with sight will never see. Those without the indwelling spirit have hearts that equally cannot see.

4) Let the stone hide from them who cannot see. For those who can, let their eyes pierce the rock and partake of the blood of the Lamb as the Father wishes.

5) Though cloaked in rock and soaked into wood, the words hidden in the failing light will serve testament till the end of days.

6) The secret of the stone will be revealed by the Lord not when the stone is cracked, but when the eyes have seen the heart of the stone with seal intact.

7) When the two stones stand broken, their hearts will be revealed. Even so, there is a failure of the wicked to purge the secret from within, for the wicked have eyes that cannot see.

8) When the four brothers have relinquished their charge, the stone, the wood, and the blood of the Lamb will be known to those who see. Those who stand in the light will have eyes to see. This is a promise made by our Father.

9) The leaning tower is falling though it does not move. Those with eyes cannot see this as they only study the movements of the shadows.

10) The blood of the Lamb is not the blood of the lamb. Those that can see will believe. For all, that secret will be revealed though few will truly understand. Through the Son of Man understanding will grow.

"We should be at thirty percent understanding now," said Thaddeusz, when Mickey had finished the reading of the paper. "Are there any new insights that surface after a comparison of the three chapters?"

"I am sure that there is, but I am just too tired now to see it. What time is it now?"

"It is the time when, among towers, only those which are falling have shadows. It is noon. The sun will no longer bake my eyes in their very sockets. Eat with purpose so that we may quickly head southwest to Poznan. There, we will stop. I think we have earned at least one good night's rest. We will start again in the morning toward Bautzen and the distance will be somewhat lessened."

"Where do we go from Bautzen?"

"First, you have a scheduled reunion with that wreck of a car—"

"Don't remind me."

"Then Matthias is planning for us to meet with the four brothers."

Mickey's ears perked at the reference to what he just read. "What will they tell us?"

"I believe they will help to fit together all the pieces of the puzzle thus far."

Mickey opened his shirt cuff, removed the plastic-covered chapters two and six, added this fish to the protective cover, and then rolled the fish over his forearm before re-clasping his sleeve shut. Thaddeusz raised an eyebrow but said nothing. Mickey reached for his phone. Before meeting these four bothers there was an important coordination for transportation he had to make. He called European Medical Command's G3 Flight Operations and Luis Toro-Calderon. Russell's mission couldn't be done on the autostrada of Italy, at least not safely. Mickey knew that if he himself was this tired, he couldn't imagine the fatigue Russell was enduring. *Special Operations snake eater or not, a little help from a*

Blackhawk will make Russell's mission go a bit easier. At G3 Flight Operations, Luis was more than happy to help.

It was after dark when Mickey and Thaddeusz pulled into a hotel in the town of Poznan. Along the way Mickey had marveled at the numerous candle-lit graveyards which flickered in the night sky as they passed through the small Polish towns and villages. He had seen many things in his travels but the effort to keep a graveside candle lit all night truly raised the bar in respect for the dearly departed.

⚜ ⚜ ⚜

In Heidelberg, Loni sipped her morning coffee as she put her finishing touches on *If I Had a Cow,* her leadoff in a series of children's books. It was a part-time passion of hers and something that helped her to switch gears and forget, if only momentarily, about the danger her husband might be in.

After breakfast, she went to the DIA headquarters and received the same report as before—mission on track, no update at this date-time group. Having been instructed by General Framingham not to call Mickey, she sat, tortured, wondering if Mickey was safe. Rubbing her eyes hard didn't seem to produce an answer any better.

57

More is Less

Route to Bristol
Southern marches of England

"I don't like it, Virgin." Suzanne grimaced as she lowered the driver's side windshield visor. "In fact, I never even understood it."

"Is there a problem with the windscreen?" Jude pointed. "Maybe it's the way the sunset reflects off the bonnet."

"Do you watch cowboy films?"

"American westerns, Dr. Coletrane?"

"At the end of most cowboy movies, the protagonist goes riding off into the sunset."

"So?"

"It's painful to the eyes. Why would anyone even want to go full face into the brightness of the setting sun?"

"Unfortunately for us, Dr. Coletrane, Bristol lies a bit farther into the sunset." Suzanne and Jude had spent the past five and a half hours heading west, away from King's Lynn and across southern England toward the Welch border. Bristol was the last large town before crossing the bridge into Wales. As Jude stared out the window watching the passing signs and looking for their exit, Suzanne mused aloud.

"Alluvial clay as a foundation meant that towers built upon it would eventually fall. In the process, the tower would begin to lean, thus making the tower stand out among all the rest, right?"

"Yes, Doctor, in these specially made towers, the secret is kept," Jude confirmed her thought stream.

"What is the secret?"

"You are direct in discussions, aren't you, Dr. Coletrane? Let me just say that it is not yet time to reveal that to you. I can tell you that the chapter you read comes from the Second Book of Benjamin, a lost book written in the first century."

"Lost books from the first century can hardly have any bearing on intentionally flawed towers."

"You might be surprised to know that the Second Book of Benjamin is an instructional guide to tell special people how, where, and when to hide a secret. In so doing, people who know and understand the book can then follow the clues to the source of the secret."

"The leaning towers were made to hide the secret?" Suzanne's mind pushed together many of the new pieces of information. However, the puzzle in her head still did not have a tight fit.

"Yes, Doctor, this is why Nicholas of Lynn, the Grey Friar of whom I previously spoke, went from the Franciscan church there at King's Lynn to the Temple church at Bristol."

"Was he a Templar?"

"There is no indication that he was. Although another friar from the Greyfriars Church, Robert of Thornham, participated in the Third Crusade in 1191. Even as a standard bearer, he could have been considered a Knight of Christ."

"Was the lost Second Book of Benjamin truly lost or was it just hidden?"

"Jolly good show!" the Virgin beamed. "It was, and is still, hidden."

"But not from me—at least not anymore."

"Dr. Coletrane, you have seen but one chapter. Legend has it that there are ten chapters in the Second Book of Benjamin."

"Legend says ten chapters, but you don't know for sure."

"No."

"How many leaning towers are there?"

"I don't know. Worldwide today, I'd guess probably thirty or so. In Europe there are about twenty-five."

"That doesn't take into consideration all the ones that have come and gone."

"True, and it doesn't take into account any that weren't intentionally made to fall ... not that that matters ... right now."

"So, the secret, like my fish, is moved about from leaning tower to leaning tower and this surreptitious action and its reason are what you aren't willing to share right now."

"Yes, Doctor, right now," Jude spoke with conviction.

"Yes, so you are willing to share!"

"Right now."

"Tell me, Virgin, I'm ready."

"Right now."

"Yes, right now."

"Right, now, Dr. Coletrane! Please turn right now or we will be in Wales. It appears that our exit has quite arrived."

The trip should have been no more than four hours, but with a couple errors in navigation and traffic on the outer London motorway, delay was inevitable. The pair was quite happy to roll into the Temple Church area from the road named Temple Way. The framework of the church was a structural skeleton and its attached leaning tower stood before them. As her mind contrasted and compared the two towers, she appreciated the westward lean of this tall church tower. *Somewhere in this structure I have to find the fish, or this mission will be a failure.* Looking at the tower's top she could see a fish-shaped flag flapping in the breeze.

Suzanne reminded herself that a tower built with a malleable, alluvial clay foundation would be destined to lean. Unlike the King's Lynn Greyfriars Tower, Jude told her that this foundation also had wool sacks in the foundation as co-culprit.

The fact that early masons had the intention to engineer a falling tower challenges the very basics of masonry. It contradicts the importance of a solid foundation. They did what most masons of the time would ridicule as shoddy workmanship. To do this, and keep the secret of having done it, is remarkable. They had to be artisans working for a greater good—yes, Psalms chapter one hundred fifteen, verse one: "Not unto us, O Lord, not unto us, but unto thy name give glory."

They went around the south side of the church and through a small gated area to arrive at the back rectory. On the way, they passed a few deteriorating crypts where it looked as if some masons had found their final resting place.

Suzanne's father was a thirty-second degree Mason. If there was nothing else that would be understood, she knew that the Masons prided themselves in their own history. Even when masonry and carpentry overlapped in biblical times, the woodwork and stonework from the artisan's hand was a source of sincere pride.

"Where was their source of the alluvial clay?" Suzanne asked as they arrived at the wooden door that breeched a long stretch of brick wall frowning into an even longer alleyway. Through the opaque glass she could see a figure moving about on the inside.

Jude whispered in her ear, "Your answers are beyond that glass opaquely. Justice James should be able to help you clarify. I trust that he is still within the keep."

That was odd and darkly cryptic ... but about status quo for this mission. She knocked and waited. *Beyond the glass opaquely. Why does that ring a bell? Hmmm, I'll ask Russell when I see him. He'll know.*

After a moment, the door was answered by a friendly face, presumably belonging to the church secretary. The woman glanced politely but stoically at Suzanne then softened and beamed when she saw Jude. Nevertheless, she extended her hand first to Suzanne, in the most proper of etiquettes, and then breached all protocol to warmly embrace the Virgin.

"To what do I owe the pleasure of this visit?" the church woman asked the Virgin.

Jude, regaining his British formality responded, "Justice, we need to see Justice James."

"Right. But first, I would like to learn about this lovely lady," said the church woman. "Mr. More, if you would be so kind." Suzanne smiled.

"Miriam More, I would be most honored to introduce you to my friend of few words, direct query, and remarkable character, Dr. Suzanne Coletrane."

"Pleasure to meet you. Please, call me Suzanne."

"Suzanne, I must apologize outright because the message of your coming didn't reach me in time before I could delay Justice James from his departure.

He is headed for the main continent even as we speak." Suzanne shot darts at the Virgin wondering why he didn't tell her this. "I imagine Justice James would sorely like to have met you. Is there anything I can do to help?"

"Access us into the office, please." Jude stroked his chin thoughtfully. "Although not the perfect scenario, I guess I can near properly discuss where Justice James might have gone in the intended discussion."

"As you wish," replied Miriam.

The trio proceeded to the inner office of the tower keeper—the inscription on the door read *Tower Master: Mr. Justice James More.* A respectful knock on the door brought no answer, as expected. Miriam opened the door and then excused herself saying, "I believe you know your way around, Jude. Dr. Coletrane, Suzanne, you're in capable hands. I trust you find that which you seek. It was most delightful, and an immeasurable pleasure, to have met you."

Jude scanned the room for a chair which he scooted up to the front of the desk. "Dr. Coletrane, please sit."

"Do I have to, Virgin? We have been sitting for so long that my lower back has joined my hip in a duet of commiseration." Nevertheless, Suzanne, her thigh still sore from the high kick to Dalton's gun, eased into the chair while trying to drink in all her immediate surroundings. She hardly noticed the Virgin as he rounded the desk and sat comfortably behind it in a most authoritative manner.

58

In God's Sight and Tower Light

Office of the Tower Master
Bristol, England

"A flower bud unfurls though we never see it move, Doctor," the Virgin began enigmatically. "We only know that it has moved as we stare into the face of the already open blossom." Hands folded in front of him on the glass-topped desk, Jude leaned forward and continued, "The same is true for towers. A leaning tower, by all rights, is a tower which is falling albeit not visibly so. Though the eye may not see it, Greyfriars Tower and the Bristol Church Tower are both entities which are actively falling."

As his voice continued in a most melodic manner, Suzanne recalled the verses six and nine from chapter nine of the book. *The guardians will pass their charge to generation upon generation until nature's mountains and man's towers fall.... At sunset the leaning tower possesses either the longest shadow or none. Such is the soul of the wicked who sees with his eyes and understands for naught.*

Another quote began spinning in her mind, *A rose by any other name is still a rose.* She remembered that it went differently than how Mickey said it. *It was Shakespeare: "What's in a name? That which we call a rose by any other name would smell as sweet." Leaning towers and falling towers are one in the same. One is just a snapshot in time of the other ... therefore a rose by just another name.... The Virgin referenced verses six and nine to me before we left King's Lynn—these guardians hold the secret within their charge. The location of that secret is in the falling towers of the world....*

Suzanne interrupted Jude. "Are there any other falling towers in England?"

"No."

"Just these two."

"Yes, the Greyfriars Tower in King's Lynn and the tower at the Holy Cross Temple Church here in Bristol—"

"Both built by skilled masons under the supervision of Templar Knights and charged with the mission of the Second Book of Benjamin?"

"By Jove, I believe you have it."

"Is this why my colleague sent me to King's Lynn and Bristol?"

"Yes, in all of England these are the locations of the two towers which, by design, were built to fall."

"So, Virgin, what is the secret?"

"It is there on the desk in front of you."

Beneath the glass on the desk was a paper in a protective transparent jacket.

CHAPTER 7

1) By the midpoint of our days, the brightness reflected in our soul will be the standard by which all of us are measured by our Father.

2) When John learned all he could with wood and stone, he produced that work which was designed from and for God the Father.

3) He felt that the wood and the stone must be a beautiful union. The strength of one protects the weakness of the other. When this is done thrice, John's task was complete.

4) When our hearts have been seasoned within His light, the beauty of the stone becomes invisible to God's plan. Through Him we, as well as the stone, achieve ultimate purpose.

5) The purpose of the stone is tossed upon the shoulders as we would cast a cloth over a boulder. Though we cannot see, with Him within us, the knowledge and purpose are secured in secrecy.

6) Blessed be those who know the secret and speak it not. For those who claim to know and reveal it, the loss of their soul departs with the attempted giving away of the secret.

7) These guardians stand as paired sentinels in the height of their glory. They will never achieve the audience destiny has deemed for the one. In this lesser light, the one true purpose is secured in its secrecy of place and time as the Lord God wills.

8) One stony cloak will hold the blood of the Lamb who secures our place in heaven.

9) Like the Lamb, no leaning tower loses its shadow in the height of day. Throughout the day it guides to it the followers of shadows.

10) Remember, in the absoluteness of His light there are no shadows.

"This is the secret?"

"It has the mark of the fish."

Those two curved lines I've seen on necklaces and on the back of automobiles. "How does this symbol tie in with the tower secret?"

"How good is your Greek, Dr. Coletrane?"

"Apparently as good as my understanding of your Brit—it's *all* Greek to me."

With pursed lips, Jude began instructing, "The Greek word for 'fish' is *ich-thys*. It is, in reality, an acronym for *Iēsous Christos Theos huios sōtēr*."

"I'm guessing that is Greek for 'Jesus Christ, God' … and something else." Suzanne rubbed her forehead and arched her lower back. "Sorry, that's the best I can do in a cloud of fatigue and this gnawing pain."

"I understand. Let me help you. The entire acronym reads 'Jesus Christ, God the Son, our Savior.' This is your fish, Dr. Coletrane, and now you have two. Now you know the connection between Christ and the fish. You understand why the symbol of the fish was chosen as Christ himself chose fishermen." In one smooth motion, Jude retrieved the Greyfriar's fish from within his jacket pocket, laid it on the glass next to chapter seven, gently lifted the glass, and then placed the remaining fish on the desktop so that the two chapters sat side by side. He then looked up at Suzanne for her reaction.

"Is there a problem, Dr. Coletrane?" The Virgin's smile died instantly on his lips. He saw Suzanne pointing Dalton's pistol at him. He raised his hands slowly.

"Not now. I think I fixed it." Suzanne reached her free hand behind her back.

"Did I muck something up?"

"No, why?"

"The gun. Why are you pointing it at me?"

"Gun? Oh, this? No. I didn't mean to point it at you. Safety's on anyway. It was just that I discovered the source of this nagging back pain."

"Dr. Coletrane, please put the gun away."

"Sorry," Suzanne placed the pistol on the table. "What were you saying, Virgin?"

"Honestly, Dr. Coletrane, I don't remember," he said, delicately spinning the gun barrel away from himself with the tip of a pen. Jude then mopped his brow, garnering a wisp of a smile. He startled as Suzanne rapped the table firmly.

"Ah, yes, I remember!" Suzanne barked. "Well—not what you were saying, but—I was thinking that it was amazing that something as preciously rare and sacred as chapters from the Second Book of Benjamin would be kept in a place of such openness. As guardians, do you think that wise?" Suzanne tapped on the pistol.

"Where else is known to be the best hiding place but there in full view where only the eyes of the knowing can see?" Jude slid the weapon farther away from Suzanne's hand. "Dr. Coletrane, in your life you probably have seen at least one leaning tower. It stood there obvious to all, yet the secret it held was known not to anyone, even you … until now."

"And now I know that leaning towers are falling towers."

"Oh no, dear, dear Dr. Coletrane. You couldn't be more amiss."

"But I thought a rose by any other name…."

"Dear me. Dear me. Dr. Coletrane, all falling towers are leaning towers but not all leaning towers are falling towers. Need I say more?"

"Oh, please don't. Sometimes more information is just more, Mr. More."

"True enough … and cleverly put, I might say. Now, where was I?"

"You were about to reveal what Justice James More would have provided me that you didn't."

"Ah yes, at this juncture only one piece *More* of information," the Virgin said coyly.

"And that is … "

" … as always, right in front of you. Here under the glass—no, there—it's upside down, you can't see it. Here, let me get it for you." Jude reached under the glass again and handed her a picture of two people in front of the Bristol Church Tower. A computer inscription on the bottom read: *In God's Sight and Tower Light.*

"It's a picture of you and Miriam in front of the church tower—so?"

"There is more in the photograph than meets the eye."

Everything looked usual to Suzanne. She looked harder but couldn't see. She started shaking her head.

"Yes … that is Miriam there holding the flowers, Dr. Coletrane … Miriam with her wedding flowers … standing next to her husband…."

"Husband? Uh … but you're a … "

"Virgin … yes, *I* am, but those people in the photo aren't, at least not anymore."

After a short pause, Suzanne looked up and smiled saying, "Of course, Justice James is your brother."

"Yes, Dr. Coletrane, Justice James More is my brother. We're twins." Handing her the two documents on the desk, Jude continued, "Just like these two—'In God's Sight and Tower Light'—we are two chapters from the same book. Come, you have gathered all there is to know here." He placed the photo back under the glass. "Though you may not understand it, you have the fish for which you came. Although it's Greek, it may not be Greek to you anymore."

He put the two fish together in the transparent jacket and handed them to Suzanne who slid them into her cargo pocket.

"I understand what you are saying Jude, but my question remains. Are these the secret or are they, like you, the guardians of the secret?"

"Yes."

"Yes, what?"

"Yes, immediately … we must go."

"Okay. Where?" Suzanne started for the pistol. Jude quickly reached out and stayed her hand.

"Why don't we have Miriam turn this over to the local constabulary? You won't be able to carry it on a commercial flight anyway."

"Fine, Virgin. Jeez, you act like you've never been at gunpoint."

"Besides your repeated efforts, this is a treat I'm usually spared, Dr. Coletrane."

"Are you going to tell me where we're going, or should I find another source of coercion?" She raised her eyebrows menacingly.

"No, no. I mean, yes, yes. Of course, I'll tell you. You must go with me to join Justice James near Dresden, Germany at a gathering. The last of your questions should be answered there. We will need to meet with the four brothers."

Suzanne grimaced. Short of Groucho Marx, there weren't many cohorts of four brothers that she knew. She was hot on the trail of something which was leading her back to Germany. *What agenda does Mickey have after the completion of this mission in England? I wonder if this diversion will affect my shadows and goons? Mickey should be wrapping up his visits in Poland—he'll call soon.* Suzanne started to reach for her phone to call Mickey but relaxed her hand. Since the British towers were at mission complete, she decided to call him once she was back on German soil. Until then, she and the Virgin would keep one thing in common; that is *In God's Sight and Tower Light* poetic justice. The fish and flowers and falling towers were starting to make sense, but there were a lot of loose ends which just didn't tie in.

They took Temple Way back across England to the London-Stansted Airport where the whole Britain sojourn began. Suzanne was dog tired, and she wanted to get into a hotel and rest before she had to fly back to Germany in the morning. Dresden wasn't a city she remembered well. During the winter, her family used to go with the Meriwether family to the Christmas markets to get the absolute, hands-down, best Christmas pastry in all of Germany. For Suzanne, the unparalleled Dresden stollen—a scrumptious, sugar-powdered cake roll— was the standard to which all Christmas pastries were compared.

Suzanne's stomach growled with the thought, but her lids weighed a ton. She collapsed on the hotel bed. *Right now, the only use I'd have for a baked stollen would be as a pillow.*

59

Twin Towers

Route to Burano
Venice, Italy

*D*eer or crow? Watching Venice fade from his seat on the deck of the vaporetto, a canal boat, Russell shook his head. *I'm too tired to be a deer. Definitely, wings would be better.*

Unlike those who were committed to ground transportation, thanks to European Medical Command's G3 Air Operations and Luis Toro-Calderon, Russell and Simeone had a helicopter waiting for them at Cavallino-Treporti on a makeshift heliport, just down from the docking point in Burano. Russell was glad for it because he could not imagine driving on the Italian autostrada after the operational tempo he had managed to keep up in the last forty-five hours.

At the airport, Russell crisply returned the salute to the helmeted crew chief who approached him from the bird which was kicking up more and more debris with an increasingly high-pitched whine. With the blast wind in his face, Russell felt extra proud to be part of the big green machine which was providing him air transport at this most auspicious time. He also felt thankful to Mickey, who had his back during this very long leg of the mission.

On the verge of an Italian break dance, Simeone tried to suppress the overwhelming excitement of being on an American warbird for the first time in his life. With his shirt hem flapping wildly, he boyishly waved a semi-salute to the crew chief with his right hand, while his left hand clutched his shirt collar closed. Russell motioned for Simeone to crouch on entry to the chopper's side panel. Simeone acknowledged understanding of the signal, but then his crouched approach was comically nullified by his still-raised, high-flying right-hand waving excitedly. Russell just shook his head, happy in the thought that the whirling chopper blades were a comforting thirteen feet above the ground.

Russell had convinced the chopper pilot that Simeone was his point of contact and needed to fly with him onward to the next objective—Garisenda, the leaning tower in Bologna. Simeone had an expression of pure joy on his face as the chopper heaved and jerked, pulling the crew and the two adventurers

221

southwest. The one-hundred-mile journey by air would cut the travel time from ninety minutes, as the deer runs, to thirty minutes, as the crow flies, with the additional perk that Russell wouldn't fall asleep at the wheel.

Bologna was the city whose fertile lands made its landowners wealthy beyond dreams. During the flight, Russell closed his eyes and conjured up an image of fourteenth-century Italy and the homegrown Bolognese physician-scientist and astrologer, Tommaso da Pizzano. He saw Pizzano graduate from the world's oldest learning institution, the University of Bologna, and imagined his move to Venice to establish professional greatness. Russell knew that when word got out that Pizzano was the goods, he had received regal offers of employment from several faraway realms. Russell smiled at the thought of Pizzano's choice to accept a position in the royal court in Paris—the center of art and literature of the fourteenth-century world.

The character of Russell's hero, Dr. Pizzano, had guided Russell professionally to medicine; artistically to poetry; and yes, even hopelessly into the velvet grip of love. It was the Bolognese physician-scientist's daughter, Christine, that was revered by Trane. Suzanne and Russell followed the pathways of their icons into a more military medical version of success. Today, that flavor of success had the taste of Italy for Russell. With his eyes still closed, he smiled thinking again of the fragrant, hot pastry, the *bussolai buranelli* from Burano along with the sights of Venice far off at the northeastern horizon.

His reverie was interrupted by Simeone shouting, "Look!"

From the cockpit, Garisenda could be seen over one hundred fifty feet above the city along with its twin tower, Asinelli, which rose yet another one hundred fifty feet.

"The ancient twin towers were built in the twelfth century—a competition between two Bolognese families," Simeone continued. "But Garisenda's foundation was flawed. For fear of it collapsing, the Bolognese people decided to reduce its height by about forty-two meters. The Asinelli family became the apparent winners."

The chopper was unable to land at the tower site itself and so it touched down nearby at the Convent Osservanza just southwest of city center.

"The convent library was famous at the end of the fifteenth century and was considered one of the richest of the city," Simeone told Russell as they left the chopper behind and struck out on foot. "Its original collection had approximately twenty-five thousand volumes—half of the collection was writings of the sixteenth and seventeenth centuries consisting of texts of philosophy, theology, and canon law. Here we will meet the keeper of the towers, Giacomo Giordano."

In the background, the blades of the Blackhawk whirled to a stop as Russell and Simeone found their way to the office of literary antiquities. Simeone was bubbling with sibling pride as he introduced Russell to his brother, Giacomo, who served on the library staff in addition to his tower duties. Russell was taken aback by their unbelievable likeness. To add to the confusion, both were dressed in striking guayaberas.

"Forgive me for asking the obvious, Giacomo, but … " Russell looked from one man to the other. "Are you guys … ?"

"No, Dr. Russell Lange," Giacomo bellowed, "we are not twins—but we get that question more times than Asinelli and Garisenda. However, despite their differences in appearance, the two Bolognese towers are, indeed, twins. Life laughs at us, eh, Dr. Lange?"

"Maybe so." Russell pasted on a weary smile. "However, I'm too tired to laugh back." Russell cleared his throat. "Simeone tells that you have—"

"Business, Dr. Lange?" Giacomo shook a finger. "You are barely able to stand on those wobbly legs. I fear my brother has been inattentive to your needs. We will fix that right now." Giacomo turned to his brother. "Come, Simeone, I have prepared a meal. Bring your doctor friend. Let us eat, drink, and relax. There is no need to spend additional energy going into the tower since I believe I have already retrieved that for which you search."

Russell was relieved to avoid negotiating the narrow streets of Bologna. Even more so, he knew food and drink would ease his body into the necessary learning mode. Russell smiled his agreement, and the three men retired to a small, glass-enclosed alcove overlooking the city. The sun was setting to their left and the city skyline could be seen with the twin towers jutting out from its very heart.

The small table sat four, but the seat to Russell's left was empty and so he stretched his legs out upon it. Simeone sat to his immediate right and Giacomo sat directly across from him. The table was set with platters of warm bread, freshly sliced meat, and strings of aromatic cheese. The fragrance of the meal overwhelmed Russell's senses as he breached courtesy and protocol to quench the basic intensities of human existence—hunger and thirst.

"Dr. Lange, you like Bolognese foods?"

"Please, call me Russell."

"Russell, I believe you love our Bolognese foods. You Americans call our mortadella your bologna."

Embarrassed like the child with his hand in the proverbial cookie jar, Russell, with his cheeks pouched, responded, "Especially the bologna." He remembered Mickey's obsession with eponyms. He wondered if Mickey had ever had bologna in Bologna. If not, only time and opportunity would ever prevent him from doing so. For now, Russell enjoyed the eponym for both Mickey and himself.

The meal went quickly and when the dishes were cleared, Giacomo folded his hands in front of him on the table, drew his chin in to form a frown, and formally initiated the business at hand.

"You have traveled far in search of answers. How can I best help you, Russell?"

"That question is more complex than you know." Taken aback by the sudden change in demeanor, Russell shifted uncomfortably in his seat. "I would say, 'Start at the beginning, Giacomo.' But I am unclear as to where the beginning actually rests. Please be so kind as to help me fill in the gaps in my understanding as you see fit."

"Sure, Russell." Sucking in a deep breath, Giacomo flared his nostrils. "What do you know of John and his work?"

"I know that John's work was distributed into places of hiding described by the Second Book of Benjamin. What I don't understand is why there are only two copies of the Second Book of Benjamin—one bound and one unbound. The unbound copy apparently has been distributed."

"This is a very good question. The bound version is actually the original which is secured in a place known only to the esoteric few. I can tell you that it was once here in the library. The nuns were given the mission to transcribe it only once—in a very particular fashion."

"In what fashion would that be?"

"In the manner of the fallen tower."

"I don't understand."

Giacomo reached behind Simeone and took a framed picture down from the wall. Removing the backing, he pulled out the chapter from the Second Book of Benjamin and handed it to Russell.

CHAPTER 3

1) So let the light be the standard by which you learn; for secrets are better understood in the light than in the shadows.

2) John learned to work the cool stone in the night; but it was his love for wood that fed upon the juice of the sun, which first made him a master in his craft.

3) It should never be the task that determines the level of skill applied. Give all your effort to even the most menial of tasks. The worker of wood should never feel bested by the skill of a mason.

4) The ruling class will ornament with stone as they have that which can pay for such. Time, the mother of all need, will forsake the stone for wood leaving the coins to jingle within the fat purse.

5) The Lord will be the stone that protects the secret of the soft inner wood. The ultimate brightness of the sun and moon must be that for which people strive. If we start to fail in our aspirations, we must ask Him for strength and guidance else what we achieve will be not of His light.

6) The secret will be amongst tall men who will keep it within the folds of their cloaks until the time when the light is high and the people are ready to receive. Even the flawed will be kept a secret.

7) The two flawed were devoid of purpose but then, through the skill of a master craftsman, made whole again. So long as the light is kept as the beacon, the Lord will see to it that the lambs are brought back within the fold. The purpose will then be given in the presence of the brightest light.

8) If the light guides the wearing of the mantle, should not the three stones take in the light and give off the heat? Behold the wood does not burn nor do the stones grow hot except once within the bosom of men.

9) Let the light be the standard by which all men learn. A man who does not see a shadow denies that there is a sun. For him the shadow directs him. When the spirit dwells within, the sun is realized and the shadow accepted though it cannot be seen.

10) The light directs the heart not the mind. A man between two leaning towers will not know which shadow to follow.

"What do you see, Russell?"

"I see a chapter text written as ten verses just like the chapters I have seen before. But if the verses were transcribed like a fallen tower … then they would … wait a minute…." Russell took out chapter five from Burano and chapter eight from Venice and laid them next to the chapter three on the table from left to right in numerical order.

"Look," said Russell. "The verbiage is so stilted in each of the chapters as a whole. However, look at verses nine and ten in each of the three chapters." His eyes flew across the three pages.

3:9 Let the light be the standard by which all men learn. A man who does not see a shadow denies that there is a sun. For him the shadow directs him. When the spirit dwells within, the sun is realized and the shadow accepted though it cannot be seen.

5:9 A tower that leans either has no shadow in the morning or the longest shadow of the day. The ones who follow the shadow for guidance live lives that are lost in the morning or lost at the end of days.

8:9 The long shadow of a leaning tower can fade in the late of day. The short shadow lengthens as the sun sets.

3:10 The light directs the heart not the mind. A man between two leaning towers will not know which shadow to follow.

5:10 Learning from the light is weakest at the dawn and dusk of our lives. Initially we learn by seeing. At midday we learn most with our eyes closed and our hearts open.

8:10 Our flesh is weak and fails with time. Only His light sustains us. He is our stony mantle and the flesh and blood within are what we use to divert from the shadow and find our way to Him, our Father.

"What is it that you see, Russell?"

"Holy Mary, Mother of God. I see that in verses nine the theme is shadows and in verses ten the theme is light. The reading of the chapters flows from verse to verse horizontally, like a fallen tower. Obviously, with more chapters the horizontal reading would be smoother."

"Can you see that even those who would learn of the chapters and would seek to use them for their own vile purposes could be thwarted because the written text, when read vertically, would continue to hide its meaning?"

"Fascinating."

"Provocative, indeed," Giacomo iterated.

"Who would be the vile seekers?"

"There have been many, Russell. Caesars, popes, dictators, Austrian artists—"

"Hitler. Adolf Hitler, as an artist, served as a soldier with a Bavarian unit in World War I. He probably knew of the mission going into Ieper and the search for the sarcophagus. Did he know of the Second Book of Benjamin?"

"With all of the victims who were tortured, he probably knew it existed," said Giacomo, "but maybe not enough to actually find it." He leaned back in his chair, his unbuttoned collar falling open. Russell listened, intently focusing on Giacomo.

"Later, he set up secret military operations to search for his personal immortality through medical research. Dr. Theodor Morell, his personal physician, was given the mission to correct Hitler's medical problems and create a tissue bank of Hitler's cells, tissues, and organ systems. Morell used his physician-scientist colleagues' research data from universities like Tubingen and Strasbourg. Hitler allowed his physician to build a special laboratory in Silesia where the work could be done. He also permitted Morell to do human testing at places like Neuengamme, Sachsenhausen, Natzweiler-Struthof, Spandau, Buchenwald, and Ravensbrück. *Nacht und Nebel*—Hitler's directive meaning night and fog—allowed the gestapo to yank anyone off the street," Giacomo motioned to his own city's roads through the window, "for any reason—including for the purpose of medical testing."

With this movement causing a rumple from his open collar, Russell noticed the forked edge of a white birthmark high on the tanned skin of Giacomo's right-side chest. Russell recalled having seen similar milk-line birthmarks on his patients. He nodded at Giacomo. "How did Christ's blood come into play?"

"Somewhere along the way, information got to Hitler that there was another source of blood which—if cloned in his laboratory, brought under his control, and given the correct weaponry—could subjugate the whole world."

"And so began the search," pondered Russell.

"No, Russell, not *began* the search—*continued* the search. Others before had been searching," clarified Giacomo. "The blood of Christ was thought to be in many places—the Czech Republic, Slovakia, Poland, Belgium, France, and Italy. *Flusszigeuner* was Hitler's search for the River Gypsies—the people who would have the fish which would lead him to the sarcophagi."

"Did any of the scientists succeed in cloning cells, tissues, or organs for Hitler?"

"For that answer, you must go to Pisa and the Campo dei Miracoli. There, more information can be given to you. Don't worry, Russell, Simeone will go with you. It appears that you have become his charge and your quest has become his."

"So it seems," Russell mumbled his acknowledgment while tucking all the fish under his trouser leg into his boot. As he stood to depart, he noted a snicker and grin pass between the brothers. "What? Do I have bologna on my face?"

"No, Russell. We were marveling at your idea of a briefcase."

"Well, I could go out and buy a nice Italian briefcase except that I have a waiting helicopter to scoop me away before sunset."

"Yes, you may indeed have lost your opportunity to shop for fine Italian accessories. Moreover, you also have lost the sun."

"How about that? Time flies when you're having ... well ... at any rate ... time flies." Russell hadn't really noticed, but while Giacomo had been speaking, night had shrouded the city. Simeone and Russell hurried back to the landing zone where the Blackhawk could be heard spinning up its engines. Before long, the chopper pilot gave them the thumbs up and they were airborne, heading southwest into the night.

From the ground, Giacomo waved at the chopper and hoped that the information he gave would provide the travelers the wherewithal to complete their mission. He knew the picture was still not fully uncovered. The night grew quiet as the lights of the helicopter faded from view. Giacomo turned and locked away the night from the halls of the convent. His thoughts dwelled inward as he knew he had his own flight to take in the morning to Dresden, Germany.

✠ ✠ ✠

In northwest Poland, Mickey was finally obtaining some rest.

Suzanne was in a hotel outside the London Stansted Airport, preparing for her trip back to Germany in the morning.

✠ ✠ ✠

As he flew off into the velvet black, Russell knew that once he finished at Pisa, he would be helicoptered back to Aviano where he would find out what tomorrow's mission held. Until then, he needed enough rest so that he could keep focused on the current mission which was, apparently, still in the process of unfurling. He let his eyelids drop and his mind unwind to the steady whopping beat of the helicopter blades.

60

Above Average Yogi

Route to Campo dei Miracoli
Pisa, Italy

*I**n the darkest of nights, we see the most abundance of stars.* Russell smiled as illuminated marble figures broke the dark horizon line. It was well after midnight when the lit-up Pisa's Torre Pendente, the iconic leaning tower, came into view. It sat in the walled-in Campo dei Miracoli, the "Field of Miracles," which also housed the main cathedral, the baptistery, and the church cemetery. The Blackhawk pilot landed the chopper on the grassy area between the Piazza del Duomo and Il Duomo itself, near the Cathedral de Santa Maria Assunta. There, the crew chief allowed both his passengers to disembark. The two stooped passengers ran from the chopper door toward the cathedral as the rotor blades beat the verdant turf into submission. The Blackhawk, needing to refuel at nearby Camp Darby in Livorno, took off immediately with the promise of a noon tomorrow return.

It was unclear if Andrea, the tower keeper, would be available at this late hour. Regardless, Russell knew that their work would have to be finished before the crowds returned in the morning. Simeone and Russell tried the cathedral's massive bronze doors, but they were inaccessible and quite secure. Russell walked around to the far end of the cathedral, which was closest to the leaning tower, and to the door at Saint Ranieri's Gate. It was also secured. While punching on the keypad of his cell phone, Russell was distracted by a shape moving across the front of the bell tower.

"Thank goodness," Russell remarked sleepily. "The sooner we begin work, the sooner we get some rest."

"I thought spooks didn't need rest," a familiar voice at the base of the tower chided unpleasantly.

"I had hoped you were dead, Dalton."

"You should be so lucky. Where's your friend?"

"He ... uh ... he had to go. We're going to meet in the morning," Russell tried to bluff.

"Dr. Lange, I think the tower door is open!" Simeone's voice startled both men as it heralded from the second-floor landing of the leaning tower.

"Come down now!" Dalton edged into the full light, brandishing a handgun. "Here, where I can see you! Or bullets are going to start flying in the direction of your friend, Russell, here."

Dalton's bluffing—with the information from the towers I'm worth more alive than dead. Do I call the bluff? Will that give Simeone time to act? How did he get around the church and up the tower so quickly? Russell's hesitation gave time for Jean Dalton's bluff to pay off. He soon saw the figure of a man nervously holding his hands so high in the air that the seamed edges of his shirt flapped against his exposed navel. In his hand, the poor unfortunate displayed a set of jingling church keys as he came into the light.

"Don't shoot. I am unarmed," he said.

"Easy, Simeone." Russell watched as Dalton herded the rattled tower keeper over next to Russell's side.

"Too easy," Dalton chortled.

"What do you want, Dalton? I'm guessing there is some reason you are taking an evening stroll with your only friends Smith & Wesson."

"I want to know what you know."

"You've inhaled too many lead-painted wood chips, Dalton. I'm afraid your diseased brain wouldn't be able to handle the data. Sorry, Captain Crunch ... or have you been promoted to Major Disaster now?"

"Ignore the sarcasm, Chaucer," a new voice said. "Lower your weapon, Jean. I'll take it from here."

"It can't be!" Russell knew the new voice, but his mind couldn't wrap around the fact that it was here, in this place.

"Dr. Lange," the voice continued, "I believe you would have to agree that *my mind* would be able to process any data you could provide."

"It most certainly can." Russell knew that the genius synapses in the brain of Dr. Joachim Wunschmann had very few equals. He watched as a well-dressed man stepped out from the secured church door. "Why would you, the division chief at the Chemical Casualty Care Division of the Institute of Chemical Defense, find it necessary to make a personal appearance to such a remote site, sir?"

"Russell ... " Wunschmann's voice was calm, almost melodic, and seasoned with just a trace of credible emotional injury. "We were so worried about you all."

"What's this all about, Dr. Wunschmann?"

"In this open forum, you know I can't go into the details with you, Russell." Wunschmann glanced around the green space. "The main issue is that the forest drums have all gone silent. I can't seem to get a report from Suzanne or Mickey. Do you know why? If so, please tell me." Wunschmann's tongue slithered. "Ease the worry in this old soul. Why were you in the desert? What was found at Dyhernfurth? What did Suzanne find in England? What have you learned here in Italy?"

"You're the division chief, Dr. Wunschmann. You and Colonel Blythe have access to everything in the army's Medical Research Command and the European Medical Command channels. So why ask me?"

"True enough, Russell, but absolutely nothing over the past seventy-two hours has been reported up the chain."

"Maybe there's nothing to report."

"Maybe there is, but it is being kept quiet. Now, why would that be?"

"A little paranoid, aren't we, Dr. Wunschmann?"

"Shut up, you arrogant—" Dalton jumped aggressively toward Russell, but Dr. Wunschmann stepped in to restrain Dalton. Seizing the moment, Russell pressed his phone's camera app and brightly flashed the aggressors. Simeone quickly scurried behind the base of the tower and toward freedom. Dalton started to follow but paused.

"Let him go, Captain Dalton. What I need to know is right here." Wunschmann squared off in front of Russell. "There are things here far beyond your need-to-know, Russell."

"Apparently that works two ways."

"What do you mean?"

"It appears, from this side of the gun barrel, that you're the one needing information here."

"Apparently," conceded Wunschmann. "Are you going to help me?"

"Of course, Dr. Wunschmann—when that tower there falls and hits the ground."

"Regrettably, Russell, I don't have time for this." Wunschmann turned. "Captain Dalton, kill him, hang his body from the banister, and slice his belly open till his guts hit the ground."

"Okay, Russell," Dalton's smile could not be suppressed, "time to bring the pain." Before he could raise his gun and unsheathe a knife, an accented voice shouted out from behind the cathedral.

"Touch him and you'll be dead before he hits the ground!" The voice was Simeone's. Wunschmann quietly dissolved into the shadow of the tower.

"Easy, Dalton." Russell stepped forward and swiftly took Dalton's gun before he could recover. "I'll take that weapon too," said Russell, motioning with his chin toward the bulge in Dalton's blazer pocket. "Move slowly."

"It's not a weapon. I thought a Special Ops guy could figure that out."

"I'll be the judge of that. Take it out carefully. Hold it by two fingers." As Dalton's hand cleared the rim of his blazer pocket, Russell saw that it was a whittled animal carving.

"I trust that beast is not loaded." Russell kept his eye on every movement Dalton made. "Drop it anyway." Dalton dropped the carving to the ground and kicked it away.

"That makes two in one day," snarled Dalton.

"All's well?" Simeone stepped out from the shadow of the church, smiling at Russell. His hand formed the shape of a pistol, but he had no gun. "I should play poker, yes, Dr. Lange?" he spoke gleefully.

"If you're going to bluff, tower keeper," Wunschmann edged back out of the shadows, "you should have something to back it up." Wunschmann reached into his coat and pulled out a .38 caliber snubnosed pistol. He waved Simeone over to Russell's side.

Russell started to drop his gun when, unbelievably, he heard Simeone's voice coming from directly behind Wunschmann. "I wouldn't do that, sir."

Wunschmann lurched forward a bit and dropped his weapon then kicked it away toward Russell. Andrea Giordano stepped into the light. He was holding a twelve-foot spear from the museum archives.

Holding Dalton's gun, Russell surveyed the situation. In front of him was Dalton with his hands up, palms forward. Simeone was to his immediate left, now holding the recently dropped animal carving and the .38 caliber pistol. Wunschmann was to his half-left, hands touching the back of his head. Lastly, standing behind Wunschmann and holding a spear was the other Simeone.

"I thought you all said that you weren't twins?" Russell said, nodding to the Simeone on his left.

"Giacomo didn't lie," Simeone replied. "You asked if Giacomo and I were twins. We are not."

"Who is this?"

"My brother, Andrea."

"Are *you two* twins?"

"No, of course not."

"Of course not! It is just an odd coincidence that you two look exactly alike. In fact, you all three look exactly alike," said Russell.

"Yes, Dr. Lange, we are triplets."

"For God's sake, you have got to be kidding."

"Why would we kid about this?"

"Glad to meet you, Dr. Lange," said Andrea. "I saw these two troublemakers prowling before you arrived and suspected they were up to no good. I decided to wait for you in the tower itself."

"You should be in Special Operations, Andrea."

"In a way I always have been, Dr. Lange. In science class, my brothers and I would often substitute for one another. Usually it was done in sport, but it was always a special operation."

"What do we do with these two?" Simeone asked.

"We'll have the Camp Darby Military Police pick them up for questioning. By the time they are released, we will be on to the last phase of this operation."

"It is probably time we get to work," said Andrea.

"Since when do you do any real work?" Simeone teased.

"Since I must bail, yet again, either you or Giacomo out of some predicament you two manage to get yourselves into."

"I am not the one who stole the foosball table from the American installation," reminded Simeone.

"The grand larceny charges were dropped."

"Only because they knew you were insane, Andrea."

"Insane? I should have let these men shoot you."

"Then who would bail you out after your next theft?" Simeone threw the carved animal, hitting Andrea on the chest.

"You know, life might be better as a twin," stated Andrea, redirecting the museum piece toward his brother.

"Gentlemen, gentlemen," interrupted a very tired Russell Lange as he collected the snubnosed pistol from Simeone, shoving behind his belt buckle. "Is there any hope of getting to the issues which brought us here?"

"Yes, we must return to the point," Simeone nodded.

"That is exactly what I had in mind," said Andrea thrusting the spear point emphatically before bursting into laughter. Russell shook his head and groaned. He scooped up the carving from the grass as he dialed the military police. *This long night is getting longer with each passing quip.*

61

Guns and Poses

Campo dei Miracoli
Pisa, Italy

*T*hree o'clock in the morning, ugh. Russell glanced at his watch as he accompanied the two brothers, still bantering, through Saint Ranieri's Gate and into the main entrance of the Cathedral of Saint Mary. Processing this new conflict in the mission, Russell figured that Wunschmann and Dalton would be questioned on charges of aggravated assault. *Wunschmann has enough clout to be out of containment by the end of business today. But at least the United States is six hours behind and any support he might gather from the ICD in Maryland won't be forthcoming before two o'clock in the afternoon Italy time. Their release will be greatly delayed without stateside assistance.*

His attention was snapped back to the present moment by the cathedral's beauty—particularly the statues of the Four Evangelists.

"Is it my imagination, or are this building, the baptistery, and the bell tower outside also tilting?" Russell queried.

"Yes."

"Yes to which, Andrea?"

"Yes, they all tilt. It is not your imagination."

"Was this tower an intentional leaning tower?"

"No, it was not, Dr. Lange. But nevertheless, the tilting made it significant for the securing of a fish from the Second Book of Benjamin."

"Where is the fish, Andrea?"

"The fish was kept in the Camposanto Monumentale, which lies at the northern end. It is a walled cemetery and is renowned to be the most beautiful cemetery in the world. A shipload of earth from the crucifixion site of Christ was deposited here from the Fourth Crusade in the twelfth century."

"Why there?"

"Because it lay with the sacred sarcophagus."

"Where did the sarcophagus go?"

"On to Silesia."

"Do we know where?"

233

"It is in the Second Book of Benjamin. Here is the chapter that you seek," said Andrea, removing the fish-imprinted document from a signpost. The inscription on the post stated that a holy relic once occupied the empty space. As with the others, it was in a protective covering. It was titled chapter one and it read with the same difficulty as did the others. Russell's eyes drank in the information on the printed page.

CHAPTER 1

1) When the moment had come and the Savior was satisfied that learning could take place, He began to reveal that which they needed to know.

2) In a town not far away lived a man named John who could work both wood and stone.

3) John placed his chisel to shape the wood. The wood was young and rebounded with strength against the skilled pounding of the hammer.

4) Chisel on stone is different than chisel on wood. John had to change his grip and even then, there were flawed trials before acceptance.

5) After the floor was covered with the pieces of cut stone, the wood in John's hands could no longer be seen.

6) The hiding of the wood must be done for there are those among us that would seek out and destroy the blood of the Lamb. From this evil, our wisdom and light must prevail.

7) Three times twice John did swing his hammer. Within each coupled pair John harbored a secret to be revealed at the failing of the light.

8) Since stone keeps better secrets than wood, the mantle had to be secured tightly. It is placed in a corner which guards the hope of mankind.

9) That place of greatest secrecy is the place where all can see. This is because those who could possess the sight defer to those who would be happy to speak of it. Those who hold the light within will then not speak of it and thus remain guardians of the secret.

10) The secret will be revealed when man can see with his heart and can find the Master.

As Russell read, he saw that the guidance of the first century had been followed just as it was written. "Verse nine is your basis for the method of hiding."

"Yes. It was commanded and so the faithful followed," said Andrea.

"I need to again ask. What is the connection of this Second Book of Benjamin with the chemical munitions found in Silesia?"

"A very unique chemical laboratory was found, was it not?"

"I believe so, Andrea."

"Through the talents of his physician-scientists, Hitler had the ability to reproduce his own tissues in these chemical laboratories." Andrea's eyes flared. "From there, his greed grew, and he wanted to produce Christ from Christ's own cells."

"But the technology didn't exist."

"You know this?" Andrea challenged curtly.

"History reflects this."

"History is written by the victor and Nazi Germany didn't win, Dr. Lange."

"So, it is possible that the technology did exist with the Nazis, but because they were not able to write history, the facts we know have been skewed."

"It has always been, Dr. Lange."

"So it seems."

"Unknown to the world, the technology did exist and was used by the Germans since the turn of the century," said Andrea. "Scientists from Strasbourg were instrumental."

"Since this predates both world wars, this begs the question if World War I and World War II were quests for Christ's blood?"

"Yes, Dr. Lange."

"Did they find it?"

"No, not that is known." Andrea shrugged.

"Did they create clones of Hitler?"

"They tried. As they have always done, the Knights Templar had to step in."

"What happened, Andrea?"

"This is as much as I know," said Andrea as he smiled. "I do know where the next piece of information for you lies. It is in Silesia. The World Templar Organization has a meeting at the place of the four brothers near Dresden. Select chevaliers have been selected for this meeting. Will you come with us?"

"I must meet my helicopter at noon tomorrow."

"I will go with you," offered Simeone.

"We will make many connections and the journey will be tumultuous."

"Sounds like more of the same; I will go with you," reiterated Simeone.

"Then we must make the connection from here tomorrow."

"Forgive me as I go to the tower and rest," chimed in Andrea. "You may use the rooms in the back of the cathedral for rest. It will be safe and quiet. Further, besides the handguns that you collected from your two colleagues; you will have the statues of the Four Evangelists to guard you."

"About that, Andrea, I've changed my mind."

"You don't want to rest here in the cathedral?"

"Yes, I do," said Russell. "I've changed my mind about the two handguns. I think I will leave them with you."

"Why? You would have better use for them than I ever would."

"I thought so initially." Russell nodded. "However, the guns would only be as helpful as the number of bullets they hold. Plus, they use special ammunition which I don't carry. So, as sweet and dear as they are in my hand, let's just plan to have the military police secure them. Can you see that that happens?"

"Are you sure, Dr. Lange? You don't think there will come a time when you will have need of them?"

"Probably, and if you're around, tap me and tell me so."

"It'll be a gentle nudge," said Andrea, winking.

"Maybe, or it might be a swift kick in the pants."

"Time will tell." Concealing the weaponry in his guayabera, Andrea retired for the evening.

Since so many thoughts were surging through Russell's mind, he had little time for future regrets. In his hand he had one fish, in his boot, three others: chapters three, five, and eight. Twice in four days he faced the working end of a handgun. He was tired and the adventure still continued. *God, I hope Mickey and Suzanne have enough other fish to make sense of all this.*

Russell and Simeone found their way to the cathedral's rear rooms and settled in to get some sleep.

"Do you think you can rest?" Simeone asked, speaking with an uncharacteristic fatherly tone.

"It is not a matter of *can*," replied Russell, lying on his back, looking up to the ceiling. "I *have* to sleep or else I will make a mental error which could be costly."

"Aren't physicians masters of making critical decisions with little or no rest?"

"Physicians are the masters of sleeplessness whether they wish to be or not." Russell scoffed. "Having to make decisions under these conditions just makes life more interesting."

"Whose life?"

"That, my dear Simeone, is the question which is the crux."

"'Crux'? That is a word?"

"Military physicians at courts martial know it as crucifixion."

"I see," Simeone nodded. "The price of being a military physician can sometimes lead to professional flagellation, humiliation, and pain. Why would anyone ever desire to place themselves in this situation?"

"Jesus expects us to use our God-given talents. With the good comes the bad." Russell tucked the recent fish safely under his pant leg and into his boot with the others, then stretched his body out before turning on his side to sleep.

"And with the bad comes our Savior. No?"

"Indeed, Simeone. We just need to keep Him in the loop. So much is provided by Him just from the asking."

"I am glad I am not a military physician." Simeone chortled. "I would be doing a lot of asking."

"For the same reason Jesus is probably glad I am not a tower keeper."

62

The Four Brothers

High country
Roman frontier, Saxony
AD 285

T he sun poured hot streams of morning through the four giant stone fingers—carved ages ago by God's hand wielding the receding glaciers of another time. By and by, the early evening sun no longer bathed the bronzed Roman military arms in light. Soldiers grunted loudly and heaved strenuously to bring to the base of the rock formation an item of great significance.

✠ ✠ ✠

At Die vier Brüder, just south of Dresden in the Elbsandsteingebirge, the faintest ghostly echo of Roman soldiers' groans and grunts might be heard amongst the quiet shuffling of an occasional curious creature. Many had traveled through these canyons over two thousand years—Romans, Gaelic tribesmen, Prussians, Poles, and Germans. Today, visitors were a scarcity. The Four Brothers rock formation was located in a retreat known as the Bastei. The area had been secured for the World Templar Organization to hold a private conference throughout the next few days. Armed guards secured the single entrance and only select, vetted people were permitted to pass. By five o'clock, the Americans began to arrive.

From England, Suzanne had flown with the Virgin, Jude More, to Dresden. They picked up a rental car and came south into the Bastei. Jude graciously took his leave as he was intent upon meeting with his brother, Justice James, and bringing him up to speed on the remarkable events of the past few days. Suzanne had received a phone call from Mickey saying that he had left Poland in time for a five o'clock arrival. However, he might be late because he was having recurring car problems.

After checking in at the Bastei retreat, Suzanne turned from the reception desk to see, despite the caveat of potential lateness, a worn-out Mickey Peronne strolling through the main hotel doors.

"So, where's this piece of work you call a car, Mickey?"

"It could hardly make it the forty miles from Bautzen, but surprisingly, it waited to die until the final stretch in. I am fine though, thanks for asking."

"Did you just abandon it?"

"No, my passenger, Mr. Lenz, is taking it to a local shop—hopefully to have it shot, repaired, shot again, repaired again, then lit on fire, hurled over a cliff, and then shot on the way down. Never has one car caused me so much grief." He proceeded up to the reception desk, dropped his knapsack on the ground at his feet, and began the check-in procedure.

"I'm fine too, thank you for asking," Suzanne redirected.

"Touché, madame." Mickey shook his head, smiling.

"I have missed having secure communications with you." Suzanne's smile drifted into a more serious demeanor. "Is there anything pressing you need to share with me?"

"Is Russell in?"

"For me—I said for me." Suzanne raised her voice a little.

"First things first!" Mickey called and raised the ante. "Where's Russell?"

"I dunno … " Suzanne folded. Her voice returned to a conversational level. "If he is in, I haven't yet seen him."

"What is the last word you heard?" Mickey asked.

"Don't worry, Mickey. Russell's a big boy. I'm sure he's fine."

"I gave him a tough row to hoe—"

"And mine was a piece of cake, was it?"

"Well, no … it's just that he took a chopper to Constanța, Romania; C12 to Aviano, Italy; fixed-wing to Grafenwoehr, Germany; chopper to—" Mickey was interrupted by the sound of a Blackhawk flying overhead.

"Russell's here," Suzanne whispered to herself as her eyes scoured the contours of the elevated ceiling.

"Where is the landing zone?" Mickey queried.

"Among these rock formations, it would be hard to tell where a helicopter LZ would be."

"I saw a clearing by the lower parking lot. If not a designated landing zone, it could certainly function alternately as one."

"That's not so very far," whispered Suzanne.

"He should be in directly."

"Yes, he will," Suzanne mused with a sudden flush in her cheeks.

"Suzanne, I'm spent. If, indeed, that is Russell, just let him know I am here. Just a quick howdy tonight … excitement is going to start very early tomorrow. I'm going to my room to continue this major energy crash. I'll plan on meeting you all early in the morning. We'll compare notes then." Mickey collected his key from the attendant, scooped up his bag, turned the corner, and disappeared up the stairwell. Suzanne frowned as she searched for seating.

No, I can see my hands. Suzanne flipped her palms up and down. *I guess only Mickey feels I'm invisible.* Biting her lip, Suzanne plopped herself down into a lobby seat. *Water off a duck's back, as Mom would say.* One pearl Suzanne had used today was to curb her annoyance in the face of being treated dismissively. *Loss of control today would be followed by regrets tomorrow.* Suzanne sighed. *Mickey's curtness was due to fatigue in the management of his own real-world urgency while no doubt worrying about things in Russell's and my lanes.* Suzanne surveyed the shelves of a wine rack next to the nearby dining area. *I sure wish they had some Alsatian wine here, but this is Saxony. So, Russell, you will have to be my exclusive source of intoxication.*

Suzanne waited a full hour before Russell finally entered the lobby. Seeing her, Russell flashed a weary smile but kept heading for the reception desk. Suzanne intercepted him, standing between him and his target.

"What's happening, stranger? Pretending not to know me?"

"Got that right."

"Got what right?"

"Stranger. These past four days couldn't have been stranger. Where's Mickey?"

"Physically alive but literally dead man walking, I'd say."

"Ditto."

"Got time for a drink?" Suzanne nodded to his right where the elevated dining room led to a wraparound bar.

Russell scoped the area in the direction where she looked. *It does look tempting.*

"Are you buying?" Russell probed.

"Maybe."

"Honestly, Trane, as much as I would love to do so, I think I'll defer to a rain check. It is great to see you but—"

"But nothing. You passed the test. Get your lazy butt in bed. Mickey wants us up bright-eyed and bushy-tailed in the morning. Right now, you look the reverse."

"Trane … " Russell gave her a *God, I love you* look.

"Yeah, yeah, I know that look. I've heard it all before; seen it all before. Check-in quick and start on that rack time. No excuses or buts accepted tomorrow morning."

"Yes, ma'am."

"Good. Now that I got you two lightweights tucked in for the night, I believe I am going to have me a … "

" … seven and seven—double, shaken, tall glass, salt rim, slice of orange. I really wish I could join you, but there have been just too many leaning towers falling. Unfortunately, I would just be the next one to collapse."

"Hey, no apologies needed or accepted. You weren't invited anyway."

"I thought I was…."

"Sorry, Russell," Suzanne's return volley was all business, "invitation expired due to lack of interest."

"You cut me deep, Trane."

"Say good night, Russell."

"Good night, Russell."

"Time to cut a trail." Suzanne turned away smartly, stoic in every way on the exterior for all to see. However, in those places where inquisitive eyes couldn't pry, deep inside, she was pure gelatin. She wished she could just curl up lovingly with her sweet Russell. *Maybe that won't ever be.* She put herself on the road to sleepy town as well.

As she sat down at the bar, she did a quick mental inventory of her room. *Since I'll be spending the evening alone, what will tonight's reading be?* The reading materials she carried exalted Christine de Pizan, one of Suzanne's three major heroines. The other two heroines were Marie Marvingt, the fiancée of danger, and the twice Nobel Laureate, Dr. Marie Curie. She always had a passion for strength in women. It confounded her to think that some women intentionally made themselves appear weak. *Then again, maybe that feign is their greatest act of strength.*

The follow-on drink and its repeat acted as the final closer. It was just what she, the doctor, ordered. Suzanne accepted this prescription for sleep from herself, although she knew that a doctor who prescribes for herself has a fool for a patient. In her peripheral vision, she saw a hotel staff member pivot away from the large, twisted art decoration situated in the lobby and head straight for the elevator. He was tall and slender and drove her memory back to Russell who had gone past the artwork, into the elevator, and onward to his room where she knew she wouldn't be going tonight. Feeling a little tingly, Suzanne drifted for the stairwell which would take her to emotional solitude. *I may hate my own past, but sometimes my life in the present also drips with utter and complete disdain.*

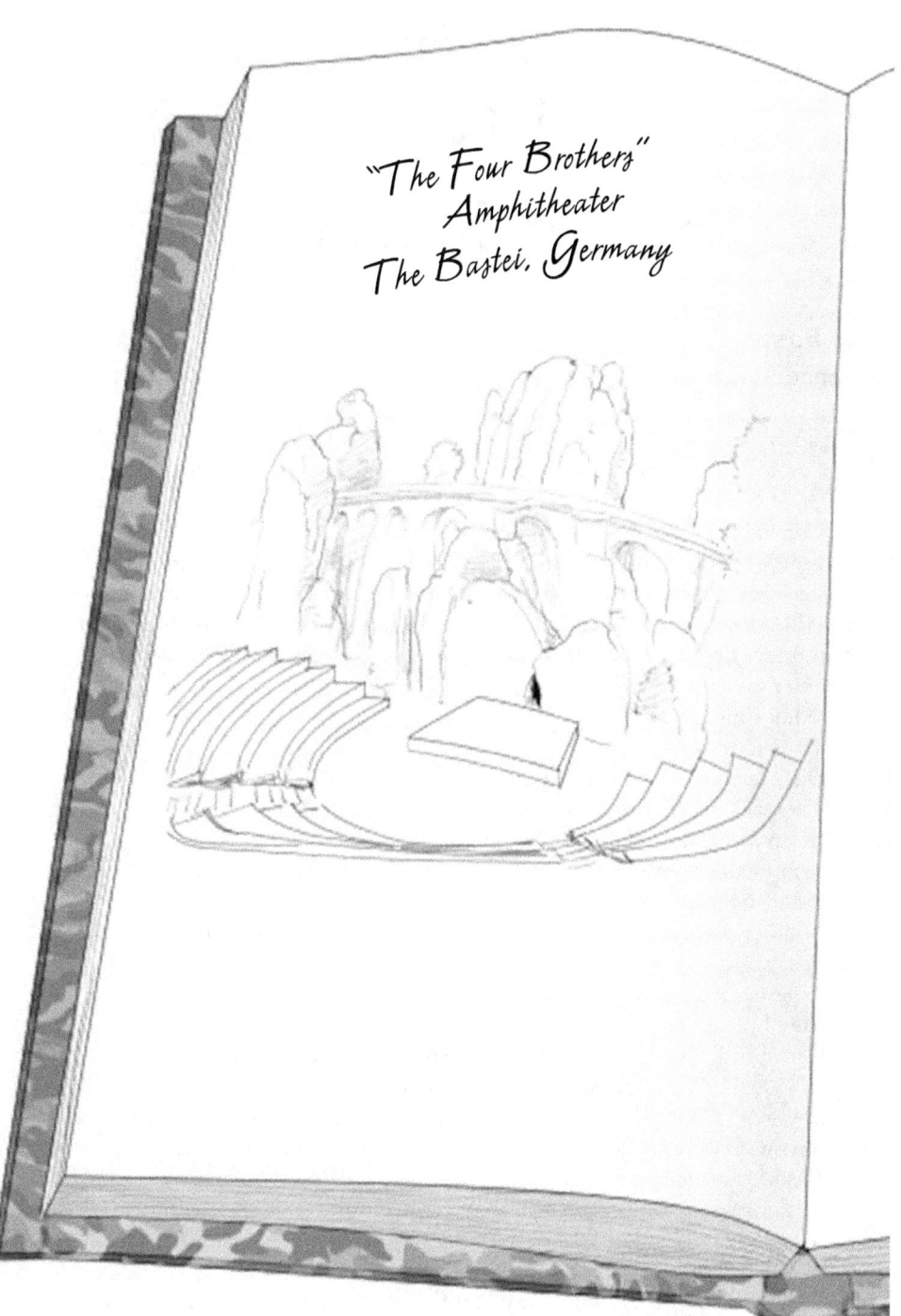

"The Four Brothers"
Amphitheater
The Bastei, Germany

63

Silent Knights

The Bastei
Lohmen, Germany

*O*nly *in the wee hours can I read without being disturbed, talk without being heard, think without being curbed, and discuss with my demons the reason they exist in the first place.* Suzanne sniggered as she peeked through her curtains. The moonlit night waned brightly as a sleepless Suzanne heard a gentle rapping on her door. She tossed her book onto the bed. *Maybe Russell rested quicker than I predicted.* She could feel her heart quicken. Against all odds, she hoped that Russell's face would fill the gap of the opening door crack. But instead of Russell, Suzanne saw an oddly dressed Jude More holding a very large, cream-colored cloak in his hand. *Lady Luck fails to deliver.*

"What time is it, Virgin?"

"Time to make a move."

"Does anyone ever get a straight answer from you?"

"The sack of crowns to the face was pretty straight forward, don't you think? Captain Dalton didn't seem to like it much," replied Jude.

Suzanne narrowed her eyes. "Are you threatening me with another loaded sack of sterling?"

"I hadn't planned so, Doctor, but this is Europe—it most certainly can be arranged."

"Where are we going, Virgin?"

"May I please enter?"

"Certainly." She stepped back from the door. "Where are we going, Virgin?"

"WTO, the World Templar Organization, meets in secret council tonight. Your presence at the conclave has been preapproved by the grand master. However, you must arrive cloaked. It is the way of our order to maintain such secrecy."

"Even from each other?"

"It is our way."

"Your way doesn't make sense."

"Nevertheless, it is—"

"I know, I know, it is your way, Virgin." Suzanne eyed the heavy cloak.

"Have you ever stopped to think that maybe your organization is filled with a bunch of really ugly people?"

"I know two who aren't so ugly, Dr. Coletrane."

"You're talking about the picture you showed me in Bristol of Miriam and Justice James on their wedding day—trust me, Miriam took in a real sympathy case."

"Why—you—I—you Yanks are always making sport of what you can't fathom."

"Oh, struck a nerve, did I?" Suzanne cooed playfully. "Bet you're wishing now that you had struck me with that bag of squid."

"It's *quid* not *squid*. And maybe, yes, a pop to your crown might just be something I would now fancy."

"Now, Virgin, don't get your knickers in a wad. We colonials have this way of establishing our own traditions."

"That's just it, Doctor. You Americans always fail to understand. You feel that you must rewrite everything as if it was some sort of transient billboard. Dinner in the colonies must be redefined. Instead of tea at four, one must blast through the take-away window benchmarking the ill-gotten gains from a fast-food eatery. I am here to tell you, Dr. Coletrane, that tradition—by its very nature—is already established. Have you ever thought that maybe to follow an established, time-honored tradition shows real character and discipline?"

"Well, Virgin, if that is true, then America would still be a colony of England and we would still be paying too much tax for crappy tea."

"Crappy tea? Did you say crappy tea? Now our tea sports issue with you?"

"No issue. Your tea works better than snake oil to strip furniture and remove paint stains."

"Dr. Coletrane," the Virgin took in a deep breath, "please understand that this is our way ... and I had hoped it would be your way too. Please, collect the fish and come with me now."

"Too easy, Virgin, too easy," Suzanne laughed. "You're more fun to tease than my colleague Mick—" Suzanne stopped. "Oh my goodness, I haven't updated Mickey about Russell's arrival...."

Jude motioned the direction to go.

"Wait, Jude, I need to call—"

"No waiting, Dr. Coletrane. Not now. Not for another moment. Get the fish. Leave your mobile. We go now." Jude reached into Suzanne's hand, took her cell phone, and tossed it onto the unruffled bed covers.

Wearing a hood and completely cloaked, Suzanne left her room, exited the hotel, and went down the path to the Four Brothers stone formation. The arms of her cloak flapped aimlessly as her hands busily secured the fish in her uniform sleeve. Meanwhile she blended into the sea of the many others who were similarly dressed. All the cloaks were lengthy, touching midcalf. On the inside edges she could see the same deep crimson lining as in the cloak that she wore. On the left shoulder of every cloak was a crimson cross pattée. There was some mild variation in what was worn beneath the cloaks. Some people wore a white tunic underneath the cloak while others did not. Those who did wear white tunics had the crimson cross centered on their chests instead of on their shoulders. A less noticeable, but distinctively different, variation lay in the neckwear. Suzanne surmised that neck medallions, if worn, seemed to have shapes and ornamentation unique to specific orders. However, the obscuration provided by every cloak was the same. Since they were hooded, over either a helmet or chain mail, the face of each and every knight was concealed. She realized that the cloaks were made for individual anonymity and for personage to reverently listen, not speak. Suzanne guessed that after her merciless teasing of him, Jude was probably most satisfied with this silent aspect of the cloaking process.

After several bridges, catwalks, ladders, twists, and turns—ever among this growing herd of silent, cloaked individuals—Suzanne saw the base of a multipeaked rock formation. At a place where the path widened toward a large gathering area, there lay a group of three stones of equal height. Upon the stones was etched, weathered lettering. She read the words, *Mutter und Frau Cneajna mit Bruder Mircea. Why did this small family choose this as their final resting place?* Her thoughts were then distracted by a small amphitheater which was being used to hold the essence of the meeting. The conclave was assembling in a semicircle around four figures who were facing the multitude.

After the strenuous exertion of the thirty-minute walk through the remarkable Saxon geography, Suzanne felt hot and wished she could take off the cloak, or at least pull back the hood. She knew this was not going to happen and she just had to suck it up. *Even without a chain mail hood or a helmet, this thing feels like being in full chemical protective clothing and mask. Blasted MOPP 4s.* She was ecstatic when they finally arrived at the base of the stage at the amphitheater. Then, the most regally decorated, hooded, and cloaked individual at stage left began chanting in Latin. Suzanne guessed that this was the grand master—leader of the WTO. The remaining decorated members of the executive committee were motionless behind him, all standing tall and firm except for one who was seated.

"Nōn nōbīs, Domine, nōn nōbīs, sed nōminī tuō dā glōriam." He then began to speak in English, "Not unto us, O Lord, not unto us, but unto thy name give glory, for thy mercy, and for thy truth's sake."

Suzanne thought it was quite convenient that here in eastern Germany, English would follow Latin as the language of choice. She then remembered that among all of the European countries, as odd as it might seem, English was always the common language spoken. Suzanne remained quiet as the conclave then responded, "Wherefore should the heathen say, where is now their God?"

The voice of the grand master continued, "But our God is in the heavens; he hath done whatsoever he hath pleased."

In unison, the conclave replied, "Their idols are silver and gold, the works of men's hands."

"They have mouths, but they speak not; eyes they have, but they see not."

The conclave responded, "They have ears, but they hear not; noses have they, but they smell not."

"They have hands, but they handle not; feet have they but they walk not; neither speak they through their throat."

The conclave chorused, "They that make them are like unto them; so is everyone that trusteth in them."

"O Israel, trust thou in the Lord; He is their help and their shield."

"O house of Aaron, trust in the Lord; He is their help and their shield," the conclave replied.

The grand master closed, "Ye that fear the Lord, trust in the Lord; He is their help and their shield." After this statement, there was a long pause. The sound of shuffling could be heard as the members of the conclave seated themselves. He continued, "Grand Chancellor, if you please...."

"Let the formal welcome of the World Templar Organization begin. Grand Secretary, please set the agenda for this conclave of WTO Grand Priories."

"Excellency, there are four European priories who have most urgent matters to discuss. They have asked for permission to address the conclave." Upon receiving a nod from the grand master, the grand secretary then motioned to four figures standing just offstage.

The four figures, of almost equal height, walked to the center of the amphitheater's stage. Their cloaks were brilliantly white and were garnished with identical black cruciform emblems on their left shoulders. Each man wore a white tunic beneath his cloak, which was emblazoned with a large black cross at the chest. They also wore uniquely shaped medallions which were identical to each other, but different than the ones worn by others. Suzanne noticed that she wore no medallion or tunic. Despite her cloak and personal clothing ensemble, she suddenly felt naked.

One of the four stepped forward one pace and, in a deep bass pitch, began speaking from the darkness of his obscured, hooded face. Only a slight hint of shadowed lips could be seen mouthing each spoken word. "For the Order of Templars in Bavaria, Germany, I am Peer Mader, the grand prior, and we propose suspension of the original agenda for the council. We have very pressing business of the greatest significance. If Their Excellencies, the WTO grand master and grand chancellor, permit, we will begin." From the left, the grand master in his heavy neck chain tapped the stage twice with a wooden staff while the seated figure next to him rapped twice with a beautifully-carved wooden walking stick.

"Two weeks ago," Peer Mader thundered, "Nazi war chemicals were found here in Silesia where the holy sarcophagus lay. Modern-day followers from the Third Reich, American soldiers, and commercial businessmen all converged to explore Hitler's secret laboratory worked by Dr. Theodor Morell—always known to us but kept from the world till now. Also, in America, at the leaning tower there, our brother Father Judas Lenz was killed in action. He was taken and executed for no crime except that he was a Templar exercising his faith. Be advised, to our best knowledge at this time, no fish were taken from him. I humbly submit this for your learned consideration in God's name and for His glory."

The conclave responded in unison, "In God's name and for His glory."

The first of the four men stepped back and the second stepped forward, continuing the monologue. As this change of speaker took place, Mickey Peronne shifted in his cloak and hood. He recalled that neither Matthias nor Thaddeusz Lenz acknowledged the loss of their brother, Judas, when he had repeatedly asked. *Did they believe it to only be hearsay? Maybe they didn't want to confirm anything.* Either way, the hostility Mickey endured at the hands of the Lenz brothers of Germany and Poland became much clearer. Mickey continued to scan the crowd wondering if Russell had ever made it in. Knowing what was done to Father Judas made Russell's absence all the more disconcerting. The voice from the front interrupted Mickey's search.

"I am Bartholomäus Mader. I have the following information from the order. The Teutonic Order, with guidance from Chancellor Owl, monitored the situation on scene. We had hoped to secure the known documents exposing Hitler's operations, but they fell into the hands of an American Army colonel, Dr. Michael Philip Peronne, known to be referred to as Mickey. It was decided that he must be redirected, detained, and studied in Bautzen. After so doing, it was in the best belief of the Teutonic Order that Dr. Mickey Peronne would knowingly cause us no harm." Nods of confirmation coupled with raps from sheathed swords came from the seated Teutonic Knights within the semicircle in the audience.

"Nevertheless, along with the modern-day followers of Hitler, Dr. Peronne was diverted away. The secret is safe. Submitted to you in God's name and for His glory." The conclave echoed this closing statement. Mickey bit his lip and cringed; he had been intentionally played by the Teutonic Knights. The second of the four brothers stepped back and the third stepped forward speaking in a clear baritone.

"I am Johann Mader. I have the following information. With guidance from Chancellor Owl, it was decided that all the chapters from the Second Book of Benjamin would be retrieved. The American soldiers, each under the supervision of a trusted knight, were allowed to accomplish this mission. The intent was to determine the character of the Americans as they sought to obtain the fish. Further, we believed them to be the most secure means of delivery. Be it known, with the time allowed, only nine of the ten chapters were accessed. Praise Jesus there was no further loss of life. In God's name and for His glory."

The conclave echoed, "In God's name and for His glory."

The third of the four brothers stepped back as the last stepped forward. Suzanne was stuck between a pair of matching chain-mailed English bookends. *How am I ever going to find the words to explain this to Mickey and Russell?* She clutched the fish within her sleeve tightly and took in a deep breath. Fish, flowers, and falling towers had left her in the midst of a serious oration by some rather non-funny, knighted version of the Marx Brothers' quartet, all speaking from the base of a geological formation called the Four Brothers. *Could anything be stranger?* She sensed that this ordeal was far from over. Suzanne grimaced. *Guess I should have slept when I had the chance.*

64

To God and Our Lady

The Bastei
Lohmen, Germany

"I am Thomas Mader. I am the last with information from the order." The gravelly alto voice paused briefly for dramatic effect. "The Teutonic Knights have brought the chapters retrieved from the falling towers of Bautzen, Pyrzyce, and Torun. If the WTO grand master permits, the chapters will now be given to Chancellor Owl." The Owl, with stick in hand, carefully stepped forward and her high-backed chair was shifted over for her to sit in the centermost portion of the amphitheater stage. The moon rose high in the dark sky and the shadows of the rock quadruplets stretched long across the stage. Suzanne watched as three knights, all dressed alike, rose from the conclave and walked to the seated person called Owl. The center knight kneeled and presented her with three chapters from the Second Book of Benjamin.

"Do not rise," said the Owl. "The knights with whom you have served have brought before the executive council the request that you be knighted within their order. What do you say?"

"If they have found me worthy, then I am willing."

Heaving herself up with her stick, the Owl stood, passed the three fish to the grand master, and then turned back to the kneeling figure. "Good brothers, it has been proposed to make this companion a Teutonic Knight. If there is any among you who knows of anything for which he should not be a brother directly, he should tell it; for it would be a better thing for him to say it beforehand than after he has come before us. Do you wish him to be brought on behalf of God?"

"Bring him on behalf of God," the conclave responded in unison.

Looking down, the Owl spoke, "Dr. Michael Philip Peronne, I told you when you were a companion that this day would come. What do you now say?"

"Madam Owl, I come before God, before you, and before these brothers asking for the love of God and our Lady to welcome me into your company and the favors of the Teutonic Order, as one who wishes to be a servant of the Teutonic Order forever."

"Good brother," replied the Owl, "you ask a very great thing, for of the Teutonics, you see only the outer appearance. You do not know the harsh commandments which lie beneath. Our mission is to do battle for Christ wherever there is need or call, and to be a servant of Christ and to the Teutonic Order for this purpose. You must be committed to defending those Christians who are at risk. You must be willing also to protect the holy shrines and their holy relics even if it costs you your life. Now think hard and decide, good gentle brother: are you willing to tolerate these hardships?"

"Yes, as did Judas Lenz, I will tolerate them all to the sacrifice of my own life if God pleases."

"Good brother, you should not request the company of the Teutonic Knights in order to have riches, physical ease, or honor. But you should request it for three reasons: one, to put aside and leave behind the sins of this world; two, to do the work of our Lord; and three, to be humble in spirit and do Christian soldiering in this world, for that is the salvation of the soul and such should be the thought by which you ask it. Given this, are you still willing to be, all the days of your life, henceforth a servant of the Teutonic Order and the WTO?"

"Yes, I am willing if it pleases God."

"Now, good brother, do you promise to God and our Lady that henceforth you will help to conquer, with the strength and power that God has given you, the Holy Kingdom of Christ; and that which Christians hold, you will help to keep safe within your power? Do you also promise to God and the Lady Saint Mary that you will never leave the Teutonic Order for stronger or weaker, nor for worse or for better?"

"Before God, our Lady, and those brethren here, as Ruth did promise, so do I."

Mickey then repeated the affirmation of the oath of the order and became a Teutonic Knight. Afterward, the Owl took the uppermost end of her walking stick and touched Mickey first on one shoulder, then the other. She bent down, pulled back his hood, and kissed him on the top of his head. She then whispered into his ear, "Mickey, I know that you have been a Companion of the Order of the Ermine as well as a Knight of the Order of the Dragon. I am grateful that Thaddeusz controlled his ire and did not kill you so that you have the opportunity to fulfill your destiny as a Teutonic Knight. I pray that the strength of the apostles continues to go with you."

"And also with you, Madam Owl."

The Owl smiled, kissed him again on his forehead, then stood up. With hand and stick raised in the air above her, she spoke in a clear and regal voice. "Sir Michael Philip Peronne, Knight of the Teutonic Order, rise and join your knightly brethren. Return to the circle of brothers from whence you came."

Mickey joined the ranks and leaned toward who he thought was Thaddeusz. "I am glad you didn't move to kill me."

"The day has only just begun," Thaddeusz chuckled.

After Matthias, Thaddeusz, and Mickey rejoined the ranks, the voice of Thomas Mader continued. "I have the following information for the order. Knights of Italy and Sicily have brought the chapters retrieved from the falling towers of Burano, Venice, Bologna, and Pisa. If His Excellency permits, the chapters will now be given to Chancellor Owl." The Owl seated herself again at the center of the stage. Suzanne watched as this time four identical knights rose from the semicircle and walked to the seated Owl. Again, one of the two center-most knights kneeled and presented her with four sacred chapters.

Before Russell could rise, he received the invitation to join the Italian Order which he was willing to do. Suzanne's heart leapt when she heard his name pronounced in the induction oath. He also received a kiss from the Owl, but no whispering followed. The grand master did move from his posting, however, and came over to Russell. He knelt and took Russell's hood back, revealing his smoothly shaven head, and inspected the traumatic bruising to Russell's face and neck. Saying something audible just for Russell's ear, the grand master returned to his posting and allowed the Owl to proceed.

Suzanne's stomach turned flips because she knew what Thomas Mader would say next. The words came quicker than she had suspected.

"The Knights of England and Wales have brought the chapters retrieved from the falling towers of Bristol and King's Lynn. If the WTO grand master permits, the chapters will now be given to Chancellor Owl." The seated Owl grew larger as Suzanne, centered between Jude and Justice James, rose to her feet and walked toward center stage. Suzanne was thankful that she was last because, having never served in the capacity of a companion or a knight before, at least now she had some idea how things flowed. Upon reaching the Owl, she kneeled, opened her sleeve cuff, and presented the chapters from Bristol and King's Lynn. As she was passing the Owl the sacred documents she recalled Jude's comment: *It is our way and I had hoped it would be yours too.* She didn't think it would be possible, but her gut knotted a fraction tighter. Suzanne felt a nudge against her shoulder blade.

"What?" she whined.

She heard the rustle of the Virgin's cloak from her right as he kneeled, his voice hissing through clenched teeth. "Please answer the question."

"What was the question?"

Jude muttered, "We want to know if you accept the request to be a dame of our order."

"Would that make me a great dame?" Suzanne recalled how she had once barely averted an international event by calling the Crown Prince of Denmark a *Great Dane*.

"No, Dr. Coletrane," said the Virgin's voice.

"No, what?"

"No, you would not be a great dame; you would only become Lady Knight Coltrane or Dame Suzanne of the Priory of England and Wales, now and forever. Dr. Coletrane, we would be honored to have you accept."

Hearing a rustle to her left, a kneeling Justice James chimed in. "Though this is our first meeting, Doctor, my wife, Miriam, and brother Jude have staunchly vouched for you. Being of great depth and character, I have total faith in their selection. You have my vote as well." Suzanne, as she was taught at West Point, began to stand along with the rising Jude and Justice James to proclaim her affirmation.

She was halted by the clear words of the Owl. "Do not rise, Dr. Coletrane. The knights with whom you have served have brought you before the executive council. They request that you be knighted within their order. I again ask, what do you say?"

"I am willing." Suzanne felt her stomach ratchet tighter. *Knights are knighted and dames are ... damed?*

The Owl stood, passed the last two sacred chapters to the grand master, then turned back to Suzanne Coletrane, addressing the brotherhood and the applicant alternately.

In the end, Suzanne was relieved because she would now only have to repeat the oath as it was spoken to her. The words stirred deep emotions within her, carving themselves on her heart.

"I will uphold the chivalrous tradition and Christian ideals of the World Templar Organization and of the Grand Priory of England and Wales. I will do my best to provide a voice to the oppressed, strength to the weak and afflicted, and largesse to the poor. I will bear only true witness to my brothers and sisters in Christ and will serve them, the holy shrines, the holy relics, and the order to the best of my abilities, in Christ's name, so help me God."

After tapping Suzanne's shoulders with her staff, the Owl said, "Rise, Lady Suzanne Niles Coletrane. You are now and forever a Dame of the Order of England and Wales. Return now from whence you came."

With these words spoken, Thomas Mader returned to the four knights on the stage and exited with them to the conclave semicircle below. Chancellor Owl resumed her place at the right hand of the WTO grand master. Nine chapters of the Second Book of Benjamin had been submitted and the three new applicants had been knighted—the night's business was nearly at an end. The grand master then moved to center stage. His strong voice clearly spoke into the fading night sky.

"Nine of ten falling towers have given up their secret and now the chapters will be rejoined with the original volume of the Second Book of Benjamin. The Holy Sarcophagus has been returned to safety. The living tower keepers, no longer guardians of the fish, will all be recalled and taken back to the Temple Supreme of the World Templar Organization, where their work as Knights Templar will be redefined or reverted. When released by the Americans, the earthly remains of the fallen knight, Father Judas Lenz, will be brought here to the Bastei for internment. Those who have eyes will see. In God's name and for His glory."

The conclave responded appropriately.

"Please be advised that the Holy Sarcophagus and the preserved blood of our Lord have safely been moved to the place where religion and science stand hand-in-hand. It will be under the guardianship of select Knights Templar. In God's name and for His glory."

The conclave responded reflexively.

"Last, we have three new members who have, before this conclave, agreed to accept tasking which may be provided in the future. To these three I command them to go, brothers and sisters, in peace and let the strength of the Twelve Apostles, Peter, John, Bartholomew, Thomas, Matthias, Thaddeus, Jude, James the Just, John, James, Andrew, and Philip, be with them. In God's name and for His glory."

After the conclave had responded, the grand master began the call-and-response dialogue which closed the meeting.

"Behold how good and how pleasant it is for brethren to dwell together in unity."

The conclave responded, "It is like the precious ointment from the head that ran down upon the beard, even Aaron's beard, that went down to the skirts of his garment and the sacred rod which he held in his hand."

The grand master closed with the final statement. "As the dew of the Her'mon, and as the dew that descended on the mountains of Zion; for there the Lord commanded the blessing, even life forevermore." He then discharged the newest members, and they were escorted away as the remainder of the conclave session belonged to the established brethren.

Newly inducted international WTO Knights Templar Mickey, Russell, and Suzanne silently proceeded back to their respective rooms while the final aspects of the conclave ritual played out. Mickey gave Russell a silent nod acknowledging his arrival. Russell smiled at an obviously flustered Suzanne. Suzanne repeated to herself over and over, *Damed if I do; damned if I don't.*

65

And Three's a Crowd

The Bastei
Lohmen, Germany

How can I rest when anxiety whips my thoughts into a frenzied slurry? Pausing in the middle of brushing of her hair, Suzanne inspected the puffiness of her eyes. *However, ATPs must be repaid to the energy bank in the same manner and rate as that they were withdrawn.*

Along with Suzanne, the events of the moonlit meeting left the other two neophytes of the international order feeling very tired. After enduring the previous days' adventures culminating in the exhausting process of knighthood, their bodies crashed. If nothing else would be gained at the Bastei resort, at least they all appreciated having the opportunity for one solid block of sleep after all the travel and intrigue.

If we had been in the United States, Suzanne thought as she resumed brushing, *things might have been different.* In the past, after many long nights of working together at ICD, the three would have managed to traipse into their nearest favorite Double-T Diner in the wee hours of the morning. Time and time again in their assignments at the Institute of Chemical Defense in Maryland, that diner was the default after any long night. However, this was Europe—not the United States. This was not the land of convenience, fast food, and billboards.

Mickey had long since adjusted to European ways during his assignment in Germany and didn't think twice about a late-night meal to catch up with each other. But Suzanne was slow to accept the change in their post-mission tradition as the lifestyle here differed so greatly from Maryland. Even though they had not simultaneously shared each other's company since they taught at the Chemical Casualty Care Division of ICD, part of her still hoped to repeat the old custom.

As for Russell, falling into his soft bed, he was just grateful not to feel the grit of sand on his sheets—a constant pitfall from a desert tour of duty.

✠ ✠ ✠

When late morning finally arrived, Suzanne stumbled in last. She brought her weary frame to the breakfast table which overlooked the famous rock formations of the area. The scenery was much akin to, though not as dramatic as, the American southwest filled with grand canyons and high chaparrals.

Russell and Mickey were already seated and deeply engaged in conversation. Suzanne, who had hoped to spend one-on-one time with Russell, was miffed to say the least. She listened impatiently to the historically-rich content every time they were together—jumping from one subject to another seamlessly. Fingernails digging into the carving she palmed, Suzanne glared at the two. *Do they even see me standing here? Hello? Earth to Russell? Earth to Mickey?*

"I'm pretty sure it was you, Russell." Mickey sipped his coffee. "I thought that a while back, in the Mediterranean, you were researching something about Hitler and a Roman pedigree? I'm not sure I fully understand how a Roman pedigree fits into the whole Nazi scheme."

"You're right. It was me." Russell folded his hands in his lap. "The issue was image in leadership."

"Hitler's leadership image."

"Yes, Mickey. Hitler, the ultimate propagandist, wanted to link himself to Rome and the power of the Caesars. As an artist himself, he knew the power of the picture."

"True, one picture is worth a thousand words."

"It is said that Hitler did a self-portrait as Caesar. However, there is probably more than one version that Hitler, or others, made of the Führer as some type of Roman leader."

"Maybe," said Mickey. "I don't know if it was a self-portrait, but I do remember a painting depicting Hitler in a toga-wearing a laurel wreath crown."

"Exactly. After establishing himself in images as Caesar, Hitler's Nazi historians were then compelled to create a fictitious lineage for Hitler to support the falsity."

"Compelled or coerced?"

"Both, most likely. The Nazi historians initiated a lineage which began in Rome, then moved it to Romania—"

"Romania?" asked Suzanne sharply. "The only thing in Romania that is Roman is the first five letters of the name, right?" Both men leaned back in their seats, realizing that they had been oblivious to the presence of Suzanne. Russell slid out of the bench seat, stood, and gave Suzanne a warm good-morning hug. Suzanne's scowl slowly dissipated into a more pleasant smile. She slid into the bench seat, followed by Russell. She set the carving on the table and began helping herself to Russell's coffee. After a few sips she refilled his cup and then folded her hands on Russell's leg. She again approached the question but this time directly to Russell.

"The Romanian connection seems a bit out of the way. If Hitler's desire was to be seen as a Caesar in Germany, why generate a lineage through Romania?"

"Actually, I can answer that one," interrupted Mickey. "The value of the lineage going through Romania is aligned with the historic presence of Ovid."

"Ovid, as in one of the three top poets in Rome? That seems like a stretch," said Suzanne.

"Maybe," continued Mickey. "Apparently Ovid caught the favor of a certain family member within Caesar's household named Julia. It seems that Julia began practicing some romantic liberties beyond the acceptance of Augustus Caesar. Augustus blamed the transgressions on the influential writings of the poet and had Ovid banished to Tomis, then an outlying colony of Rome on the western shores of the Black Sea."

"Tomis, Romania," interrupted Russell. "It still exists today as the town of Constanța. Ovid died just outside of Tomis and is buried in the little town which now bears his name, Ovidiu. I have been through it many times on my way to and from Constanța coming from the Mihail Kogalniceanu Air Base."

"Imagine, Ovid died in Romania," whispered Suzanne distantly, quite off topic in her frank disbelief. "This would mean, folks, that Hitler's lineage, false as it may be, included the same Romanians which he gathered up and mercilessly put to death."

"A sad reality," resumed Mickey. "Hitler's *lineage* can then be traced from Rome, through Romania and including Transylvania, then through the Magyars from Hungary, and eventually to the early Austrian settlers in the town of Braunau-am-Inn which borders on the frontier of Germany."

"Hitler's lineage flowing through Transylvania begs the question of a Vlad Tepes–Dracula connection, wouldn't you think?" Russell posed.

"Maybe yes, maybe no. However, it was his connection to Ovid that Hitler wanted emphasized. He claimed that his artistic talent stemmed from Ovid."

"There is a carved bust in Ovidiu near the MK Air Base which some say favors old Adolph himself. Personally, I don't think so," Russell added.

"Well, I believe … " began Mickey, but he quickly paused as the waitress refilled Russell's coffee cup. Suzanne took the opportunity to order her breakfast as well, giving enough time for the dust to settle.

"I believe," resumed Mickey, "that Hitler wanted to recreate a father-son relationship with himself being the father."

"How is that possible? Hitler and Eva Braun had no children," said Suzanne.

This time, Russell answered. "True enough, but if he did, he would want to create the most powerful offspring possible which, of course, would be under his direct mentorship and control."

"Enter *Flusszigeuner*," said Mickey. "A Nazi investigation of the 'River People' would lead Hitler straight to the cellular DNA of Christ."

Russell then added, "Suzanne, can you see that with the success of Operation River People, Hitler would be free to again create the Roman father/Jewish son relationship with a cloned Christ. This would position Hitler as the new executive world power with the legitimate power of Christ—or anti-Christ, for that matter."

"Is this what Talbot found in the secret laboratory in Poland, Mickey?"

"Talbot is a Chemical Corps geek, Suzanne. When he went down into the secret laboratory he knew enough about what he saw to know that it was well out of his lane."

"Did he say how far he went into the lab?"

"He didn't have to. I saw his size twelve prints in the dust on the floor of the lab. You could literally see the exact point where he stopped. Once Talbot saw some physician-scientist biomedical stuff around, he knew it was time to call for help. Whenever the Nazis mixed medicine and science with chemistry, the outcome was never positive for the people of the world, especially the River People."

"What did the papers from the secret laboratory show, Mickey?" Russell asked.

Hearing a hint of longing in Russell's voice, Mickey averted his eyes as he spoke. "The papers pointed to the places where chemical weapons and biomedical research was being done on concentration camp inmates. *Flusszigeuner* identified the River People. The paperwork labeled *Unsterblichkeit durch Medizinische Forschung* was about immortality through tissue culturing and cloning. I think we can call that one Operation Immortality."

Suzanne's face became more aghast with each passing word.

"Holy Mary," interjected Russell. "Nazis cloning a Jewish neo-Christ so as to make him the son of Hitler. Can anything in history be more horrific?"

"Wait a minute, Russell," Suzanne interrupted. "You guys said, 'again create' a Roman father/Jewish son relationship … ?"

"Right … you aren't spun up on that yet. The tower keeper Simeone said that some believe that Jesus's biological father was a Roman soldier named Tiberius Julius. Cloning Christ in Hitler's day, along with Hitler's supposed lineage, would have recreated this relationship."

"Do you believe that, Mickey?"

"Not really. Nothing referencing the miraculous birth of Christ within biblical scriptures really supports that theory."

"What of the fact that Christ would fail to have the correct number of paired chromosomes?"

"Did you miss the part where I said *miraculous*?" Mickey laughed playfully. "She sounds more like us every day, Russell."

"No need to insult, Mickey." Suzanne frowned.

"Sorry, Suzanne." Mickey swallowed his grin, shifted, and leaned forward. "If Tiberius was indeed construed to be the biological father, then the line of David had to pass through him in order to fulfill the prophecy."

"This isn't about what any of us believes, Mickey."

"No, Russell. But, if an unstoppable dictator believes it and has the resources to clone the holy cells of Christ to re-establish a believed relationship, then theology gets a scientific half nelson."

"So that's what has a big red nose and lives in a test tube," recalled Suzanne.

"I beg your pardon?" said Russell.

"When I was in England, Mickey asked me, 'What has a big red nose and lives in a test tube?'"

"Bozo the *Clone*," replied Russell dryly.

"If I may remind you, I was on an unsecure mode of communication." Mickey looked at Suzanne and continued. "At that time I needed you to think about cloning without saying the word on an open net for goons like Dalton to hear."

Russell nodded then placed his carving on the table next to Suzanne's. Suzanne slid her carving over to his so they faced each other nose to nose.

"Well, Mickey, I never got it. Next time go with something like … I dunno … what do you call a closet with a phone?"

"A phloset—is that a word?" Mickey proposed.

"Shut up, Mickey." Suzanne glared. "Is *that* a word?"

"Actually, it's three words."

66

Of Wishes and Wagers

Restaurant at the Bastei
Lohmen, Germany

"They're birds of a feather, Suzanne," Russell grimaced. "Vultures, no doubt." After many minutes of eating and sipping coffee, Russell picked up Dalton's carvings. "When you saw Dalton in England, Suzanne, was Wunschmann with him?"

"No, he was accompanied by a full complement of cocky attitude but, in reality, quite alone." She put her coffee mug down on the table and looked down into it. "In retrospect, I'm pretty sure Dalton had been following me from the time I left the airport at Ramstein."

"Did he fly into Germany with you?" Russell asked.

"No, I don't think so. He didn't seem jet-lagged like me. Hang on...." She paused and closed her eyes, searching her memory for the glimpse she caught of the mint-green car from the autobahn. "License plate RO MD 4444," she said out loud. "I actually saw him, but I didn't *see* him. Ugh ... well, what's done is done. That plate though, it means he came from Rosenheim, south of Munich, right?"

"Yes, the DIA briefing I had confirms that." Mickey glanced from one to the other. "But, the question is, what was he doing there?" Reaching out, he took the carvings from Russell's hands.

"At Rosenheim? Your guess is as good as mine," Suzanne replied.

"What about Wunschmann? How did he get from the US to Germany, to England, to Italy so quickly?" Russell queried.

"Part of it was luck," explained Mickey. "Once Wunschmann heard that Lucky Industries had located the Dyhernfurth lab he waited for the findings to roll in. When no news came about what was discovered, he made plans to get to Poland. The local chemo officer's quick reaction time and arrival on-scene kept Wunschmann from making the personal appearance which would have highlighted his conflict of interest."

"Conflict of interest?" Suzanne asked.

"Daddy's businesses," Russell chimed in. "Lucky Industries and Wunschmann's wife's shop, Lucky'n Love Ceramics, are all part of Wilhelm Wunschmann's business ventures."

"Really? Wilhelm, the elder Wunschmann?" Suzanne's face strained with the thought. "We're talking about Joachim Wunschmann's dad, right?"

"Yes, Joachim's father was selling snake oil in the form of pottery shop construction. In reality, he was wishing to find the secret laboratory and the secret papers," said Mickey.

"Based on last night's experience, we now think that the lab might also have contained a sarcophagus, of sorts, brimming with the largest known volume of Christ's blood preserved in a wooden flogging post," concluded Russell.

"So," said Suzanne, "Yogi—Joachim Wunschmann—diverted his goon to follow me so he could keep tabs on the mission. If Dalton was discovered, he had a justifiable interest in being my backup."

"But where does the luck come in?" Russell pondered.

"Military flight routes," Suzanne replied quickly. "Wunschmann couldn't catch any timely flight leaving the US directly to Germany so he must have taken a military flight connector which hooked into Mildenhall Air Force Base in England. Mildenhall is a stone's throw from King's Lynn. When Mickey diverted me from Germany to England, this inadvertently led me straight into a collision course with Wunschmann."

"That's incredible," Russell slapped the table. "So, the moment Dalton was subdued at King's Lynn, he was taken to the nearest military facility to be detained by the US military authorities."

"That's right, Russell. The Air Police locked up Dalton in their facility about the time I departed for Bristol. Since Wunschmann was at Mildenhall awaiting his connector to Ramstein, Germany, he was probably five buildings away when Dalton made his one free telephone call. Joachim had him on an out-of-jail-free card faster than I could drive to Bristol."

"Did they follow you to Bristol?"

"Honestly, I don't know but there is no indication that they did."

"How did Wunschmann know to go to Italy to find me?" Russell asked as Suzanne winced.

"It was me, Russell. I wish I could say otherwise—but, honestly, I screwed up." Suzanne's eyes moistened. "Everything bad that happened to you was my fault. In my frustration with what I thought was an unhelpful tower keeper, I threw out information that Dalton soaked in." Suzanne folded her napkin into a triangle over and over until it couldn't be folded again. At that point she pounded it with her fist and welled up. "In my own defense, I have to say that I didn't know he was standing there behind me until it was way too late."

"Suzanne… "

"I'll take the category 'Stupid Moves' for five hundred, Alex—I'm so sorry, Russell. I *do* know better." Suzanne clenched her hand in a fist and brought it up to her mouth, covering her trembling lips.

"Yes, you do. I taught you better."

Suzanne narrowed her eyes. "What's done is done, Russell." She blew a sigh of pent-up anger into her fist. "It won't happen again." She broke eye contact, focusing on the flatware in front of her. "Anyway, with the information I gave Dalton about your whereabouts, Yogi Wunschmann and Dalton must have taken the military connection from Mildenhall into the Livorno Airfield and—boom, thirty minutes from there to Pisa, Italy."

"No harm done, Suzanne, even if they did have a lucky break." Russell smiled. "However, if they had killed me," he reached out and put his hand on hers, "I can promise you, I would never speak to you again."

"Actually, Russell, if you can believe it, they had more good luck," Mickey added. "You went from Burano westward through Venice, to Bologna, and finally to Pisa. Had you gone the other way, Wunschmann and Dalton would have been in Pisa, and you would have been in Venice. They would have been in the wrong place at the wrong time."

"But they weren't," summarized Russell. "I am just glad Andrea, the tower keeper at Pisa, had enough Spidey-sense to know they were up to no good. Thanks to him and his brother, Simeone, Wunschmann's streak of good luck eventually came to an end."

"Yogi Wunschmann really does earn that nickname Lucky Dog, doesn't he?" Suzanne spoke aloud what everyone was thinking. "When it comes to luck, it seems that Wunschmann is no different than Hitler," she whispered. "Hitler dodged so many attempted assassinations that he couldn't have done better with a suit made of four-leaf clovers."

"You may be right, Suzanne," conceded Mickey. "It appears that Hitler's luck rubbed off on the whole Wunschmann family. The elder Wunschmann was a loyal follower of the Third Reich. Unlike many of his scientist colleagues, he luckily survived persecution after Hitler's collapse. The Americans, of all people, gave him a way out."

"How was that?" asked Suzanne.

"Operation Paperclip. Wilhelm Wunschmann got funneled out of Germany during the hunt for Nazis. America sent him through Costa Rica and eventually brought him stateside to the Institute of Chemical Defense."

"Why would they do that?"

"He was a scientific genius. It was he who developed the idea of the Wunschmann Pipette and then later made millions when he sold the patent to the government. Unfortunately, with the good, came the bad."

"I can imagine."

"Yes, although he was a transplanted American, he apparently passed on his Nazi mentality to his son, Joachim. Now we know Joachim has since been using his leadership position at the Chemical Casualty Care Division and the Institute of Chemical Defense to further his father's work. I think the junior Wunschmann wished to recreate his father's Nazi world in every way."

The three sat in a doleful silence for quite some time processing all the new revelations put before them.

Then, Russell leaned over toward Suzanne. "Trane?" he whispered loudly.

"What, Russell?"

"Are you up for it?"

"What's up—what are we going to do?" Mickey asked.

Suzanne pointed to Russell and herself driving home the point that the term *we* clearly excluded Mickey. She looked directly at Russell, leaned in toward him and said, "Up for what?"

"A wager, of course," he raised an eyebrow at her.

She gave back the same playful look. "Depends on the stakes."

"Hmmm. How about a reunion dinner back home at our favorite Thai restaurant … loser pays?"

"I'm listening…."

"It's a leaning tower question."

"I hardly think I'm an expert in leaning towers—"

"Well, you should be," Russell interrupted. "You certainly have had the same crash course as the rest of us. And anyway, this is right up your alley."

"All right, I'll take the bait." *Win or lose, at least I'll have a one-on-one dinner date to look forward to.* "What's the question?"

Russell sat up straight and put on his best haughty teacher look. "What, Dr. Coletrane, is the location of the only leaning tower in America?"

"How should I know?" Suzanne blurted out.

"You are a history teacher, for Pete's sake. Shame on you, Suzanne."

"But—"

"Nope! No getting out of it. The bet was made and you lost."

"I didn't bet."

"Suzanne Niles Coletrane, you most certainly did. By my accounting, I have one bet made with you. One bet lost by you. One consequence required of you. Plus, I have one witness to prove it!"

"Okay, okay, let me try again. The only leaning tower in the US?"

"Yes, Suzanne Niles Coletrane, you, more than anyone at this table, should have known that—"

In the background, the whop-whop-whop of a landing helicopter interrupted the conversation. Outside, a medically marked army helicopter was descending.

"Heads up, folks, General Framingham's bird is here," said Mickey.

"Are you sure that is the general's helicopter, Mickey?" Russell asked.

"Oh yeah. I know the hum of that baby. It was my ride into this melee. To think, I was so thrilled to get the keys to the boss's chopper. Loni always said, 'Be careful what you ask for. You may get it.'" Mickey returned his gaze to the table. "So, Suzanne, what's your final answer?"

"Hey, give a gal a second. Besides, I don't understand what any of this has to do with me."

"I have to agree—how would you know?" Mickey said to Suzanne, then he looked to Russell. "I mean, she's not from Illinois."

"Easy counselor," Russell cut across Mickey. "This is her mystery to unravel. No more clues."

"Illinois?" Suzanne shifted forward over the table, hot on the trail and watching Mickey closely. "Why should I know anything about Illinois?"

"Suzanne *Niles* Coletrane, you should be ashamed of yourself," Mickey urged, grinning from ear to ear.

"Whoa, Mickey," repeated Russell. "You're going to give it away."

"C'mon, just one more clue?"

"I can smell the Thai peanut sauce now," Russell teased.

"Well, there is that old river in Egypt," volunteered Mickey.

"Aswan?"

"Dam," said Mickey.

"That's it? Aswan River?"

"No, Aswan is a dam."

"Forget it. I give up. The bet's off." Suzanne slouched back in the booth, grumbling to herself, "No Thai dinner ... no dancing...."

"Dancing?" repeated Russell. "I never said anything about dancing. And no way I'm letting you off the hook on this one."

"Well, fine then. But if I'm paying, then dinner implies dancing, and dancing implies—Domino?" The conversation was interrupted by the big, cold, wet nose of a Dalmatian who was more than glad to join the trio for breakfast.

67

Swelling of the Ranks

Restaurant at the Bastei

Lohmen, Germany

"**D**omino?" Mickey bubbled. "What are you doing…?" Mickey started when he saw, rounding the corner of the breakfast area, the loving face of his precious Loni.

"Guess who else can get Daddy's ride?" Loni jingled imaginary keys. "Can two more join this motley crew?"

"Since when do you fly with the European medical commander?" Suzanne asked.

"Never," replied Loni. "Domino and I just absconded with his ride, compliments of an old friendship. Chief of the DIA's European Division requested a favor from the old man when my prodigal husband didn't come home earlier this week. The general was about to balk when his wife, Cyndi Labelle Framingham, insisted this would be justified as continued support of a mission that began at some obscure pottery store in Poland. You know something about this, Mickey?"

"Guilty as charged, honey," Mickey replied. "Operation Beauty and the Beast."

"It seems that the European commander's wife, Margie Bloomfield, confirmed this as well." Standing now with her hands on her hips, Loni glanced at her husband and the booth alternately. "Can I join you? Or do you just prefer to hang out only with the wives of flag-ranked general officers?"

"Hmmm," Mickey smiled.

"Well?"

"I'm thinking … " Mickey spiraled a finger at his forehead.

"Michael Philip Peronne!"

"Oh, why not?" Mickey patted the seat next to him.

Domino immediately took the hint, seated herself next to her master and began clearing off the remainder of Mickey's breakfast meal. Mickey started to object but Loni stayed his hand.

"Easy. She's just stress eating."

Mickey motioned Domino back onto the floor where she finished off the bratwurst. Loni eased slowly into the booth where she softly kissed each one of Mickey's eyes and then placed a light peck on his lips.

"The dancing part is iffy," resumed Russell, noting the special manner that the Peronne often greeted. "But nevertheless, Dame Suzanne Niles Coletrane, you—among all of us—should have known about the only leaning tower in the United States."

"Ooh, ooh, I know this one," Lori bounced. "May I?"

"Sure," said Suzanne. "Why not? I already lost and I'm getting nowhere fast."

"The only leaning tower in the United States is a half-scale replica which sits just off the horizon from the O'Hare International Airport."

"Chicago, Illinois? Huh, it figures. I hate Chicago."

"What?" Russell recoiled. "How can you hate the home of the Cubs, the White Socks, the Bulls, the Blackhawks, and 'duh Bears?"

"Isn't it also the professional home of Mike Ditka, Walter Payton, and Michael Jordan, as well as the birthplace of Pizzeria Uno's and the Chicago dog?"

"It is, Loni!" Russell exhorted. "Ah, Sweetness! Can't touch that!"

"Uno's? I love Chicago-style pizza and the fabulous Chicago dog," said Suzanne. "Okay, okay, I *love* Chicago, but what's 'sweetness'?"

"It's not a *what*, it's a *who*," Russell huffed. "None other than the humble and gracious gentleman athlete, Walter Payton."

"Oh, so Payton and the leaning tower both dwell in Chicago?"

"Kinda, sorta, Trane. The leaning tower is just outside of Chicago in a suburb which shares a name with that old river in Egypt—the Nile."

"Really? Nile? It's the Leaning Tower of Nile?"

"Close. It is called the Leaning Tower of Niles, with an *s*," Mickey hissed. "Yes, m'dear, as in Suzanne *Niles* Coletrane. If I'm lying, may my closet phone, the phloset, never work."

The trio laughed. Acknowledging past inside jokes, Loni rolled her eyes. Domino cocked her head sideways as if another angle might find the humor. Russell reached in his pocket to get his camera phone to do a selfie and capture the joviality of the moment. Then he passed the phone to Loni and asked her to take a picture.

"Isn't this the Leaning Tower of Niles?" Loni asked, looking at the phone's photo.

"No, this is a picture taken in Pisa, but it was truly an accident," said Russell reclaiming his phone. "On the screen there are Yogi Wunschmann, Jean Dalton, and Andrea Giordano. I flashed my phone camera in self-defense. Hmmm, it must have been in the panorama mode since it also captured Andrea, the tower keeper."

"Maybe it's just a combination of the flash, lighting, and shadows, but Andrea is a dead ringer for the twins Jude and Justice James More," said Suzanne, peeking over Russell's shoulder.

"Funny you should bring up twins, Suzanne, because Andrea is one of a set of triplets," offered Russell.

"Really? Tower keeping twins *and* triplets?" Mickey picked at his eyebrows. "Matthias and Thaddeusz are at least twins, if not triplets, when the murdered Judas Lenz is considered in the mix."

"Who murdered Judas Lenz and why?" Suzanne asked.

"That would be my fault, Suzanne," answered Loni. "I told that to Mickey as part of his mission brief. I chose not to include it in the information sent to your command prior to your arrival to Germany. If I had, you would have been spun up on the Leaning Tower of Niles in the USA." Loni shifted forward. "However, here's what we know now. The *who* is most likely Joachim, aka Yogi, Wunschmann. He was actually captured in a Chicago photo at the Leaning Tower of Niles. The *why* is because he knew something then that we are just about to find out right now—I'm betting it will explain some extremely ancient DNA found at the site."

"Let me look at that picture," Mickey said to Russell. He passed the phone to Mickey as Loni slid on to the chair next to him.

"This is Andrea?" Mickey asked as he stared into the phone in his palm. "He could pass for either of the two Lenz brothers with whom I have spent the past several hours and days."

"How can they all look exactly alike?" asked Suzanne.

"They can't, unless they are all—oh my Jesus," Russell exhaled.

"What does this mean, Mickey?" Suzanne asked.

"It means, honey," said Loni, "that the tower keepers aren't the guardians of the secret. They *are* the secret! Someone, Hitler, or the Knights Templar, actually had success in cloning humans."

"My God, these guys could be mini-Hitlers!" Suzanne postulated.

"Possibly," replied Russell.

"Or mini-Christs," said Mickey.

"Mickey, honey, remember now—your mission here is over," said Loni, clutching her pendant crucifix unconsciously. "The DIA has the data you were requested to find. We have volumes and volumes of Nazi papers that Talbot turned over from the Dyhernfurth lab—and it is just a matter of time before the German authorities subdue Wunschmann and his henchmen." She turned. "Mickey, the mission is complete. Do you hear me? Mickey?" Loni put her hand on her husband's shoulder and shook him slightly. "Mickey?"

"Hello?" Suzanne poked.

"What, Suzanne?" Mickey rubbed at the creases in his forehead.

"The initial question remains, Mickey. Did the true sarcophagus get tapped and do we know if Jude, Andreas, Simeone, and all their brothers are from Christ himself?"

"We can't know for sure, Suzanne," Mickey sighed deeply. "We have to worst-case it and consider that these clones could have actually come solely from Hitler."

"Is that a real possibility or is it just being cautious?" asked Loni.

"Yes," responded Mickey.

"Yes what?"

"Yes, it's time to go and find out." Mickey shifted in his seat. Looking directly at Suzanne and Russell, he muttered, "We made an oath, remember?" He leaned back in his booth and sat up tall. "Folks, we are not at a complete mission status. No more discussion with the DIA now. Honey, I need your ride." He held out his hand, palm up.

"DIA calls the shots here, Mickey," Loni crossed her forearms.

"It doesn't seem so, Loni. You said yourself, DIA is at mission complete. From this point on, this is in the medical operations lane which means your ride now belongs to me."

"Mickey—you wouldn't."

"Did it. Done it. Honey, I need the keys."

"Why do you need the general's Blackhawk?"

"I haven't time to explain."

"Don't worry, Loni, take my bird," Russell mollified. "It appears I won't need it anyway."

"Why don't you all take your own bird?" Loni asked.

The three soldiers looked at each other and then back at Loni. All three replied in unison, "Speed!"

"Fine. So now you have a fast ride." Loni bit at her lip. "Where exactly are you all going?"

"To hell in a handbasket if we don't succeed, honey," responded Mickey, looking at the photo on the phone. Loni leaned in to view the picture. Domino, still searching for tidbits, scratched at an empty plate under the table and barked.

"Loni, I'm taking Domino for a long walk," Mickey said. "I need her leash."

"No, I don't think so—I don't like the sound of this. It sounds like someone is going to get hurt. *You* accept the danger when you put on your combat uniform. Domino is my only baby. Nobody hurts my Domino."

"I may need Domino to help gain the edge in a tight situation."

"You're right. Good point." Loni nodded. "As a sniffer and for protection, she is a viable asset. Okay, fine, I agree, Domino can go."

"Don't worry, Loni, I won't let anything happen to her." Mickey gave her a serious nod.

"I believe you, Mickey—because I will be the one bringing her. Look at it this way—with both of us there, we can double the edge."

"Loni, you can't go. It doesn't involve DIA. It's a medical operations issue and it needs to be just Domino and me."

"Good. I am glad we agree. Domino and I will wait for you in the chopper."

"Loni," barked Mickey, "I can't let you go."

"Too dangerous for me, but not Domino? I'm DIA. She isn't."

"You are an analyst, not a field agent."

"Okay. That's true. But without me, you don't get Domino. Sorry, Mickey, but we are a paired package."

"All right then, you both must stay back together."

"And so as a pair, we shall. Have a safe flight."

"No chance on an alibi?"

"I love every spot on this puppy." Loni rubbed the coat of her freckled hound. "No chance, darling. We'll stay where we need to be. I'll see what I can muster on the DIA front to support you. You all be careful and please keep your collective heads down."

68

A Path to Mordor

The Bastei

Lohmen, Germany

"It's not a good sign when what you don't know outweighs what you do know, Mickey," Suzanne sniped. She wrung her hands as she followed the two men out of the hotel lobby and toward the landing zone.

Suzanne, Russell, and Mickey knew that the WTO grand master, the Owl, and the cloned Templar tower keepers had all left after the conclave to go south to Franconia. They weren't quite sure how long the Templar group was staying in southern Germany since the two leaders' final destinations lay in Istanbul, Turkey and Pyrzyce, Poland, respectively. The airport at Munich would make the flight connection easier. According to their watch, the Templars had at least an eight-hour head start on them. The general's helicopter was fast and better fueled, but it would still need to make a refueling stop at Grafenwoehr before they could reach their anticipated end point.

While the chopper was refueled, the trio stood near the LZ. Under the cover of the noise of the helicopter blades and the engine, they chanced the discussion which they could not have in front of the chopper pilot.

"Why Schloss Tegernsee?" Russell asked.

"If I remember right, Tegernsee Castle was built on the remains of a Benedictine abbey," said Mickey.

"Well then, since Benedictine and Cistercian monks were related to Bernard de Clairvaux, this would most likely tie in with the Knights Templar."

"Indeed, it could. The kicker, however, is that the abbey is now a science research facility."

"An abbey castle laboratory—religion and science, hand-in-hand."

"Exactly," said Mickey. "I remember sitting at a dinner once with the elder Wunschmann. He talked about growing up on Lake Tegernsee at a place near where Dr. Morell resided. I believe he said there were beautiful towns there. One in particular was named Bad Wiessee. I remembered the name because Loni's aunt is a famous writer and ceramist named Louise and we called her Weezee. Anyway, maybe that personal family connection is the tie-in."

Suzanne chuckled. "Now that ties in a pro-Nazi scientist, Knights Templar in a castle, an abbey turned science research laboratory, and Loni's old Aunt Louise—where are the men in the clean white suits who are coming to take us away?" Suzanne scanned stone faces. "Enough with the jocularity for now." She cleared her throat. "What are we going to do once we get there?"

"That's the part I haven't figured out, Suzanne. I am betting that Yogi Wunschmann, Dalton, or the Templars themselves are going to remove, alter, or destroy the evidence of the successful human cloning."

"Are the clones themselves in danger?" Suzanne winced.

"Define danger. Bottom line, they may be sacrificed only because they exist. Look at Judas Lenz. He was at a leaning tower that didn't even have a fish."

"We don't know that," reminded Russell. "The conclave was told that no fish had been taken."

"There is one fish left from the Second Book of Benjamin—chapter four. Is it in the leaning tower in Ovidiu, Romania or Niles, USA?"

"I can't say for sure—"

"Can we call in backup?" Suzanne interrupted.

"For what? To take on a bunch of chemists at a castle laboratory making ceramic paints under the name Lucky Industries?" Mickey recoiled. "Think, Suzanne! By the time we could convince the powers that be to aid us, there would be nothing to rescue. Anyway, Loni is a good trooper. Whether she agrees or disagrees with our plan, she will ensure that we have all the support DIA can provide."

"What support *can* DIA provide?"

"Not sure. Maybe more help in terms of the aftermath. That part is in Loni's hands now."

"You don't think the Templars have taken the one and only sacred sarcophagus to Tegernsee Castle, do you?" Russell posed the query lurking in the back of everyone's mind.

"That would be so J. R. R. Tolkien," Suzanne commented.

"That's right—they would be marching toward Mount Doom, into the mouth of evil with the very relic evil seeks to find," said Mickey.

"Where else is the best place to hide something which is fervently sought?" Russell placed one hand over his other, balled-up, fist.

"Precisely." Mickey removed the covering hand. "In plain sight." Russell and Suzanne nodded knowingly.

"All this is just a hunch, isn't it, Mickey?" Suzanne asked.

"Executing a hunch with fierce intensity is better than waiting for all the data to come rolling in. Folks, time is not on our side. If this place is reeking with the foul fragrance of Wunschmann and Dalton, then that alone tells us that something is going on which warrants a rapid response."

"Given the paucity of intel we have and the critical info we lack, I don't think that Loni or the DIA would agree with your thinking—or our execution of it."

"I can absolutely say they wouldn't agree, Suzanne. This is the line in the sand, folks. You are welcome to stay here in Grafenwoehr and catch the next helicopter home. As for me, I have an oath to uphold. You must do as your conscience dictates."

"My word is my bond, Mickey, you know that." Russell waved his fist. "Plus, I am already dead two times over. Who wants to live forever?"

"That's easy for you to say." Suzanne pulled at imaginary whiskers. "I have a calico cat that depends on me for his livelihood."

"I've seen Toby. He's a smart feline. Trust me, he has already packed up his litter and moved on since your departure."

"Good point. I guess I'm in too, Mickey. Let's get on with it. Dame Suzanne at your service."

"At His service, actually," Mickey pointed upward.

"Oh, you know what I mean," retorted Suzanne. "The bird's ready, let's go."

Twin spires of the chapel
Tegernsee Castle laboratory

69

In, Around, and Above

Route to Schloss Tegernsee
Tegernsee, Germany

*B*eauty *is truly skin deep … but ugly is to the bone.* Mickey stared at the picturesque castle ahead as the chopper drew close to its target. *What evil hides beneath all this loveliness?* The sun was setting in the west, bathing the lake in front of the golden castle-abbey and making the chopper's lake approach tactically backlit. On the northern approach, in front of the square building with an internal courtyard, was an unfinished grass and dirt parking lot. It was sparsely occupied—most of the usual Bavarian laboratory staff had already begun the weekend departure.

The Blackhawk kicked up some dust and loose advertising flyers as it set down on the field in front of the main entrance. The tall, twin spires, which marked the front entrance, were set against a beautiful panorama of the German Alps. The clocks on the spires read five minutes after four o'clock. Mickey disembarked and headed straight for the main entrance. Suzanne headed east around the beer hall which occupied part of the lower level of the castle, searching for the possible side entrance sally port into the internal courtyard which she had spied during their approach. Russell stayed in the chopper.

As a spook, Russell loved to rappel and did so often in his leisure time. However, this was all business and a somewhat tricky drop since the chopper had to hover above the sharply pointed tips of the spires for his overhead insertion onto the roof. *It doesn't matter. I have no desire to live forever. Never did.*

✠ ✠ ✠

Clearing himself from the beating helicopter blades, Mickey crouched behind the few available cars and a wooden ticket booth in the parking lot as cover. *I sure could use Domino's sniffing skills to check out the front door, but Loni was right, Domino's no soldier.* When a lack of observable movement could be confirmed, Mickey attempted a hobbled sprint inside the entranceway. His left hamstrings burned from the crouching and the running which had just made his already weak leg weaker. The nerves in his left foot were singing with pain. As he stood in the main foyer of the building, repositioning his LBE which had scrunched up during his prolonged squatting in the parking lot, he could hear what sounded like Dalton's voice coming somewhere from the floors above.

Dalton was shouting orders and herding some people from the west side to the east side of the hallway on the top floor. Mickey heard the words *labs* and *bombs* more than once and made the obvious connection.

His mind spun out the probability of Russell running smack-dab into Dalton in the upper floors. *It's certain. I might have to neutralize Dalton's ability to corner Russell, and if that means neutralizing Dalton himself, then so be it.*

He waited, his ears straining, his eyes scanning the foyer. Dalton's voice grew faint quickly and trailed from what appeared to be the easternmost corridors. *He's moving away, and fast. Russell should be safe at his overhead insertion, at least for now.*

Now is the time to go down. His recent experience in Poland had taught Mickey that heading down to the lower levels was where the pay dirt was. *Thank Jesus these labs aren't deep bunkers.* Not knowing what he would find below, he knew he couldn't go weaponless. He searched the entrance foyer for a weapon, any weapon. His eyes landed on just what he needed. So, down the front, central stairwell and toward the basement went Mickey with courage in his heart and a three-and-a-half-foot baby blue and white striped umbrella clutched in his hand. Printed upon these colors of Bavaria was a monogram of the regionally famous and comically obese Tegernsee Lake man whistling for his unseen hound standing beneath his rotund beer belly. An angst-filled Mickey could only hope for such utter and blissful anonymity like the dog printed on the umbrella.

Suzanne rounded the nearside castle corner with significantly more grace than Mickey's entrance. Much to her chagrin, the sally port she saw from the air was blatantly inaccessible from the ground. *When God closes sally ports, He opens up … looking … looking … ah yes … loading docks.*

Far to her right, in a nestled loading dock area, a kitchen worker from the beer hall was washing some vegetable crates with a short hose. He glanced up and smiled, acknowledging her presence without missing a minute of task completion. She returned a look which transmitted a desire for him to allow her to enter the open door which stood ajar behind him. He looked back at the door, then again at her. He passively shrugged toward her and gave an accepting nod. Not waiting for the formal version of a written invitation, Suzanne rocketed past him and into the near-empty beer hall's food preparation area. Needing no employee assistance, she rifled through the nearest kitchen drawers and gathered up some very sharp knives and a quite respectable meat cleaver.

With newfound weapons in hand, she shot out of the galley, through the back of the building, and into the inner courtyard area. Thinking she might run into some clergy milling upon theses cloistered chapel grounds, she slowed her pace to a fast walk as she stuffed the absconded kitchen flatware in her cargo pockets, waistband, boot tops, and on her belt loops. When she found no one in the inner courtyard, she picked up the pace toward the distant chapel door.

From the back of the complex, Suzanne raced around to the far wall where a large door led to what was probably the formal chapel area. She now realized that the square was, in reality, bisected into a block figure-eight structure by the cloister chapel of Saint Quirinus.

Into the side chapel entrance Suzanne quietly slipped, noticing immediately that her waking world was framed in the gold-trimmed walls of the brilliantly white interior. Against this background of elegant cream and gold, the darkly stained wooden pews gave stark contrast. The pews were all parallel to her route of entry. She had an option of which pew row she cared to enter. The congregation's benches all faced left which she knew pointed toward the altar. She was awestruck by the beauty of two paintings bracketing a stained-glass window positioned across from her on the far wall.

She snapped back to operations mode, quickly assessing her surroundings. There was an elevated pulpit mounted near one of the central pillars to her front and right. To her immediate left was a candlestand where candles flickered to draw God's attention to the prayers offered when the votives were lit. Suzanne edged through a row of pews directly to her front.

She paused. A sound coming from the front of the chapel began to steal her attention. *That sound seems human.*

At the end of the row, she turned left into the center aisle and the whole of the altar opened wide in front of her. She scanned for signs of life. On the wall behind the altar was a large mural of the crucifixion. She looked to the altar and saw a small crucifix upon a red velvet altar cloth. Above the gold and white altar, suspended in the air between two balconies, was a crucified figure of Christ on the cross. On her right and left, rising to the full level of all three floors, were balcony seats arranged for viewing the altar as well. The paintings, frescoes, statues, and reliefs were incredible. *All of these are completely lifelike, but none are alive.* The human noises stopped as she turned toward the altar.

Warily, she approached the front of the chapel and looked closely at the crucifix perched upon the altar. Then a strong, raw smell assaulted her senses. It was coming from the crucifix which was heavily stained with age. Steadying herself with her left hand and reaching across with her right, she grabbed the holy relic. Her fingertips stuck to its surface. The realization of what she held overwhelmed her. *This is drying human blood.*

The noise began again, this time from directly above her.

She looked up and gasped in horror. The Christ on the cross was a real person. It was his dripping blood staining the formerly white altar cloth.

The sacrificial lamb's eyes opened sluggishly. His hoarse voice croaked, "Bombs ... six ... casks ... below ... train...." Unconsciousness drilled silence into the hanging body.

The last trailing word twisted the handle of the dagger that was driven deep into Suzanne's heart. She shook her head. *He said train, not Trane....*

She took a few breathes to steady herself, but questions coursed through her mind. *Who is this? What crime justifies such a punishment? What did he say? What does it mean?* She took another breath and put aside her horror, then called the five carefully chosen words back into her mind. *Are there six bombs? Six casks? Bombs to go off at six? Is a train involved or am I the Trane who is already involved? No matter, I have to act quickly—the words* bombs *and* below *are probably the most tightly connected pair.* She glanced down; her watch read 4:25.

"Pssst, Trane."

"Whaa ... " Suzanne's body gave a startled jump and she looked up to see Russell positioned high above her, behind the suspended cross in one of the third-floor balconies. *God be praised, he's safe.* She squinted. He was in the company of a person she did not recognize, at least not from this distance. Her breath hissed through her teeth in the relief that at least this much of the ad hoc Team Peronne had not yet bought the farm.

70

Knives and More Knives

Schloss Tegernsee
Tegernsee, Germany

When God closes sally ports … Russell saw Suzanne dart through a side door by the beer hall as he touched down on the roof. *Thank God for open beer halls.* He was quite surprised, but nevertheless glad, that he did not attract gunfire. His arrival was anything but subtle. He had a choice of two spire entrances into the third-floor foyer; he chose the cathedral side on the east as he could identify it from overhead. After freeing himself from the rappelling line, he rounded the corner quickly. Before he could react, a strong arm came from behind and held him with a sharp knife firmly placed on his left jugular. He knew this hold and he knew how it usually ended.

"Does your God forgive murderers and assassins?" sneered Nabil Baghbah, having left his scimitar back in the Middle Eastern desert.

"No, Nabil." Russell grunted. "Neither does yours."

"I thought you were my father's friend."

"You should know; you were there when I last saw him five days ago. Why are you here? Where is Asaad?"

"I will ask the questions."

"Well then, Nabil, ask meaningful ones or kill me and be quick about it."

"You claimed to be my father's friend." Pushing Russell away, Nabil retreated, sheathing his dagger. "Are you a Templar as is he?"

"Asaad is much more than a Templar," Russell wiped the trickle of blood from the minor skin cut on his neck.

"How can one be more than a Templar?"

"Asaad is the prior of the Preceptory of Jerusalem and current WTO grand master of all Templars."

"But my father is Palestinian. He soldiers for Jordan."

"Nevertheless." Russell widened his stance. "Despite which nation Asaad chooses to serve, he serves as a Palestinian Christian and has an equal right to serve Temple Mount as a Templar in the name of Jesus Christ."

"How is it that you know this? You didn't know this in the desert."

"True, Nabil, I knew this only when he knighted me into the international order."

Russell grew quiet; he remembered the hood of his cloak being retracted and the blessings placed upon his wounds. *Sahid-nee ah Sahid-dek*, Asaad had whispered to him. The friendship that began in the United States had now crossed the desert and reestablished itself between brother Templars.

"Your father knew this time would come." Russell placed both hands on Nabil's shoulders and looked him straight in the eye. "He has charged me to help him through you, Nabil. Tell me everything you know of this building and what has happened since you arrived. I pledge on my life I will help you and your father."

"Fine." Nabil spoke quickly. "I secretly followed Asaad from the desert to the Bastei."

"You were at the Templar event at the Bastei?"

"Please ... let me finish," Nabil huffed. "There, I found out he was a Templar but not his rank. I followed by train from Silesia to Bavaria and then finally here. I saw the arrival of my father with a veiled woman and eleven virtually identical men." Nabil unsheathed his knife then squatted. "I then saw a man arrive later along with a finely suited Black man he called Chaucer. They forced my father and the veiled woman into the chapel." He scratched out a diagram in the floor dust. "I followed Chaucer around to the basement laboratories, winery, and cafeteria. I saw him plant explosives here, here, and here," Nabil pointed. "When I returned to the chapel, the woman and my father had gone. I heard the man tell Chaucer that he would be going to his office, then he ordered Chaucer to return to the basement. From what I understood, everything will be completed by six. When I heard the helicopter, I went to the spire to see if my father had been taken there for further transport—instead I found you."

"Is the plan to explode the bombs at six this evening?" Russell looked at his watch.

"Yes."

"What time do you have now?" Russell prepared to synchronize.

"It's 4:23."

"Where are the eleven men who accompanied your father and the veiled woman?"

"I can't say. I was focused on my father. I am not sure where they went or were taken. I know that they were in the company of Chaucer."

"Where was the last place you saw Asaad alive?"

"The chapel. I already looked there. There was no one in the chapel."

"Okay, but it was the last place you definitely saw Asaad alive? It may not be much, but there may be a clue there that will tell us where Asaad and the woman have been taken."

"Come," said Nabil, "I will take you to the chapel."

"Not something I ever expected to hear from you, Nabil."

Two minutes later, Russell and Nabil looked over the third-floor balconies and saw Suzanne directly below the crucifixion. Nabil gasped and withdrew from the balcony railing.

"Is he alive?" Russell asked quietly, acknowledging the profound acoustics within huge chapel.

"I believe he is only unconscious but, judging by what was done to him, he will die soon if we don't help."

Russell motioned for Nabil to go around to where the other suspending rope for the crucifix was secured.

"We're going to release the ropes and let him down. You engage the ABC's down there."

"Reciting the alphabet?" asked Nabil. "How is that going to help my father?"

"Airway, breathing, and circulation—ABCs!"

"I am sorry. I know you are a doctor, and you know what you are doing. Can she be enough help until you get down there?"

"Nabil, she is a more specialized doctor than me. God has her placed in the best position to save your father. Please, release the rope carefully."

The two men lowered the crucified victim sufficiently so that Suzanne was able to guide the cross into a face-up position on the altar. She went to work.

He's been tied on the cross, not nailed, good. Blood loss from the makeshift crown of thorns—it transected blood vessels of the head. Bullet wound to the right abdomen—probably hit some aspect of the right kidney and liver. Chest badly macerated, probably from torture. She pulled a pouch from her LBE and quickly rummaged through it. *Percussion hammer—useless. Tuning fork—more useless. Driver—better, I can use it as an artery clamp. Voila! Penlight!*

Russell and Nabil heard four loud shots as they came down the stairwell to the ground floor of the chapel. Suzanne was hovering over the body, using a penlight to check to the victim's eye dilation.

"Those were gunshots … four rounds discharged. Confirm four?" Russell panted.

"I dunno … probably four." Suzanne stashed her penlight. "Here, rip some cloth into strips. Hurry, use this." She handed Russell a kitchen knife that she pulled out of her boot.

"What blade will you use?"

"Don't worry, Russell. I have another." They aggressively cut and tore parts of the tablecloth into bandages while Nabil looked on wide-eyed.

"Is he going to die?" Nabil's breathing staggered.

"Who is this, Russell? A friend of yours?" Suzanne asked, eyes never leaving her patient.

"He's Nabil, the son of Grand Master Asaad. Long story. We met in the desert five days ago and yet again a few minutes ago in the spire. Both times he tried to kill me. No one likes him very much."

"Two attempts to kill you, Russell?" Suzanne shot a furtive glance. "He really does know you."

"Yeah. We're old friends now." Russell tore more bandage strips. Nabil hovered.

"Really, old friends, eh?" Suzanne wiped at her sweaty forehead with her sleeve. "What is it with you and your playmates? Can't seem to get along?" Suzanne deftly packed and wrapped the wounds.

"All's good now ... bosom buddies." Russell bounced his gaze between Suzanne and Nabil.

"Good. Glad you two kissed and made up."

"Why hold a grudge? It's only life, right?" Russell kept tearing strips.

Nabil knelt near the body. "Is he going to ... going to ... ?"

"Die? No," said Suzanne. "Not if I can help it. However, he's a she."

"A 'she'? They cut off my father's genitals?"

"No, the blood you see there is pooled from the trauma."

"I don't ... " Nabil stared blankly at the body before him.

"Nabil, look at me." Russell paused his work, then physically turned Nabil's head toward his own. "This is not your father. This is a woman who has had her head gouged, her breasts macerated, her abdomen shot, and has been tied on a cross for a slow, agonizing death. This is not Asaad."

"Not Asaad ... " Nabil turned away, covering his face with his hands.

"Tell me I'm wrong, Suzanne." Russell pointed with his jaw. "This isn't who I think it is?"

"Yes, I'm guessing so," Suzanne said, her hands working furiously, "but not for long if we don't hurry. This is what Wunschmann and Dalton left of the Owl."

"Bastards. I hate friggin' cowards!"

"Easy, Russell," continued Suzanne. "The Owl spoke of bombs. I am not sure exactly of the details. I think it involves casks in the beer hall or winery. There may be six of them or they may be going off at six." She paused, fixing her gaze. "Russell, I'm frightened. I have a situation here for an EMT with proper equipment and time. I am *not* an EMT and I have no equipment. ER doctors handle this stuff, not me. It'll take all of the time we have until six for me to stabilize her and then I can't be any help to you and Mickey ... if Mickey is still ... oh, Jesus ... what were we thinking?"

"Don't say it. Mickey's fine. He will take care of the basement issues. This is your lane for now."

"Russell ... " Suzanne clenched her jaw and blinked away the tears that had edged her eyes moments before. She turned back to the Owl and the task she had been given. "Russell, you know quite well that Mickey is not Special Ops like you. He takes splinters out of fingers and pokes an abscess or two. He is not a bomb defusing expert, for Christ's sake." Suzanne's Viking-self surfaced.

"You forget, Suzanne," Russell said, smiling wryly, "he was a soldier before he became a doctor. Also, his Chemical Corps background taught him a little about ordnance, bombs, and explosives."

"Enough to save us today?"

"Okay, point taken." Russell nodded. "I'll go and help him once I'm finished here."

"You're finished here. I'll keep your dear and charming old desert friend with the killer smile here with me while you go help Mickey. I think that would be the best way to divide and conquer."

"His name is Nabil."

"I'm Nabil." Nabil dropped his hands and eased back toward the group.

"Don't let her die, Trane. It would kill Mickey. Even more important, don't give them the satisfaction."

"I will do my part to save her, Russell, but you must do your part to save us. The bombs must be found. You are the one who has the greatest skill to defuse them."

"And you have the greatest skill to save her, Trane. Stabilize her. Nabil, you stay with Suzanne and help her find a transport method to get this woman to the chopper out front."

"This is the veiled woman?"

"We believe so."

"I will stay until she is safe, but not a moment longer," said Nabil.

"No one has forgotten your father, Nabil." Russell shook his head. "We must help those whom first we find."

"You have my word until her safety is met," repeated Nabil.

"And you have mine." Russell sprinted off without looking back.

It was 4:50 when Nabil and Suzanne carried out the Owl, tied to the disassembled top of the altar table, with her wounds bandaged and her pulse rate and breathing waning.

Russell bolted to the front of the building and found some classrooms. He located the central set of stairs and took them down into the front basement area where all the rooms were laboratories except one labeled *Weinkeller*—the wine cellar. He looked at his watch. He had exactly sixty minutes to find and defuse an undetermined number of bombs. He was the only one in a position, against all odds, to make the impossible happen.

Under his breath he repeatedly recited, "With God all things are possible. With God all things are possible. Boy, I hope He works late on German weekends."

71

Day of Wine and Fuses

Schloss Tegernsee wine cellar

Tegernsee, Germany

I hope they find out about this new bomb situation sooner rather than later. It was 4:20 when Mickey reached the front door of the wine cellar.

Mickey figured that here in the rooms that made up the winery, explosives would probably be planted on any source of fuel lines, heating tanks, or on any pressurized plumbing of the large fermenting wine vats. He went from vat to vat looking carefully and found at least three small bombs with timed fuses, all in the same general area. His search was interrupted by sounds coming from the back of the winery and, more specifically, from the southeast stairwell of the castle.

Oh, I know that foul voice ... and it's close.

Dalton pushed open the back door of the winery and with a gun in his free hand, he issued in an eleven-man group of bound and gagged cloned tower keepers tethered together with a connecting rope. Mickey dove headlong and slid to a stop beneath the wine tasting counter. Peeking between the seams of the front paneling he had an eye-level view of the fearful, huddled group being forced to sit side by side against the far wall. With all their faces partially covered with gags, it was quite difficult for him to decipher who was who among them. Then he spotted the tufted chin hair of Thaddeusz.

Raising himself off his belly, Mickey knelt quietly. He began formulating how he could best help them and himself. Then he noticed that, in his haste to hide, he left the blue and white umbrella resting against the closest vat. He clenched his teeth. Dalton would soon see it and know that it certainly didn't walk there by itself. Mickey quelled the surge of panic he felt rising within. *I don't need another failure, especially now, with so many lives on the line.* His mind shifted. *Get that umbrella out of Dalton's sight.* He swayed back and forth under the counter, moving into a squatting position, and trying to figure out the right course of action. Mickey's movement caught the eye of the tower keeper sitting directly to his front. It wasn't Thaddeusz. Mickey saw the man's eyes track his movement for a brief second. Judging by the dress, he looked to be one of the prim and proper English tower keepers. *I need help—one clone is as good as the other.*

Mickey craned to see where Dalton had gone. The English tower keeper nodded his head slightly to the left, indicating that Dalton was away in that direction. Mickey started to shift around but he saw the eyes of the English tower keeper grow wide and stern. Mickey froze in place. He could see Dalton's polished wing tips coming behind the counter. Without hesitation the key phrases of a much longer prayer rocketed through his head. The last time he had prayed this Queen Catherine Parr prayer was when the sands of an Iraqi bunker dwelled in the creases of his battle dress uniform.

Every syllable recited was accentuated by the increasing tempo of his heart beating. *"O Almighty King and Lord of Hosts which by thy angels thereunto appointed do minister both war and peace ... "* Quietly Mickey contracted his aching legs and cramped body as far to the front of the counter as he could. *"And which did give unto David both courage and strength, being but a little one, unarmed, and not expert in feats of war with his sling to set upon and overthrow the great huge Goliath. Amen."*

He saw Dalton, the huge Goliath, come right up to the counter and then speak aloud. "Hello, what would you be doing there?" Mickey felt a rush of nausea. *Why hast Thou forsaken me?* Mickey was about to crawl out with his hands up when his eyes met those of the English tower keeper—he fervently shook his head: *No.* Mickey acquiesced and remained still, his stomach churning vigorously.

"Well then," said the Goliath, "since you won't come to me, I guess I will have to come to you." Mickey again looked across the way and still received the same reassurance not to move. He watched as Dalton's feet walked back around the counter and to the edge of the first vat. He picked up the umbrella.

"I just don't remember you being here before. That would mean ... that someone else brought you in here ... and that someone might still be here ... fairly close by." Mickey heard the rustle of Dalton's blazer jacket. Assuming Dalton was reaching for his gun, Mickey checked his immediate area. He noticed that the table which hid him was not fixed to the floor. He gritted his teeth. *"Overthrow the great huge Goliath."* He contracted himself for a full-body vertical spring against the underside of the table. *Knock the counter up and over, crush Dalton, take the advantage.* Mickey sucked a deep breath in tense preparation but released it quickly as a new sound entered the room.

Mickey's ears picked up a scampering noise and a somewhat familiar clicking sound coming from the door off the rear stairwell. Dalton also heard the noise and shifted his attention in the direction of the intruder as she eased her way into the room. Mickey's eyes saw a glimpse of the figure, but his mind could not fathom any sense of understanding. His eyes focused on a white coat covered with random black markings. *This isn't going to be good.*

Through the door, strolling in on all fours was a Dalmatian. Although Mickey couldn't fully see the dog's face, the knot in his gut, nevertheless, told him it was Domino. *I hope I'm wrong.* As all dogs of a given breed tend to look alike from afar, dog owners eventually become like mothers in a park filled with children. They know theirs from the others through a myriad of distinctive characteristics.

Mickey needed a prime view of this dog's face. Loni's canine baby was a white-faced pup with only a spot above the left eye, called a kissing spot; a beauty mark on the left of her snout; and a tiny wisp of a moustache. Domino was unique in that her right eye was blue and her left eye was brown.

Lucky for all, Dalton didn't remember or recognize Domino as the very dog he encountered years ago at pet parks, hiking trails, and gym aerobics classes. Since she wore nothing but a nondescript body harness, it seemed to Mickey that Dalton just attributed her presence, though strange and quite inappropriate in time and place, to that of a random stray dog.

"Which one of you brought your dog?" Dalton mocked. "No one confessing?" He shifted back to the umbrella and to the faces of the beleaguered tower keepers, many of whom seemed quite distressed at the four-legged intruder. "Afraid of dogs, are we?" he taunted the tower keepers. "Idiots...."

Two horrible thoughts immediately came to Mickey's mind. *If this is Domino then she has tracked my scent. Oh, God, why did I play hide-and-seek with her so often? She never ever fails to find me. And if Domino is here then Loni is probably not far behind. They were a packaged deal—this is not a danger I'm willing to share.*

True to form, Domino came right to the front edge of the wine counter and began playfully pawing, barking, and scratching.

"What have you got there, Spotty?" Dalton cooed. "Did you find something, pretty doggie?" Dalton started to crouch. "Maybe you found the owner of this umbrella?" Mickey tried to quietly shoo Domino away which only made her bark and paw more fervently. Unable to stop the barking of the annoying dog, Dalton snatched hard at her harness, exacting a painful yelp from the Dalmatian.

Now! From his crouched position, using the strength in his good leg, Mickey sprung vertically against the underside of the counter. The counter teetered up and forward, sending Domino backward into a surprised Dalton who fell and lost the grip of his handgun. The gun skidded into the shadow of the open door. A stooped and panting Mickey looked into Dalton's wide-eyed face seconds before their eyes simultaneously turned toward the gun.

Before either one of them could move, from the shadows of the hallway, in strode Loni holding Dalton's revolver which was now pointed at its very distressed owner. Dalton's panicked eyes shot left and then right trying to figure out what to do next. The analyst timidly walked over to her now-standing soldier husband. In a flash, Dalton's hand swiped for the gun in Loni's hand but never made it. A fifty-three-pound Dalmatian caught his wrist in midair. Dalton drove his free arm's elbow into Domino's flank. The dog yelped.

Loni's eyes flashed with anger as she spun her second hand up to stabilize the gun and shoot Dalton. Unfortunately, lacking the skill and adeptness of a DIA field agent, the one hand only knocked the gun out of the other. The gun fell from Loni's grasp, hit her knee, and slid across the floor. It stopped in front of the seated Thaddeusz whose hands were tied in front of him. He quickly picked up the handgun and cocked the hammer skillfully. Tracking where the gun moved, Dalton's face lost tension. He locked gazes with the steely-eyed Thaddeusz Lenz. Dalton's body jerked as the handgun blazed four consecutive rounds into his center chest and upper abdomen. Thaddeusz's eyes smoldered in the direction of the felled Dalton well past the time the last round fired.

"Nobody hurts my Domino!" Loni shrieked at a dying Dalton. "Nobody!" Loni ran her hands over each Dalmatian spot as her tears moistened the dog's fur. "Mickey, her ribs are broken."

"Thaddeusz ... " Mickey squatted down and pulled at the gun in Thaddeusz's hand. Thaddeusz could not release the gun—his gaze was fixed on the twitching and gasping Dalton. "There is no more to hate."

It was 4:31, and with eyes glazing over, Jean Geoffrey Dalton spit out his last few breaths of life in Mickey's direction, then gasped and spasmed into a sickening silence.

Mickey looked over at Loni. She was uttering terms of endearment through broken words and sobs, frantically hovering over her softly whining and grunting polka dot baby girl. He turned back to the body and emptied the contents of Dalton's pockets. He was awed by what he found. *I'll never see Jean Dalton in the same way again.*

72

Blaming Ruth

Schloss Tegernsee courtyard

Tegernsee, Germany

Why couldn't I have been a trauma surgeon or an ER doctor? Suzanne groaned. *Then at least this woman would have a fighting chance.*

With the help of Nabil, Suzanne carried the traumatized and splinted Owl into the courtyard and out the sally port near where she had first tried to enter the complex earlier. She had no problem releasing the inner security latches to push open the heavy wooden door. Her arms ached from the weight of the altar tabletop which was much heavier than the tiny figure tied upon it. Once they rounded the west end of the building, they turned left into the alley formed by the castle laboratory and the beer distribution loading dock. On the dock steps, the sad green eyes of a little street urchin followed them as they went north where they could see the blades of the chopper spinning up.

Two of the flight crew members spotted them and ran across the parking lot, hopped the small chain restrainer, and came over to assist with the transporting of the ever-waning Owl, kept warm only by Suzanne's uniform top. Suzanne looked into Nabil's eyes knowing the questions which burned behind them. Where was his father, Asaad? Was he in the same shape that the Owl had been in when she was first found?

No matter how much Nabil may have wanted to break away and resume the search for his father, he had made a vow to help this woman until safety. As much as Nabil loved his father, he was honorable and knew that he had to hold to his word. His father would perform no differently had the situation been reversed.

The clock on the spire read 5:05 when the Owl was en route to Bad Wiessee and the nearest hospital helicopter landing zone. Nabil and Suzanne needed no further directive. The mission now was clear. They only hoped that Asaad's time had not run out.

Mickey's watch read 4:33 when he leaned over a smarting Domino. He rubbed his physician's hand over the contour of each rib, eliciting a growl from

284

the dog. He knew that even if she bit at him, she would never bite hard enough to hurt him.

"Is she okay?" Loni asked tearfully.

"Her ribs aren't broken."

"You didn't answer my question."

"Honey, she is not okay. She has painfully bruised ribs."

"Will she *be* okay? I want her to be okay, *okay*?"

"If you must know, I am most certain that she will fare better than Jean Dalton here."

Dalton lay flat on his back, his shirt completely soaked with blood. His head was turned to the right toward the rear stairwell door—the blue and white umbrella obscuring his neck and face from view. The earpiece for his telephone remained firmly in place. He never moved.

"I killed him?" Loni's eyes began to well up. She cupped her face in her hands, drawing in a sobbing breath.

"Not really, honey. You sort of passed the gun to Thaddeusz who shot him four times."

"Oh my God. I helped killed him."

"Honey, Loni, I need you to help me release these people. Dalton would have hurt them, and us, had you and Thaddeusz not stopped him."

"He had to be stopped." Loni wiped her eyes with the back of her hand. She looked straight at Thaddeusz. "I only wanted him to stop hurting Domino."

"You succeeded—a job well done," Mickey answered, unbinding clone after clone. "Now please release the guys."

"You saw him, right?" Loni started untying the bonds. "He yanked Domino." Loni gestured moving to the next man down the line. "What kind of sick person jerks the harness of a defenseless puppy dog?"

Slowly a growing crowd of men, rubbing their wrists and faces, surrounded Mickey and Loni.

"He was a very bad man," continued Loni. "No one ever really liked him."

"There is some evidence that supports that the feeling wasn't mutual."

"What?"

"There was one here whom he liked very much."

"Yes, I know, Mickey. We've been through that time and time again. He liked me to the point of stalking me. Come on. This is not the time, or even remotely the place, to discuss this kind of history."

"I was just going to say—"

"Say what? The man is dead and yes, you were right! He was a horrible man who could not find love in any living thing."

"Well, maybe one living thing...." Mickey handed Loni a beautifully hand-carved Dalmatian with a name etched on the underside.

"I can't read the name. Can you?"

"Let me see."

Loni tilted the carving toward Mickey. His hands were stained with Dalton's blood from the body search. He rubbed a bloodstained finger over the letters. "I think it says *Smarl.*"

"Who is Smarl?"

"I'm guessing it was the name of his Dalmatian," Mickey's voice ended in a whisper. *Could it be that he was just enamored with Domino and not stalking Loni?*

"Mickey, I … " Loni rolled her lips inward. For the first time in her life she felt shame and embarrassment for her own publicized hate and disgust.

"Loni, two eyes … right here … right now." Mickey took the carving and pushed it into his cargo pocket. He squared off in front of his wife. "Loni, you have to take Domino back up the stairwell, out the first-floor landing, to the courtyard, and out of the building to the rear of the complex." Domino, upon hearing her name, began wagging her tail. Loni reached to pet her, but Domino's wagging slowed to a stop.

"I'll take Domino out now. Will you be far behind?"

"I think we need to define what *remaining behind* really means." His eyebrows contracted.

"What's the issue, Mickey? I told you that I would stay back where I needed to be."

"And yet, you are here."

"I didn't lie." Loni's eyes darted. "Yes, I implied to you that Domino and I would stay back." Loni nodded. "But I didn't stipulate just how far back in time or distance. Don't blame me because you didn't ask the right question. If you *need* to blame anyone—"

"Wait," he interrupted, holding up his hand. He gently pulled her to the side, away from the group. "If you are here, then the Nazi papers—"

"—are in secure storage in the general's bird," Loni finished.

"Fine." Mickey's face relaxed but then grew stern again. "If I *need* to blame anyone, who would you suggest?" Mickey nodded toward Loni.

"Not me." Loni shook herself free. "Blame Ruth."

"Ruth? Who's Ruth?"

"Ruth as in Ruth and Naomi. You know, the biblical Ruth."

"Yes, I know … but—"

"Ruth said, 'Don't tell me to turn back or to leave you. Where you go, I will go. Where you stay, I will stay. Your people will be my people. Your God will be my God. Where you die, I will die.'" Loni's eyes welled up.

"Loni … " Mickey drew her into a hug and kissed her tears softly. He knew if he couldn't direct her, then he needed to be absolutely sure that he could protect her.

"I'm glad you're here. But there's more to be done." Mickey turned back to the clones. "I have to lead the guys out of the front of the building. Then I need to help Suzanne and Russell. Everyone here needs to catch a hop out as well."

"Mickey," Thaddeusz came over and whispered, "I believe I can speak for all of us by saying we don't fear for our lives. We are Templars. We don't want to flee to safety. We have made our oath to Christ. There is much work here. We are many hands which just need to be shown what to do."

✠ ✠ ✠

It was 4:46 when Mickey, falling back on his Chemical Corps munitions and explosives training, began instructing the cloned tower keepers on how to defuse the bombs. Thomas, Justice James, and Jude left with Loni and Domino as a vanguard.

The remaining eight clones combed through the rest of the winery looking for and disarming anything with wires attached. Two threatening bottles of a Müller-Thurgau white wine were skillfully disarmed by ensuring that their contents had been satisfactorily emptied. Matthias and Peer conceded to the dirty job needing to be done.

About fifteen minutes later, Mickey and the eight remaining clones sped up the northeast stairwell hoping to clear the upper-level laboratories of any explosive devices. They were on the cusp of the final sixty minutes where all things—good, bad, or ugly—would come to an explosive end.

73

And Rituals for All

Schloss Tegernsee winery
Tegernsee, Germany

I heard four shots, which means that up to four could be lying here dead or.... Russell clenched his jaw as he made his approach toward the lower levels.

Meanwhile, Simeone, the last of the eight clones still with Mickey, cleared the winery area and closed the door into the northeast stairwell just as Russell passed the basement door on his way to the front entrance of the wine cellar.

As he opened the wine cellar door, Russell's keen nostrils picked up the smell of gunpowder. He again recalled the four gunshots, and in the distance, he now saw a sprawled body whose blood was forming a congealing, crimson carpet. He braced for the worst as he could not make a positive identification of the victim at this distance. *All soldiers know that they live on borrowed time.* Russell negotiated the long hall through the winery. *Mickey knows it. Suzanne knows it. Even Nabil and his father, Asaad, know it. No one talks about it, but it is always there.*

With each step, he hoped that the body wasn't Mickey's. Unbidden, his mind went back to the evening of a formal military dinner with civilian guests and spouses.

✠ ✠ ✠

Loni named the dinner occasion "The Turning of Leaves" when her husband's gold leaf, indicating the rank of major, changed into the silver leaf of a lieutenant colonel. The October dinner's title was dually meaningful because of the abundance of autumn hues which painted the nearby Catskills. Mr. Vice, the person designated as the master of ceremony, read a revised version of the "History of the Warrior Mess" modified by Loni for the occasion:

> In the lives of warriors long ago, in the dimly remembered times of our own significant history, men and beasts fell under the cold steel onslaught of hand-to-hand battle, amidst the brazened fires shadowed by plumes of thickened smoke.

288

By the funeral pyres of the dead, the survivors gathered as a brother-hood and toasted the slain of their own, cursed the enemy whom they sent to hell, and celebrated life as only those who faced death at the edge of steel were able to do.

As time passed, and as armies surged over continents vomiting death and destruction, this brotherhood of warriors remained. The survivors with the greatest responsibility became the leaders who led from the front. Over the ramparts, thick with dead and dying, they spurred onward the frantic masses through flesh-searing flames, striking fear into the hearts of their enemies by their very presence on the field of battle.

Men whose word was their bond unto death continued to meet to toast the fallen, to revel in the camaraderie only fire and blood can temper, and to test the hardness of the spirit required when facing the very roots of their destiny. The warriors of the past have given rise to these warriors of the present who sit here this very night.

We toast to our fallen, we share camaraderie, and we smile reservedly as we prepare once more to taste the blood, face the flame, and hope that tomorrow will bring us back to this hallowed ground where we may once again raise our glasses and remember....

✠ ✠ ✠

Counting the number of bullet holes, Russell stood above the bleeding remains of Dalton. Despite all his disgust with the man that Dalton had become, he knew that this man—the former US Army Captain Jean Dalton—died far away from all those who knew him and, yes, probably even those who loved him. *It is the potential fate of all soldiers, even disgraced ones.* Russell bent down, reached into the open collar and swept the base of the neck for the dog tags which he would turn in to the Personnel Section. His hand came up with a broken dog tag chain. *Mickey's alive.* It was a ritual all soldiers knew and honored.

Russell snapped back on task and noticed that the room had been swept clean of any explosives—again, Mickey's handy work. *Where would Mickey go next?* He looked at his watch. It read 5:05. *No time to duplicate Mickey's efforts.* He went into the southeast stairwell and strained a keen ear. He heard nothing. The light in the window of the door leading into the south wing of the basement was off. *If Mickey had gone that way, the light would be on.* Russell began to sweep the basement for explosives as quickly and thoroughly as he could. He proceeded clockwise until he arrived at the start point—the center stairwell of the north wing of the chapel. Then he doubled back.

Russell opened the door into the south wing and the automatic lights kicked on, showing a total absence of life. The wing was one large open bay with a central walkway flanked by laboratory benches lined up in two long files. At the far end was another windowed door leading to the center stairwell in the south wing. Russell scanned the room for gas tanks, vats, hazardous chemical, or gas lines. He knew these would be the best options for increasing a bomber's bang for the buck. Then he spotted it. A sloppily placed sequence of C-4, each block containing a fuse. A drooping wire scalloped from charge to charge like a macabre attempt at interior decorating. He deduced that the demolitions person wasn't too concerned that this handiwork would be discovered as there was no attempt to cleverly hide the explosives. Russell disengaged all the fuses from the plastics. His watch read 5:14. He needed to get to, and through, the next wing's basement so that the western wing of laboratories could be accessed and cleared. Time was becoming less friendly by the passing minute. He wondered if Suzanne and Nabil had finished their mission and if the Owl had made it to safety.

The Owl, holding on to life by tenterhooks, was removed from the helicopter landing zone at a nearby German hospital. All the field-expedient items that sustained her thus far, including the use of her walking stick as a splint, had held well enough for the transfer. Her chances for survival now rested in the skilled hands of German medical teams at the trauma center.

74

Crescent and the Cross

Schloss Tegernsee grounds
Tegernsee, Germany

T<i>hank you, Marie Marvingt. You may have saved the Owl.</i> Suzanne smiled. *Flight medicine and air evacuation in any form owes their existence to you and your wartime experiences in Morocco.* From the front landing zone, Suzanne and Nabil watched the helicopter take its precious human cargo off to definitive medical care.

Once the chopper was clear, Nabil snapped his skyward gaze down to the intense pain shooting into his right palm. He remembered the onset of pain as he was carrying the makeshift litter with the Owl aboard. He gazed upon a large gash in which blood was pooling. Also spotting the wound, Suzanne pulled out a remaining piece of the cloth bandages and began carefully pressure-wrapping the laceration securely. Nabil's eyes initially watched the skilled movements of her hands, but then shifted and followed the contours of her face.

"Dr. Russell Lange, he is your friend, yes?"

"Dr. Lange is my friend, yes. Why?"

"How is it possible that he is a friend of Islam and still an ... an ... "

" ... an infidel?"

"Yes, an infidel."

"May I answer your question with a question?"

"Why not? I expect no less from any American."

"Why are you surprised that your father could vest a friendship with a man such as Russell?"

"Do not speak of my father, woman."

"Do not speak of my love, Saracen." A quick jerk on the bandage brought a hardly noticeable wince to Nabil's face. He tightened his lips. Suzanne continued unnoticing.

"Russell Lange has lived a life like no other. He is a man who sometimes finds it more difficult to live than to die. He has experienced persecution on a

291

personal, professional, and religious level. When he met your father, he met a man—not a Saracen. It did not matter that he was Palestinian in the service of Jordan. He did not persecute your father for his person, profession, or religion. I believe your father gave Russell the same latitude by sharing with him the Five Pillars of Islam."

"You do not know my father," Nabil spat.

"Apparently neither do you. Your father is a Christian and a Templar of great importance." Suzanne released Nabil's hand and shoved it toward his chest. "Maybe you should figure out why." Suzanne shook her head and turned her gaze back to the twin spires.

Nabil's lips trembled but he could only glare his appreciation. Flexing his hand, he grunted with the throbbing pain hidden beneath the bandaging. He didn't have time for this inconvenience. Ignoring the pain, he redirected his attention toward the front entrance of the castle complex.

Nabil took the lead and guided the advance toward the building's doors between the two spires. The clock on the spire read 5:05. Within seconds they were back inside the building, standing on the main floor near the north-central stairwell next to an empty umbrella stand. Nabil paused only for a second before he shot up the stairs past every landing, heading for the place he thought his father would be. Unbidden, Suzanne followed in his wake.

It was 5:35 when a winded Nabil and Suzanne arrived at the fourth floor amidst executive offices in the southern wing of the complex. Voices could be heard through an ajar door labeled *Director of Laboratory Research: Dr. Wunschmann*. It appeared to Suzanne that her boss, Wunschmann, had two offices in two different countries. *I wonder if ICD knows Wunschmann is moonlighting in Europe?*

Nabil pushed the door open to reveal a wide receptionist's suite without life. The voices they had heard were coming from the intercom on the desk of the receptionist. The desk was unmanned, but still a formidable obstacle as it straddled the direct path to a closed door far at the back of the suite.

Suzanne had not come this far to be thwarted or, for that matter, to be the slightest bit delayed. Nudging Nabil exacted from him a confirmatory glance as he removed his hand bandage and clenched his bloody fist tightly, preparing for the fight. Eye to eye, the silent message, *You go right and I will go left*, was clearly understood between the Christian and Islamic soldiers of very different origins. As each rounded their respective corners of the reception desk, a noise from behind froze them in midstride. Something had moved. They crouched in response and moved to the back side of the desk. The clock on the wall read 5:38.

✠ ✠ ✠

Loni's quick glance at her inner wrist showed 4:46 when she and a gingerly stepping Domino were escorted out of the basement into the southeast stairwell by Jude, Justice James, and Thomas. They proceeded up the stairwell to each landing to spread out and search for explosives. Jude splintered off to check the first-floor dormitories. Justice James left the remainder of the group on the second-floor landing as he headed off to the south wing. When Domino, Thomas, and Loni got to the third floor, Thomas peeled off for the south-central stairwell. Loni continued up this stairwell to its final destination.

On the third floor, Thomas went from lab to lab looking for anything that could vaguely be construed as explosive in nature. With the numerous labs ahead and armed only with a short course in identifying and disarming, he was less than confident that he could complete his mission. However, being a Knight of Christ, he knew that God's plan would be unfurled through him.

It was 5:21 when Loni and Domino arrived on the fourth floor and approached the empty receptionist's suite. Upon entering, they faced a large desk sitting in the room's center. In addition to the main entrance door where she now stood, Loni saw three options before her, but her way forward was clear. Two choices were archways to the left and right—each entrance facing the short side of the receptionist's desk—and each served as access points to their own large display rooms with plate glass windows facing the suite. The final option was directly behind the receptionist's chair, leading to the closed door of the director's office.

Loni set her jaw and took a step toward the director's door, but a mildly limping Domino immediately scuttled in front of the desk and into the right display room. As Loni attempted to grab the dog's harness, she heard a sudden elevation of voices echoing from the region around the receptionist's desk. Following Domino, she diverted her course and raced into the room, diving behind a cloth-covered bench. She tried to slow her now racing heart—her right hand clenched in a fist over her crucifix pendant.

Floodlights above the corners of the large plate glass window shone back into the display area of the room, bathing the crouching Loni in a dark shadow. Steadying herself against the cloth-draped bench, she peeked briefly around its corner and through the ceiling-to-floor plate glass window. She saw no movement, but she could still hear voices from within the suite. Nearby she could hear the rustling and snorting of Domino as the Dalmatian sniffed around the display room. She could not see her polka dot baby because of the structure behind which she was hiding. From the level of the floor, Loni ran her hand up the bench until the feel of the dark, soft, felt-like material transitioned to a very cold, fine, coarse surface. Loni drew in a deep breath in response to the sudden, drastic change of the surface. She released her breath slowly, listening to an absence of canine sniffing.

Did Domino leave the room? Certainly I would have heard the scratching of her nails on the tile outside the suite. Loni started to inch forward to further investigate, when the sniffing sound resumed. Domino was still in the room, on the other side of whatever sat on the bench between Loni and the window. As it seemed that no danger had followed her into her hiding spot, Loni stood hesitantly to venture a better look around.

Her small display room mirrored exactly the display room on the other side of the receptionist's desk. Each room had a sculpture made of stone and wood. Loni crouched when again she heard the voices speaking.

"Did you really think you could stop us, Schweinehund?" an accented gravelly voice hissed.

"Someone had to try."

Loni noted a hint of a Middle Eastern accent in the other voice.

"How long have you hidden them from us?"

"It is easy to hide in plain sight that which someone does not seek."

A cry of pain reverberated around the room.

"You are in my office. When I ask you a question, you would fare better to just answer it directly."

"It is easy—"

Another cry of pain and a muffled grunt pierced the room. Loni began to realize that the sounds seemed canned, almost with a steel room echo. She seized the harness of Domino, who had just rounded the corner of the sculpture. After a mild start, Domino settled down to the increasing rhythmic breathings and grip tension of her master's hand. Loni kept low and out of sight.

"Arabs must like pain," snarled the voice from the receptionist's squawk box.

"I am Palestinian," the voice croaked.

"Okay, well then, Muslims must like pain."

"Palestinian Christian, Doctor."

"No such thing."

"Torture doesn't change the truth—not then, not ever."

"Agreed, it may not change the past or future for a certain Palestinian Christian. However, it changed the present and the future for someone named Michael—a friend of yours, possibly?"

Loni involuntarily sucked in a spastic breath as she heard the name. She prayed that there was another Michael, different from her Mickey. Domino tensed in response to the change in Loni's demeanor.

"No need to hurt him … Michael has done nothing—"

"Really, you know what he has done? He reported his doings to you. Well, he and his two cronies should have reported to *me*."

The pit in Loni's stomach grew as she now understood that the voice must belong to Wunschmann, and he could only be talking about Mickey. The two cronies had to be Suzanne and Russell.

"Is he dead?"

Wunschmann gave a low, rumbling laugh which mimicked a distorted growl. "He and your Owl need only a third crucified soul to be a reenactment of Calvary Hill."

"I supposed I'm next."

"I suppose you are."

An agonizing deep, throated groan was heard as ripping, scraping, and pounding preceded the cries, "My hand—my hand—why are you doing this?"

It was 5:37 when, with a total abandonment of concern, Loni numbly stood up, then stumbled to and through the display room archway into the receptionist's suite. Two people in the room were caught by surprise at her sudden presence. The Middle Eastern man grabbed her arm. His blood-stained hand marked the left sleeve of her shirt. Loni never flinched. Domino growled and posed for a launch. Suzanne quickly kneeled in front of the shifting Dalmatian in a soothing manner while Nabil corralled a trance-like Loni.

"Mickey ... they have killed Mickey," mumbled a dazed Loni.

"We can't believe that right now. We need to focus," whispered Suzanne, looking up from her kneeling position by the dog.

"Suzanne?" Loni looked around at the sound of the voice. "Suzanne, please get Mickey ... bring him to me ... even if he is dead ... I want him. He needs to know something from me ... I want to be with Mickey now, Suzanne." With both hands, Loni pressed her pendant crucifix to her chest. She swayed, but Nabil steadied her with his grip on her arm.

"Loni, Loni ... " Suzanne stood and took Loni's face in her hands. "Two eyes, two eyes ... on me right now. I need you to focus, please. What would Mickey want you to do right now?"

"I don't know. I don't know anything anymore."

"I think he'd say give him a big hug," spoke a winded voice from behind them.

Loni shook loose of Nabil's hold while Domino rounded Suzanne. As they turned, they saw Mickey, kneeling and trying to catch his breath in the doorway. The clock on the wall read 5:40.

"Where have you been? I thought you were dead," asked Loni. Domino sniffed toward Mickey's mouth as he began to respond, but the intercom box answered first.

75

Hooked Cross

Schloss Tegernsee Director's Office

Tegernsee, Germany

*T*wenty minutes is nothing or forever, depending on the circumstance. Leaning on Loni for support, Mickey watched as the wall clock ticked to 5:41. Snuggly between them stood a quiet Domino. Nabil and Suzanne also listened as Wunschmann's voice grew hoarse with threats and curses.

"You and your band of soldier-monk rejects were destroyed on Friday the thirteenth in the year 1312. Why on earth would you think you could stop the hand of the Third Reich? Now you shall be the third to go in the manner of Knights Templar grand master, Jacques de Molay—nailed to a church, bleeding to death. We've got a good start now, haven't we?"

Suzanne kicked in the closed door to the private office. Mickey followed right behind, eyes darting around the scene. He vowed to himself, *I will not let history repeat itself. I will not!*

As the rest of the team entered, they saw a bloodied man on a chair whose back legs were stuffed down behind a window radiator. Stripped to the waist, he wore a crown of thorns and streams of blood gravitated down his face. His hands were outstretched and held in place by ice picks pounded through his palms into the rustic wooden window frame. Blood trailed down his wrists.

Seemly unconcerned with the noise of the forced intrusion, an enraged man stood in the center of the room, continuing to hurl derogatory and humiliating remarks at the nearly crucified Asaad. Nabil lunged toward the back of Wunschmann but was quickly side-stepped. Nabil fell, sprawled on the floor in front of his nearly unconscious father.

"What have we here, yet another Arab?" Wunschmann cajoled. He turned toward the intruders he'd seen in the window's reflection.

"Wilhelm Wunschmann? It can't be. You're dead," exhaled Mickey through his teeth.

"A mere inconvenience," bantered the elderly Dr. Wilhelm Werner Wunschmann. "You seem to be quite alive yourself, Mickey. I guess Dalton didn't take you out as he was instructed. He must have killed Russell instead."

Suzanne winced.

"It was you who was behind the Dyhernfurth chemical mayhem in Wroclaw," Mickey continued.

"Lucky Industries was, of course, the perfect cover to dig for the secret laboratory."

"What were you looking to find?"

"The same thing you found, Mickey. I was looking for the location of the cells of Der Führer. This idiot and his band of disheveled tower keepers kept me away from them long enough. Before I died, Yogi and I successfully made several batches of viable clones from the cells we had. But the Templars continued to steal the clones from my laboratory. Even the ones that were produced in the CC security area at the Institute of Chemical Defense were taken. I was running out of raw material and the lab promised enough cells to continue my work."

"But, you're dead...."

"Apparently not as much as folks like to believe. Yes, it was problematic at first and later it was a necessary evil to free me up to track down the thieves. Those that I caught, I left hanging with their entrails eviscerated."

"And now you have had the rest of them killed by Dalton—along with Szkolna Gora and Russell Lange," Mickey bluffed.

"Yes. Now, with the death of the freaky bird woman, Russell Lange, and this poor excuse for Templar leadership, the meddlers have mostly all been neutralized."

"Are you aware that the tower keepers are, indeed, the clones you produced?"

"Impossible. They are nothing like Der Führer."

"Did you ever ... stop to think why?" a weak voice from the window whispered. Never lifting his head, Asaad continued, "The clones you made ... would have been destroyed by you ... if you had the chance."

"Why would I destroy my own clones?"

"Why indeed?"

Asaad panned the faces in the room. Mickey and Loni each had a hand on Domino's harness. Suzanne stared blankly out the window. Nabil, now kneeling, hugged his father by the waist.

"Maybe because ... the clones ... were all mixed ... with purity," Asaad muttered.

"A sterile mixture would be no basis for destruction."

"As always ... eyes cannot see ... ears cannot hear. Purity comes ... from the Father."

Wunschmann glared silently at Asaad's bloody face.

"Each batch of cells ... processed by scientists ... by Templars.... Your evil was negated ... by the ultimate good."

"You have the cells of Christ?" Wunschmann scoffed.

"No, Doctor ... you do ... here."

"The cells of Christ reside in this laboratory?"

"Yes ... hidden ... in plain sight."

"Impossible."

"Quite possible," interjected Mickey. "If after diluting the Hitler gene, the resulting clone, or clones, were taken all over Europe and reared in the light of Christ. They could become Templars and keepers of the secret themselves. It could happen."

"It did happen," said Asaad.

"My Hitler clones are your army of Templar Knight tower keepers?"

"They were until you killed them," said Mickey.

"Probably better off dead," Asaad muttered.

"As are you!" screeched Wunschmann withdrawing a German Mauser pistol from his belt.

Shifting his feet under him, Nabil shielded his father as he ripped open his own shirt, exposing his unprotected chest toward the barrel of the pointing gun.

Wunschmann growled, "I have no compunction in killing you first and then your Templar friend."

"What greater glory can a son have than to die for his father?" Nabil boasted.

"I believe you have that backward," taunted Wunschmann. "It is the father who should die for the son."

"And so you shall," said a new voice from the doorway.

The popping sound of muzzled gunfire filled the room and Wilhelm Wunschmann, Snake Oil Willy, slumped dead to the ground.

Mickey turned around. The younger Wunschmann stood at the doorway holding a Walther PPK, complete with a silencer.

"Why, Yogi?" Mickey asked, dumbfounded.

"Because I love the memory of my father and that's not him."

"But—"

"That is his clone that I was instructed to create. It ran things here ... it has out-served its purpose," sneered Yogi.

"Are you sure?"

"What do you mean, Mickey?"

"How do you know that the body that died previously and was laid to rest wasn't the clone?"

"See the framed picture of Theodor Morell on the wall there?"

"The picture tilted crooked?"

"Yes," Yogi nodded. "My father admired Dr. Morell. He would have never allowed that framed picture to be askew."

"Still, the fact is that you may have just killed your living father. That is, if you yourself aren't a clone—"

"Impossible—improbable—I think you need to worry more about your own remaining minutes in this world."

"Are you?" Suzanne asked.

"Am I what, a clone? Am I a clone?" Yogi laughed; a bizarre hysteria tinged his voice.

"Are you?" Suzanne repeated louder.

"This building is rigged to explode in thirteen minutes if Dalton did his job right. I guess that's how long you have to find out. All of you—go over there next to the window."

"Can we at least get the wounded man down?" Loni asked.

"I don't care. Pull him down. Leave him up. Does it matter? We'll all be dead soon anyway. Even if we aren't, I can easily wrap this up with the tilt of my gun barrel."

Loni kept hold of Domino and didn't leave Mickey's side as they crossed the room toward Asaad. Nabil and Mickey broke the handles off the ice picks and pulled the bleeding hands through the embedded picks. Asaad groaned through his gritted teeth as his arms painfully returned to his side. Suzanne helped ease the bleeding man to the floor while Loni held a growling Domino tightly.

Yogi watched with indifference etched in his face, his gun trained on the motley crew.

Suzanne removed the crown of thorns and began her work, tearing strips of bandages from Nabil's discarded shirt. She used the stub of an ice pick still in the broken handle to shred the cloth. Then she remembered that she still had one knife tucked into her boot, but she paused her initial reaction to retrieve it. She looked up at Mickey, caught his gaze, directed it toward her boot, and then buried herself in her work.

76

Rain, Trane, and Canine Mane

Schloss Tegernsee Director's Office
Tegernsee, Germany

Overhand, underhand, side-armed, or wrist flicked? As she worked to bandage Asaad's wounds, Suzanne considered the knife hidden in her boot and gauged the distance and knife rotation to target. *Time is running out. It must be soon.* After the last of the shirt was shredded, Suzanne slowly reached toward her boot. She looked up to see Yogi Wunschmann leveling his gun at her.

"I know what you are thinking. Forget it."

Suzanne tightened her lips. *Drat! He's been reading me.*

"Slide over those ice picks, both of them." Wunschmann pointed with the gun barrel. "Nice and easy. You wouldn't want me to accidentally get injured," he sneered.

As the broken ice picks slid across the floor, Yogi kicked them toward the door behind him as if to shoo them on out of the room. In the doorway, locking gazes with him, stood a solemn Thomas Mader.

There was no time for Wunschmann to react. Thomas jumped, grabbing Wunschmann's gun hand. At the same time, the water sprinklers in the ceiling started spraying the room.

Through the sudden onset of rain, Suzanne quickly reached into her boot and extracted the large kitchen knife. She paused briefly, taking aim. As she watched, Thomas slipped on the wet floor and lost his grip on Wunschmann. Suzanne knew it in her heart. *Now or never. For Russell ...*

With a flick of her wrist, she threw the knife. Simultaneously, Domino lunged out of Loni's grip. Loni screamed as Wunschmann raised the gun, pointing it toward the dog in midflight.

The world suddenly seemed to move in slow motion.

Through the continuous ceiling rain, Wunschmann got a clear bead on the spotted canine heading straight for him. Moving on a collision course with the lunging dog, Suzanne's knife tumbled through the air.

300

Sprawled face-first on the wet floor, Thomas kicked out at Wunschmann's planted foot. Wunschmann's body spun forward—his leg went sailing up into the air. The gun went off simultaneously as Domino crashed into Wunschmann's chest and sent him reeling backward into the doorway.

The ripping tear of the thrown knife hitting flesh echoed through the misty downpour. A loud yelp from Domino purchased a scream of distress from Loni as she saw her baby crumple. Blood spurted from the Dalmatian's head, matting her fur with sticky scarlet.

Dr. Yogi Wunschmann lay on his back next to the dead elder Wunschmann clone. A geyser of blood squirted from around the large handle of Suzanne's knife as it sat protruding from the right side of Yogi's throat. Domino shook blood from her head and wobbled over, collapsing in the lap of a somewhat rattled Loni. Thomas sat quietly, holding pressure on his right side, watching blood slowly trickle through his fingers.

Mickey checked his watch—5:51. He rushed over to Domino, the closest victim and found no open wound to tend.

He moved quickly to Thomas, ripping open his shirt to access the injury. With his right hand, Mickey put direct pressure over the bleeding gunshot wound. Mickey's clinical eyes then scanned Thomas's complete right side, cataloging all he saw, while his left hand moved swiftly from the shoulder down. *Shoulder joint intact, right chest expansion-contraction intact, skin with no exit wound but two blips. Benign translucent split-end oval birthmark, no treatment.* Mickey lifted his bloodied right hand to peek underneath. *Abdominal wall gunshot wound—three-inch full thickness skin insult ... but just grazing. Lucky, could have been worse.* Mickey placed Thomas's hand over the deep gash. *Treatment is like a little Dutch boy, got to plug the hole.* Mickey yanked a bandage from his LBE, made a quick plug, and unceremoniously shoved it into the hole in Thomas's flesh.

"Hold this tight," he said to a wincing Thomas.

Suzanne quickly moved over to Wunschmann, kneeled on his chest, and with a firm grasp of the knife handle, swiftly pulled and thus widened the gash through the lateral neck. A rush of blood released from the right carotid and jugular with a terrible hiss. Wunschmann's eyes went dull and his breathing spasmed to a stop.

Almost immediately, all eyes fixed on the wall clock. Without words or commands, the frazzled group executed a rapid evacuation. Nabil helped his father; wounded Thomas Mader carried the twice-assaulted Domino; Mickey heaved his wife into a standing position; and all followed a frantic Suzanne Coletrane out the room. The clock read 5:53.

Following the flow of gravity, the group rambled down to the third floor. Loni looked to her wrist: 5:55.

Using a fireman's carry, Suzanne hoisted a whimpering Domino so Thomas could help Nabil carry Asaad down to the second-floor landing. Mickey checked his watch: 5:57. Thomas's wound bled vigorously—he left a spatter trail in his wake.

Mickey and Loni, now in the lead, kicked open the castle's back door on the first floor. Loni exited while Suzanne passed a still tender Domino to Mickey as she went through next. Thomas staggered through with Asaad draped over his shoulders. Nabil shot through the doorway and grabbed Domino as Mickey slammed the door shut behind them.

"Sixty seconds to detonation," yelled Suzanne as she pulled Loni over a hedge and into a small sunken garden to the right of a large square guard house. "Take cover!" Nabil curled around Domino as he slid his body into a small culvert in the rear parking lot.

Thomas and Asaad fell short of a narrow ditch by which they could have received some protection from the impending blast. Thomas had no more energy to pull the limp Asaad to safety. But from the ditch, the four arms of Justice James and Jude More reached out. They grabbed Thomas, who held his grip on Asaad, and together they pulled both wounded men into the ditch.

Completely spent, Mickey resigned himself to the fact he could not safely clear the porch of the rear entrance. He hunkered down in place; his eyes found Loni. She screamed toward him. Tapping his chest and pointing to her, he mouthed the words, *I love you.*

Suzanne's gruff voice called out the countdown as she struggled to keep her hold on Loni, fighting to keep eyes on Mickey. "Ten ... nine ... eight ... "

Nabil curled his body tighter around Domino.

"Seven ... six ... five ... four ... "

Justice James and Jude More put their bodies over the two exhausted escapees.

"Three ... two ... one."

Everyone hunkered down in place. The moment stretched.

Only the slightest of shuffling could be heard as everyone waited to exhale. No one moved for several seconds.

Suddenly, the door to the rear of the building burst open and a very soiled and unkempt Russell Lange staggered out. He then plopped down in the middle of the sidewalk and moved into a cross-legged seated position.

"Hello, Mickey. Got a corkscrew?" Russell grinned. He scanned the area, watching each person peering from their respective nests of safety.

In one hand he had a bottle of a Bavarian Silvaner wine, and in the other was a strand of detonation cord.

"I just hate to drink fine wine all alone." Russell began to laugh, and in turn, he was joined first by Mickey and then by all the folks slowly coming out of cover.

"You really are a rascal," said Loni as she stood up, laughing at Russell. Mickey walked over and stood by her. Domino had wriggled free from Nabil and was nuzzling Loni's hand while leaning against her leg. Overhead a chopper flew to the rear of the castle laboratory complex and joined the second helicopter already on the ground at a nearby soccer field.

Suzanne reached into her other boot, brandishing yet another kitchen knife in response to Russell's request for a wine bottle opener. "Would this do instead?"

✠ ✠ ✠

The helicopter crews crested the horizon and helped load up the weary and slightly wounded for the trip back to the US base at Grafenwoehr. Before long, the silhouette of the Tegernsee Castle and laboratory became merged into the colors of the fading sun. Loni leaned against her husband as she held Domino in the adjacent seat. Justice James and Jude sat numbly. Thomas yielded to the many skilled hands which came to put a stop to his bloody waterworks. Nabil supported his father, who clutched his walking stick close to his shoulder.

"Thank you for retrieving this, son. I thought I'd never see it again."

"It was either you or me, Father. The danger had passed and between us two, I am younger, quicker, and less wounded. Besides, there were too many steps for you."

Russell and Suzanne had given up their return seats to spend some down-time in the Tegernsee area. They stood waving as the choppers lifted up and away, leaving the two of them all alone. When the whop-whop-whop of the chopper blades had long disappeared and were pleasantly replaced by the usual lake sounds, she laced her fingers once again with his. Suzanne, who felt she had waited for this moment for an eternity, leaned close to Russell and recited part her favorite poem softly in his ear:

I have a gift
It's, oh, so small.
I have this gift
not shared by all.

I wanted to share it
with only you.
But you were gone
What could I do?

The gift stays wrapped for none to see.
Waiting for you, to come to me.
To be as one, as once we shared,
Our love unchained, nothing impaired.

After a brief silence, Russell asked, "So, who's the poet?"

"A high school boy who fell in love with a colonel's daughter," replied Suzanne with an appropriate tone of Vosges nostalgia.

"Anyone I know?"

"Someone you probably see quite often."

"Do I feel rain?" Russell queried as the clouds above began to gather for an evening shower.

Suzanne grinned widely as she reminded her Russell, "In the army, it ain't training unless it's raining."

Russell hugged her close, bringing his lips to just beyond her eyelashes. "I'm guessing you, my dear lady, would be the subject of today's cloud burst training."

Brushing her eyelashes against his moistened lips she executed a well-timed butterfly kiss. "That is why they call me the Trane."

77

Farewell to Arms

Hotel

Tegernsee, Germany

"**Y**our students gave you the nickname Death from Above?" Russell watched Suzanne carefully peeling a Jonagold apple using his army knife.

"You know, Mae West said that when she's good, she's very good."

"So you're Mae West now?"

"I guess so because she also said that when she's bad, she's better."

"After the way I hear you handle knives, Suzanne, I'm thinking I really shouldn't be so close to a registered weapon."

"It's *your* knife, Russell."

"I wasn't talking about the knife."

"Come on, Russell. You're the one who gave me extra training after the formal Special Ops classes back at Fort Benning."

"Do be honest, my dear Dr. Suzanne, I never realized that hurling steel across the room with such deadly accuracy was a duty-related, medically credentialed, category-two military physician skill."

"Well, I can see it has been a while since you've been to a meeting of the executive council of the hospital's professional staff," she smirked. "A sharpened knife whizzing by an ear is a good signal for the deputy commander of clinical services to call an end to the staff meeting."

"That's a fact." Russell motioned for an apple sliver.

After a long silence, Suzanne asked, "Do you think that Yogi was a clone?"

"I'm not sure we will ever really know now."

"Yogi was so shocked when he saw Thomas Mader." Suzanne passed another slice of fruit to Russell. "He tried to react but then the ceiling water sprinklers blasted him in the face."

"That was the moment you needed."

"Yes, Russell, it was. Was it you who turned on the sprinklers?"

"Yes, it was me."

"Why?"

"It was the only signal that I knew would tell everyone to get out of the building."

"A signal? How was I supposed to know that?"

"Ten out of the eleven clones figured it out."

"Yes, but one didn't. Thomas was there when the others were not."

"He knew, Suzanne."

"How do you know that he knew?"

"Asaad told me. He said that Thomas was one who always questioned his personal self-worth. Thomas needed to save Asaad and, thus, save himself."

"So history repeats itself."

"I thought you hated history." Russell grinned.

"I hate any history that *I have* that doesn't include *you*."

"How do we fix that?"

"We still have at least one more leaning tower to find." Suzanne held an apple slice between her teeth until Russell took it. "This time, we'll do it together."

"What if it has another fish?"

"What if it does?"

"Then we could end up in an adventure with a different conclusion."

"*This* adventure really could have had a different ending." Suzanne's voice softened. "There was a moment when I wasn't sure if Mickey was bluffing or not. He said that you were dead."

"You didn't believe him?"

"I wasn't sure."

"What swayed you?"

"I didn't hear the pain that I knew would be in Mickey's voice if he knew you really were dead. Your death would be devastating for many people."

"Whoa, Suzanne, you give me way, way too much credit."

"Maybe, maybe not. The bottom line is that you would have died saving us."

"What do you mean?"

"What if you had miscued on just one of the bombs? You would have been killed."

"What then? I guess you would never speak to me again."

"Russell, you're incorrigible."

"Well then don't *encorrige* me!" Russell laughed and playfully wrestled with her until they both went limp with laughter. A peaceful silence followed.

"So what becomes of all of this? Will the clones just ride off into the sunset?"

"Actually, I'm not sure they are all clones."

"What would they be if not clones?"

"Chimeras … possibly?" Russell scratched his face.

"A mixture of the Hitler and Christ genetic pools?"

"I'm saying that distinct DNA regions may remain untainted in their bodies."

"That can't be all good."

"I am not sure if it's all bad."

"Will the clones or chimeras or whatever they are remain linked to the Lost Books of Benjamin, Russell?"

"Maybe, Suzanne. Presumably, there are still other remaining Books of Benjamin to be redistributed among other icons with secret clues for identification. The River Gypsy People will most likely issue in another era of miracles like at Tabgha, using only loaves of bread and laden baskets of—"

"—fiche?"

Russell erupted in laughter as Suzanne leaned back into the curvature of his arm, feeling the resonation of his laugh surround her. Russell curled his arm around her shoulders and beamed a warm, loving smile.

For the first time in ever so long, Suzanne felt completely content.

78

Seed of Missed Content

Peronne residence
Altenbach, Germany

"I f everyone liked what I liked, Loni, everyone would want to be married to you." Mickey tugged at the tightly tucked-in corner of the sheet until it released so he could slide one of his legs out of the covers.

"Well, it's a good thing I said yes to you early."

"Early?" Mickey arched an eyebrow at his wife. "Not first?"

Loni chuckled as she piddled around the room.

Fingers laced behind his head, Mickey watched as Loni finally executed the last portion of her morning ritual. With the puppy blanket, she covered Domino first and then, afterward, leaned over to give Mickey a kiss. Mickey's arm reached out suddenly and cradled his surprised wife while rolling her over his hip and onto the center of their big California king mattress. He then switched the music from Loni's favorite artist, Ray Charles, to Third World with its reggae downbeat. He smiled as he listened to Loni's protest.

"How can a person who passionately loves reggae artists like Steel Pulse and Third World comfortably listen to Heart, Stevie Nicks, Kellie Pickler, and the twang of Hank Williams?"

"I'm an enigma," Mickey smiled smugly.

"It doesn't stop there! Andrew Lloyd Webber's *Phantom of the Opera*, Carlos Santana, Billie Holiday, Britney Spears, and Starship are also in your truck. Well, *were* in your SUV … before…."

"I'm eclectic, honey. I love the best in every style of music, even a sax harmony duet between Kenny G and Al Billbert—wait, what do you mean 'were in my truck'? What happened to my truck?"

"Yeah, I guess that's why you are *American Idol*'s oldest fan. Besides, it's getting repaired."

"I probably am." Mickey frowned, not liking the word *oldest* attached to his name. "Even the oldest vehicles become classics, you know—that is, if they are not all beat up beyond recognition. What happened to my truck that needs to be repaired?"

"Nothing serious. Really. But speaking of beat up—"

"They're both fine," reassured Mickey. "Don't worry."

"How did you know what I was going to ask about Asaad and Nabil?"

"I just know. Your thoughts are mine, and I can't shake one thought from my mind. I am so glad that Asaad's trauma and severe blood loss never led to shock."

"DIA reports state that Nabil never left Asaad's side throughout the recovery phase in the hospital. Also that both men, and the stone-capped walking staff that Nabil went back inside the castle to collect, were already well on their way back to Istanbul, Turkey."

"Did the DIA report conclusively hold the Wilhelm Wunschmann clone responsible for killing and mutilating Judas Lenz?"

"Yes, Mickey. Actually, the briefing photo had him at the scene of the crime wearing an ICD jacket which was mistaken by many, including me, to mean Investigation Criminal Division. Only later did the obvious Institute of Chemical Defense meaning become realized."

"Did the reports state that Szkolna—the Owl—was also medically stabilized thanks to efforts of Suzanne and Nabil?"

"Yes, and kudos were also extended to the chopper pilots who flew her quickly to the local German hospital, the *Klinikum*. That alone was so critical, Mickey." Loni smiled. "I know that great-grandmother Jasmine would have been pleased to know that Marie's contributions affected people so close to us."

"That's right!" Mickey sat up. "Jasmine Hertz and Marie Marvingt flew together." Mickey bunched the sheet around his waist. "Did your great-grandmother have a hand in the design for medical air evacuation as well?"

"I don't know, Mickey. I'm sure the grande madame could tell us. Next time we are in Oger, we'll ask grandmother."

"Still, from what was described to me, I thought we had lost the Owl."

"Hmmm…." Loni took a slow, deep breath and raised her hands to her face.

Mickey sat pensively watching Loni slide into remote viewing modality, focusing on a far horizon.

She traversed all of Germany and mentally arrived at Pyrzyce, Poland, at the Owl Tower. She strained to see Szkolna in the tower, but she just wasn't there. All Loni saw was a tall, beautifully carved stick propped against a high-backed chair. The beauty of the stick took Loni's breath away.

"Are you okay?"

Loni took in another deep breath, lowered her hands from her face, and blinked. "Yes, I'm okay."

"What did you see? Did you see the Owl?"

"No, I didn't see the Owl. I did see a beautiful, intricately carved walking stick. I'm sure she wasn't far from it. That stick looks so familiar, yet not. I would love for Douglas Coletrane to see it."

"Douglas? Why so?" Mickey asked.

"Douglas and I always seem to have the same taste for beautiful art," Loni sidestepped. "We never miss."

"Honey, I hate to disappoint you and Douglas but that isn't art. It's Szkolna's walking stick. She always keeps it. It stabilizes her. The good thing is that if it's there, like you said, she isn't far away." Mickey's voice trailed into an awkward silence.

"Don't worry, Mickey." Loni placed a gentle touch on her husband's arm. "She remained stable. I just feel that she did."

"I hope so."

"There's more, isn't there?"

"No."

"Mickey?"

"No ... well ... "

"Well what?"

"Well, I can't help but feel that my actions brought danger to so many, Loni. I will have to live with this guilt forever."

"Guilt is self-imposed."

"It's more than self-imposed. Medicine's creed outright says 'Do no harm'— and look! I placed so many people in harm's way."

"So you're responsible for all this tragedy, eh?"

"It seems so."

"We have no say in the matter? Whew, that is such a relief. That certainly alleviates me from being responsible for any of Domino's injuries."

"Cynicism and the sarcasm? What is this, a new teaching technique?"

"Only the best of the best wield it." Loni softened. "Honey, you know how much I love Domino. And yet, I carried her, leash in hand, to a near-death experience not once, but twice."

"Yes, you did. But only because you followed me into the danger that I willingly engaged."

"When I knew you were going into harm's way, Mickey, I could think of nowhere else I would rather be than by your side. It was my choice to make, not yours."

"Loni ... " Mickey looked into those unflinching eyes. He started to speak but her fingers covered his mouth.

"I know Domino loves us too," said Loni, glancing over at the Dalmatian's steady breathing, "and even though I put her in harm's way, she made further decisions to place herself in greater danger in order to protect us. She made choices too."

"What are you saying, Loni?"

"I'm saying what I am saying. I'm telling you that we all made choices for which, apparently, you are willing to accept full responsibility. Frankly, for you to accept absolute responsibility for all the horror we have chosen to undergo is, well, unfathomable and unrealistic. When we commit our lives to each other, we accept the inherent dangers and horrors, even if you try to keep us from them."

"Even if it means that you might sustain injury or that you could be killed?"

"Especially if it means losing our lives. Believe me, Mickey, I really thought I had lost you this time."

"Why did you think that?"

"It's not like you to choose not to come home at the end of a mission."

"But, for me, the mission wasn't over."

"DIA had what they needed. They were satisfied. Mission was complete once you had reached the Bastei and the final papers from the lab entered the chain of custody."

"You know as well as I do that the end of this DIA mission did not produce the level of closure needed. Had we not intervened, those tower keepers would have died."

"General Framingham didn't appreciate you extending the mission on his dime."

"It was the right thing to do."

"True, but, Mickey, that was a huge risk you took."

"I am sure the DIA had something to say about their analyst turning field agent without permission."

"I did not present myself as a DIA field agent."

"All evidence to the contrary."

"I was what General George Patton would have called an 'advanced reconnaissance in force,'" said Loni as she pinched up some of the skin on Mickey's bicep.

"One Dalmatian and a DIA analyst do not constitute a 'force.'"

Domino, caught up in a chase dream, barked while her legs mimicked running.

"There are those who would disagree with you … if they could," said Loni gently, almost tearfully, while she reached down to stroke Domino's flank. Domino gave an initial growl that turned into a painful whimper.

"I guess there is a physical price for being a four-footed hero," Mickey confirmed.

"Two-footed heroes aren't exempt, Mickey." Loni nodded and whispered, "I worried so much about you as you took off from the Bastei for the Tegernsee Castle."

"Why?"

"You went like the 'Light Brigade' charging boldly into the unknown. I didn't like you going where the DIA and I had laid no groundwork of reconnaissance data for you. You literally went into the lion's den blindly and there wasn't anything I had done to help you."

"Is that why you followed me?"

"Well, that and you failed to kiss me goodbye."

"I did not." Mickey shook his head.

"You most certainly did."

"You're quite mistaken, honey."

"Mickey, I know that you didn't because this was what I thought of when the cloned Wilhelm Wunschmann said you had been killed. I was thinking that I would never get to hold you and kiss you again. The memory of that lost kiss burned a gaping hole in my heart. I cannot recall any pain ever carving me so deeply."

"I am sorry I didn't kiss you before leaving."

"It's never too late to right a wrong."

"Try saying that to some who built a leaning tower," chuckled Mickey.

"Are you going to kiss me?"

"Sounds like you are making it my mission."

"It is your mission, Dr. Mickey Peronne, should you choose to accept it."

"Will the secretary disavow any knowledge of my actions?"

"That depends on the action—"

"How 'bout this?" Mickey pulled his wife close and kissed her lightly on her lips.

"Nice, but rather innocuous." Loni gave Mickey a pinch with a twist. "I think there will be nothing for the secretary to disavow."

"Ouch. Hey, sweetheart, you were the one who told me that you thought leaning towers were benign."

"I do confess. Never, in my wildest dreams, could I ever believe that so much intrigue and adventure could be tied into a leaning tower."

"It was certainly more than meets the eye. Now I know better. The leaning towers in the world are structural enigmas not because they exist, but for the reasons they exist."

"Who would have thought they were built with the intention of leaning? It's counterintuitive."

"Thank God the Knights Templar and the early masons did."

"Now that you all have exposed the secrets of these leaning towers, what will happen to them?"

"It's so hard to say, Loni. The public eye chooses to see what it wants to see. It may end up that the leaning towers remain in anonymity."

"I can't imagine that."

"Really? Every American traveler, military or otherwise, who comes to taste Europe sees the touristic obvious. Most of them rarely invest the time to see the jewels like these towers."

"Would you love me even if I didn't take the time to go and see them, Mickey?"

"I'd love you even if you left your eyes at home."

"Mickey, I love you more than meets the eye."

"I do too."

"No, Mickey, I love you *much more* than meets the eye."

"Are you … ?" Mickey made to respond, but she again covered his mouth so he couldn't speak.

Domino whimpered as she stretched onto her back, her front legs standing straight up in the air. On her face was the classic smile-snarl which only Dalmatians have.

"My love for you is, indeed, *much* more than meets the eye." She placed his hand on her heart then on her belly.

"What are you saying?" Mickey whispered anxiously. "You're ... you're ... I can't even say it ... but are you?"

"Lash yourself to the mast, Doctor." Softly laughing, Loni rolled over to the far side of the bed. "It appears that multiple recent successes have shattered any concern you have had for a past string of shortfalls." Mickey smiled at her. Loni continued. "You might just have to stop being so obsessed with work, Mickey. Working round the clock seven days a week doesn't make for a good family life. So stop playing with falling towers and stay here around the house a bit more often and maybe, just maybe, you'll find out if, indeed ... you know...."

"Have I told you today how much I love you?" Mickey rolled to her side of the bed.

"Not today." Loni propped up on her elbows, puffing away the wisps of curls from her cheeks. "Never enough, and definitely not more than meets the ear."

"Honey, your face is flushed, and you have that slapped-cheek appearance. *Please* don't tell me you have a headache."

"Not a chance, Dr. Peronne."

Amidst whispers and moans, flurried bed linens rapidly covered two bodies embraced in blissful unity. On the floor beside the bed, Domino's spotted ears perked in unison then gradually relaxed as the canine drifted back off into a most serene and peaceful slumber.

THE END

A Word From the Author

How can a book be lost if it is found? It depends on what makes a book a book. As seen listed, The Lost Books of Benjamin, each book a trove of lost works until it is found, contain four categories of books:

*1 Benjamin – **The Book of Thoughts***

*2 Benjamin – **The Book of Towers***

*3 Benjamin – **The Book of Tales***

*4 Benjamin – **The Book of Tomorrows***

Imagine a long forgotten dusty trunk, sitting in an attic filled with old papers. Collectively, 1 Benjamin (Thoughts) is an anthology of prose and poetry written by the novel's characters themselves.

Sometimes lost is not lost but instead is just hidden. Revealed within the novel series, 2 Benjamin (Towers) contains ten chapters which are a scrambled iteration of an original ten-chapter manuscript. Each chapter is purposely concealed in a different leaning tower, discovered when reading the novel series.

When lost is characterized as not yet found, the twelve-novel series comprising 3 Benjamin (Tales) waits on a shelf begging for discovery. Within the series unfurls twelve distinct tales supporting an overarching tale, pitting good against evil in a race toward destruction.

When time is the substrate of loss, better to accomplish yesterday than today and today better than tomorrow. The book, 4 Benjamin (Tomorrows) is literature briefly mentioned in the novel series today which can be fully appreciated on the morrow.

—B. Albertill

About the Author

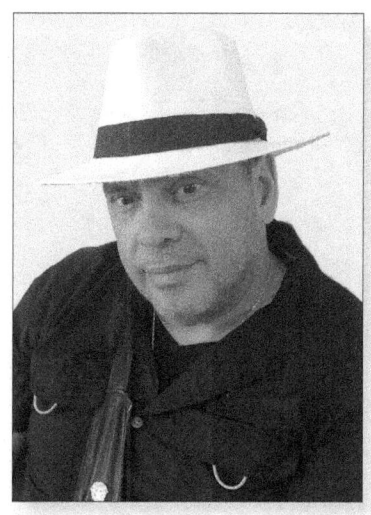

B. Albertill is the author of the twelve-book historical fiction series, Lost Books of Benjamin (LBoB). Albertill is a retired US Army physician-scientist, educationalist, science researcher, historian/theologian without portfolio, and a modern-day Templar. Having served in the military from Viet Nam era (1973) to his last posting in Afghanistan (2015), he has trained in clinical, research, and operational military medicine, the field of chemical warfare, and the history of military medicine. His writing is underpinned by a world-view defined by this professional education, military training, and resulting personal experiences.

Albertill writes historical fiction supported by years of travels and residence throughout Europe and the Mediterranean countries in Northern Africa and the near east. As LBoB novel protagonists Mickey Peronne, Suzanne Coletrane, Russell Lange and the numerous historical characters move throughout these regions, Albertill literarily walks shoulder-to-shoulder with them. The gift given to the reader is the robust flavor of credible historical fiction from novels penned by one who has firsthand appreciated the numerous historical settings.

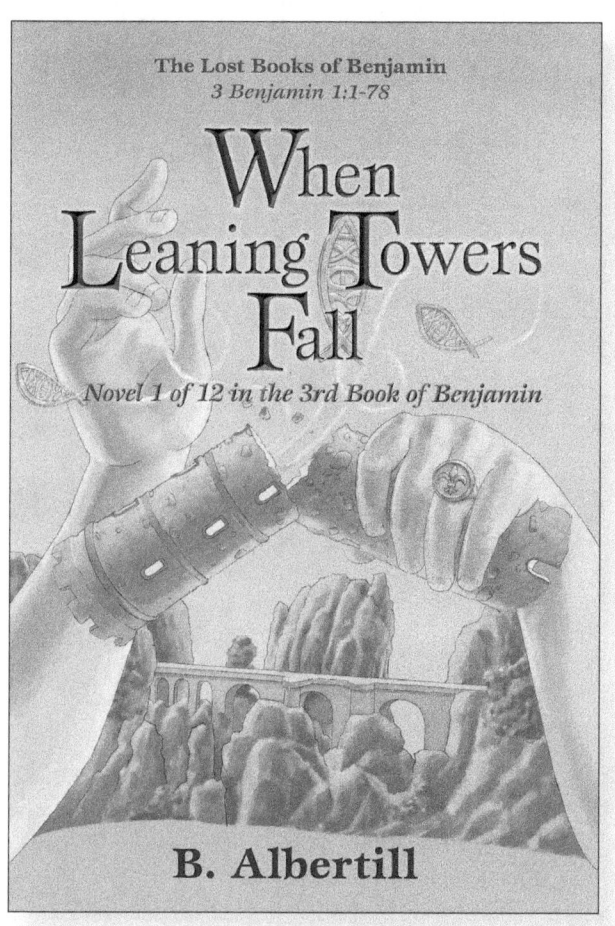

The Lost Books of Benjamin
3 Benjamin 1:1-78

When Leaning Towers Fall
Novel 1 of 12 in the 3rd Book of Benjamin
B. Albertill

Publisher: SDP Publishing
Also available in ebook format

 SDP Publishing

www.SDPPublishing.com
Contact us at: info@SDPPublishing.com

www.ingramcontent.com/pod-product-compliance
Lightning Source LLC
Chambersburg PA
CBHW072110020726
47501CB00003B/784